10/14

FRONTIER FURY

Center Point
Large Print

Also by Will Henry and available from
Center Point Large Print:

Medicine Road
A Bullet for Billy the Kid

FRONTIER FURY

A Western Duo

Will Henry

CENTER POINT LARGE PRINT
THORNDIKE, MAINE

This Center Point Large Print edition
is published in the year 2014 in conjunction with
Golden West Literary Agency.

The text of this Large Print edition is unabridged.
In other aspects, this book may vary
from the original edition.
Printed in the United States of America
on permanent paper.
Set in 16-point Times New Roman type.

ISBN: 978-1-62899-250-2

Library of Congress Cataloging-in-Publication Data

Henry, Will, 1912–1991.
[Legend of Little Dried River]
Frontier Fury : a western duo / Will Henry.
pages cm
Summary: "Two stories dealing with the Indian wars in the Colorado Territory and the Pacific Northwest in the mid-1800s"—Provided by publisher.
ISBN 978-1-62899-250-2 (hardcover : alk. paper)
ISBN 978-1-62899-320-2 (pbk. : alk. paper)
1. Western stories. 2. Large type books.
    I. Henry, Will, 1912–1991. Frontier fury. II. Title.
PS3551.L393L43 2014
813'.54—dc23
                                                    2014025803

Table of Contents

THE LEGEND OF
LITTLE DRIED RIVER

I

High on the lonely reaches of Horse Creek, lost in the tawny sea of the buffalo grass, stood a small island of timber called The Cottonwoods. It was here that Preacher Nehemiah Bleek built his mission school for the Indian children orphaned by the warfare between red man and white then firing the south plains. This was scarcely an ordinary undertaking, but then Bleek was scarcely an ordinary man.

To begin with, he was a preacher who never preached. Believing literally in God himself, he never argued the case with others. He was ordained by no church, seldom opened his Bible. If necessary for the peace or protection of his dark-skinned flock, he would alter the text of the Good Book to suit the emergency. It was said of him, beyond his ministry, that he had an infallible eye for a fast horse, a hard bargain, a good white man and a bad Indian, and an accurately aimed set of rifle sights. He was, withal, as gentle as a lamb. But what a lamb!

Nehemiah Bleek was six feet three inches tall. He weighed 238 pounds. No man knew his full strength. His very appearance was enough to halt most enemies in their tracks. Full-bearded and brawny as any blacksmith, his head was huge, ith a mane of red hair. The face was square, ...omely, spattered with freckles. His small blue eyes danced with that inner spirit that the Indians called *hotoma*, but his trust of friendship, once bestowed, became the chanciest of gifts.

"That crazy preacher," the white settlers said of him, "he will kill you if you cross him."

By this they meant that, if they lied to him, or tried to steal from him, or cheat him, or, above all, if in any manner they threatened his Indian orphans, men would find themselves in real peril from Preacher Bleek.

"He will as soon break your back as your arm," the settlers angrily declared. "He's crazy, plumb daft!"

The burly giant from Horse Creek presented no such social problem to the Indians. They said of him only that he was touched by higher power. This did not make him crazy, but simply distinguished. They never used the harsh word, *mashanē*, sick of mind, when they spoke of Bleek. They called him by his English name, Preacher, and they were always glad to see him and to make room for him in their camps.

But the whites, particularly the Indian Bureau and War Department men, saw Preacher Bleek in quite another way. To them, Bleek's presence in the country was sinister and dangerous. His mission school served as a refuge for wanted hostiles, as well as for their unwanted war

orphans. It was, they said, an intelligence po?
from which the defiant red warriors might safely
plan and launch their bloody raids on the settlers'
homes and the stage stations of the Arkansas
River valley. Specifically Preacher was accused of
encouraging the Indians to think along lines other
than surrendering to the Army commanders and
going to live on the arid and desolate reservations
set aside for their captivity.

"He constantly stirs them up," the officers
charged, "by telling them that the real aim of the
white man is not to improve the lot of the red man,
but rather to imprison the lot of them."

What Nehemiah Bleek was in honest fact
attempting to do, of course, was to teach the
orphaned Indian youngsters how to live as the
white man lived. He reasoned that if the children
could be so taught, they would have a chance to
survive in the coming time of the white man,
whereas their red parents, refusing surrender, must
certainly perish.

But the newly appointed commander of the
military district of Colorado had a pet theory of his
own for the best care and education of Indians,
large or small. "Kill them all, little and big," he
said. "Nits make lice."

The Indians understood the new commander's
beliefs. Wherever his troops ventured, red mothers
desperately hid their little ones, or fled with them
as far and as swiftly as they might.

"Mashanē is coming!" became a cry to strike error into every unsurrendered heart.

The year was 1864, the month November, the Heavy Frost Moon. In the summer just passed, the Cheyennes, the Sioux, and the Arapahoes had raided the white settlements of the valleys of the South Platte, the Smoky Hill, and the Arkansas Rivers. Particularly were the Cheyennes guilty of this warfare. Too long had the cavalry troops pursued them. Too long had the commissioners of the Indian Bureau cheated them of their lands. Too long had the settlers driven them from their hunting grounds. The Cheyennes could stand no more.

If an Indian fought, he was tracked down and punished. If he obeyed the white man and camped peacefully, he was attacked. If he came in and made a treaty to go on the reservation, he was tricked and lied to. If he then tried to leave the reservation, he was shot down. His Sioux friends from the north advised the Cheyennes to come up to their country and make a new home. But the south plains were the home of the Cheyennes by this time, and they would not leave. So they went on the war trail to defend their freedom and to keep their wandering way of life. This determination made the times risky for Preacher Bleek and his Horse Creek missionary school.

Every cavalry patrol that came toward The Cottonwoods were of the regular Army, in the field for the reasonable purpose of keeping track of the movements of the various large bands of Indians known to be in that southern part of the Colorado Territory. Yet Bleek had no way of being certain when any given patrol would be of this proper origin, or one of local volunteer troops with secret orders to kill Indians wherever found. And now, with the snows of the Heavy Frost Moon beginning to whiten the buffalo grass, Preacher had sudden new cause to fear the latter possibility.

All Colorado troops were called home from the north, where they had spent the summer chasing the Sioux, and were ordered south to the Arkansas. At their head came the Colorado commander himself, the officer the Cheyennes had named Mashanē, Sick Mind. From the day of his return, the Indians felt the chill of the presence of this man. The uneasy peace that had been established in his absence by Major Wynkoop, of the regular Army, commenced to melt away at once. "Mashanē has come back," said the People, and the mothers watched anxiously where their children strayed, the herd guards held the ponies close by, the warriors nodded grimly and oiled their guns.

The friendly Cheyennes who passed his way continually warned Preacher Bleek of such things; thus it was that he knew Mashanē was back from the Platte and had bivouacked his main body of troops in Bijou Basin, east of Denver. He also had been told that the dangerous commander was presently away from that big camp, out somewhere on the prowl with one of his killer patrols. This worried Bleek, since he was much concerned at the moment with the nature of the troops that Mashanē had brought down to Bijou Basin.

The 3rd Colorado Cavalry was a volunteer organization. As such, it differed greatly from the regulation pony soldier regiments and was never to be confused with responsible commands like the United States 3rd Cavalry. The Colorado troops had uniforms and were in truth authorized by the United States government, but in all other respects they were vigilante troops in the darkest tradition. Their members were enlisted for but 100 days, a span of time seen as ample to "clean out the redskins along the Arkansas Road." Moreover, many of these 100-day volunteers were the draft dodgers of their time. They sought, by enlisting with the 3rd Colorado, to avoid the War Between the States and service to their country. This questionable patriotism, together with the fact that they were local men with a background of hatred for the Indians, was what multiplied Bleek's fear of them.

Thus, when he heard that Mashanē was in the field with a patrol of these men, he took all due alarm. But it was only when he received the subsequent report of that patrol's whereabouts and direction of travel that he understood the full nature of menace to his beloved red orphans.

"Beware, Preacher!" cried the Cheyenne scout, reining in his lathered pony only long enough to shout the news. "He is riding for the upper waters of Ohecmoheno!" The Indian waved his war lance and spurred his mount away from The Cottonwoods. Bleek sympathized with his haste, for in Cheyenne *ohec* meant creek and *moheno* meant horse. Mashanē was coming to see Nehemiah Bleek at Horse Creek.

II

But another commander had heard of the big white man's mission school at The Cottonwoods and had started for it sooner than the commander of the 3rd Colorado. He halted now with his two fellow riders on an elevation of the prairie over-looking Horse Creek. It was a cold dusk. All day the wind had been spitting a sleety rain at them. The horses were tired. They were tired. Now all of them hoped that this was the final rise to be ridden over, the final silence to be peered warily into.

"There," the leader said, pointing. "That's it, over where the stream turns toward the sunset. That dark spot of timber. That is The Cotton-woods." By the darkening light his companions saw him straighten. "Mahesie," he said to the smaller one, who was only a boy, "you are a

15

Cheyenne. Remember that. There will be times ahead when you will need to remember it."

The boy nodded, thin shoulders squared bravely. So they had come to it at last. Down there lay The Cottonwoods, the destination of the ride that had begun in high Wyoming many days before. The wonderful time of his wild free life was finished. He would be like a captured mustang down there.

"Uncle Maōx," he said, "I don't want to stay here. I am a northern boy. My mother was a northern woman. My father, your own brother, was a northern man. We have no people here in the south country. I will die of loneliness at the white man's school."

The tall warrior reached out and put his arm about the boy. "Listen," he said. "Don't you think that I have studied this a hundred times during our journey? Yet each time I say again to myself that you must do it . . . you must stay here and learn the white man's ways. We are too old to learn, Kōvohe and I. But for you there is time."

"Uncle, what I wish to learn, you and Uncle Kōvohe could teach me better than any men. I want to be a fighter, too."

At this, the third rider shook his head. He told the boy that he must not think to be like Maōx and himself. He insisted that they had made war all their lives and had little to show for it. They did not have many horses. They were not important chiefs. They had poor robes, no squaws, not even a lodge of their own. They really had nothing whatever.

But the boy said that, on the contrary, they had all that he wanted. They rode where they wished. They hunted or took the war trail and touched the brow in servitude to no man. Every Cheyenne knew their names. He asked only the same life for himself—not to be sent into slavery at the white man's mission school, not to be abandoned in this alien southland.

The youth's plea held enough truth to disturb the two gaunt warriors. As Cheyennes they knew well how he felt about freedom. Kōvohe sighed deeply. "You make me sad, Mahesie," he said. "I want to weep for you, for all of us."

Maōx took his own blanket and put it about the boy's shoulders, for it was very cold. "It is a dark night, Kōvohe," he said. "Go ahead and weep for our people. No one will see you or hear you."

"Bah!" snorted the other warrior. "You know, Maōx, for a fighter with your reputation you are soft as buffalo grease. Who cares about the People? I worry about me! And it is colder up here on this rise than the rump of a wet dog in a snowbank. Come on, let us ride down out of the wind."

Maōx turned his spotted buffalo horse down the slope. The other mounts followed without urging from their riders. Swiftly they went forward through the growing prairie darkness, the unshod hoofs soundless on the dead grass of autumn. The rain came on once more, heavier now, whipping the horses' flanks, gluing their manes to their wiry necks.

"Maheo's navel!" swore Kōvohe, spitting away the cold drops of freezing water. "We will get lost in this strange country. I cannot see my hand before my face for this rain!"

The boy, Mahesie, put out his small hand.

"Do not be afraid," he said, touching the fierce warrior. "My uncle is leading us."

When Bleek heard his dog bark outside, he knew that the visitors were not white men. The dog was an Indian dog; it barked one way for the white man, another for the red. "It's all right," he said to the children. "Only some Indians coming."

They were gathered at the fireplace in the main room. Each night before bed they came there and Preacher told them wondrous stories. He spoke sometimes in Cheyenne, again in hand signs, mainly in simple English. The children seemed to understand him as well one way as another. They laughed or clapped their hands or wept as the circumstances of the tale required. But Bleek seldom told them sad things. "You've seen enough of that," he would say.

Now, however, despite his assurance, the children began to leave the fireplace. They had heard too many Indian dogs barking in the night. But Bleek held up his hand. Out in the clearing before the school, the dog was changing the tone of his bark once more. Now it was quick, excited—a sound of greeting, not challenge.

"Hah!" Preacher said. "Real Indians. That's a northern dog. He is smelling northern Indians. What bark is that he is giving now, children?" His blue eyes darted among them. "Ohes," he said. "You tell me."

The youth, a boy of about six, rubbed his head. It was a notable head, as bare of hair as a bladder. His name translated Young Buzzard, and came from the bald head, a relic of the raging fever with which his mother had brought him to Bleek and never returned for him.

"That is the friendship bark," the boy finally said with pride. "We know his tail is making little wagon circles."

"Good." Bleek nodded. "Now you must all be quiet until I have greeted our visitors. Do you know why? Hehēn?"

Hehēn, whose name meant Blackbird and whose father had been an escaped slave, was only seven. He was ebony-dark and kinked of hair, looking like some young Bantu or plantation boy, but answering in Cheyenne as alien and guttural as any full-blood's. "Hēhen, Preacher," he said. "Children should be seen only and not talk."

"Good, good," said Bleek, moving for the

door. "We speak when spoken to, that's the rule. *Zepeva?*"

"*Zepeva*," chorused the children, and surrendered to the slash of the rain against the cottonwood logs of the building and to its drum on the prairie sod that made the snug roof. At the door, Bleek hesitated.

A slender tot by the fire nudged her companion.

"I'm glad it's Indians," she whispered. "Aren't you?"

Bleek turned quickly. "Soxoenos," he reproved the child, "what is it that we don't do?"

"We don't whisper," lisped the little girl, then giggled and held her pudgy hands to her face. Her name was Sunflower and she was Bleek's secret favorite. An Arapaho waif, she had been found abandoned on the prairie with a broken leg suffered in the flight of her people from soldier pursuit. The leg had not healed right despite Bleek's every effort to set it and care for it. But Sunflower had a disposition that shone through any handicap, leading the Horse Creek missionary to give her the name she bore.

"That's right," Bleek now agreed. "Be still now, all of you."

The obedience of the children was matched by the falling away of the wind and the rain for a moment. In the heavy silence, Bleek swung open the thick plank door.

The indrawn—*"Ah!"*—of the children picked

the lock of the moment's stillness. The missionary himself stepped slightly backward.

Painted against the blackness of the storm by the brush of the firelight stood a Cheyenne warrior taller even than Nehemiah Bleek. On the warrior's right was a boy of about ten or twelve, on his left a thick-chested brave with the evil features of a gargoyle. All three stood in dignity, blankets plastered on them by the rain, heads held erect. They made no movement to come in, or to ask permission to come in. Bleek understood this.

"*Nomoto, nomoto!*" he said. "Welcome, welcome!"

The tall warrior nodded and made a sign with his left hand, accepting. He came into the room, followed by the boy and the second warrior. Just within the door, they halted. Behind them, Bleek closed the door. At the sound, all three wheeled instinctively, then relaxed and waited for the missionary to come around and face them.

The latter did so, informing them that he was Preacher Bleek, a friend of the Cheyenne people, and that they were to think of his home as their own. "These are my children," he added as he noted the tall warrior eyeing the little ones. "They have forgotten their manners. Children, what do we say when guests enter?"

"*Nomoto, nomoto,*" murmured the flock obediently, but refused to leave their various retreats.

Now the tall warrior, with his face seeming sculptured of stone, held up his arm toward the children and smiled. It was a beautiful smile, startling for having appeared upon such a brooding and fierce face. "*Nihehozetaz*," he said. "I come to you for help. Do not be afraid of me."

This great dark northern chief coming to them for aid? This vast fearsome figure from out of the stormy night, seeking assistance from them, from little children? Slowly they came forward, bunching behind Bleek like a covey of prairie chicks.

The big Indian—his voice was deep as thunder, yet soft as thunder far off—spoke now to the missionary.

"I am Maōx," he said. "These with me are Kōvohe and the boy, Mahesie."

Bleek made a sign to the second warrior, Kōvohe, and said: "You are welcome, Picking Tooth." Patting the boy on the head, he added: "And all children are welcome here, little Red Dust." Then he turned back to the leader. "Maōx?" he said, frowning. "I don't remember a Red Nose among the northerns. Is that the right translation?"

"There is another translation." The tall Cheyenne nodded.

"Yes," said his companion, Picking Tooth, showing a wolfish grin. "You have the nose part right, Preacher, but the red is wrong. Study that

22

noble feature. Observe its size. Note the hump, especially, of the bridge bone. What do you call a horse with a nose like that?"

Bleek's frown lingered another instant, then cleared. "Of course, of course!" he said, striking his forehead with the heel of his hand to show his ignorance. "What a poor mind I have. Here, let me have those wet blankets. Come to the fire. Children . . . Sunflower . . . run and bring some water for the kettle. Quickly, quickly, everybody to work."

The Indians came to the fire, yielding their sodden blankets with gratitude. The children scuttled this way and that, raising more dust from the earthen floor than adding of substance to the comfort of the guests. As for Nehemiah Bleek, old as he was at these things, Picking Tooth's identification of the tall warrior had caused an odd sensation in the stomach. It was as though one were looking at a wild animal not in a cage. As though the view were very close. As though the big room of the mission building had suddenly grown quite small. And as though everything in that room had been touched for the moment by the sweeping freedom of the far places.

The reason was there, warming at the fire. Roman Nose—greatest fighting man of the fighting Cheyennes, a legend and folklore in his own time.

III

Bleek brought out and gave to the Indians some of his best Burley tobacco. With such guests one did not offer the poor quality of harsh trade weed common to the frontier. The northern Cheyennes accepted the gift, and the lending of two pipes to smoke it in, making no undue acknowledgments. To them, it was merely *hotoma*. Had Preacher come to their lodges and had they such fine tobacco to give him, then he would have been given the fine tobacco.

When the pipes were going well, the blue smoke curling, the bowls glowing, the dark faces knowing content, Roman Nose spoke.

"Preacher," he said, "we have come a long way to ask a thing of you."

"Ask it." Bleek waved, puffing his pipe.

"No, first let us talk a bit."

Bleek nodded. The children waited, big-eyed, watching the foreign Indians, the strangers from the north.

"These children," Roman Nose continued, "are yours, you have said. They look more like mine."

Bleek smiled his rare shy smile and agreed. He explained his relationship to the Indian youngsters, concluding with a shrug: "As they do not know their own fathers, I am their father.

Sometimes there are more of them here, sometimes less. These are the ones who stay with me the entire year, the ones who really are my children. Mine and Maheo's."

"Good," said Roman Nose. "I'm glad you mentioned Maheo. The Allfather is the parent of each of us."

"He is," agreed Bleek.

"Good," said Roman Nose again, and after eyeing him: "If a man doesn't believe in God, I won't believe in that man. We understand each other, Preacher?"

Bleek was by no means sure that they did. What he was certain of was that he should give no hint of this doubt. "I am your brother," he said. "Go on."

Roman Nose then told him that tales of his school on Horse Creek had spread to the north. The southern Cheyennes had said that the big white man who lived at The Cottonwoods was protecting Indian orphans and instructing them in living as white children. It was said by the southerns that the big white man was also the enemy of Mashanē, who was the enemy of all Indians and most of all the enemy of the Cheyennes. "Is all of this true?" the tall warrior concluded.

Bleek answered that it was not entirely so. He said that he was not the enemy of Mashanē, but that Mashanē believed all Indians, "little and

25

big," must be destroyed or there could be no peace. Hence, since Bleek's life was devoted to his Indian and half-blood outcasts, it was inevitable that he and Mashanē should not be friendly. "But I would remind you," he told Roman Nose, "that most of the settlers and the soldiers agree with Mashanē, not with me. I would also remind you that the warring of the Cheyennes this past summer has been a shameful thing. You yourself have been in it. If you say to me that there is no blood on your hands, I will not believe you. You know I speak the truth."

At this, the huge warrior shook his head. "You do not know the truth," he said. "The truth is that the red man and the white man are not alike. Maheo made the difference in them . . . I did not."

"No," said Bleek. "You are wrong. Maheo sees us alike, red man and white. We are both only men."

Roman Nose grew angry. He put down the borrowed pipe and came to his feet. Red Dust and Picking Tooth also arose.

"The southern Cheyennes have lied to me," growled the war leader. "Those old fools, Black Kettle and White Antelope, have grown soft in their heads. They told me you had *hotoma*, that you were a Cheyenne in your heart. They lied to me. You are a white man."

"Yes," replied Preacher. "And you are a red man."

"I am going," said Roman Nose. "Where did you

26

put our rain-damp blankets? We won't stay in your lodge."

Bleek did not move to fetch the blankets. He sat puffing his pipe. "Now you are behaving as a white man," he told the scowling Indian. "You won't listen to the other side."

Roman Nose stopped on his way to the door. "What do you mean?" he demanded.

Preacher Bleek shrugged, blew upward a curl of smoke. "I said the red man and the white man are no different beneath their skin," he said. "They are not." He turned to Blackbird and called the half-blood boy to come and stand with them. The youth did so, pleased to be singled out. Bleek asked Roman Nose to observe that Blackbird was as dark as a lump of coal. Next, he requested the Indian to explain what difference there was, then, between the half-Negro youth and a white child of similar age.

Roman Nose scowled yet more fiercely. He stared hard at Blackbird, who only grinned happily back at him. And he looked hard at Nehemiah Bleek, who nodded pleasantly and waited. Finally the tall warrior admitted that there would be no important difference—both were but children, no more. "But I do not see," he concluded, "what this has to do with the discussion, Preacher."

"Just this," answered Bleek softly. "They are not just children . . . they are our children, yours and mine."

27

"Hah!" snorted the gaunt brave. "Yours and mine and some buffalo soldier's!"

"Precisely so," granted Bleek. "And if our children are no different, red or black or white, then you and I are no different. Do I lie to you?"

"I don't know." Roman Nose shook his head. "Your words confuse my mind. I am not a great talker."

"No," said Preacher, "you are a great fighter, and this summer just past you fought on the South Platte River, and in the fight white children were killed. These were little children, with their mothers, each no different, save for the color of their skin, than Blackbird, or Blackbird's Cheyenne mother, or than Sunflower, here, and her Arapaho mother. Again I say, can you tell me that I lie to you?"

Roman Nose narrowed his eyes. He was thinking very hard. The children fidgeted. Two of them had fallen asleep. In the stillness Sunflower slipped her hand into that of Red Dust. The northern boy did not even notice it. He was too absorbed watching his famous uncle. It seemed to him that the moment was here when they would get their ponies and go away from the big white man's mission school. When they would ride joyfully back to high Wyoming, and home.

But the uncle of Red Dust was not a simple man to know. He lived much within himself. Now, unexpectedly, he said to Preacher Bleek: "Your tongue is straight, you do not lie."

"Then you understand," Bleek asked, "that Mashanē feels about the white child as you do about the red?"

At once Roman Nose was scowling again. "No, no!" he denied. "Not Mashanē! You, Preacher, yes. But not that devil, Mashanē. He is a killer of women and small children!"

"Yes, Roman Nose," said Bleek quietly. "And what are you?"

The Indian could not answer Preacher's question. "Why do you defend Mashanē?" he challenged Bleek, unable to admit his own guilt.

"I don't defend him," said the missionary. "But Mashanē is a war leader like you . . . a fighter. I wanted you to see that, to think about it. How is it all right for Roman Nose to see a little white child scalped or his mother carried off to slavery, while for Mashanē to order his men to shoot Indian women and children is a vicious and terrible thing?"

Now the tall brave nodded very slowly. "I see," he said. "I begin to see. . . ."

Bleek could sense that, insofar as the great warrior was beginning to see, it was not a sight likely to alter his career of killing and raiding and making war. But the thing of the moment was to implant the doubt of Indian righteousness in the fierce mind. The gamble, always, was to get these wild people to stop and start to think—to think how the white man saw things, not just act on their savage impulses as red men. Where the Cheyennes had done this, notably under the two peace chiefs of the southern branch of the tribe, Black Kettle and White Antelope, a good commencement had been made. Those particular Indians, committed as a tribe to live peaceably with the whites regardless of provocation, had the best chance to survive the war of extermination—extermination or life imprisonment on some reservation—that Preacher Bleek knew to be coming to the valley of the Arkansas.

Bleek believed this pacifist course to be the only one that provided the Indian a chance to escape annihilation along the Arkansas. He had talked with the honest Indian Agent Colley at Denver, and with the decent Major Edward Wynkoop of the regular Army before that officer's transfer out of the area. He had talked, as well, with Major Anthony, the officer sent into the area to replace Major Wynkoop. All had left him convinced that the unchangeable policy of the government was to put the Indian under restraint on reservations in Oklahoma and Kansas, or to kill him in the process—with the choice being generally given to the particular troop commander in the field. Hence, as he now waited for Roman Nose to conclude, Bleek knew a considerable anxiety. The question was not if the huge warrior was beginning to see, but what he was beginning to see. Would he now again demand return of the drying blankets, only to stalk out into the gusting night? Would he "see" that Bleek was still a white man at heart, not a friend of his red people? Or had he actually had a glimpse of the truth—that a little child dead by Indian hands was the same as one destroyed by the guns of Mashanē's soldiers?

The pause was now stretching beyond need. Afraid of whatever dark thoughts might be forming in the warrior mind of Roman Nose, Bleek urged him gently, carefully. "What are you seeing, brother?"

In reply, the huge brave held out his hands, showing them to the bearded missionary. "These hands," he said, "have never touched a little child in anger. Not a red child, not a white child. I thought they were clean hands, but they are not. What I am beginning to see, Preacher, is the blood you have shown me on these hands. I will think a long time on it."

"This is a good thing, brother," said Nehemiah Bleek. "Will you now sit on the robe again? I want to help you, to hear what it is you have come so far to ask of me."

Before Roman Nose could answer, another less troubled warrior spoke for him. Picking Tooth, that realist by any skin color, grinned and patted his dark stomach.

"All this talk, *hai*! Listen, Preacher, you and this great fighter talk later. My belly is as empty as a white man's whiskey bottle washed up on a riverbank. How about some food, eh, Preacher? All you have been feeding us is hot wind and words. We didn't ride down here ten sleeps from Platte River just to gnaw on argument bones. Come on, now, where are you hiding the buffalo tongue and the hump ribs?"

It was the right thing to say at precisely the right time and put in exactly the correct spirit of human complaint. At once the air seemed to grow lighter in the log-walled room. The mission children commenced to laugh. Sunflower gave Red Dust's hand a friendly tug, and batted her long black lashes at him. The Cheyenne boy snatched his hand away indignantly, yet in the same moment weakened enough to lick his lips and watch to see what the host was going to do about Picking Tooth's reminder of food.

As for Preacher Bleek, he shouted out a good loud honest Cheyenne shout and clapped his hands and began to order this child to run that way and bring something, and that child to dash this way and fetch something else. In no time at all the tea was set to steep, the fresh buffalo tongue and the juicy hump ribs were broiling on the rack. Even the precious white sugar was brought out from Preacher's padlocked iron cabinet—where the whiskey for medicine was also kept—and every person there, young and old, waited in happy anticipation of the feast, and shared meanwhile the heart-warming glow of the fire and the return of the good Cheyenne *hotoma*.

All except one of them. The boy, Red Dust, knew what it was that Roman Nose had come to ask Preacher Bleek. He could not laugh with the others, or share the *hotoma* with them. It was the best he could do not to cry.

IV

After the last of the tasty buffalo ribs had been gnawed bare, dry blankets were brought and spread on the warm hearth, where the visitors from the north preferred to sleep for the night. The mission children then bade their guests good night and retired to the adjoining dormitory.

Here, in the "sleeping room," as they called it, were bunks of planking built against the log walls. Each bunk was equipped with a buffalo robe and a mattress of old canvas stuffed with prairie hay. The robes were the product of Preacher's hunting and tanning skills, the grass-filled pallets the work of the mission orphans. In one way or another, the room was furnished by those who used it, and loved by them as the only real home they had ever known.

Now, young health being what it was, excitement soon blended into sleep. In minutes, only the visiting northern Indians and Preacher Bleek were awake. It was time to come to the serious business of the evening.

Roman Nose was brief with it. It seemed to him, he said, that where one white soldier was killed, ten sprang up to take his place. At the same time, if an Indian warrior were slain, no other warrior leaped to do battle in his cause. Soon the Indians would be gone. No one would be left to fight for the free, wild life that the Cheyennes treasured. This was why Roman Nose had come to see Preacher.

After the past summer of killing along Platte River, it was certain that there must be a terrible revenge of the pony soldiers upon the Cheyennes. For himself, Roman Nose did not fear. But the boy, Red Dust, had been given into his keeping by the lad's dying father, and the boy must live. He was only eleven summers. He was a bright boy, very quick to learn, very slow to forget. He was not war-like in his ways, but believed in gentleness. Such Indians were the first to be slain by the white man.

Roman Nose himself spent ten moons of each year on the war trail. He had no home in which to keep the boy. His fire was wherever darkness caught him on the prairie. He had no woman to mother the boy. His vows of chastity to his warrior society forbade a mate. One day, perhaps, when the wars were over, he would take a squaw and have a lodge. But what of the boy, meanwhile?

It was at this time of worry that he met White Antelope, who had journeyed to Wyoming to plead with the northern Cheyennes to end their war and make peace with the pony soldiers.

"Your madmen will get us all killed!" the old chief had cried. But the young fighters had hooted and jeered him and told him to go home to the Arkansas. They called him peace-talker, and coward, and old woman.

But Roman Nose spoke with him about Red Dust, whereupon White Antelope had told him of Preacher Bleek's school for Indian orphans. He promised that if Roman Nose would bring the boy to Preacher's school, White Antelope would be camped nearby, probably at Little Dried River, which the white man called Sand Creek. Thus, if there were any trouble with the boy at the school, White Antelope could give him an Indian home until such time as a party was riding north and could return him to his Uncle Maōx.

"Now, Preacher," concluded Roman Nose, "we come to the question which brought me here . . . will you take the boy and teach him your ways . . . the white man's ways . . . until I return for him when the grass is new again?"

Bleek hesitated, seriously concerned. Red Dust was older than he liked. He preferred to get his children when they were much younger and could be taught more easily. Moreover, this particular boy was quite wild and shy. He had been nervous from the moment he came into the building. He had not laughed once, or smiled, or uttered a solitary word. Finally he was a fighting Indian by birth—born free among a people who valued liberty above life. There was the look of eagles in his dark eyes, the crouch of a wolf cub in his wary walk. No, this one could not be tamed. It was too late.

Carefully he explained his fears to Roman Nose. To his surprise, the warrior agreed with him. "Yes," he said. "You are correct, Preacher. The boy is as you say. Now you know why his uncle has ridden ten sleeps to bring him to your school."

Bleek puffed furiously at his pipe. He wanted time to think of the best way of refusing the boy. "You take a pony," he said to Roman Nose. "What is the proper age for first training? Please answer that."

"Very young is the best time," the Cheyenne replied at once. "The first spring after the foaling, if possible."

"Shall we say a yearling, then?"

"Yes."

"Very well. In a boy, now, how many years equal one pony year?"

"My people say seven years."

"That is right." Bleek nodded. "So you see what I mean about the boy. He is too old for the best training."

Preacher thought that he had trapped Roman Nose with this logic, but he had much to learn of the great fighter.

"All right," said the latter. "But what makes the best-grown horse, the most trustworthy in all trouble? The one to be depended on beyond any started as a mere yearling?"

"Why," said Bleek, "the one you start as a two-year-old, of course."

"Aha!" cried the stern warrior. "You have lost, Preacher. In terms of pony years, Red Dust is just exactly two years old. *Namea*, white friend! I give the boy to you."

Bleek raised his pipe. He intended to wave it about in protest, while he thought of a way to escape. But he had no more than stabbed the air with it than the dog in the outer yard commenced to bark snarlingly.

"Zehavseva!" said Picking Tooth, reaching for his rifle. "Those are white men coming!"

Preacher Bleek was at the plank door in the next instant. Swiftly he dropped its heavy locking timber into place. Behind him, Roman Nose and Picking Tooth crouched with rifles ready. Red Dust had no gun, but in the winking of one coal in the fireplace he drew his knife and joined the two warriors. Almost in the same breath of time, a heavy cavalry boot *thudded* against the door panels from the outside, followed by a hoarse-voiced order: "Open up!"

The missionary called out that he would obey, asking his callers to be patient for a moment.

Crossing the room, he signaled the Indians to stay where they were, making no move, no sound. Then he disappeared into the dormitory, reappearing shortly dressed in a flowing old-fashioned nightgown and carrying a lighted candle in a tin tray. He had a sleeping cap with tasseled tip on his head, and was yawning mightily.

"All right, all right," he told the soldiers. "Quit smashing at my door with your blasted boots. Can't you give a man ten seconds to get out of bed?" Pausing by the fireplace, he told Roman Nose and Picking Tooth that they and the boy had one chance: to get down into their blankets on the hearth and pretend that they had been aroused by the knocking from a sound sleep.

Roman Nose at once ordered his companions to do as Preacher said. Bleek waited until the three were in their places, noting that the warriors took their rifles with them, and the boy his knife. Then he was at the door and had unbarred and flung it open.

Into the fire-lit room, with a bluster of windy rain, stomped three cavalrymen. Two were ordinary troop sergeants. The third was what the Cheyennes called an "eagle chief," a full colonel. All three were wearing the uniform of the dreaded 3rd Colorado regiment.

Nehemiah Bleek, himself a very large man,

could only stare at the officer. Six feet, seven inches tall, clad in a winter great coat of wolf skin, he loomed as a veritable Gargantua against the blackness of the outer night. The fearsome impact was not lessened by the craggy features, the huge head, the jut of the heavy brow, the burning intensity of the eyes, and the wide, merciless set of the thin-lipped mouth.

The boy, Red Dust, had never seen him before but had heard of him in the tales of terror told by Cheyenne mothers. He knew him at once. "Mashanē," he gasped, and shrank back.

Preacher Bleek stepped forward. He bowed to the gigantic officer, welcoming him with a diffident sweep of the candle.

"Good evening, Colonel Chivington, sir," he said. "Please to come in, gentlemen, and permit me to close this door against the rain."

Chivington said nothing to Bleek. His unblinking eyes ran over the room. He stood motionless, like some hungry prowling cat come into a warm barn full of fat mice.

"Skemp," he ordered one of the sergeants, "arrest those Indians by the fire. Durant," he told the other sergeant, "get our horses into the Preacher's barn, then bring the men inside. Shoot those Indian ponies where they stand."

The second sergeant saluted and went out.

Skemp moved to the fire. Ignoring the two

grown Cheyennes, he put the muzzle of his carbine to the head of Red Dust. Chivington nodded watchfully.

"If either of the devils moves," he said, "kill the boy."

His command was three times punctuated by pistol shots from the outer yard. The Cheyennes by the fire moved only their eyes and the muscles of their faces, but it was as though the shots were going into them rather than into their beloved shaggy ponies.

In the muttered thunder of his voice Roman Nose said something slowly and with great distinctness, but in his own tongue. Instantly Chivington wheeled on Bleek.

"What did he say?" he demanded, lashing the question.

Bleek shrugged. "A prayer for the ponies," he answered. "I reckon we wouldn't understand it, Colonel."

Chivington stared at him. "We may understand it better than you think, Bleek," he said. "That was no prayer. Skemp."

"Yes, sir."

"Did you catch any of that?"

"No, sir. I ain't no good with Cheyenne. Just a little 'Rapaho and Comanche, sir."

"Did that sound like a prayer to you, Skemp?"

"Not hardly, Colonel."

There was a pause. During it Chivington seemed

to be studying the situation. And Nehemiah Bleek was studying it. The missionary could smell the danger.

"All right," said Chivington, breaking the stillness, "we'll see if we can't get a little better Indian translation. Skemp, bring me that boy. He can be our interpreter."

Nehemiah Bleek saw the look of wildness that came into the face of Roman Nose at the officer's reference to Red Dust. In the same glance he noted the way in which Chivington was watching Roman Nose and Picking Tooth, and he understood what it was that the commander of the 3rd Colorado was doing. He was trying to make the warriors move. His hand was at the butt of his revolver. He wanted the Indians to do something, regardless of how trivial, when Skemp seized the boy. In his cold-eyed cunning, he knew that of all things calculated to snap the thin string of civilization restraining such horseback hostiles, the most certain act was to touch one of them in roughness—and especially a child.

But if Colonel John Chivington knew Indians, he did not know Nehemiah Bleek. Few men did. The Horse Creek missionary was standing behind Chivington, near the front door. The first hint the officer had of anything amiss was when he heard the *thud* of the door bar dropping home. He wheeled about, hand closing on the revolver butt. But the hand did not continue with the movement to draw or to fire.

From beneath his long white nightgown, Preacher Bleek had produced an ancient flintlock pistol of awesome bore. The distinctive scraping *clink* of the big spur side hammer being put on cock was not lost on Colonel John Chivington.

At the fire, hands outreached to grasp Red Dust, Sergeant Skemp hesitated. He had set down his carbine to take up the boy. Now he did not know whether to leap to retrieve the weapon, to seize up the youth and use him as a shield, or to stay poised as he was. Bleek relieved him of the decision.

"Now, Colonel," he said quietly to Chivington, "happen you touch your pistol, or your sergeant touches that there boy, I will touch off this here blunderbuss, and God Himself will judge the consequences."

Chivington's glare was that of a cornered thing. His face was dead white.

"Bleek," he said, thick-voiced, "you're crazy. You can hang for this!"

The bearded missionary shook his head. "Hang, Colonel?" he said. "For saving your life?"

He waved the horse pistol, uttered a Cheyenne phrase to Red Dust. Reaching down, the boy took the corner of Roman Nose's blanket in one hand, the corner of Picking Tooth's blanket in the other.

"Go ahead," said Bleek gently. "Pull them away."

The boy drew the blankets off, not quickly, but

slowly and with his dark eyes never leaving the giant cavalry officer and Preacher Bleek.

Chivington saw the rifles of Roman Nose and Picking Tooth come into view. He saw the bores of both weapons aimed at him. He saw the red fingers on the triggers, the red thumbs hooking the hammers back. And he saw the look in the eyes of the two Cheyennes. In the hush of that seeing, he felt the barrel of Bleek's flintlock ease into the small of his back.

"Unfasten your revolver belt and let it drop," said the Horse Creek missionary.

Chivington was in a dark rage. It was a fact that Bleek had just saved him from the certain death hidden beneath the Cheyennes' blankets. But now Preacher had gone beyond this fact and had put a gun on an officer of the United States and was unlawfully disarming him in the presence of the enemy.

"Bleek," he said coldly, "do you know the penalty for insurrection?"

"Colonel," answered the missionary, "I ain't even certain that I know what insurrection means. Drop the belt."

"It means," said Chivington through his teeth, "armed uprising against established authority. It means," he added icily, "pulling a gun on an officer of the Third Colorado Cavalry. It means the rope."

Preacher Bleek shifted the horse pistol, but only

to press its muzzle more deeply into the officer's back.

"You won't hang me, Colonel. Not tonight, anyways."

"Bleek, for the last time . . . I warn you!"

"Drop the belt, Colonel," repeated Preacher. "And that's my last warning to you."

V

Slowly Colonel Chivington obeyed Bleek's order. The heavy cavalry revolver, with its belt and holster, *thudded* to the earthen floor. Preacher carefully kicked it aside. But in the moment that he did so, Sergeant Skemp dived for his carbine resting against the fireplace. Once more he was too late. Roman Nose instantly swung the barrel of his rifle, striking the sergeant across the shins just as his fingers clutched the carbine. The trooper's feet were knocked out from under him and he fell heavily, hitting his head against the stone corner of the fireplace. He lay motionlessly on the floor, either dead or unconscious.

"Preacher," said Chivington, white-lipped, "if Sergeant Skemp is dead, so are you. If he is only hurt and these Indians are known hostiles, which I assume they are, then I am going to put you in a federal prison for the rest of your natural life." He paused, the seething fury of a proud and ruthless commander still paling his face. "Only," he said, "you won't find it a very natural life, Bleek. I will see to that. Now put that rusty horse pistol away and unbar that door for my men. You are under arrest."

Nehemiah Bleek shook his head. "It's been said, Colonel, that you don't cherish the idea of taking prisoners. That being so, I don't cherish the idea of being taken prisoner by you. Furthermore, Mashanē," he said with meaningful emphasis, "let me advise you that, if you were to try to put in arrest those two Indians by the fire, you would be killed instanter. In fact, sir, I'm not even convinced I can hold them off of you in any event. Your only chance . . . and you'd better hold to it hard, Colonel . . . is to order off those men waiting outside. These Indians are northerns, as you have guessed. They don't have a treaty with the government, and to them Mashanē is a foul word."

Chivington now was so beyond himself with anger that he whirled about on Bleek, ignoring the latter's cocked pistol. At once, both Roman Nose and Picking Tooth leaped up from the hearth and came after him, closing on his rear like two red wolves. Their rush was as silent as it was deadly. Bleek saw them in time to cry out stridently in Cheyenne that they must not kill Mashanē at any cost. It was a tribute to the profound friendship of the Cheyenne people for the proprietor of the Horse Creek school that the savage warriors obeyed him.

Shifting their rifles from firing to clubbing position, they swung them against the back and shoulders of Chivington, driving the giant cavalryman to his knees, dazed and shocked.

Bleek knew, however, that the killing blood was up in his dangerous guests. He had not been deceiving Chivington in his doubts of controlling the wild visitors from high Wyoming. The hated Mashanē's life was still within the crushing drive of either of their rifle butts.

"Maheo be thanked," he told the warriors in Cheyenne. "You are true friends. Quickly, now, we must save the children and save ourselves. There is no time to think of Mashanē or his sergeant. It is our own lives we must worry about."

"What are we to do?" asked Roman Nose.

"Yes," said Picking Tooth, "what? Those soldiers out there will kill us. There are too many of them. We can't fight them. They will corner us in here and send for more soldiers and we are dead in the end, anyway." He turned to Roman Nose. "I say kill Mashanē, Maōx. When will we have another such chance?"

"I agree with you," said Roman Nose. "What is your idea, Preacher? You had better hurry with it."

In a lull of the wind, they all heard the voices of the soldiers growing louder outside. Next instant the door was tried, and, when it did not yield, Sergeant Durant knocked sharply on it and called for Chivington's further orders.

Chivington, head clearing now, stumbled to his feet. The Cheyennes turned wild. The excitement of Durant's pounding on the door, the plain intent of Chivington to answer that pounding, to unbar the door—he was starting for it even then—proved too much for nervous systems conditioned to kill or escape at the hated cry of pony soldiers.

Roman Nose's deep voice was a hoarse snarl. "Get out of the way, Preacher," he raged. "We are going to kill Mashanē. Get down, get down . . . !"

Bleek leaped in behind Chivington and struck him across the back of the head with the barrel of the horse pistol. The huge officer buckled and slid to the floor, but he was not unconscious. Like some great felled ox he began to stumble once more to his feet. Bleek was astride him instantly, jamming the pistol against his temple.

"Colonel, if you don't stay down and you don't do precisely what I say, those Indians will kill both of us."

From somewhere, Chivington regained the clarity of mind to understand the danger he was in. Both Roman Nose and Picking Tooth were telling the Preacher to get away from Mashanē, that they were going to shoot him. The Indians had a wild sound in their voices, a wild look in their glittering black eyes.

47

"All right, all right!" the officer cried out. "Durant!"

"Sir? What's the matter?" the soldier answered from outside.

"Shut up, Durant!" Chivington shook his head, clearing away the remaining webs of confusion. "They've taken me hostage in here. Do whatever they say."

"They, sir?"

"Preacher Bleek. Do what he tells you. If I come to harm, charge him. He incited these Indians in here. They jumped us."

"Is Skemp . . . ?"

"Skemp's unconscious or dead, I don't know. One of the Indians hit him. Talk to Bleek."

But Preacher did not wait for Durant. He spoke first and rapidly to the Cheyennes. After a moment, the two warriors lowered their rifles and moved away from Chivington. The officer got to his feet. He weaved a little, but seemed to have recovered himself enough to understand his situation.

Roman Nose and Picking Tooth had him under guard. There was no doubt that they would fire into him at the first excuse. Yet, also, he could see that their killing urge had passed. He realized that this was the work of Preacher Bleek. The missionary had almost certainly saved his life twice within as many minutes. But it was the same Bleek who had put his life in jeopardy to begin with by permitting the Cheyennes to have their rifles under their blankets when admitting Chivington and his sergeant. In such a case, any white cavalry officer must proceed with extreme caution the rest of the way.

Accordingly Chivington asked Bleek for permission to sit down in the chair by the table where the missionary had his few work tools of teaching—two or three primary readers, an atlas, a picture-book geography, chalk, hand slate, erasers, his tattered old Bible—and, once seated, made no more resistance. "Sergeant Durant!" Bleek called to the soldier outside. "Can you hear me?"

"Yes, sir, go ahead."

"Where are your men?"

"I've stationed them around this building. You're surrounded, Preacher. There had best no harm come to the colonel."

"None will, if you do exactly as I tell you."

"Is that so, Colonel?"

"Do as he says, damn you!" flared Chivington. "I've already given you that order."

"Yes, sir. All right, Preacher."

"Hold a moment," said Bleek.

Turning to the Cheyennes guarding Chivington, he asked them if he could trust them to obey him now.

They looked at one another, thinking over the question. The truth of the matter was that, whether by courage or ignorance, by clever mind or simple one, the big white man had risked his life to save their lives. Any long-time fighters of the pony soldiers knew what penalty Preacher would pay for helping hostile Indians escape through holding Mashanē hostage. When Roman Nose and Red Dust and Picking Tooth were all safely home in high Wyoming, Preacher would be hanging in the prairie wind by his neck from an Army scaffold outside the stockade at Fort Lyon.

"All right, Preacher," said Roman Nose. "We will obey."

Bleek at once turned to the door and told Sergeant Durant to come inside. The trooper hesitated and was ordered by Chivington to obey. Bleek admitted him and re-barred the door. He then pointed out concisely to the sergeant the position of his commander. Durant was an intelligent man. He nodded quickly, and Bleek continued.

Safe passage must be granted the two warriors and the boy. They were on a friendly visit and could not be surrendered to Colonel Chivington. The sergeant would understand this, of course. Again Durant nodded. Chivington said nothing, but the look he gave his sergeant was enough. Here was a man who very plainly, or at least properly, did not subscribe to the no prisoner philosophy of his commander. That understanding nod of Durant's to the impossibility of giving over Indian captives to Colonel John Chivington was going to cost him his chevrons, and perhaps a great deal more. But the colonel wisely kept his anger to himself, and listened with Durant to Bleek's proposal.

With the Cheyennes, the latter now said, must go Chivington himself. This was only to make ironclad the assurances to the Cheyennes that the soldiers would attempt no pursuit. To protect Chivington, Bleek would also go with the Indians. Durant would stay behind in command of the troops at the mission. Trusting Durant, Bleek would give him the exact destination of the retreating Cheyennes—the big southern camp on the Black Butte Fork of the Smoky Hill River—but would caution the sergeant at the same time to bear in mind that this confidence was not blind generosity. It was a calculated risk. Not only Colonel Chivington, but also the reputation of the 3rd Colorado was being held for ransom.

If the patrol stayed in the field until it had Chivington safely back, who need ever know of the affair? But what if the patrol, or some member thereof, should return to the base camp at Bijou Basin to report the incident, or to seek reinforcements toward its revenge? How would it benefit the 3rd Colorado to have it known that Colonel John Chivington and an entire scout patrol of his brand-new volunteer cavalry had been outwitted by a jackleg preacher, two visiting Cheyennes, and a small boy? How would such knowledge affect the 3rd's relationships with such as Major Anthony, Agent Colley, Governor Evans, or General Curtis and the Department of the Platte? What would be the result for Skemp and Durant? For Colonel Chivington? For the men themselves?

As for Nehemiah Bleek, he realized the implications of his own part in the night's work. He wanted only for Durant to know—for the record—that he had done what he had done solely to prevent the murder of Chivington by the Cheyenne hostiles he had surprised at The Cottonwoods. Beyond this statement, Bleek had no defense.

Skemp had been unconscious during the critical actions. He could bear witness neither for nor against Preacher's story. Only Chivington himself knew the truth, and Bleek would never expect him to testify against his own cause in any military court that might try the Horse Creek missionary for what Chivington had already promised him would be a hanging offense. The simple fact was that Bleek could not trust his life to the mercy of Mashanē, any more than he could the lives of his Cheyenne friends. Neither, and indeed above all, could he or would he entrust the lives of his children to this wicked man. He believed that Chivington was possessed. He understood now why the Cheyennes called him Mashanē. Bleek paused, studying both Durant and Chivington.

The commander of the 3rd was breathing

heavily. He looked at Bleek with sick fury. His massive face was the bad color of a fish belly. His eyes were fixed, staring. Durant was sweating profusely. He was also ill, but in another and normal way; he was sick with fear of his commanding officer.

Bleek knew that the matter had come down to the last question. "Well, Colonel?" he said.

VI

Chivington, his mind on the quality of mercy to be expected from his Cheyenne guards, told Durant to proceed.

The sergeant called in the men from the outside, had them stack their arms, and stand away from them. Then Chivington informed them of the terms under which Bleek would attempt to leave the mission with the Cheyennes. There were threats and muttered hardnesses at this, but the huge officer said that he was briefing them and not soliciting support. He made the men see, far better than Preacher might have done, why it was to the advantage of all of them to accept the plan for the safe passage of the hostiles. The troopers were not dull-spirited regulars. Local men, they had seen much of the Cheyennes, could appreciate their colonel's agreement to go along with the crazy Preacher's hostage suggestion.

53

Moreover, they read between the words of Chivington's instructions to co-operate with Preacher Bleek, the message of hatred and vengeance that the 3rd would one day wreak on the Horse Creek schoolmaster and his red friends. Chivington was as well known to his men as he was to the Indian mothers who hid their children at the whisper of the name Mashanē. The colonel was utterly without compassion. From the hour of his release near the Cheyenne village over on the Smoky Hill, the hunt for Preacher Nehemiah Bleek would begin. Nor would it end until the Horse Creek missionary had been tracked down and executed.

But the men, lacking a spokesman, still hesitated. They were not convinced how Chivington meant his orders to be obeyed. Sergeant Durant, who might have supplied the momentum for acceptance, refused the responsibility. Preacher Bleek had read him correctly. He was a decent man and no fanatic where Indians were concerned. His instinct here was to do exactly what his commanding officer ordered him to do, and volunteer nothing. Accordingly he stood rigidly facing the men, back to Chivington. If he were doing anything, it was praying that Nehemiah Bleek knew these fierce red people as well as local legend said he did. Chivington did not miss this deliberate obduracy on the part of his second sergeant. Noting it, however, was all that he could then do. The situation continued at stalemate and the hard-eyed hostiles with the rifles were becoming extremely nervous again.

Bleek barked something at the Indians in Cheyenne, then wheeled on Chivington. "Better make it an order to get this thing moving, Colonel, and make it quick."

He spoke quietly, but the officer was not misled by that. He merely nodded and said: "All right, men, this is an order. Do exactly what Bleek tells you."

The troopers eyed one another, shuffled their feet. Some saluted, others merely nodded, or waved awkwardly.

Chivington shifted his glance to the unhappy Durant. "Sergeant," he said, "you will be in charge here, as agreed, and will be responsible in my absence. Have you any questions?"

Durant turned and saluted. "No, sir," he said.

Chivington nodded with evident satisfaction. When he spoke to Nehemiah Bleek, the disquieting chill of his original stalking entrance had returned. "Very well, Preacher," he said evenly, "do your damnedest."

The children, of course, were long since awake. To get them dressed and ready to depart took only a few minutes. While Sunflower, the seven-year-old "mother" of the group, supervised this phase of the abandonment, without anyone telling him Red Dust began to help the children.

Rather, he began to help Sunflower help them.

The little Arapaho girl was not giggling now, and the Cheyenne boy appreciated this. It was a good kind of girl who could work hard and be serious when that was what had to be. Red Dust thought it was remarkable that a young child could laugh so easily one moment, and be so grown-up and efficient the next. But he had only started to learn about little Soxoenos, the Arapaho Sunflower.

It was true that Preacher had only told the children they were going on a surprise visit to the big Cheyenne camp on the Smoky Hill. As a result, the mood of the youngsters, while sleepy-eyed—until they saw all the pony soldiers in the big room—was nevertheless the usual mood of children going on any kind of journey. There was a lot of chattering and tussling and failure to pay attention to the work at hand. How many times in such a young life would one be awakened in the middle of the night and told to get ready to go and see one's Indian kinfolk far away on the great Smoky Hill River? But Red Dust took charge of this nonsense and the mission tots, all of less years than he, and most impressed with this slim wild cousin from the north country they obeyed him and got all of their things piled on the floor and ready to be loaded.

While Red Dust and Sunflower did this work, troopers under Sergeant Durant were hooking up the mission wagon and bringing it around in front for loading. This vehicle, canvas-topped and gaunt-ribbed as some bleaching buffalo skeleton, had been suffering the pangs of age when the Santa Fé trade was still flourishing. From whence Preacher Bleek had rescued and restored the old prairie schooner, no man could say. How it continued to roll over the plains without accident was another unanswered mystery. "A matter of faith," was Bleek's explanation, and scarcely arguable at that. Certain it was that its shabby age would have discouraged even a wolf hunter or hide hauler. Its wheels were bowed in the front, cow-hocked in the rear. Its hickory running gear and bed frame, yellow pine bed and siding, ironwood tongue and whiffletrees all were warped and shrunken and bleached and blasted by the snows and sands of a thousand journeys over rock and river and desert. It was not a real wagon but the ghost of a hundred Conestogas broken or burned or abandoned along the Arkansas Road since William Bent had built his fort and opened the country to the white man some thirty-five winters gone.

But if the Argonaut, as Bleek had named the old wagon, was ancient and questionable of pedigree, the teams that towed it through the seas of buffalo grass surrounding Horse Creek would, by com- parison, make the Argonaut a thing of grace and loveliness. The wheelers were called the Kiowa

Ladies. A set of twin Indian foals, they had been travois animals among the Kiowas when acquired by Bleek. Smoky white in color, freckled and speckled, rat-tailed and -maned, they had been together since being dropped on the prairie by their wild dam, and to attempt to separate them for any reason was tantamount to war. They would bite, kick, fall down, roll over, squeal, attack any adult on foot and within reach—save for Preacher Bleek—and were guilty of but one softness toward humanity, an abiding love for small Indian children. Bleek had named them Salome and Sheba.

The leaders were Samson and Delilah, the former a giant black Spanish jack, the latter a diminutive piebald Comanche jenny with one sky-blue and one canary-yellow eye. Samson wore his mane unroached because Bleek believed that cutting it might sap the jack's enormous strength. The bristles of this fearful crest stood straight on end and were no less than an arrow length in height. So black and so vast was Samson that all who saw him vowed he was no male jackass but a Percheron mule sired out of some settlement plow mare by Satan's own Spanish jack. In temper toward mankind, the Spanish jack and the Comanche jenny were the equals of Salome and Sheba. Trusting no man beyond Nehemiah Bleek, they were like affectionate camp dogs with the mission children.

This, then, was the caravan of Preacher Bleek and his unwanted orphans of the Argonaut, the ark in which they would now set sail through the stormy dark toward the Smoky Hill River and whatever of God's will awaited them in that distant place. Bleek understood that he would never see his school again—or had to guess, at least, that he would not.

In the final moment of his arrangements with Durant and Chivington, something had happened to guarantee this unhappy likelihood. Skemp had regained consciousness.

VII

With Skemp recovered, Durant was detailed to accompany Chivington as a fellow hostage, "to provide added security against Indian treachery." Bleek felt that he could not argue this change except at the price of losing his tenuous control over Roman Nose and Picking Tooth. But he had known in the moment of Skemp's leering acknowledgment of Chivington's parting advice to "take care of things" at the mission, that all he had counted on of decency from Durant was doomed. The hope for a realistic delivery of the captive officer, with no senseless deviltry thrown in, had vanished.

Skemp was of the vigilante breed. Like

Chivington. He had no stake in the land. He felt no love of hearth. No need to build and defend a home. Skemp and his kind were freebooters, soldiers of fortune. They were on the Arkansas to find a fortune or to thieve one from someone else. They sought to adventure merely for the sake of helling and hard riding. They warred against a nomad people who had no modern firearms, a people of no military organization, no common leadership, no tribal bond save blood, no mutual creed beyond love of freedom and native heath. But Skemp's kind, as Chivington's, would leave the land when they had violated it; they never stayed on to rebuild, to pay back, to belong. Knowing this, Nehemiah Bleek made the preparations for departing The Cottonwoods guided by his assessment of 1st Sergeant Skemp.

Into the Argonaut went all of the school's robes and blankets, and a hay mattress for each child. What supplies Bleek had on hand of foodstuffs were also stowed aboard. Into the buffalo-hide 'possum belly slung under the wagon went the mission's tools, all of the shovels, axes, saws, adzes—everything of use that Bleek had made or traded for in his lonely years on Horse Creek. In the side box by the water barrel were packed the few books and other meager trappings of his teaching, barring only his dog-eared Bible, which he put in the bosom of his bear-skin winter coat. The children were the last of the cargo, and to judge from the good cheer and the Cheyenne banter with which the brawny missionary helped them over the tailgate and into the tumbled mountain of robes and hay pallets within the canvased cavern of the old wagon's bed, it could be assumed that the Smoky Hill visit was as innocent as the prairie orphans had been told.

A closer look at the broad, bearded face, when the last child was loaded and the tailgate tarp drawn closed against the lashing rain, would have shown the harsher truth. It was not an easy thing for Nehemiah Bleek to say good bye to The Cottonwoods. A part of his life had gone into this crossroads of the wilderness. That part would stay here when he now turned away; it would be buried there at The Cottonwoods, unmarked and unmourned, but it would be a part of the crazy preacher from Horse Creek, and it would be dead.

"Preacher," called the strained voice of Sergeant Durant, "we had best be going! Your Indians look to be getting edgy again."

Bleek went around to the front of the wagon. All seemed in readiness. Astride Samson sat Colonel Chivington. The black Spanish jack was Bleek's own saddle mount, and a fit brute to bear such a burden as Mashanē. Flanking Chivington were Roman Nose and Picking Tooth, astride borrowed cavalry horses. The hostage's hands were free, but his booted feet were tied beneath Samson's hairy belly. The Cheyennes rode with their rifles held across the pommels of their saddles. The range between them and the commander of the 3rd Colorado was powder burn close. Any desperation move by the captive to free himself, or by his troopers to do so, would carry the certainty of blasting gunfire into the colonel's back.

As though to remind of this guarantee, Roman Nose kept cocking and uncocking his rifle in cadence with a prayer chant monotone that Chivington found more chilling than the November rain. On the passenger side of the wagon seat, Sergeant Durant waited with vast unease. He was not restrained in any way except as he might be sobered by the 238-pound presence of Nehemiah Bleek on the driver's seat beside him. Yet he found this bond as effective as his commander did the cocking *click* of Roman Nose's rifle hammer.

Making a last examination of these preparations now, Bleek nodded and commenced to climb up to take the lines. As he did so, Sunflower's small voice called urgently to him in Cheyenne. Bleek stopped and smote himself on the forehead with the heel of his hand, despairing of his stupidity. He had forgotten the dog.

Going back to the brute's kennel by the mission door, he released the animal but kept his chain firmly in hand. Only when he had returned to the wagon and re-chained the Cheyenne wolf dog to the tailgate, did he feel easy. The dog had an Indian name and deserved it. It was Hokomenònika, Lamewolf.

Lamewolf had been crippled in a white man's spring-jaw trap when young. Since that time, he had hated the scent and the sight of the *veho*, the pale-eyed men. It was not safe to release him in the presence of white men. Bleek he would tolerate, even partially trust. But his major love was reserved for the little Arapaho girl, Sunflower. For her, his savagery turned to total servitude. His wildness became that of a lap puppy, his ugly temper no fiercer than a dove's. Bleek believed that this was because both Sunflower and Lamewolf had been injured by the white man. "Made to limp," as the bearded Preacher put it, "in the same hard track of life." For whatever reason, the wolf dog was the slave of Sunflower. "Watch after him," he told the little girl. "See he doesn't jump in the wagon and get everything all wet."

He spoke in English now. He did that with Sunflower, who was his pet and pride, and a fast learner who could understand and speak the white man's tongue in only three years with scarcely a trace of Indian gutturals. That is, she could if she wished. But Sunflower was a very independent little person. Right then she answered Preacher in a chatter of thick-voweled Cheyenne that sounded as though she had never been a day away from the cowhide lodges of her northern nomad kinfolk.

"Heathen!" growled the big missionary, and

turned and went back up to the front of the wagon.

Again he had one foot on the hub of the wheel. And again he struck himself on the forehead with exasperation.

"Hold a moment, friend," he signed to Sergeant Durant, who was holding the lines for him. "I must be getting old. Be patient, and don't try anything with those Cheyennes. I've forgot the medical supplies."

Returning to the school, he entered the main room. It was by agreement deserted, the troopers of the patrol being confined by barred door to the dormitory. Bleek had given them a small axe and said not to start chopping their way out until the caravan was clear of Horse Creek. This was, of course, to assure the Argonaut sufficient start to disappear in the rainy darkness before any immediate pursuit might be mounted by Skemp. Such, anyway, was the faith of Preacher Bleek.

Crossing the darkened room now, he approached what he had taught his Indian children to call his "padlocked Holy Medicine cabinet." In reality, this was an old cast-iron stage depot safe locked with a combination. Where Bleek had come upon it was one of his several state secrets. The safe's contents, however, were well known.

Spinning the numbered dial, Preacher swung open the safe door, reached in, and brought forth the nearly forgotten treasure of medicinal spirits. He raised the bottle for a fond moment to the firelight, so that the dying glow could show him the beatitude of the soul-restoring legend blazoned on its side—Old Crow. Then he put it to his lips and took a single unpausing and prodigious draft. He stood a moment permitting the great jolt of the whiskey to invade his toes, his fingertips, the last grateful vacuoles of his weary brain.

"Ahhhh!" He smiled, and put the bottle inside the bear-skin coat with his Bible. Blowing out the smoky oil lamp on the schoolmaster's table, he went out into the raw bluster of the night cheerfully whistling a march-step chorus of "The Battle Hymn of the Republic."

The rain had slowed to a tinny drumming on the wagon's canvas top. Its steady sound soon lulled the last child—but one—to an untroubled sleep. Red Dust could not shut his eyes. He sat by the tailgate, peering out through the pucker hole, thinking of a hundred ways in which he might escape. It must be, he thought, fully three wagon rides to the Smoky Hill River. Three entire days and nights imprisoned in that little rolling lodge? With those seven little children giggling and roughing around? And that foolish small Arapaho girl grinning at him and blinking those great black eyelashes of hers and sliding her fingers into his and patting him on the knee and advising him—him, Red Dust, the nephew of Roman Nose!—not to worry, that she would see that no harm came to him? *Eotohesso*; it was amazing.

But Red Dust's wonderment over Sunflower was only in its most innocent stage. He had no more than thought of the little Arapaho girl when he felt her hand touch his and heard the suppressed sound of her contagious giggle. She put a finger to her lips, warning him to make no noise. Then she slid past him and wriggled out the pucker hole of the wagon. Popping his head out of the pucker hole, he saw the girl lying half over the shelf-like box Preacher had built onto the Argonaut's rear as a sort of baggage boot similar to the ones on the stagecoaches that plied the Arkansas Road. Red Dust thought that surely she would fall and be hurt, and could not imagine what she was doing. As he hesitated, he saw her begin to slip, and without thinking he leaned out and seized her ankles to hold her up. This brought another giggle and in a moment she had twisted back up atop the baggage box and was holding up the harness snap and the pinion end of the dog chain that fastened Lamewolf to the wagon's rear.

In the next breath the great shaggy brute had leaped up on the box, joining Sunflower. From here, the Arapaho girl ordered him to jump in through the pucker hole and he obeyed, landing very nearly in Red Dust's lap. Once inside, the freed wolf dog shook his burden of mud and rain all over the rear compartment of the Argonaut. Sunflower now followed him in through the pucker hole, while Red Dust was still spitting muddy water out of his mouth and saying things in Cheyenne that no nice boy should ever say in front of a little girl.

Sunflower, a creature of impartial good heart, patted Lamewolf on the head with one hand and Red Dust on the head with the other hand.

"You are both good boys," she said. "Now we can all go to sleep. My friend, Lamewolf, won't be wet and muddy any more. Thank you, Cheyenne boy, for holding onto my feet. We always bring Lamewolf into the wagon when Preacher isn't looking. Happy sleep to you."

Red Dust said nothing. Perhaps it was as well. If Sunflower's friend, Lamewolf, was no longer wet and muddy, her friend, Red Dust, was very much so.

VIII

Now, in truth, Preacher Bleek did not know what lay ahead. They had come four miles through the night with no mishap and that was a thing for which to be thankful. The rain had stopped and the stars were out. On the seat beside him Sergeant Durant sat like a man of wood. He had spoken no word, nor had Bleek, since the outset. Preacher knew that the soldier was thinking very hard about something, and would talk when he was ready to do so.

But presently the clouds returned, blotting out the stars. The temperature fell ten degrees in as many minutes. It began to snow. The flakes were hard and small and stung the skin like needles. Durant glanced nervously ahead, where Chivington rode on black Samson. Then he leaned close to Bleek.

"I want to talk, Preacher," he said, "but I don't know how to commence."

Bleek nodded quietly. "It will come to you . . . just continue to think on it."

Durant returned the nod, but his mind remained troubled and his tongue mute. He was a soldier, and had joined up to ride against these hostiles that Preacher befriended. He was a family man, with three young ones and a fine wife. These Indians, some of them like these very Cheyennes of Bleek's, were killers. They did attack homes like his and Durant had no sympathy for them. Neither did he think that Preacher was right in shielding them, or in harboring their young ones. The Indian kids were in fact red nits, just like the colonel said, and they would grow up to make hostile lice the same as Chivington vowed they would. At least they would, unless the daft Preacher actually could redeem them with his far-fetched idea of educating them to behave like white folks, or to get by with the white folks. And Sergeant Durant had no more real illusions on this latter score than did his grim commander, or than Sergeant Skemp, or any of the wet and cold troopers locked in Bleek's dormitory room back at the schoolhouse. But it was not Bleek and his orphans that bothered Durant, and that prevented him from talking to the big missionary.

What bothered him was Colonel J.M. Chivington. He knew the man. He had known him for a considerable time. There was little about Chivington, an ordained minister of the Methodist Church, that deceived the quiet 2nd sergeant of the scout patrol. The fact that the cavalry officer could be called preacher by rights, whereas Nehemiah Bleek was only a self-declared man of God, did not change a thing. When Chivington put on that uniform and that long sword, he was no man of any god. And when he grew silent and abandoned his usual angry way, he was thinking of just one thing—revenge. In the present case, it was Preacher Bleek who had humbled him, and, unless Providence intervened, Durant knew what had to happen to Preacher Bleek; Chivington would kill him.

One thing might save Nehemiah Bleek. That would be if Durant could talk to him and convince him to let Chivington go, and to flee for his own life, then and there, never returning to Colorado Territory. But the miles fell away; the snow deepened. Preacher Bleek was forced to halt and make camp in the shelter of some scrub timber, and the opportunity was lost.

Once in camp, with the cold eyes of Colonel Chivington on him, the simple-hearted soldier could not bring himself to speak to the Horse Creek missionary. Durant knew the price of being caught at such merciful work by his commander. Chivington would destroy him as quickly as he would destroy Nehemiah Bleek, or any man alive who might stand in the way of Mashanē's vengeance.

Next morning, the skies had blown clear. The air was sharp and winey. Only an additional light blanket of snow, enough to make a fairyland for the children of the prairie's ordinary dreariness, had fallen during the night. The start from the shelter camp was made in as good spirit as was possible under the onus of Mashanē's continuing refusal to talk to anyone save Sergeant Durant, and only to the trooper privately.

Some changes were made by Bleek in the march order soon after setting out. He had been watching the skyline to the rear, toward Horse Creek. Reaching an elevation above the creek's drainage a mile to the east, he was given a better view. At once he stopped the teams.

The greasy tumor of smoke growing against the raw blue of the morning sky to the west ballooned and burst higher even as he was swinging down from the driver's box. He said nothing but trudged up to where Chivington sat watching the smoke

70

from Samson's back. The giant cavalryman had an expression on his face that would have maddened a saint. And Nehemiah Bleek was not canonized. Nevertheless, he kept his own voice and attitude as quiet and controlled as Chivington's had been.

"Colonel," he said, "is that Skemp's work, or yours?"

"A good man, Skemp." Chivington licked his thin lips. "He knows what to do."

"Is that your answer, Colonel? Is that why you left Skemp behind, rather than Durant? To burn my school?"

Chivington looked down at him. His features were contorted but the voice was calm. "Damn you, Bleek," he said. "Get on with it."

By this time Roman Nose and Picking Tooth were crowding their ponies in more closely. In Cheyenne they inquired of Preacher if something were wrong. Bleek told them that it was a thing between Mashanē and himself.

The Indians nodded and touched their fingers to their foreheads, respecting their good friend's answer. Roman Nose said in his wonderfully deep voice: "We are sorry about your school, Preacher. We know what it is to see the black smoke of a man's lodge rolling against the sky. If you wish it, Preacher, we will kill him for you right here."

Bleek thanked him, saying that such a thing could not be done in front of the children. To this, Picking Tooth observed that the pony soldiers

71

did it all the time in front of the Cheyenne children. He suggested that Preacher reconsider his charity toward Mashanē.

"Let us shoot him for you, Preacher," he urged. "I would like to have that wolf-skin coat of his. It's going to be colder very soon, and Maōx and I did not come south with warm enough things to wear. Move to one side just a bit more, eh?"

Again Bleek declined, explaining that Mashanē's whole value was as a living pawn in their risky game against the rest of the pony soldiers. He was all, really, that could get them safely across the plain to the Smoky Hill. As warriors, how could they argue this matter?

They could not, Roman Nose admitted. "Go ahead," he told Bleek. "Do it in your own way."

Bleek ordered Durant to drive the wagon. He himself would go on foot ahead of the caravan, scouting the way. Picking Tooth would ride back on the trail to watch for Skemp and the patrol. To be sure that the troopers would see that Chivington was alive and in good condition, the officer would be taken off Samson and made to walk out ahead of the wagon teams. This time his feet would be freed and his hands bound, with a rope running from his hands to the horn of Roman Nose's saddle. And across that saddle horn would still be the rifle of the Cheyenne warrior. In all of this, of course, the white names of the two braves were not used, all talk being in Cheyenne and using the northern names Maōx and Kōvohe. Bleek well understood the excitement the legendary Cheyenne warrior's name would have created in Chivington and the troopers of the 3rd Colorado—knowledge that might easily have altered the entire complexion of the 3rd's conduct. It might still do so, if carelessly disclosed. It was God's own grace, the Horse Creek man thought, that neither Roman Nose nor Picking Tooth spoke a word of English. Their comprehension of Bleek's Cheyenne, however, was perfect. Instantly they obeyed his new orders, if not exactly. The big missionary had said nothing of pulling Chivington off Samson so suddenly and so hard that the huge officer would fall under the Spanish jack and get himself stepped on by 1,200 pounds of black jackass. Nor had he specified where Picking Tooth should jab Mashanē with his rifle muzzle in encouraging that officer to rise up out of the snow and present his hands for binding. Neither was it in Preacher's instructions that the hench-man of Roman Nose should peel Chivington's fine wolf-skin winter coat from his back and don it himself before remounting to ride off on his rear scout. But Preacher did not intervene.

The Indians were being Indians now. They were working at their own trade—war—and for Bleek or any white man to halt them at its rough inter-play would be more than foolish. Bleek would have said nothing had they wanted to strip Colonel

73

Chivington to his long-handled underdrawers. Just so they did not harm him, or inflame their mercurial tempers, or decide in the impetuously direct manner of their nomad kind simply to knock in the head of the hated pony soldier chief and be done with the entire business. This was all that Nehemiah Bleek could pray for—that he could continue to protect the life of John Chivington—and it was all that he was thinking of right then.

When, at last, Picking Tooth was gone and Roman Nose had the rope on Chivington, Bleek went to the rear of the wagon. There he unfastened Lamewolf from his chain.

Seeing Sunflower and Red Dust watching him from the tailgate, he grinned and reached inside the pocket of his coat. Sunflower understood what the gesture meant, and sent up a signal squeal that brought Blackbird, Young Buzzard, and the others all tumbling to hang and shout over the tailgate. Preacher knew the mystery of making rock candy. From his white sugar and certain other *veho* magic, he fashioned these gleaming crystals of pure happiness and, on such rare occasions, out would come the ancient gold poke in which he carried the treasure.

Now, giving each child a portion, he told them to be good and not to stray from the wagon. He was going to take Lamewolf and go out hunting. If he did not tell them for what he would hunt, perhaps it was wisdom, perhaps only oversight. In any event, the gift of candy crystals was sufficient to cover his retreat back to the head of the wagon. There, he told Durant to kick off the brake and go forward, following the same buffalo trail they had been taking on the previous night. Moving on up to the lead team, he smuggled a lump of the rock candy to black Samson without his mate Delilah seeing the reward.

As the Spanish jack rolled his wicked eyes and puckered his ape-like lips in pleasure, Bleek reached up and bent down one of the ragged hairy ears.

"That's for stepping on Mashanē," he whispered, and, before Samson could even grunt in reply, he was gone on past Roman Nose and Chivington in a swinging dog trot, Lamewolf loping by his side.

On the wagon seat of the Argonaut, Sergeant Durant watched the big man and the wolf dog dwindle against the snow-bright swell of the prairie. Behind him, in the wagon's covered bed, the Indian and half-blood children laughed and tussled among the buffalo robes. But, behind them, the smoke from the burning mission school on Horse Creek still rolled, black and ugly, against the lovely stillness of the morning sky. And somewhere between that smoke and those children Sergeant Skemp would be riding with his Indian-hating scout force of 3rd Colorado Cavalry.

Suddenly Sergeant Durant wished very much

that he had found the will to warn Preacher Bleek. But maybe there was yet time. Maybe he could find the way and the will at the next stopping place, the next camp spot. Maybe he could, if Skemp did not find that place or that spot before they did.

IX

They continued toward the Smoky Hill, watching for Skemp and the patrol. By noon halt, when no pursuit had developed and there was no news of Picking Tooth, Bleek was growing increasingly aware that something had gone wrong. He was forced to curtail his forward scouting because of his fears that Roman Nose might kill Chivington, or that the officer and Durant might make some try to get the big Cheyenne. As Roman Nose spoke and understood no English, the two white men could easily converse over his head to set a concerted effort of some kind.

When Picking Tooth still had not appeared after an hour's uneasy wait, the march order had to be changed once more. Chivington was bound hand and foot and placed in the bed of the wagon. Durant was manacled to the wagon seat with a set of rusted old Spanish leg irons that Bleek dug out of his toolbox. He could not move more than three feet in any direction. Preacher took the reins once more. The boy, Red Dust, and the little Arapaho girl, Sunflower, were told to take Lamewolf and go ahead of the wagon, letting the savage Cheyenne wolf dog smell out the way.

"I will have to tell you what it is we are hunting now," Bleek advised them. "We are hunting pony soldiers." He stepped to Red Dust and put his big freckled hand on the slender youth's shoulder. "The girl goes along only to handle the dog," he explained. "You are the warrior."

"*Haho*, thank you," said the boy, the first words he had spoken directly to Nehemiah Bleek.

The Horse Creek man further admonished the lad that he was to watch the dog constantly. At the first hint of the brute's smelling soldiers, Red Dust and Sunflower were to turn about and race for the wagon. Preacher would decide what next to do at that time.

"In no circumstance," he repeated, "are you to go forward once the dog has growled. Do you understand?"

"*Hēhe*," replied the boy. "Yes."

It was then time for Roman Nose to depart. He was going back to look for his friend, Picking Tooth. In parting, he and Bleek could not know whether they would meet again, or whether either of them would ever see the other in that hard life, or if either one, for that matter, would see Picking Tooth alive and well again. Roman Nose rode his horse up to the wagon and sat him a moment, looking at Bleek. He was plainly framing words, but he was never the orator. He was a simple fighting man. He found words poor weapons. Finally he scowled and put out his hand as a white man would. Surprised, Bleek took the dark hand and shook it with great strength. He could feel the Indian returning his grip with equal emotion.

"*Nataemhon,*" said the burly red-bearded Preacher. "Good hunting."

"*Haho,*" said the tall warrior. "Good hunting to you, also, Preacher." He swung his horse to depart but held the mount in at the last moment, watching his nephew and the small Arapaho girl march away through the snow with Lamewolf on the chain. His fierce dark eyes moved back to study the homely broad features of Nehemiah Bleek.

"Preacher," he said, "if I do not return, take the boy as your own son. Tell him that I said it."

Without words, Bleek touched the fingers of his left hand to his forehead. The gesture was the Cheyenne bond. Nothing could break it.

Roman Nose nodded and turned his horse away.

In the nature of the country there was no hiding the passage of a tall-wheeled old prairie schooner. The swells of the land lay across their route. Each stream crossing meant two skyline etchings of the caravan, once going down to the water, once coming up away from it. And between Horse Creek and the Smoky Hill River were no less than nine such crossings.

Bleek's only consolation was that these same

conditions of unlimited visibility protected him from any trick by Skemp. There was no way in which the troops could get around the slow crawl of the Argonaut by daylight. What would happen during the darkness of the coming night was another matter, and one that Nehemiah Bleek was content to deal with when tomorrow's sun came up. God, or Maheo, would take care of Preacher Bleek and his brood.

But the afternoon wore along with still no word from Picking Tooth or Roman Nose. The way now stretched unbrokenly toward their night's camp spot, the fringe of timber on the middle fork of Rush Creek. Halting the teams, Bleek called in the children and Lamewolf. Both Red Dust and Sunflower were glad enough for the signal. They had walked nearly twenty miles, with no food and no fire to warm by, and the afternoon wind was beginning to rise.

"Turn the dog free," Preacher told them, "and get in the wagon and rest. The road is clear now, and all downhill to wood and water. Not a pony soldier in sight all day."

Too weary to ask questions, the children went to the tailgate and climbed over it. Even Red Dust, worried and afraid over the long absences of his fierce uncles, could not avoid the embrace of the wagon's warmth. He was fast asleep in a dozen turns of the wheels. Sunflower slept beside him, and as soundly. Their hands were still clasped.

Preacher Bleek looked back at them from the driver's seat. He nodded to himself, feeling strong and good in his heart. But then his eyes fell on the cold, impassive face of Colonel John Chivington regarding him from his prison place behind the wagon seat, and the good feeling vanished.

As the hours and miles creaked by, grave doubt came to Nehemiah Bleek. Perhaps he had made a bad mistake at the mission school. He thought he had acted to save the Indians from Chivington, and to save Chivington from the Indians. But now it seemed that what he had done might have been precisely the wrong thing. Might not Roman Nose and Picking Tooth and Red Dust have survived Chivington's questioning and been permitted to stay at the school, to depart next day and in peace? No, Preacher knew better than that. Chivington had been as good as a dead man in that moment. But Roman Nose and Picking Tooth would have been dead men had they fired on Mashanē.

In the end, it was Nehemiah Bleek who had taken the burden of decision from all three men, and placed it on his own broad shoulders. Now he was guiding the Argonaut down the long plane of the prairie to the middle fork of Rush Creek, and he was all alone. Picking Tooth was gone. Roman Nose was gone. Preacher Bleek was a dead man, unless some miracle should save him.

"*Ho-shuh, ho-shuh*!" he called to his teams. "Do not hurry, be easy as you go. Steady, steady!"

The Kiowa Ladies looked back at him. Samson and Delilah stared resentfully in their turns. Bleek, sensitive to all things four-footed, chuckled at the mixed looks of censure flung back at him. "Forgive it," he told them, still in Cheyenne. "You are absolutely right, my friends. Take your own pace. You know what to do. I'm talking to the wind."

The sound of his voice brought Lamewolf circling back in to the wagon. The big wolf dog ran alongside the wheelers, looking up at his master above. He growled in a way like that of no civilized dog. Bleek waved at him and answered, not with words but with a growl very like the brute's own. Satisfied, Lamewolf barked and ran off. Bleek barked after him, the imitation so perfect yet so eerie in its animal sound that Chivington, watching him uneasily, shook his massive head.

"Crazy," he said aloud. "Bleek, you're crazy."

Bleek glanced around. He appeared surprised rather than offended.

"Crazy, Colonel?" he said. "Me?"

He looked down at himself, puzzled, as though wondering what Chivington could be thinking. He still wore his long white nightshirt over his clothes, having had no time to remove it since pulling it on to make the cavalry patrol imagine it had roused him from his bed. Over the night-shirt, of course, he wore his bear-skin winter coat. Why not? It was cold.

As for that garment itself, fashioned for him by a Cheyenne squaw in gratitude for his extraction of a soldier bullet from her small son's back, making the boy to walk again, it was certainly nothing to call a man crazy over. As a matter of fact, Bleek rather liked the way in which the woman had designed the sleeves with the bear's forelegs and paws intact, and with the hind legs and stumpy tail dangling down in the back. How many winter coats along the Arkansas had rear legs and a tail? Was a man to be called crazy because, viewed in haste or ignorance, he might be taken for a two-legged grizzly bear in nightgown and cap with a War of 1812 flintlock pistol stuck in one pocket, a bag of rock candy and a bottle of bourbon whiskey in the other, a Bible snug at bosom, and smoking a foot-long Arapaho ceremonial pipe? Fair was fair.

"Colonel," said Nehemiah Bleek, shaking his head in mild reproof, "I just don't rightly see how you can call a man of my everyday, ordinary qualifications crazy!"

X

Roman Nose rode his borrowed cavalry horse very hard. Something was making the tall warrior apprehensive in his heart. Always a religious man, even a mystic among his people, the famed fighter was now feeling premonitions of *nāevhan*, of death. The bad visions were of his old friend, Picking Tooth, and of the pony soldiers. Had Mashanē's men caught Kōvohe? Was the dear companion of his youth already stiffening in the alien snows of the Arkansas, ten long sleeps from Wyoming and from home? Had he ridden into a soldier trap on the back trail of Preacher Bleek and the ancient prairie wagon? Why was everything so still now, as Roman Nose loped westward along the wagon's tracks? Why had he not long ago seen the troopers following those same wagon tracks eastward? Where were those troopers? Had they not left the mission school of Preacher? Had they lied about following Mashanē to Smoky Hill River? Were they rather fled back to the Bijou Basin main camp of the Colorado Cavalry? Who might say?

Roman Nose only knew that his heart was bad for the safety of his friend. He knew, as well, that something was quite wrong about the emptiness of Preacher's back trail. Those men of Mashanē's were up to something. Roman Nose cursed himself for not shooting the narrow-eyed sergeant who had sought to put hands on Red Dust. His instinct had told him to do it, but his respect for Preacher had delayed his hand. Well, it was the last time Roman Nose would ever listen to a plea from a white man—even from Preacher.

The sad thing was that Indians and white men,

no matter the goodness of their hearts toward one another, did not think of things in the same ways. What was good to an Indian, was evil to a white man. What a white man would accept with a smile, an Indian might greet with a gunshot or the slash of his knife. The white man kept talking about loving all brothers, the Indian and the white, the black and the Mexican, and sharing the good things of his wealth with his poorer neighbor. But when the Indians said "yes" to this, they could find no white man who would give up anything of his wealth to the Indian in return for the Indian's generosity. The only time brotherhood was practiced by the white man was when the white man had nothing to give in exchange for the goods he expected the other man to give him. Preacher was a wise man who understood this failing of his fellows. But what the Horse Creek missionary did not seem to understand was that the Cheyennes had quite a different idea of brotherhood than Preacher had. The Indians believed that only the weak loved their enemies. Only the mad ones felt that their enemies could be changed into their friends by sweet words. The fighters ruled, and the Cheyennes were fighters. Yet where had war brought Roman Nose's people? Had it led the white man to deal with honor with the Indian? It had not. When the red man at last came to him seeking that peace so widely offered by the white man, the white man raised his gun and shot the

Indian dead. That was simply the way that things were: the white man hated all Indians, the red man hated all whites. It came in the end to the friendship of one man for another man of his own kind. Like the friendship of Kōvohe and Roman Nose. Cheyenne to Cheyenne. Red brother to red brother. Same blood to same blood. There was no other defense against the white man's wickedness in the names of peace and brotherhood.

Roman Nose raised his fierce head. His eyes stared ahead toward the distant embers of Preacher's burned-out school. He thumped his heels into the ribs of the cavalry horse he was riding.

"*Enševao*," he said to the animal in Cheyenne. "Move faster. If we find my friend Kōvohe dead, we will leave a white man dead in his place."

Private Obie Jenks was not ordinarily an ambitious soldier. But that was beginning to change. Obie Jenks had finally carried out an important order on his own. He had burned down the Horse Creek school and he had done a fine job of it. It gave him his first feelings of the power of command.

Of course, in leaving him behind, Sergeant Skemp had told him exactly what to do. Skemp and the patrol had lit out the previous night, right after chopping free from the dormitory. The sergeant's idea was to get around Preacher Bleek in the darkness. Then, when Preacher saw the smoke starting up next morning, he would think that the whole troop was just leaving to set out after him, after putting the torch to his place. At least that was Skemp's plan to throw the big missionary off guard. And Skemp was smart. He was meaner than a badger, too. It made him the ideal sergeant for Colonel John Chivington and that last part of it is what was getting to Obie Jenks as the forenoon wore on. Maybe now, blast it, Chivington would notice how bright Obie Jenks was, and give him a sergeant's stripes and pay. This whole plot had depended on Jenks and he had surely burned down that orphans' schoolhouse exactly on schedule. If Skemp caught up to and ambushed Preacher Bleek, the credit ought really to go to Private Obie Jenks—no, make that Sergeant Obie Jenks.

Presently the forenoon was gone and the fire was settled down to where the sills and the lintels of the little building were all that remained. The charred roof timbers had come down with a grand crash twenty minutes ago. It was time for Obie Jenks to get his horse out of Preacher's barn and ride hard after Skemp and the patrol, as ordered.

But on entering the barn, he received a bad start when he thought he saw a human figure scuttle away into the cottonwood trees beyond the structure. Yet when he ran out to investigate, he saw nothing. Suddenly afraid, he hurried with the saddling. Maybe he should go for help rather than following the patrol. It would be a lot safer and it might be smarter, too. Obie Jenks was not quick of mind like his sergeant, but he was tricky and mean in the same manner. The opportunity for promotion waiting for the man who might be first to report Chivington's capture to the Bijou encampment kept gnawing at Jenks's imagination. Finally, when he swung up on his mount, it was the ominous stillness that hung with the smoke over the burned-out school that decided him. He had better run for his life. To follow Skemp was to risk running into hostile Cheyennes. For a lone soldier that would be certain death. Moreover, suppose they caught him here at the school? How would the Cheyennes feel about the cavalryman who had burned Preacher's Indian orphanage? No, it was no good—Obie Jenks would ride for Bijou Basin.

And why not? The Cheyennes wouldn't be thick in that direction and for a story for the officers he could say that the dirty redskins had set upon him at the mission—that he had been forced to retreat the one way that was open, toward Bijou Basin. He could then report the danger in which Chivington and his patrol stood—the danger from the huge band of hostiles that had jumped brave Obie Jenks all alone at the burned-out school— and Obie would get rated a hero, or at least get some sergeant's stripes, or anyway $5 extra pay.

It was when he turned his gelding away from

the school that Obie Jenks saw the Indian slide out of the cottonwoods beyond Bleek's horse barn, and go skulking into that building. His first thought was one of intense fear, almost panic. But after he realized that the Indian had not seen him, Jenks's newly discovered ambition overcame his natural cowardice. There was a much shorter ride he could make to earn those sergeant's stripes. It was only back to that horse barn of Preacher's. One Cheyenne scalp for three cavalry chevrons. It ought to make a fair exchange.

XI

When the soldier disappeared beyond the trees, Picking Tooth came out of his hiding place in the brush near Bleek's horse barn. The Cheyenne was glad that the trooper had left. He had certainly not wanted to harm the fellow. But he had wanted to get in close to the burned school so that he might study the tracks of the cavalry patrol leading away from the mission.

Right now all was fine. There were still enough hard tracks around the building to tell him that the main patrol had gone many hours before—long before that morning's sun. He was able to see, also, in which direction the patrol had gone. It had turned down Horse Creek, south and east, rather than crossing the creek to take the old buffalo trail followed by Bleek and his orphans with the ancient Santa Fé wagon. This meant that Sergeant Skemp was cutting around the wagon, circling like a wolf. He was swinging wide to come back in again far ahead of Preacher and there to lie in wait for him when, all unwary, he came to that night's camp. The only blessing in the matter was the fact that Picking Tooth was in time to return to Preacher with the warning. Or was he? The brave had forgotten the quick passage of the November daylight.

Now, reconsidering, he realized that there was no blessing in the situation. His pony was not fresh. It would never last for a hard-driving ride back to the wagon. Preacher would have to depend on the eyes and instincts of Roman Nose to protect him and the Indian children from the ambush by Sergeant Skemp and the pony soldiers. Well, that was another blessing in its way. To have Maōx out in front of any caravan was protection only to be exceeded by the eyes and ears of Maheo himself.

It made no difference for that day. Picking Tooth could do nothing now but return to the wagon and to his friend Roman Nose with the information he had found at the school. That was why he had been sent out, to scout back and see what he could find, and he had done this job well.

Oh, he could easily have killed the solitary soldier. Roman Nose would have done so. But Picking Tooth was another man than Maōx. Taken in the Cheyenne view, he was what Maōx called "a good brave coward." So he had let the soldier go, and was happy he had. Now he himself would depart and no one harmed in the business of doing his duty. Let's see. Where had he put down that rifle of his while getting down on all fours to inspect and sniff at the old pony soldier tracks? Ah, yes. It had been back there by the fireplace. He had leaned it against the stark column of sooted chimney stones. Nodding to himself, the good-natured brave turned about and went toward the gutted chimney. He was humming a little Cheyenne "stout heart" tune, to ward off the loneliness of the ruins of Preacher's burned school at The Cottonwoods.

He was still humming it when he rounded the chimney's corner and Private Obie Jenks, waiting there for him, shot him three times in the stomach from a distance no greater than the reach of a rifle's barrel.

Obie Jenks whacked and hacked and cursed the time he was losing. His sheath knife was not sharp and was not designed, either, for this sort of work. The blade wasn't the right shape and the lack of a proper guard made his hand keep slipping up over the blade when it would hit the hard skull bone under the Indian's hair. Taking a scalp was not as easy as it looked. But one thing was for certain: there wasn't going to be any officer or man of the 3rd Colorado that wouldn't know Obie Jenks had killed and scalped himself a full-grown Cheyenne buck.

The trooper cleaned his knife and his hands in the snow. The blood would not come off his coat sleeves, but it would dry there and look impressive back at Bijou Basin. He tried to tie the scalp lock at his belt, but could not manage it. It didn't seem to hang just right. Glancing around the school clearing, he hurriedly stuffed the long black braid into his saddlebag. He was self-conscious about it, as though someone might see him and ask him what it was. Then he seemed to realize how foolish this was, standing there by a burned-out rock chimney in the Arkansas wilderness, half a hundred miles up Horse Creek. Throwing back his head, he laughed aloud. It was a wonderful joke. There wasn't another white man within a five-hour ride, one way, and a long day in the saddle, the other way. As for Indians, the same thing went. There had been one, but old Obie had taken care of him. If there were any more of the red devils around who wanted a dose of the same medicine, all they had to do was let old Obie know about it.

Suddenly Jenks realized that he had not been merely thinking these thoughts, but actually talking them out loud. The echo of his own voice frightened him. It bounded around among the fallen roof timbers. It played into and out of the charred fireplace. The rising wind picked it up and flung it about. It came back in the weirdest way. As though it had been changed into an Indian voice. Into the guttural accents of Cheyenne, in fact. And of Cheyenne spoken in a voice so deep and rare as never to be forgotten, once heard. And Obie Jenks had heard that voice before.

He whirled. In his desperate mind was but one thought—to reach the chimney rocks where he had leaned his repeating carbine to begin the scalping of Picking Tooth. But another was there before him. It was an Indian, a Cheyenne.

In the whirling of the ground snow he had come up behind the trooper like a ghost. One moment no one was there and Private Obie Jenks was laughing wildly and talking to himself. The next moment the ghost was there, and it was not talking to itself. It was talking to Obie Jenks.

"Nāestoz, it is death," said Roman Nose, and struck his ten-inch skinning knife into the stomach of the soldier and ripped upward to the breast bone.

Obie Jenks stared stupidly down at himself. He was a dead man, and he knew it. He shook his head at Roman Nose and slid slowly into the snow.

The Cheyenne stood above him, no sign of mercy on his dark face.

"Nahoxemo," he said to Obie Jenks. "Farewell."

XII

The short day of the early winter was nearly over. Preacher Bleek was glad. The last of the fifteen-mile slope down which he had been lagging all afternoon now lay ahead. It could not be more than a mile to the fringe timber of Rush Creek. Soon they would have a good fire going. The children could get warm, hot food could be prepared, the good Cheyenne *hotoma* returned to the weary company. It was well enough. The weather was changing again. The wind, on the rise all afternoon, was now spitting sleet between its teeth. It would be a bad night. Bleek raised his face to the gray skies and thanked his Lord out loud for the fine campsite ahead.

In that moment Rush Creek, usually the most forlorn and desolate of prairie outposts, looked like an oasis in the land of Canaan to Nehemiah Bleek. Yet the fact that there could be a serpent in that prairie paradise was not lost on Preacher. Bleek had been searching the grove through his brass-bound telescope for the past hour. Neither in the timber nor on the open plains about it had he been able to discern a sign of the missing cavalry patrol. He was now certain that Skemp and the troopers had deserted Chivington. Most likely they had cut and run for home. It would be a natural thing for volunteer troops to do. Such men weren't like regular Army troops. Once their officers were removed, they tended to drift like sheep, or to huddle, but not to act together. If they had gone back to Bijou Basin to get help, it was no blessing to Preacher Bleek, however. It would only mean that he would have to get his cargo to Smoky Hill even more quickly.

By now, of course, he had despaired of seeing Roman Nose and Picking Tooth again. Either they had been ambushed and killed by Skemp, or they had decided to work some independent war plan of their own. If they were dead or had deserted and did not return, Bleek would be faced with the problem of holding Chivington hostage without any Indian pressure to make the situation real. This he knew he could not do. If Roman Nose and Picking Tooth were still missing the next dawn, and had Skemp and the patrol not put in their appearance, then Bleek would have to set Chivington free. He would have to give him a horse or leave him in the Rush Creek timber on foot, but with gun, ammunition, food, and matches. As for taking him on to the Indian camp, this was completely impossible. That was why Bleek had tried to be so careful in setting up the plan whereby the patrol would follow in sight of the Argonaut and thus be ready to receive the hostage when the Cheyenne encampment came into far view, and Bleek and the children would thereby be guaranteed their decent chance to reach the Indians and temporary safety.

Without the patrol to take Chivington's release, and to guard that release from Cheyenne attack in the retreat to either Bijou Basin or Fort Lyon, nothing would work. All of Bleek's risks, taken to help his children and Roman Nose and Picking Tooth and Red Dust, would have been gambled in vain. It was a bitter thing for Preacher to dwell on, and with his customary good spirits he now refused to do so. That was why he had just lifted his face to his Lord and spoken out his thanks, aloud. And it was why he now waved upward in friendly acknowledgment of the nearness of heaven.

"Amen, amen!" he called after the wave, which was made left-handedly and much like an absent-minded salute.

Then in a sober aside to his seat companion, Durant, he added thoughtfully: "How about you, Sergeant? You much of a praying man?"

Durant started to reply, interested enough. But he looked around and saw that Chivington was watching him. Bleek, sensing the silence, glanced about. His blue eyes caught the cold stare of the captive officer.

Chivington nodded to him with no change of expression. "How about you, Bleek?" he said. "You much of a praying man?"

Nehemiah Bleek did not consider that he was

afraid of Chivington. But no man could be indifferent to the menace of that vast body and strange mind. When such a troop commander had behind him the full authority of the state, there were no definable limits to the hell he could create. Bleek understood this—understood that beneath the controlled quiet of the question a devil's broth was brewing in the sleepless brain of Colonel John Chivington. But Bleek was Bleek, too. He would not lie down and roll over to any implied threat of dead dog.

"No sir, Colonel," he said, "I don't rightly reckon I practice the Word near hard nor frequent enough to be called a praying man."

The huge officer studied him a long, uneasy moment. Then he nodded slowly. "Well, Preacher," he said, "you had better start rehearsing. You are going to need the practice."

Roman Nose built a "skunk," a Cheyenne funeral pyre, for his friend Picking Tooth. He used Preacher's winter woodpile to lay the cross-locked frame of the skunk on the hearth of the school's fireplace. Preacher would not care. He would never need the wood for his own burning. Not that winter. He would be happy, Roman Nose knew, to supply the cut wood for the last journey of a good man like Kōvohe.

Arranging the dead brave's body in the proper manner, the tall Cheyenne placed it atop the stacked cordwood of the pyre. The wood was beautifully split by Preacher's powerful axe, and it was dried by the long hot Arkansas summer. Roman Nose knew that it would burn fast, and he was glad. His friend would have a quick journey.

Ordinarily a pony would have been left—the pony most beloved by its departed master—at the foot of the burial scaffold. This was to provide transportation for the sleeping one up the steep pathway of Seameo, the Road of the Dead, the Milky Way. But in this case there was no Indian pony to leave with Kōvohe. There were only the three cavalry horses, that of the dead soldier and the two Roman Nose and Picking Tooth had borrowed. Or at least he hoped that the mounts of his friend and of the soldier were tethered in the timber somewhere near at hand. He had an urgent use for those three strong pony soldier horses. Lives other than his own depended on those big cavalry mounts. How might he spare one of them to tie at the foot of Kōvohe's scaffold?

Roman Nose raised his head to seek guidance of Maheo in the matter. As he did so, his dark eye fell on the snow-mounded forms of the three Cheyenne ponies shot by Mashanē's order just outside the school's doorway.

"*Haho*, Maheo," muttered the big warrior. "It is a miracle. I ask for one pony and you send me three!"

Now quickly he knelt in the snow. Scraping

away the flakes, more of which were falling with each moment, he made a small patch of bared earth. This he dug at with his knife until he had loosened a handful of dirt. Going to the scaffold, he placed Picking Tooth's shield on the dead brave's breast, then mounded the handful of *hesec*, the mother earth, on the shield. Taking from the mound four tiny pinches of the soil, he tossed one pinch in each of the four cardinal points, north, south, east, west.

All the while, he was chanting and grunting the ritual prayers that, as a holy man of his people, he knew in all their pagan complication. At the last words of the prayer, he broke off to glance quickly about the deserted ruins. Reassured that he had no audience save the soft fall of the snow, he bent quickly to the ear of the silent warrior and whispered: "Listen, Kōvohe, I hope you understand about the ponies. I'm not certain it's a right thing to do, but let us both trust in Maheo, eh? After all, it was He who sent me the sign, wasn't it? *Haho!*"

As quickly as he had bent down, he straightened and sped on with the work of lighting the fire. There was no difficulty here. Embers and coals of Preacher's log and plank building were hissing out beneath the new blanket of white flakes all about him. Seizing up a smoldering brand, he whipped it about his head until it burst into bright flame. Plunging the torch into the dried kindling of the pyre, he stepped back ten slow paces. Here he stood, arms upraised to his friend's rising spirit, until the pyre's building flames had reached and engulfed the homely "good brave coward" who had been the heart companion of his Wyoming boyhood and the staunch comrade of the grown years on the war trail.

When he could see the body no more, when he knew that the bursting flames had wafted its inner spirit upward, Roman Nose said softly: "Good bye, old friend. One more of us is gone."

Then he turned swiftly for the winter-gray trunks of the cottonwood trees behind Preacher's horse barn. When he had found the hidden mounts of Picking Tooth and the pony soldier, he led them on the trot back to his own mount, waiting at the school ruins. Roping the spare horses together, he swung up on the freshest of the three—the mount of Private Obie Jenks—and kicked the animal hard in the ribs. "*Vovehe!*" he shouted. "Run!"

XIII

Bleck halted the teams, set the brakes, wrapped the lines. They were still on the slope, still a quarter mile from the Rush Creek timber. Nothing had been seen or heard from that timber, but Preacher was not satisfied. Too long on the prairie to trust an absolute stillness like this one, he had to make one more probe, try one more test.

"Listen," he said to Sunflower and Red Dust in Cheyenne, "I am going to take the dog and go forward. I don't like to leave you alone with the wagon, but this white man"—he indicated Durant by tapping him on the shoulder—"is a decent man and I will have to trust him. I trust you and the Cheyenne boy to keep the children quiet and out of trouble until I get back. I am going to scout the timber with Lamewolf. Now keep the children in the wagon, and do not be afraid of the three-stripe soldier."

Sunflower, by the eloquent roll of her big dark eyes toward Chivington's place behind the wagon seat, indicated that the Indian's concern was not for Sergeant Durant. Bleek did not miss the unconscious flick of the glance.

"Mashanē is bound like a dead buck to a carrying pole. His feet and hands are held with rawhide I tied myself. You have seen me tie a deer, Sunflower. You tell the boy that Preacher's knots yield only to the knife."

"Yes, Preacher," agreed the little girl. "If you say I am not afraid of Mashanē, then I am not afraid of him."

"Good," said Bleek. "Now be alert, both of you. I shall return in moments only."

Taking his rifle, he whistled up the dog and started down the slope. The sleet of the earlier afternoon had now become a light whirling fall of snow. In the gray darkness of the nearing twilight, the burly form of the Horse Creek missionary was soon shrouded from view.

The moment that it was, Chivington strained forward in his bonds, eyes glaring, voice shrill. "Durant, this Cheyenne boy has a knife. Jump him and cut me loose!"

"By heaven, Colonel, I can't do it. He's clean to the back of the wagon. These here Spanish leg chains won't reach more'n three, four feet."

Chivington was furious. He never used profanity but helpless anger was glazing his features. "Durant," he hissed, "do something! Call the Indian boy up to you. Smile at him. Offer him something!"

"Colonel, sir," pleaded the trooper, "look back there at him. He's watching you wilder than a wolf whelp right now. He ain't about to do nothing we tell him, sir."

"Durant, you're refusing an order. You'll face a court-martial! I'll see you swung alongside Bleek at Fort Lyon. I'll see . . ."

"Colonel, sir, please . . . if you don't slack off, you'll see that Cheyenne kid going out over the tailgate and off down the hill after Preacher."

Chivington swung the blaze of his eyes to the slope beyond Durant.

"That's it!" he cried. "We'll go down the hill after Preacher! Grab the lines, Sergeant. Kick off the brakes. Whip up those teams, man!"

Durant, not a quick-minded fellow, hesitated. Instantly Chivington was snarling at him. "That's an order, do you hear me? Get this filthy wagon rolling!"

He was literally screaming now. Durant knew that one more refusal, one further word of doubt, and the raging threat of the gallows at Fort Lyon would no longer be a wild man's fancy but a military fact.

"Yes, sir," he said between clenched teeth.

He sent the surprised teams and the overloaded wagon into a lumbering downhill plunge. Behind him, Chivington laughed and yelled unsteadily.

"Good man, good man!" he shouted. "Don't you see, Durant, don't you see? Skemp will be down there waiting. He's in that timber. He's got to be, he's got to be!"

The trooper nodded, fighting to stay upright on the pitching seat of the Argonaut. He was pale and sweaty, appearing ill. Durant knew well enough that Skemp might be waiting in that timber. Back at the mission it had been Durant himself who passed Chivington's secret orders to Skemp. It had been Durant, too, who ever since had yearned to confess the possible trap to the simple-minded Preacher. To warn him and his forlorn brood of orphaned Indian kids of the likely ambush at Rush Creek. But in the end it was—it had to be—Durant's own fear of Chivington that over-whelmed his compassion for Bleek and the Indian children. No man hung himself.

"Hee-yah, hee-yah!" the sergeant yelled at black Samson and china-eyed Delilah. And drove them and the Kiowa Ladies with all his skill headlong toward Rush Creek and the last crossing of the Argonaut.

Bleek slowed when he reached the low bluffs above the creek's channel. The nearest trees in the bottom growth were less than fifty yards distant. To the Preacher's right, the trough of the buffalo road went down and over the dry bed of the stream. At this time of the year, so far up its course, Rush Creek had no flow. There was a big pool and spring at the crossing, which was why the buffalo and Indian trail ran that way in the beginning. This water lay out of Bleek's view, below the crossing. He could not approach it from the downstream side, as the bluffs failed there, permitting anyone in the grove to see up the incline of the long slope he had just come down. Hence, he would have to depend on the dog to go on in from where he was, scouting the grove for him.

The dog was a good dog. But the children had spoiled him a great deal. As a tracker and trailer, particularly as a scout dog, he had had little work the past four winters. Now Bleek had no real idea how well the animal might respond to the order to "go ahead," to "scout out," the common commands of a hunting dog reared by the Cheyennes. Well, the time to find out was right then.

"Lamewolf."

He murmured the name, unleashing the chain. He made the "go ahead" sign. The wolf-like brute crouched and growled. Bleek made the cut-off sign.

"Be still, be still," he whispered, and the dog quit his chest rumblings.

"*Naasenēnàno*," he commanded. "Go on, leave. I order it."

Lamewolf regarded him steadily, his yellow eyes burning in the dusk. Then he whined and turned away. Sliding over the edge of the bluff, he leaped to the smooth sand of the channel bed, started slinking down it toward the crossing and the grove near Big Spring. When he was midway in the buffalo trail, he flattened to the ground behind a hummock of snowy grass. Bleek could see his busy tail sweeping snow dust. But he was not wagging the tail in friendship. He was jerking it in nervousness, the way a stalking wolf or coyote will do.

"Dear Lord," muttered Bleek, "there is something in there."

Before his fear could mount higher, Lamewolf had left the snowy hummock and was returning upstream, ghosting along the white-blanketed sand. When he scrambled back up the bluff and dropped at Preacher's side, his roach was standing on end from skull base to tail root and his deep growl was vibrating in anxiety.

"Come on," said Nehemiah Bleek, "we're getting shut of here, old dog."

He started quickly back up the slope, Lamewolf slinking at heel. Fortunately there would be time to turn the teams and cross at Soda Springs, a salt lick about ten miles upstream. There was no timber there, but plenty of buffalo chips for fuel and the cutbanks of the streambed for wind shelter. They would be all right even in a bad storm.

It was as this comforting thought took shape in his mind that Nehemiah Bleek heard the rumble of wagon wheels and, glancing in dread up the slope, saw the dim shape of the Argonaut bounding down upon him in runaway wildness. So close was he that he could also see Durant driving the teams and the white face of Colonel Chivington crying him on from within the wagon.

Bleek quit thinking, then, and began to run. Not away from the wagon. Not out of the way, but directly at the madly careening teams and the swaying freighter. As Samson and Delilah burst upon him, he wheeled in the last fraction of time and reversed his speed to run with them. In this way he was able to seize the collar of the black Spanish jack and swing himself up on the hairy withers. In the same motion he grasped the cheek straps of both animals and virtually lifted their forehoofs off the ground.

Delilah squealed and planted her rear hoofs. Samson did the same. Behind them, the Kiowa

Ladies sat back on their haunches to obey the bracing of the lead team. The Argonaut rode up on their rumps, teetered, leaned, slewed around, and crashed over on its left side into a gully full of fresh snow. The impact spat Chivington out into the slush and mud of the gully. Durant, being leg-ironed to the seat, stayed with the wagon, escaping serious injury. The Kiowa Ladies were down and thrashing to free themselves. Bleek leaped in with his knife and slashed their tugs. The Indian mares scrambled up, little the worse for the hard use. There was no time to inspect for wounds among the children. The best that could be done was to take all of them that could move and try to escape on foot with them up the streambed and into the snow flurries before the troopers in the timber could mount up and rush the slope to see what had happened.

It was in the process of hauling the children out of the rear of the wagon that the red-bearded missionary realized that the troopers were not going to rush that slope—not on horseback, anyway.

"*Zetōxz!*" cried Red Dust who, with Sunflower, had escaped unharmed. "Look there, Preacher!"

Following the boy's excited point, Bleek saw a sight that could be nothing less than a visitation of the mysterious ways of the Lord. From out of the grove, up the buffalo trail with a burst of snorting and neighing that would raise the hackles on a dead wolf, came the horses of the scout patrol of Chivington's 3rd Colorado Cavalry. They were running in a gob, all still strung on the rope line of their camp picket. It was beautiful. No scattering, no confusion, no loss of precious time, no herding required. It was a work of pony stealing that only an Indian could have engineered, and very few Indians at that. This Indian, however, was of the few.

Behind the stolen cavalry mounts he came, standing in the stirrups of the cavalry saddle of his borrowed horse. He was raw-boned, tall, fierce of face and eye, dark-skinned as any buffalo soldier. But he was no buffalo soldier. He was a Dog Soldier. A Cheyenne of the north.

"*Hešeo, Hešeo!*" cried Red Dust. "Uncle, Uncle!" Leaping past the gaping Bleek, he raced toward the great towering form of Roman Nose, charging up the snow-blown slope, driving before him the seventeen stolen cavalry horses of Sergeant Skemp's patrol.

XIV

The capture of the horses changed everything. The first thing was to gentle down the run-off cavalry mounts. This was speedily accomplished by Preacher, Red Dust, Roman Nose, and all the children working at the same time. It was only minutes before the horses were quieted and the cut picket line retied, this time to the overturned Argonaut.

Chivington was then retrieved from his muddy resting place, very nearly strangled in the cold slime and snow where he had alighted. Durant was unlocked from the front of the wagon, relocked to the tailgate. All that Preacher ever said to either of them was: "Well, Colonel, I don't rightly know how to tell you this, but we're going to have to leave you and go along," and then sadly to Durant: "I reckon we all make mistakes, Sergeant. You were one of mine. I figured you for decent." Then he was busied with what he must do before Skemp recovered nerve enough to send his troopers looking for horse tracks. But even though Bleek labored hard and drove the children without stint, there was that in the twinkle of his small blue eyes, the tilt and bloom of his big red beard that said clearly that old Preacher was returned to his flock and no one need be afraid to go to sleep that night.

The plan was simple enough; with plenty of horses for everyone, they would all mount up and run for it. As for the Argonaut, she was done for, her running gear not repairable in the time left to them at Rush Creek Grove. The teams were unharnessed. The Kiowa Ladies were turned loose. Samson was saddled for Bleek. Blankets and food were packed on the two Indian mares and the pinto jenny Delilah. The other cargo of the Argonaut was left beneath the canvas cover of the top and in the overturned bed. Likely when the spring melt set in and the new grass came, the Smoky Hill Cheyennes would wander this way and help themselves to what had wintered through. They were welcome and more than welcome to anything of Preacher's.

It was not important. The important thing was that Maheo had answered the prayers of Roman Nose. He had let the tall warrior ride the three-horse relay from Horse Creek to the Rush Creek camp of the ambushed patrol of 3rd Colorado Cavalry in the very nick of time. *Haho*, thank Maheo! It was a sad thing that Picking Tooth was dead, and a grim thing that Roman Nose had returned with not only his friend's hair, but also that of Private Obie Jenks dangling at his belt. But this was the way of things, red man against white, in the Arkansas valley of 1864. The thing to remember was that Roman Nose had saved them all from the pony soldier guns, and brought them the wonderful tall strong horses of the cavalry to ride on the rest of the journey to Smoky Hill River.

Vovehe! It was time to ride. Chivington and Durant were set free, leg-ironed together at the ankle. Preacher gave them a maul and a cold chisel and said no word to them as he did. But it was a small maul and a dull chisel. They would be until daylight freeing themselves.

When Preacher turned away from giving the tools to the colonel and the sergeant, he went up to Roman Nose and announced in a deliberately loud voice that he would be the last one to advise a famous colonel of the 3rd Colorado Cavalry on how to conduct himself in the field, but that, if he were such an eagle chief, he did believe that he would take his scout patrol and his two sergeants and march for Fort Lyon the fastest way he knew how.

Roman Nose nodded soberly. For a moment there in the growing darkness, Bleek saw the grim Cheyenne smile. Speaking and understanding no word of English, he had translated Bleek's harangue perfectly. It was an old Indian trick, used when haughty chiefs wanted no word with each other, yet knew also the need to communicate with one another.

Roman Nose knew that Preacher was advising Mashanē, through him, what he wanted the eagle chief to know.

"Tell me," he rumbled, when Bleek had concluded and while Chivington was still answering his suggestion with raging promises of being hanged or shot down on sight, "what was it you advised the pony soldier chief to do?"

"A very simple thing." Nehemiah Bleek grinned. "I told him to take his men and run hard all the way to Fort Lyon. Is that all right with you?"

The trace of a smile, if that was what it had

been, vanished from the dark face of the Cheyenne. "Mashanē should be killed," he said.

"No," said Bleek. "That would be murder."

"You will be sorry, I will be sorry, we will all be sorry," complained Roman Nose. "This man should die."

"He will die," answered Bleek, "but we will not kill him. Come, my friend. We have our own lives. We have these children to look after. I ask you to help me."

Roman Nose looked beyond Preacher Bleek at Colonel John Chivington. He stared in silence. There was death in the glance, and the giant officer could feel its cold hand upon him. He stood back against the fallen wagon, crowding close to Sergeant Durant. His heavy breathing and the soft hiss of the falling flakes were the only sounds.

"In God's name, Bleek," pleaded Chivington, "call him off of us. He means to kill us . . . or me."

Bleek moved forward, touched the tall Cheyenne on the arm. "My friend," he said, "it is time to go."

Slowly Roman Nose nodded. His fierce gaze, so intent on murder but the moment before, seemed shifted far away. He was looking to the north, toward his home, and he was seeing that land. "Yes," he agreed, "it is time. Kōvohe is dead. My heart has gone with him. I want to go home."

He turned away from Chivington and went and took his horse from the boy, Red Dust. Swinging to the saddle, he told Bleek that he was ready to go on to Smoky Hill River. "All right, Preacher," he said. "You are the chief of this party. Go ahead and lead the way."

"With the Lord's will," answered Bleek, "I will do it."

He got up on Samson. The black brute turned at once for the buffalo trail. Behind him came Delilah and the Kiowa Ladies, unroped, moving freely, following like dogs. The cavalry horses carrying the Horse Creek orphans came after them obediently. The children scarcely had to guide them at all.

Once down into the streambed by the easy way of the old buffalo road, Samson turned sharply left and bore away up the dry bed to the north. Fifty yards away, their shaken nerves just calming enough for them to have gathered some small driftwood and started a blaze to warm and recover by, the troopers of the 3rd Colorado, never by sight or sound were the least bit aware of the passage of their stolen stock. Sergeant Skemp, in fact, had only begun to exhort them to "rally up and foller me" in some delayed pursuit of the lost horses when Chivington and Durant staggered up to the fireside in their chains.

"It's him," breathed the sergeant. "It's the colonel."

Chivington did not answer him. He held out the maul and the chisel, and pointed to the Spanish leg irons. "Start cutting," was all he said.

Bleek was certain that there would be no immediate pursuit. A scant three miles upstream a feeding halt was called. The place was where an overhang of bluff provided a scoop for the wind to hurl the snow up and over the channel and make a tiny haven from the storm beneath the bank. Here the horses were given a good ration of rolled oats while their riders chewed handfuls of buffalo jerky and drank scalding tea that Preacher brewed with melted snow.

Directly the blankets were unfurled. Dead grass was gathered from beneath the snows, shaken dry, and piled in a Cheyenne nest, a big ball of grasses looking like a giant tumbleweed. Now, well fed and full of hot tea, the children were piled into the center of the grass ball and sealed there with the blankets. For the hardy waifs this was a king's couch. Preacher had the happy light back in his blue eyes. His red beard was bristling like a chestnut burr, as it should be, when he was sure of their safety. And there was the great tall warrior, Roman Nose, also to guard them and to guard, too, the fine stolen horses of the pony soldiers. Thanks be to Maheo. A small thank you, likewise, for Preacher's Lord God Jehovah. The spirit of *hotoma* was back among them and Mashanē was far, far away. Sleep came fast, and it was deep.

Some, however, did not sleep. Bedded under the bank between picket line and grass nest was

Lamewolf. His yellow eyes were open. They moved, with his sharp ears, to every scent or sound penetrating the curtain of snow that closed them off from the plain about them. Perhaps pursuit by the pony soldiers was not to be, but there were still seventeen cavalry horses to watch over, and still plans for the remainder of the flight to be drawn by the two men at the buffalo-chip fire. The old dog was not new to this game. Not any more so than were his master, Preacher Bleek, or the Cheyenne warrior, Roman Nose. When the enemy's horse herd has been run off and the retreat only beginning, vigilance was the price of pony flesh. And not only of pony flesh, but also of human flesh. Yes, and of dog meat, too. Lamewolf growled deeply in his throat.

By the fire, Bleek noted the sound of the growl and nodded to Roman Nose.

"He says all is well. But for us not to count the horses until we are home."

"A smart dog," said the tall warrior. "But then he's an Indian dog."

Bleek spread his hands and shrugged, as if to say: "Of course." Then he said aloud: "Well, brother, we had better do some talking. God has been good to us, but I think we should give Him a little help, too."

Roman Nose bobbed his head in agreement. He and Preacher spoke a common tongue. They came quickly to their decisions.

The single bag of oats brought from the Argonaut had been consumed in the one feeding of the cavalry horses. The wind was dropping, the cloud cover thickening. This meant heavier snowfall. Drifts could be formed that would block the prairie trails to horse travel. Where they huddled now was midway of their journey. It was forty miles back to the school, forty miles on to the Smoky Hill. South lay the Arkansas, half a hundred miles. North, three times that far, was the South Platte. No wonder the wind sounded lonesome and the old dog growled deeply in his throat. They were stranded in the empty stomach of *emhätō*, of nowhere at all.

"In about two hours," said Roman Nose, "I think we had better wake up the children and leave this place."

Bleek nodded. "I will watch first," he offered. "You sleep."

Roman Nose watched him a moment, then agreed. He immediately pulled his blanket about him and lay down nearly in the ashes of the fire. He seemed unconscious at once.

Bleek eyed him carefully, almost craftily. When his breathing became deep and regular, Preacher smiled with compassion for the weary and the worn. He even reached across the fire and pulled a corner of the blanket over the warrior's face, then quickly lifted the corner and peered closely at the dark features. He lowered the blanket again, assured that all was well.

Into the bosom of the bear-skin winter coat went the big gnarled hand. Out came the bottle of Old Crow. Up went the hand to hold it to the fire's light for the tantalizing view of the sainted label, before the quaffing.

In the moment of this delighted anticipation, a lean and muscular red arm shot out of the blanket across the fire and speared the bottle from Preacher's startled grasp. Roman Nose did not even bother to sit up, but took his drink from the bottle without moving from the flat of his back. As ungraciously, the red arm extended back across the smoky buffalo chips and returned the bottle to the hand of Nehemiah Bleek.

Preacher looked at the badly damaged storage level. He studied the motionless Roman Nose.

"Ahhh," he said, "true brothers . . ."

And raising the bottle to a juggler's tilt with head thrown back and blue eyes lidded blissfully, he drained the remaining contents.

XV

Chivington was a hard man who lived in a hard land during a hard time. What he was doing in Colorado Territory was no more than what he considered his natural and legitimate duty. The pursuit of the Indians he believed to be the first order of state business in the due process of frontier law. As always in a raw land, the Army arrived before the settlers. In Colorado Territory, between the South Platte and the Arkansas, Colonel John Chivington was the law. Or divined that he was.

General Curtis, of course, stood ahead of him in actual military command. Officers such as Major Scott Anthony at Fort Lyon were his peers in the field. Governor Evans and Agent Colley for the United States were his superiors in the matter of local and national authority in civil affairs affecting Indians. Yet Chivington saw beyond these restraints. He understood his fated rôle more clearly than those above him. Curtis, Anthony, Evans, Colley, and before them Wynkoop, that stout champion of the Cheyennes—all were hamstrung by the legal responsibilities of their appointments. It was Chivington who acted for them. It was Chivington who not only was the law, but also was beyond the law. It was he who served silently the purposes of the state, and without warrant. He who went in the night and suddenly on his missions of enforcement. He who held no paper that said he might do the things he did, but who held in his Spartan mind the unwritten permission—some said explicit encouragement—of superiors and peers alike, to pursue the enemy in accordance with the dictates of his own relentless conscience, and those dictates were plainly known to all: kill Indians. Kill all, little and big. Nits make lice.

And Colonel J.M. Chivington, called "Butcher" Chivington by some and Mashanē or Sick Mind by others, was a man who did not falter in his duty. Neither did he fail his conscience. Of the many things he was, or might stand accused of being, coward was not one or liar another.

With the first gray of daylight he was marching from Rush Creek Grove. But he was not marching, as Bleek had warned him to, toward Fort Lyon and the aid of the regular Army troops of Major Scott Anthony. He was marching due west back over the ancient buffalo road to Horse Creek. He was going straight to Bijou Basin to get his own troops. He was risking his life and the lives of his dismounted patrol to do it. The stakes disturbed him not in the least. He knew his business, and his business was not getting killed by Indians.

He was going to get the 3rd Colorado Cavalry and go and kill himself some Indians of his own. Any Indians. The first ones who got in his way. Just so long as they were Cheyennes. And it was a dark night.

Preacher roused Roman Nose about 10:00p.m. They made some more tea and awakened the children. Another shred of jerky was shared.

As foreseen, the temperature had moderated. Great fat flakes had replaced the small and dry ones of the earlier fall. The snow was piling up.

A little after 10:00, all were mounted and moving out once more. The direction taken by Preacher in the lead was due east. Behind him came the twin Kiowa pack mares. They were faithfully followed by the line of cavalry horses carrying the children. Bringing up the line was Roman Nose.

About midline, where Red Dust and Sunflower had been told to ride and police the behavior of the other children, Lamewolf trotted at the heels of the Arapaho girl's mount. Now and again he would range out a bit on the flanks of the column to scout the night. But for the most part he held close to the horses where the snow was packed and the going made easier. Lamewolf had come to that time of life where wisdom was replacing ardor, and the old brute knew from instinct that they had a far trail to follow before the next sleep.

He was right. With but one stop to boil the last of the tea and inspect all of the stock, there was no halt in the march to Smoky Hill River. Three quarters of the distance was covered by break of day. Then the wind rose, the skies cleared, and the early sun shown on a prairie world of glittering frost-white beauty. The children were delighted, but Roman Nose and Preacher exchanged anxious glances and increased the gait of their wearying mounts. Old Lamewolf growled in his chest, complaining at the forced pace. It required him to lope rather than to trot. Moreover, like Roman Nose and Preacher, he was commencing to read the wind.

They were going to need luck and good leadership to make those last miles to the Cheyenne camp. The wind was east, northeast, and northwest by freakish turn. It made the prairie seem like an ocean of snow. Combers, breakers, swells, and great mountains of the white surface uplifted in minutes. A spot that appeared to be thinly covered as the party would dip to a low place in the buffalo road would be waist-deep when they arrived. Again, a bad place might be blown free for them just as whimsically. But the deep drifts were more in number than the thin spots.

It was now that the canniness of Nehemiah Bleek was tested. The column was stalled, the animals all panting from the fight to breast the deepening snows. There was still a long rise of prairie between them and the valley of the Smoky Hill's north fork. If they could make the crest of the rise, they should find the north slope of the elevation clear of deeper snows. But the way to that rise lay up the south slope, already drifted high and piling higher by the moment.

Now it was made plain why Preacher's blanket roll behind Samson's saddle looked so bulky. The burly white man unslung the blankets and extracted from there a pair of beautifully made

Indian snowshoes. Putting on the rawhide webs, Bleek waved and called to the worried children to lay aside their concerns and watch Preacher break the trail for old Samson and the rest of them.

"*Nahetotaneševe!*" he cried cheerfully. "Come, let us all attack that hill in a happy way. Up we go. *Hai!*"

In thirty minutes Preacher Bleek stomped a trail up the south slope of the divide. It was through deep and heavy snows, but such were the weight of the Horse Creek man and the brute quality of his strength that he drove the webbings of the snowshoes hard enough to pack the going for Samson which followed him and which weighed 1,200 pounds.

Roman Nose had never seen a man of any skin color do such a powerful thing. The Cheyenne was an extremely large man himself, yet he could not have broken the way up that snowy slope. Not if given the whole of the remaining day. The strange schoolmaster from The Cottonwoods had something to his medicine besides *hotoma*.

Roman Nose, as they all rested at the crest, was so curious as to the source of such strength that he went up to Preacher and sniffed his breath. Having done so, he scowled and shook his head. Wrong again. It wasn't *véhoemáp*, the white man's water, the whiskey. Was it, then, the strength of a mad-man? Was Preacher truly a crazy one, as the whites said of him? Roman Nose knew that crazy people sometimes had enormous strength—did amazing things, wild things, unexplainable things and fearsome. But by the way Preacher returned his look when he drew back from the breath-sniffing and by the way the small blue eyes sparkled and from the rare sound of the big white man's laughter as it boomed out on the morning's stillness, the Cheyenne warrior knew that this huge red-headed preacher was not crazy. He was, in fact, just what the southern Cheyennes said he was: touched by God.

Roman Nose acknowledged his respect with Indian dignity. To show him there was an equal return of the feeling, Bleek waved graciously for him to take the lead. It was only fitting that a Cheyenne of such fame should have the honor of heading the column into the village of his kinsmen. Especially when such a Cheyenne had just stolen seventeen horses and put Mashanē and a whole patrol of his best pony soldiers on foot out in the middle of the Rush Creek buffalo pasture. *Ih hai*! Go ahead, warrior. Ride out!

Roman Nose drew himself to his full height. He shook the snow from the eagle feathers in his long braids. He glanced around and gave the forward sign to the Indian children. The company moved off, all of its members doing as the great Maōx was doing, sitting tall for the entrance into the Cheyenne village down there on the north fork of Smoky Hill River.

Watching them go past him, Bleek was touched. Something, a tear or a snowflake, melted a drop of moisture down his cheek. He brushed it away and, as the last child filed past him, he spurred black Samson and rode on down the north slope as tall in his saddle as any of them.

XVI

In the Cheyenne village on Smoky Hill River, the news of Mashanē's return was received with alarm. The band quickly agreed to take the orphan children from Preacher and pass them along to Indian camps in Kansas, where they would be out of Chivington's reach. After a suitable time, Preacher could gather them up once more and start another school. As for Preacher himself, he must move on with equal swiftness. The reason was Mashanē's nearness in Bijou Basin. It was a certainty that such a man as Sick Mind would never forgive Preacher for what the Horse Creek schoolmaster had done to him. Nor would he forgive any people who gave Preacher shelter. Both Bleek and his Smoky Hill friends understood this hard fact of their lives. No time was wasted in false sentiment. But when it came the turn of Roman Nose to speak his views of the situation, it was another matter.

"My brothers," he said, "you are wrong to talk

of peace and of running away. You cannot hide from Mashanē's kind. Now I want you to think about that, and I want to tell you something else." He paused, letting his fierce gaze wander over them. "Before I came down here, I saw an Army paper up north. It was shown to some of us by Guerrier, who you all know. Guerrier would not lie to us. He is one-half our blood. That paper said that the Army chiefs should befriend the Indians. They should begin this by stopping the roaming pony soldier troops that do not know one tribe from another and that go about killing everything in the shape of an Indian. This Army paper ended by warning the soldier chiefs that it would take only a few more murders by these roving troops to unite all the tribes in war, and it would be a bloody war." Again the northern warrior paused, then concluded, voice rising with passion. "My brothers, hear me. I say to you that there do not have to be a few more murders to start this war. There have already been far too many murders. I do not lie. Over at Preacher's schoolhouse at The Cottonwoods my own friend, Kōvohe, lies dead, shot three times in the stomach by a soldier of Mashanē's roving troops. Kōvohe had no gun in his hand. It was murder. Now I am going home and I am going to bring my people back down here when the new grass comes, and we will find Mashanē and those soldiers of his and kill them all. Maybe if we do that, the Army will let us alone and will stop killing our women and children. I ask you southern people to be ready to join us when we return. War is the only tongue the white man understands."

When Roman Nose had quieted down from his excitement, Bleek tried to reason with him. Neither Roman Nose nor all the northern and southern Cheyennes together were going to kill Mashanē and all his pony soldiers. Roman Nose himself had said that there were too many soldiers to destroy—that was precisely why he had brought Red Dust to Preacher Bleek, so that the boy might learn the white man's way and not die fighting pony soldiers who had more numbers than the blades of the buffalo grass. But to this sober plea the famed Cheyenne fighter had a warrior's reply.

"Kōvohe is dead," he said, "and Roman Nose wants to die."

"What about the boy?" demanded Bleek accusingly.

"Treat him as your son," replied the other. "You have already told me that you are going now to find your old friend, Major Wynkoop, over in Kansas. You say that Wynkoop is at Fort Larned. You say, if you find him there, you know that he will help you start a new school for the children, and that he will not permit Mashanē to harm them no matter what happens. Have you then lied to Roman Nose?"

Preacher at once protested the question. There

was no doubt, he said, that Wynkoop would help the children. The good major was the enemy of Colonel Chivington. Their feud was over Chivington's underhanded part in taking away Wynkoop's power to protect the Indians in Colorado Territory. It was Chivington who had caused Wynkoop to be sent away to Kansas. It was Chivington who had put Major Anthony in command at Fort Lyon. No, Preacher had not lied about Wynkoop. If the brave officer could be reached—if he was, as the Smoky Hill people said, at Fort Larned—then there was indeed a last desperate chance to re-gather the orphan children and bring them to final safety in far Kansas.

"So then," promised Bleek, "you have my word on it, Maōx. If it can be done, it will be done."

"And the boy, Preacher?"

"It will be as you say. If you do not return with the new grass, he will be as my own son. Here is my hand on it."

Their grips met, held firm for a long moment, fell apart.

Roman Nose touched his fingertips to his forehead, saluting Preacher Bleek. The latter returned the gesture of simple human respect, one man for another. And that was the whole of their parting.

After that camp, they never saw one another again.

• • •

The seven children of the Horse Creek mission school to reach the Smoky Hill winter camp of the southern Cheyennes in late November of 1864 were the following: Ohēs, Young Buzzard, the bald-headed boy, of Kiowa-Comanche blood; Hehēn, Blackbird, the Negro-Cheyenne youth; Mocenimoe, Little Braid; Kamax, Wooden Stick; Ookat, Bareskin, and Ešxovevemàp, Sugarlump, all pure-blooded Cheyennes, and, of course, Soxoenos, Sunflower, the little crippled Arapaho girl.

Although the Indians loved children—indeed, made the love of their children the center of their culture—they never made the white man's mistake of confusing love with law and order. In the Indian society the child was not consulted about its past, its present, or its future. It was told what to do and it did it, until such an age where it was told it was old enough to act for itself. In no other way than this total discipline could the children be expected to survive the dangers of their nomad life. Incredibly spoiled in many ways, in the matter of obedience to elders and respect the Indian child never hesitated. He was not confounded by kindness and affection, not made either a brat or a simpleton by doting over. He knew his time to command would come. He bided that time in obedience to parental rule as naturally as the bear cub to the mother bear, the fawn to the doe, or the wild foal to the mustang mare.

So it was that when the children were divided, this one to go to that tribe, this one to the other tribe, they did not contend the decisions, but accepted them. Preacher did his best to assure them that the danger would pass and they would all be united again when Mashanē was gone and a kinder man had come to take his place. For Bleek this was a lie. He did not believe Chivington would be replaced, but rather that the warfare along the Arkansas would grow worse. In fact, he knew that it would. Bleek had met several of the important people in the Arkansas region, either by way of soliciting their aid for his wilderness school or by virtue of their own curiosity that had led them to visit the mission on distant Horse Creek to see for themselves the "daft and odd bear of a man" who neither preached nor prayed but called himself Preacher, and whose schooling was said to "defy the law and endanger the peace" of the entire frontier.

Some of these visitors went away dismissing the proprietor of The Cottonwoods as a harmless crackpot. Some others felt, but did not reveal the fact, that he was doing a good and charitable deed but was of course quite mad. Still others sided with the military view that held the school should be closed and its head given a one-way stage ticket out of his Arkansas parish. Occasionally, though, a man would meet Nehemiah Bleek and see something in him that solicited neither laughter nor pity or censure, but demanded admiration.

Two such men were the Indian agent, Colley, and Wynkoop, both majors in rank, yet both reasonable and good men of the kind all too often found in the military but scarcely ever exalted by it. As in most professions, including the "praying practice," as Bleek called the ministry, goodness and light were seldom the heralds of success, the frontier Army being no exception. It was the "hellers" and the "devils" by Bleek's description who "garnered the main gravy." The "wheel horses," on the other hand—the Colleys and the Wynkoops—were given only the "teepee scraps and weed chaff" for their labors. Universally labeled "Indian lovers," their unfailing reward, in Bleek's opinion, was to have the tobacco juice of public ire aimed constantly at their reputations. "Splattered," in the more precise translation, "all over their hard-working backsides." It was the Chivingtons and the Anthonys who were the darlings of the Arkansas.

Understanding this, Bleek was prepared to lie to his children in telling them good bye. He thought that it would be kinder than telling the truth. Moreover, there was still that small hope of finding Wynkoop and then, with that hope gone, there was always the eternal star of faith. "Remember Maheo," he intended to tell the children, "and never forget the Lord God Jehovah."

XVII

Bleek, however, did not say farewell to the children that day, or the next. It was five days later that he managed to get away from the big camp on the Smoky Hill. Delaying him had been a second heavy snowfall setting in even as he planned his route to Fort Larned. Realizing that any weather that would challenge Samson's vast power to plow a track line would also inhibit a cavalry horse, he had not worried about being caught in the village by any troops that might be alerted by Chivington's return from his Horse Creek scout. What was it the Bible said about the rain falling the same way for everybody? Well, if it went for rain, it would go double for snow. Preacher surely could count on having a good jump on any new scout patrols coming up to reconnoiter the Smoky Hill Cheyennes. He could depart in confidence. It was just the Spanish jack and himself against the ordinary hardships of a winter trail. Of course, it was a long trail, and time was an unknown menace to his plans for seeing Wynkoop. It was 200 miles to Fort Larned—likely a little more, allowing for bad trail detours. But Preacher believed that Providence had sent that extra snowfall to slow the enemy, or perhaps it was that Maheo had struck a blow against Mashanē.

Thus armed in spirit, Bleek prepared to set out. He chose to depart the camp after darkness. If by some outside chance the cavalry had found the village and were watching it, they would not see him leave. Hence, the Indians would not be punished for harboring a man wanted by Colonel Chivington and the 3rd Colorado. The children were to leave later that night and for the same reasons of secrecy and fear of Mashanē's return.

What could be done had been done. No man knew better than Bleek the odds faced in the 200-mile ride to find an officer who might or might not be where Cheyenne rumor had located him. This doubt weighed mightily in the big man's mind as he sought out the children to say his farewells.

The latter were staying in the lodge of Preacher's old friend, Honeheonoz, Wolfbag. The wife of Wolfbag was a northern woman, a half-sister of Red Dust's mother. She and Wolfbag had no children of their own. They had been pleased to shelter the little ones of Preacher Bleek until they might be sent along to the other tribes for safer keeping. Now Bleek was pausing outside the lodge of these good friends, composing himself for an entrance that would hide any of his doubts from the children who trusted him in all things. He stood with head down. Whether praying, or gritting his teeth, might have been a difficult decision to make for one who knew him well.

However, Hotamemaes, the chief scout of the

Smoky Hill camp, was not familiar with the Horse Creek missionary. Thus he came trotting up to the head-bowed Bleek with a sharp command for the white man to step aside and unblock the way into the lodge of Wolfbag. Hotamemaes bore important news.

"Hotamemaes?" inquired Bleek, raising his head. "Dog Chips? What a fine name for a respectable man. May I ask what important news it is that brings you through the night at such speed?"

"Of course," said the brave. "As war chief of our camp, Wolfbag must tell us our plans for avoiding the troops, or for fighting them. I have just come up from the Arkansas and I saw something big down there . . . that good oak leaf chief has come out of Fort Larned over there in Kansas and set up a camp down below Fort Lyon. He has not many soldiers with him, but the Arapahoes tell me that he has sent them word that he will protect them. Little Raven and most of the Arapaho lodges have gone down there from Fort Lyon and camped near the good chief. *Ih-hai*! Wouldn't you say that was something big?"

"Praise God!" cried Nehemiah Bleek. "Do you mean Major Wynkoop? Is that the good oak leaf chief you mean?"

"That's the one," answered Dog Chips. "Now will you stand aside and permit me to go in?"

"Hallelujah!" breathed Bleek, voice lifted with happiness. "Major Wynkoop only sixty miles away, rather than two hundred? The Allfather is certainly working for his red children tonight!"

"*Haho*, thanks be," muttered Dog Chips, and ducked in through the entrance flap of Wolfbag's lodge convinced that the strange-minded schoolmaster from Horse Creek was indeed, as his people said, touched by Maheo.

As for Bleek, he stood a moment motionlessly. Then he made the Sign of the Cross on his broad chest and raised his face to the clearing starlight overhead.

"Thanks be for me, too, Lord," he said softly. "I reckon me and Samson will give that devil Chivington a real race now."

Outside the lodge the wind moaned restlessly. The wife of Wolfbag, who had been instructed to mind the matter of preparing the children of Preacher for traveling before daylight, was restless. She wanted to go to the next lodge where she knew her sisters were gathered to discuss the news from the Arkansas. Their husbands, of course, had gone to the meeting of the Dog Soldiers over at the medicine lodge. Finally the woman decided that she would risk her husband's wrath. The men would be talking war until all hours, anyway. The little ones, bless them, were all sound asleep.

The squaw took a final close look at the slumbering children, wrapped her blanket against the cut of the wind, and slipped out through the entry flaps. *Brrrr!* It was cold! That simpleton of a preacher had selected a fine frosty night to start out for the Arkansas. *Ih*, these white people were all crazy!

It was as well for the woman's peace of mind that her thoughts had already dismissed the sleeping children. No sooner had the entry flaps fallen behind her than Sunflower was sitting upright in her blanket and whispering to ask of Red Dust if he, too, were awake.

He was, he admitted. What did his Arapaho sister wish?

It developed that Sunflower wished to escape the lodge of Wolfbag and his woman and go and try to find Preacher. Preacher was her father, she said, and her heart was not easy away from him. She was afraid without Preacher near. Would Red Dust help her to go and find him? Could not the nephew of the great Roman Nose follow any trail and fight any bears or wolves that might come upon them?

Red Dust was not a shrewd boy, but he was gallant. He asked some hard questions. How would they catch up to Preacher—fly? How could they track him in the dark—by crying out for him to wait for them? What would they tell him when they came up with him—that they were surprised to see him, and very glad?

Sunflower's mind was as quick as the trap that had twisted her leg. To catch up with Preacher they would take the spotted Delilah. This beast would trot all night to be up again with her black mate, Samson. As for following the trail in the dark, Lamewolf could do that for them. As for a story for Preacher when they came up to him, leave that to Sunflower. She knew where the soft spots were under the schoolmaster's great muscles and his grizzly-bear winter coat.

Red Dust wanted to go badly enough, but it was taking the little Arapaho girl with him that worried his Cheyenne mind. Women were never taken on the war trail. Also, this little girl was *voxkatae*, a crippled one. Not, indeed, that this was a criticism. Never that. But a leader had to look to all his party, to the good of the group. No, he finally said, he would not do it.

But Sunflower said that he would. She said it with two big tears and a trusting patting of his hand, and the boy was beaten.

"Don't cry," he pleaded. "We will go."

But then, as they started up from their beds, Hehēn, the Blackbird, awoke and wanted to know where they were going. Sunflower told him the truth, promising that they would find Preacher and come back for Blackbird and the others. But the Negro half-blood depended on Sunflower. She had been his small mother at the mission school, as she had been to the others. He could not see her go.

While Sunflower hesitated, trying to think of a

good argument, the other half-blood boy, Young Buzzard, sat up, blinking sleepily. So they had to tell him also of the plan.

Now both boys insisted on going and Red Dust was growing very nervous. Sunflower could see that in a moment the northern boy was going to quit the scheme, or else run out of the flaps and make his separate escape.

"Listen," she said, eyes gleaming, voice held to the lowest of tense whispers, "I have thought of something to keep us all together. You and I, Red Dust, will ride the spotted jenny, as we said, but these two here can then take the Kiowa Ladies and away we will all go on mounts anxious in their own hearts to rejoin Preacher and the black Spanish jack. Isn't that a wonderful idea?"

Red Dust doubted that it was. But by this time the thought of running away was getting into his wild blood. He agreed to the suggestion. Taking what they needed of food and blankets from the lodge, they gathered up the bridles and saddle pads of Bleek's animals and set out toward the pony herd. Their luck ran good and they found Sheba, Salome, and Delilah within minutes. Sunflower merely pursed her lips and made a peculiar sound like a rabbit being stepped on by a grazing buffalo. It seemed that the Kiowa Ladies and the calico jenny materialized out of the dim mass of the horse herd like three ghost ponies. Even Red Dust was impressed.

"Very good for a girl," he said. "Come on, let's get on them and ride far away from here."

The children climbed up on the two old Indian mares and the little pinto jenny. Red Dust led the way to the camp's edge whence Preacher had departed that dusk. After a little searching they found Samson's hoof prints. The huge jack's track line stretched away and away into the murk of the starlight. Back near the Cheyenne village a dog barked and was answered by the yammering of coyotes from the outer prairie. Far over toward Rush Creek a timber wolf took up the refrain. A second howl and a third replied to the lobo, but these howls were nearer and were to the south, down where Samson's track line led.

"I don't like wolves." Blackbird shivered. "They're bad friends."

"Yes," said Young Buzzard, "why don't we go back to the lodge of Wolfbag and his woman and talk some more about this journey?"

"Be still," ordered Sunflower. "Do you want this northern boy to think we have no spirit?"

"I don't care what the northern boy thinks," answered Young Buzzard honestly. "It's those wolves that concern me. What are they thinking?"

"Of something to eat," interrupted Red Dust grimly.

"Exactly!" cried Blackbird. "That's a smart boy, that northern boy. Let's go back! I don't want to be wolf food, do you?"

"Listen, you southern people," warned Red Dust somberly, "if you want to go back, it's too late. We have set out to find Preacher and we will find him. Nobody turns back."

"That's right," said Sunflower. "Let's go, Lamewolf!" she called to the Indian dog that sat on his haunches, panting and yellow-eyed, pluming the snow with his tail. "Take the trail, here. *Hai*!" She slid off Delilah's rump, over the jenny's tail, and seized the savage dog by the scruff of the neck and dragged him whimperingly over to the track line. There, she shoved his nose into the snow, giving him the scent of Samson's rear hoof prints, where the odor was strongest. "*Ai-hai*!" she said excitedly. "That's it . . . go now, find Preacher!"

Lamewolf growled uncertainly. The look he shot at the little girl was one of pure doubt. But she shook an impatient finger at him and stomped her twisted foot in the snow, and he dropped his hackles and his tail and put his black nose to the track line and slinked off along it like a puff of prairie smoke. Sunflower ran to the spotted jenny and took Red Dust's hand. The Cheyenne boy swung her up behind him. She put both arms about him and gave him a happy squeeze. "*Hai*!" she said. "Let's go, warrior!"

Red Dust looked around at her as questioningly as had Lamewolf. But in the end he was no more the match for those big brown eyes than was the vicious old wolf dog. Sunflower merely giggled and gave him another squeeze and kicked Delilah in the flanks, and away they went.

The two half-blood boys were sharing looks of gravest question, too, of course. But the Kiowa Ladies, waiting for no approval from them, shot after Delilah. All at once the fears of the night and the wolf howls vanished. The air was cold and the Ladies and Delilah were fresh by five days of rest with the Cheyenne herd. No boy could sit to a rocking lope along a mysterious track line leading toward runaway adventure for long without responding to the spirit of such things. Within a mile everyone was happy and chattering together, telling of the great times they would again have with Preacher when the morning's light should come to show them where he was—right there over the next rise, not far at all—and let them ride up to him crying out the good news to him that it was they, his own dear children, caught up with him and come to help him look for Major Wynkoop and all those good new pony soldiers down there where Little Dried River ran into the Arkansas, below Fort Lyon.

XVIII

The children did well through the night. Red Dust, no stranger to the hard trail and the cold, had borrowed a large woven grass pannier from the implements of Wolfbag's squaw. Into this basket he had put a supply of the woman's best dried buffalo fuel. Now he and his friends were glad for this northern foresight. It permitted them to find shelter and make a warming fire against the mid-blackness of the morning. They started on with renewed sureness, although Lamewolf had a few minutes' seeming difficulty in finding the line of Samson's trail after the halt. Soon enough, however, he quit whining and let out a *"whoof!"* that announced he was back on the scent again. Red Dust, peering down at the single line of tracks, nodded in relief. That old dog had worried him a little. But it was all right. The track line went on south as before. It lay as clearly in the snow as if it wanted itself to be followed without fail and by poor light. Red Dust could have stayed with that track line without Lamewolf. It was easy.

Easy, perhaps. With the first gray light of daylight, the hoof prints were wandering a little and the children, sleepy-eyed and long past the first flush of adventure, were continually falling into little catnaps in the saddle. Even Red Dust was having trouble keeping his eyes open and upon the veering trail. Then, suddenly, he was not having that trouble any more.

The tracks wavered up a long swell of the prairie to disappear over the snowy crest of the rise. When the Indian boy reached the top of the incline, the tracks ran only a few feet and stopped—stopped with the creature that had been making them—a very old and gray-bearded rogue bull buffalo that now had faced about to make his stand against his trailers.

The other Indian children came to the crest, their mounts halting. Delilah, the piebald jenny, snorted loudly.

The bull dropped its great head, pawed the snow in clouds over its neck hump. Mules liked buffalo for some strange reason and would run off and join the buffalo herds with great obstinacy. This endeared them little to the Indians, perhaps explaining the Cheyenne dubiety toward the breed. It endeared them still less to the buffalo, which were quite afraid of the mule smell and tended to stampede at the first hint of it. But this old bull had traveled far and he was tired.

He stood and pawed and stared and snorted back at the spotted jenny and the four Indian children and the two Kiowa mares. Lamewolf, that great tracker who had led them so far astray and so wrongly during the dark hours, was also old and tired and had traveled far. He showed no more interest in a battle than the ancient herd bull. He sat down in the snow with a weary grunt, eying the shaggy traitor who had caused him to get on its cross trail. It was Red Dust, finally, who decided what must be done.

"See," he pointed out to the children, "Uncle Hotoa wants only to be left alone. He has come away from the herd to be alone and to die. The buffalo do that. It is a matter of pride with them. Come, we will not disturb this old man."

"But what will we do?" demanded Sunflower with a darkly reproachful look at Lamewolf. "If the dog has lost us, how ever will we find ourselves again?"

Red Dust pondered the question. He was a boy who had been taught to think of his words before giving them. As he hesitated, Blackbird and Young Buzzard encouraged him.

"Yes," said the first boy, "where are we? Are we going to wander on and die like the buffalo? In all of this land I see only blue sky and white snow."

"That is so," agreed his comrade quickly. "I can't see anything but sky and snow, either."

"Never mind," said Sunflower, elevating her plump chin. "Red Dust will see something else."

"Hah!" said Blackbird. "Let him name it to me!"

"And me!" challenged Young Buzzard. "What do you see, northern boy? Magic signs in the snow?"

"Yes," replied Red Dust, straightening. "And all we must do is follow them. Come on."

"Where?" demanded Blackbird.

Red Dust kneed Delilah into a turn. He started her along the back trail of the buffalo's track line, giving them his answer in that act. They were going to have to follow the tracks back to wherever they had crossed lines with the tracks of black Samson, probably at that place where they had built the fire and where Lamewolf had showed uncertainty. All of the children understood this fact in the moment of the northern boy's turning of Delilah. It was an Indian thing. They could see it clearly when it was shown to them. Tired as they were, they picked up their spirits once again and started kicking the Kiowa mares and the little pinto jenny a lively tattoo of heel thumps in the ribs. As quickly as they had lost their Cheyenne *hotoma*, they now recovered its inner-warming courage.

"*Nanehea, nanehea*! Let us all follow Red Dust quickly."

The three mounts began to canter. This was sight-tracking in bright, growing daylight. No need to trust an ancient dog's wheezy old nose any more. No chance for trails being crossed here. This would be a sure thing. Only follow the northern boy and raise the good spirit yells all the way.

The children commenced to utter the high yipping noises of the Cheyenne "hurry up" call.

This sound always served to stir the heart of the downcast, to lift up the will of the weary. But in the present case it stirred and lifted up something else, something that brought Delilah and the Kiowa Ladies to a snow-showering halt, their eyes walling with fear, their ears pointing. Those were timber wolves howling their hunting song back there! They were coming on the trail they had made following the old bull.

In the stillness, the hoarse baying of the gray brutes seemed only over the rise, only just beyond where the bull's tracks disappeared across the snow crest. It was a moment of real terror for the children. They swung their widened eyes toward Red Dust, throats dry, voices locked in their clenched teeth. The northern boy was taking out his knife, spitting on its keen blade.

"Arapaho girl," he said swiftly to Sunflower, "will that dog of yours bait a buffalo? Will he take hold of a bull and hold him for the hunter to get behind?"

"I don't know!" cried Sunflower, very frightened, "I don't know! Will you do that, Lamewolf?"

Red Dust was swinging the spotted jenny, motioning for Blackbird and Young Buzzard to turn the Kiowa mares.

"He had better do it," said the northern boy grimly, and led them on the gallop back toward the lone shaggy figure of Uncle Hotoa.

When they came once more to where the old

bull stood, they found him ready for the wolves. He had put his rump to the wall of a little dry wash just beyond the big rise. Here the pack could not come at him from behind. Here the magnificent old lord of the prairie was prepared to face his enemies to the last.

Red Dust slid from the back of the spotted jenny. Talking in an even tone, he told Sunflower to take the two half-blood boys and quickly ride on down the wash. The bed of the depression deepened to the south and made a hairpin turn to drain toward the small stream beside which they had made their night fire. Around that bend, they were to wait and watch. If Red Dust could do what he must to the old bull, he would run and join them. If he failed and the wolves then came up to surround him, they were to go at once down the deepening wash, and get away if they could. He would try to occupy the wolves.

Sunflower began to cry out against this, but the northern boy ordered her to go. Another burst of howling from the wolves, much nearer now, decided the girl. Shouting to Blackbird and Young Buzzard, she drove Delilah off and around the bend, the half-blood boys following her on the Kiowa mares.

"Now hold hard to those ponies when you are hidden!" Red Dust called after them. "They will want to break away from you when they get the wolf smell!"

The Cheyenne boy had seized the rusted chain of Lamewolf's collar in the beginning, so that the brute would not desert him when Sunflower rode off. In the excitement of shouting after the departing children, Red Dust realized he had dropped the chain hold and freed the dog. But now his heart rose within him, rather than failed.

Lamewolf was making no sign to go after his Arapaho mistress. He was looking from Red Dust to the sound of the wolf howling to the snorting and snow-pawing of the cornered bull. This was no dog that was going to run away. Seeing this, the northern boy threw a glance upward toward Maheo.

"Thank thee, Allfather," he said. Then, softly and with a quick pat on the dog's broad skull: "Come on, old fighter, let us see what two Cheyennes can do together."

The moment the boy moved forward, knife in hand, toward the buffalo, Lamewolf dropped to his furry belly in the snow and rushed in upon the bull. Attacking the bull's head, he got the great animal to lower his horns and come out a step or two from the wall of the dry wash. Red Dust, circling to the rear of the huge beast, slid along the wall behind him. The straining muscles of the animal's rear quarters, the twisting and thrusting of its tremendous body—all were within touch of Red Dust's outstretched fingers. If the bull came backward, the boy would be crushed in the instant of the maneuver, spread like a bug upon the dry earth of the prairie cutbank by the scraping force of 2,000 pounds of bone and horn and shaggy black hide.

But the great beast did not turn. In the instant of the sliding behind him, Red Dust whistled to the dog with fingers between lips and made the seizing shout in Cheyenne. From some dim cranny of his Indian youth, Lamewolf called up the meaning of the whistle and the shout and hand signal of the northern boy. In he went to the left of the bull's lowered head. The bull swung his gleaming horns to follow the movement. Instantly Lamewolf shifted to the right, and, when the brute's head came back toward him, the dog's jaws closed on its black nose and held there. With a thunderous bellow of anger and pain, the bull set itself on its haunches to raise its head and dash the old dog to the ground for stomping. And that was the moment of Red Dust's prayer.

When the rear quarters bunched and set themselves, the boy dived in between the great bull's planted hind hoofs and slashed, once, twice, with all his force to drive the knife through the hock tendon of each rear leg. The old bull never felt the knife.

He knew only that the dog had let go of his nose and that there was a small Indian boy running out from behind him and that there was blood on the snow and it was his blood. He tried to lunge after the boy and the dog, but something was wrong. His rear legs would not work. They buckled beneath him. He struggled up on the front legs, sitting like some enormous black-maned dog on the snow. It was thus the wolves found him, racing up but moments after Red Dust and the old dog had vanished around the bend, into the deeper course of the dry wash.

The pack was not fooled by the wounded bull. Three or four of its members split off and began to run the tracks of Red Dust and Lamewolf toward the bend. But the northern boy had won his gamble. They had no sooner veered off from the pack than the pack had gotten the sight and the scent of the freshly shed blood in the snow about the old bull and was raising a hideous yammer of snarls. The other wolves now whirled and turned back from the track line of Red Dust and the children, to be in at the kill of the buffalo.

As Red Dust had foreseen, the blood could not be resisted by the gray killers. As for Uncle Hotoa, the great old bull had died that four of his small Indian comrades might live. Maheo would understand that and would bring old Hotoa to see it likewise. Meanwhile, the courage of the northern boy had purchased the time for his companions and himself to escape—or so he urgently prayed as he led the other children in the flight.

His prayers were heard. By the time the

paunches of the wolf pack were bulging with sweet buffalo beef, the matter of the human prey was completely forgotten. Moreover, that prey was far away. Hidden by the ever-deepening walls of the dry wash, Red Dust and the others had ridden their mounts many miles and were now nearing the end of the wash, where the walls of the depression vanished and its channel widened to join that of Ponoeohe, the Little Dried River, that south-running tributary of the great Arkansas that the white man called Sand Creek.

Preacher, traveling south through the night, made good time. He had brought his Ute snowshoes with him, and, when Samson gave sign of wearying, he donned the webs and trotted ahead of his mount. The Spanish jack followed him like a dog. In this sharing way they were far down the Indian trail to the Arkansas before daylight. Only one thing worried Preacher. He had been fooled by the bad snows up on the divide country near Smoky Hill River headwaters and the Cheyenne village.

The higher country up there had caught much heavier falls than the lower prairies toward the Arkansas. It was nearly open going, once they had struck the valley of Little Dried River and were on the main Indian trail to the big river and the rumored camp of Major Wynkoop below Fort Lyon. If those lighter snows and nearly bare earth

149

conditions held also to the west, toward Bijou Basin and the field bivouac of Chivington's 3rd Colorado, then only God would know how long ago Chivington had reached his main troops, had reached those troops and sent the vengeance patrols looking for Preacher Bleek and his scattered brood of Indian orphans. But the Lord had been with Bleek so far, and the big Horse Creek man was not going to begin doubting Him now.

He and Samson went on, only hurrying more than they had before the snows thinned and the thoughts of Chivington returned. With the first faint streaks of dawn they were on the Arkansas. By sunrise they had found the white tents of Wynkoop's temporary field headquarters and Bleek was breakfasting with the "good oak leaf soldier chief" from Fort Larned.

The meeting went well. Wynkoop listened with keen understanding to Preacher's report of the school's burning and of his abduction of Chivington as hostage for the escape of the visiting Indians and of his own orphans of Indian blood. Wynkoop was aware of Chivington's standing order to the 3rd Colorado. He was not a soft man on Indians himself. In his day and when the depredations of the Cheyennes and the Arapahoes against the whites of Colorado had warranted it, he had issued his own "kill Indians on sight" orders. But these had been temporary

150

actions designed to quell bloody outbreaks in local situations. They were never blanket conceptions of a method of warfare that amounted to extermination of the red man wherever encountered.

"I believe your story," he said to Bleek, when the Horse Creek schoolmaster had concluded. "Moreover, I am going to issue you a written pass to go up to Pueblo and see Colley. I will put in that pass the order that you are to be given any of these children you may find along your way to Pueblo. Particularly any of them that may have been brought in to Fort Lyon. I will address this communication to Major Anthony at Lyon, requesting his co-operation. I expect, too, that he will furnish it."

He made the last statement with something of a warm wrinkling of the crows-feet at his eye corners, and Bleek queried him on it.

"I am satisfied," he answered, "that Anthony understands that I am not down here setting up this field camp for the protection of the peaceful Indians on my own. He will be forced to assume that I am acting under higher authority than his by the mere fact that he was not consulted or advised in any way on the matter. This fact alone must lead to his honoring of this pass and order I give you, the regular Army being what it is and Anthony being of the regular Army. Now, Bleek, there is no more I can do for you. I am going to assign two troopers to ride with you for your own protection. Anthony I do not fear, but Colonel Chivington is another matter. I suggest that you avoid him. As for your request in regard to a new school site near Fort Larned, the best I can offer is to say that I will be happy to entertain the idea if you will come and see me at the fort after this Indian matter is settled here. Meanwhile, your wisest move is to collect your children and report to Agent Colley at Pueblo. He will advise you from that point. He will also instruct Chivington of my order, and no doubt of his agreement with it. Again, this will ensure that the children are to be brought in unharmed if found in the field. Now, sir, I hope that you have enjoyed your breakfast and that your opinion of the military and the Indian Bureau are, alike, somewhat improved."

Bleek thanked him humbly. He did not like, he said, to press a matter when the major had been so kind, but it was going to be necessary that he be provided with some transportation to Pueblo. Might the major spare a good mount in a good cause? Bleek's own black jackass had covered sixty miles in one long night, and was used up.

"We can do better than that," answered Wynkoop. "The Pueblo stage is due past here within the hour. It stops at Fort Lyon and at Bent's Ranch only. You will be with Major Colley this time tomorrow morning. You can't beat that, Reverend."

Bleek blushed at hearing the title, but Wynkoop was not insincere in using it.

"Yes, sir, I reckon that's first-class, Major, sir," he said. "I and my little ones won't forget you. God willing, we'll come and tell you so, too, down to Fort Larned like you said, Major." He turned to peer off down the Arkansas, squinting against the early sun. "Begging your pardon, Major, but don't you think you'd best write out those orders for me? Isn't that the Pueblo stage coming yonder?"

It was the stage, and Wynkoop nodded quickly.

An orderly brought the materials and the officer made out the document. He sanded it and gave it to Bleek.

"Don't show it except as needed," he said, "and don't surrender it to anyone save Agent Colley. Good luck, Bleek. These are bad times. We can only do what we think is right. You understand that you will face some sort of inquiry over this affair with Chivington. I am taking your word for what took place, but even so the circumstances warrant complete investigation."

"Yes, sir, I know that, Major. What I did wasn't right, I reckon. It was like you said, Major. I did it because I thought it was right at the time."

"I'm satisfied that's the case," said Wynkoop.

The stage was swinging into the camp then, and Bleek was knuckling his bushy brows and making one parting request of his quiet-voiced benefactor.

"Major, sir, might I tie on that old jackass of

mine to the back of the stage and tow him along to Bent's Ranch? I can leave him there. Me and Colonel Bent, we're old friends, sir. You know, on account of the Cheyenne Indians and like that."

Wynkoop glanced at Samson. He had not previously studied the latter, and now his hand waved emphatically.

"Good Lord, yes, Bleek," he agreed. "Take him along by all means. In fact, sir, that's an order!"

Nehemiah Bleek grinned, did his ham-fisted best at a proper salute. Taking the black jack, he went to meet the halting Pueblo stage. Ten minutes later the stagecoach, with Preacher Nehemiah Bleek aboard, had cleared the camp and was rolling for Fort Lyon.

"Praise Jehovah," murmured the man from Horse Creek, and with a sigh that blew dust from the tattered upholstery of the opposite seats, he lay back against the cushions of the old Concord and fell fast asleep.

XIX

When Red Dust and the mission school children rode out of the dry wash, into the open lands of upper Sand Creek, they revealed themselves to another group of prairie travelers brought out by the good weather. Coming up Sand Creek were Sergeant Skemp and a new search patrol on the prowl for "any Indians, so long as they were Cheyennes," as ordered by the enraged Chivington.

There were eight troopers with Skemp, including ex-Sergeant Durant, now reduced to buck private and put in Skemp's patrol for punishment and penalty. Skemp and Red Dust saw each other's group at the same time. Even as the northern boy turned the pinto jenny and fled with his companions for the high ground north of the wash, Skemp was shouting his troopers into hot pursuit. It was not a routine running down of fleeing children; it was a hard, gun-firing chase. If the troopers, taking separate decent actions, were firing into the ground or over the heads of the fugitives, Skemp was not. He was aiming to hit, as he had ordered his men to aim. Only the uneven ground and twisting course of the Indian mounts prevented him from wounding or killing the children or their saddle animals.

Riding up beside him, Durant called out for him to stop shooting. In the name of God, couldn't he see that the kids were unarmed? That they were terrified? That they could not possibly get away from the better-mounted patrol? His answer was a snarl from Skemp and another round fired at the children. It came to Durant, then, that the sergeant meant to kill those poor wild orphans of Preacher Bleek's, and to do it in the chase so that he could so enter it in his report—*Shot While Attempting to Escape: We couldn't make out too clear that they was only kids, General, sir. Our orders was to shoot any hostiles we saw, sir, and it all happened so quick like we didn't hardly have no real chance to be certain if they was growed bucks, or whatever. You know how it is with them crazy devils, sir. You give any of them the benefit of thirty seconds' doubt and they'll shoot you from the back quicker'n a drunk Mexican.*

Durant could see the words. He could hear their pious delivery before the court of inquiry that would look into the murders. It was as clear to him as though he were already there, as the witness he would undoubtedly be required to be. He knew, too, what the court would rule. Also, what would happen to witness Durant should he presently persist in any course of obstruction to Sergeant Skemp's plain intent to kill Indians.

He pulled his horse back, reining him away from Skemp. But he would not touch his carbine's trigger, not even to fire, as his fellow troopers were firing, to make the sergeant think that his order was being obeyed. Curse the court of inquiry! And curse that murdering Skemp. Private Durant had fired at his last fleeing Indian, tame or hostile, man, woman, or little child.

But now the chase was closing. The two Indian boys on the dirty gray mares, single-mounted and very light in weight, were going to make it safely away, Durant saw. The little spotted jenny, however, small anyway and carrying two children, was falling behind and would be caught. As he noted this, the trooper saw the little crippled Arapaho girl jump off of the pinto jenny and go rolling head over heels along the bare hard ground. Miraculously she got to her feet and began to limp toward the edge of the dry wash bluff. The northern Cheyenne boy was fighting the jenny, trying to get her turned about so that he could go back for the girl. But before he could control the animal, Skemp had drawn within fifty yards of the Arapaho child.

Sunflower was trying to get over the lip of the dry wash wall, to hide there and to lead the soldiers after her so that Red Dust might win free alone on Delilah. But the walls of the dry wash were too steep and too high. There was no place to climb down, no niche, even, to hold her slight body below the edge of the prairie, out of the gunfire. As she hesitated, Skemp's last shot struck her. She spun three times around and fell sprawlingly over the bluff top, into the deep wash. The sergeant slid his horse to a stop, dismounted, and ran stumblingly toward the edge of the depression, levering the spent shell from his carbine. The dismounting gave Red Dust time to turn Delilah and spur her toward the cursing Skemp. The latter heard the drum of the jenny's trim hoofs but thought it was one of his men coming up. He turned in the last second, but was

157

too late. Knife bared, the northern boy leaped from the jenny's back down upon him.

Skemp writhed violently, managing to keep the blade from burying itself between his shoulder blades, where Red Dust had aimed it. But he took a nasty ragged gash on his left arm before he could throw the Indian boy away from him and pick up the carbine he had dropped when the boy's knife struck. With a foul oath, he started toward Red Dust.

Yet, as he raised the gun to fire at the boy, Lamewolf, having run like a coward at first rifle burst, came racing back to leap and bury his fangs in the wrist of Skemp's right arm. Screaming with pain, Skemp literally lifted the wolf dog over head and flung him down the bluff. But he had dropped the rifle again and now, before he might recover it the second time, Red Dust had kicked it over the edge of the bluff and followed slidingly after it, to tumble and fall to the floor of the wash below.

He lit almost atop Lamewolf in a drift of soft snow two feet deep. To his joy, he saw there in the same drift, her fall also broken by the snowbank, the crumpled figure of Sunflower. The Arapaho girl was bleeding from the gunshot wound and could not walk, but she was alive, and Red Dust seized her and carried her back in under the overhang of the bluff. There he found some rocks and weathered ledges, with a dark hole that smelled and looked like a wolf's denning place.

Up above, he could hear the raving of the wounded Sergeant Skemp as the latter roared at his men to hurry up, to bring him another carbine, to get up there on the double and start shooting. The northern boy was desperate.

He saw Lamewolf totter up and out of the snowbank and look around. He whistled for him and the old dog heard him and limped into the rocks to join his small people. In the same glance Red Dust saw the pony soldier carbine sticking up in the snow, and ran out and brought it back in under the overhang. He patted the hand of Sunflower. He put his arms about the little girl and hugged her hard.

"Lie still, little sister," he told her. "We have a gun now, and a place to fight. Don't move. It makes the bleeding worse."

Sunflower smiled, or tried to smile. But the pain was very bad where the bullet had struck her. Her best effort was to reach out and pat Red Dust's hand in return. She was so weak, so shaken, that her voice would not come.

Lamewolf crept to her, whining deeply in his throat. She put an arm around the furry neck. The old dog crouched and laid his head by her side so that she could hold onto him, could feel his warmth and strength there beside her.

"Give her your life, old dog," said Red Dust. "I will give mine to both of you. I am going to kill that pony soldier sergeant, if he comes down here."

159

Skemp, meanwhile, was coming down. He seized a carbine from one of the men and ran along the wall of the wash until it lowered and he could jump down into its bottom. Then he raced back up toward the overhang and the rocks of the wolf denning place where Red Dust waited for him.

When the sergeant came, cursing and glaring, to a halt, looking around for the fallen children, Red Dust stood up from behind the rocks and pulled the trigger of his carbine. There was only a loud metallic *clink*. The carbine was empty.

Skemp laughed and raised his own weapon to shoot. In that instant, Lamewolf rushed past Red Dust and attacked the sergeant once more. This time, however, Skemp was ready for him and shot him in mid-air. The bullet seemed to take off the top of the old dog's head, fur flying as if the lead had exploded upon contact. Lamewolf hurtled past Skemp into the snowbank, never twitching after he fell.

Mercifully Sunflower did not see her friend struck down. The Arapaho girl had fainted from pain and loss of blood. Red Dust could not say if she, too, were not gone like the brave old dog. He only knew that his own time was staring at him from the muzzle of the pony soldier's gun, now looking point-blank into his dark face for the final breath.

The nephew of Roman Nose took that breath and stood up straight, waiting for Skemp to pull the trigger. But Skemp's finger did not close. Another calvaryman's carbine barked from atop the bluff. Skemp's gun flew apart, stock shattered. Skemp looked at his empty, numbed hands. His face, dead white beneath its four-day filth of beard, turned upward. Red Dust heard the voice of one of the soldiers up on top. It was giving an order to the sergeant. And the northern boy saw the sergeant step back and slowly raise his hands in response to that order.

That was a real stillness. During it, Red Dust came out from beneath the overhang. He saw the soldier up there on the bluff. He saw the white smoke of the gunpowder still curling from the muzzle of the soldier's carbine. And he saw something else. He knew that soldier. It was the quiet man, Durant. The one who had driven the wagon for Preacher.

The troopers went with Durant down the bluff to where Skemp waited. They followed the private because men will always follow other men who seize command. But they were already commencing to suffer doubts.

Durant understood this, being a man who thought and felt things beyond his apparent simplicity. The sergeant had clearly gone berserk in the pursuit of the Indian children. These other men—most of them anyway—were decent enough. It took the leadership of such as Chivington and Skemp to bring out the cruelty that lurked in them, as in most men. They had sided instinctively with Durant's rebellion in their first disgust with Skemp. But now, as they came up to Skemp outside the wolf den, Durant did not know whether he could hold them any longer.

Skemp, the old sneer back on his dirty face, was certain that the troopers would not stay with Durant. They all knew Colonel Chivington too well for that. But Durant still held the carbine on him, and the men were only wavering as they drew up and halted.

"Sergeant Skemp," said Durant, "you're under arrest."

Skemp laughed. "Do you hear that, boys?" he asked of the silent men. "Old Skemp's under arrest. Now, I wonder what the charges might be? I don't mean against me, boys. I mean against you, when I tell the colonel about Private Durant shooting at his sergeant. Eh? How about that, Binford? You, Morissey? Heckert, you think the colonel's going to forgive you?"

"Binford," ordered Durant, "tie his hands behind him. Heckert, you and Morissey take him up above and get him on his horse. We're taking him in to Fort Lyon."

"Fort Lyon?" The troopers echoed the question as one.

"That's right. I'm turning Skemp over to Major Anthony with my charges. Turning myself in, too. I'll stand trial for what I've done, and those of you as want to can witness for or against me. But Skemp is going in. Now tie him up."

None of the men moved.

Skemp laughed again. "Go ahead, boys," he said, holding out his hands. "Do what General Durant tells you."

Durant knew that this was the time. He knew, too, that he needed help from some source not evident among the weakening resolves of his fellow troopers. It was then that his glance fell on Red Dust. The Indian boy stood waiting. He stood as straight as a rifle rod. Something in his dark face, his dignity, tugged at those chords of human charity in Durant's breast that had brought him to shoot the carbine out of Skemp's hands.

"Binford," he said, "I want you to go back in those rocks and bring that little girl out here."

Binford looked at Skemp.

"Sure." The sergeant grinned. "Why not? Poor little thing. That's quite a tumble she took. I wouldn't be surprised but what it had kilt her."

Binford went up into the rocks. Presently he came back out from under the shadows of the overhang. He stood in the morning sunlight, the fragile Indian child in his arms. She looked as though she were asleep, a broken and tortured Arapaho doll, now at peace. Binford's jaw muscles were shivering. His face was white with righteous anger. He looked at Skemp and this time there was no question of the trooper's feelings, or his decision. Binford was a big man. He was rough and coarse, and he had killed an Indian in his time. But this was different. This was not an Indian. It was only a little baby girl.

"Sarge," he said to Durant, not Skemp, "she don't hardly weigh no more nor a broke-wing bird."

"That's what she is," agreed Durant. He turned back to the other troopers, low-voiced. "Arrest Sergeant Skemp," he said to them, and now the men went forward and took Skemp hard by the arms and shoved him away down the wash and toward the horses, and Skemp understood in his skulking way what had happened there in that moment of sunlight below the overhang, and he went with the men not saying anything, and in fear for his life.

XX

Durant made a wide circle away from the Sand Creek trail, cutting overland to intercept the Arkansas stage road below Fort Lyon. He traveled with intentional slowness and great caution. He could take no chance of meeting other patrols of cavalry. He knew that his only course with Major Anthony lay in voluntary surrender. He must make it into the fort on his own, and tell his own story, before anyone else might tell it ahead of him.

When the early twilight came on, they were still some miles above the Arkansas. Camp was made in a small growth of brush beside a small tributary of Sand Creek. Durant did not recognize the little stream, nor did any of the men. They made a fire and ate a cheerless supper. After full darkness, it began to snow lightly. The leafless scrub did little to shield them from the rising wind. The men became surly. They sensed that Durant was leading them by the long route, that they ought to have been snug and warm in Army bunks at Fort Lyon by this time. Nothing was said, but bad feeling was in the air.

Skemp had not uttered a word since his capture. His wily brain had evidently told him that silence was his greatest menace to the worried men.

The troopers slept quickly enough after supper. The last one up was hulking Binford, who tarried to be sure that Sunflower was made as comfortable as could be beside the fire. Durant told Binford that he appreciated his help. The big soldier nodded, glanced uneasily toward Skemp, who was bound securely to a nearby sapling.

"Listen," he whispered, "don't let on I'm saying anything to you, Sarge. But the boys ain't to be trusted tomorrow. Maybe not even for the rest of tonight. You'd best get out of here if you can. I'll mind the baby girl for you."

He trailed the words off and got up and went over to his blankets. Rolling up in them, he was snoring before Durant could fully absorb the several implications of his friendly attempt at warning him.

He looked at Skemp. The sergeant was wide-eyed, watching him. He had the wild shadows of the firelight glittering in his deep-set eyes. Even bound to the tree, he seemed crouched, ready to spring. It came to Durant that Binford was right. He had to get out of this camp, and quickly. But he must take the Indian boy Red Dust with him, and he must take the little girl Sunflower. To leave either with Skemp, Binford's good-hearted assurances to the contrary, was unthinkable.

But how? How was he to do it with that devilish Skemp watching him without blinking the whole night through? Sleep was the answer. Skemp must somehow be put to sleep.

He poured a cup of coffee and took it over to the prisoner. Putting the cup on the ground, he unsheathed his knife. "I'm going to cut you loose, Skemp," he said. "Just be quiet and don't wake up the men, eh? This here coffee will go good on such a cold night. Have I got your word you won't try nothing?"

"Sure, soldier," Skemp answered. His narrowed eyes swept the sleeping camp. "You know me. I'm obliged for the coffee."

Durant went behind the tree to which Skemp was tied. Without a sound, he drew his long-barreled Colt cavalry revolver and struck the sergeant across the back of the head with the weapon. Then, and only then, did he cut the ropes. Skemp's unconscious body slid to the ground. Durant had brought him that sleep which was required for the escape.

Awakening the Indian children, he spoke to Sunflower, who translated the news of their flight to Red Dust. The Arapaho girl was weak from loss of blood, but her wound had proved to be less serious than feared. Her mind was bright and clear again, and she could be carried without harm. Red Dust was overjoyed at this and at the word of the good soldier, Durant, that they were going away into the night. In Indian silence he untied Delilah from the picket line, while the white trooper freed his own horse. Mounting up, they stole out of the camp, Private Durant in the lead, Sunflower cradled in his strong arms.

Durant had no certain hope that they might find the Fort Lyon trail by darkness and with snow falling, but he knew one thing beyond all question. If he could safely bring these Indian children of Preacher Bleek's into the custody of the regular Army commander at Fort Lyon, he would be a far better man than he had been on the day he joined Colonel John Chivington and the Volunteer 3rd Colorado Cavalry to "kill all Indians, little and big." And this was the thought that kept him warm through the long and icy night.

• • •

Durant was looking for a place to halt and get down. He had not struck the Fort Lyon trail he was probing for and the little Indian girl needed to be warmed and rested. For the past hour the snow had increased. If a man were now to be honest about it, he was lost; he was as lost as Bo-peep's pet sheep. He had better get in out of the wind, build a fire, and wait for daybreak.

A good idea. But the wind kept building and the snow changing directions. Shortly it occurred to Durant that this might be a delusion. Perhaps it was he who was changing directions. Watching the wind for the following few minutes, he was convinced. That snow wasn't switching on him—he was riding in a circle.

The fear of this crawled up inside him. It wasn't that he cared about himself. But he did want to bring that little girl through. Yes, and the brave boy, too. What then? Make a bivouac there in the wide open country with only their horses for wind-break and warmth? No, that wouldn't do. There was no wood, no buffalo chips, not even any burnable grass for fire building where they were wandering. It was a barren part of the prairie and the wind kept sweeping it down to its hard flinty crust just to remind Durant of the poverty of the wilderness he had led these poor small Indian kids into. What a hero he was! And what a soldier!

He pulled his horse to a stop. Red Dust brought

the pinto jenny up alongside of him and said something in Cheyenne to Sunflower. The girl told Durant that the boy wished to know if he were lost. Abjectly the trooper admitted it. The girl then said that the boy agreed. That he, too, was lost. However, he had a friend who was not. Surprised, Durant straightened.

Red Dust nodded and patted Delilah on the neck.

"He says the *āevoham* knows where to go," translated Sunflower.

"The what?" said Durant.

"The little spotted mule," answered the Arapaho girl. "She wants to lead. Red Dust thinks she has winded something."

Durant tightened the blanket about the child, held her more closely in his tired arms.

"All right, sweetheart," he said. "Tell the boy to turn the little jenny loose. Let's all pray she's smelling friends."

Delilah started off through the whirling snow, going upwind. She kept sniffing and snuffling and never broke her quickening trot. In three or four minutes they all saw the dim star glow of a campfire haloing through the snowflakes. In another five minutes the jenny had led them down into a shallow wash and up that sheltered course to a sharp bend that hid the fire. When the spotted jenny brayed the next moment, she was answered from beyond the bend by twin shrill whinnies of glad welcome.

"The Kiowa Ladies!" cried Sunflower, and that was indeed the case. Around the bend of the wash, they found Blackbird and Young Buzzard cozily dug in under a dry bank with a good fire. The two Kiowa mares were munching at a fine pile of gathered prairie hay. The half-blood boys were in good condition and spirit, barring the belly hunger and sadness of heart that would now vanish with the return of their lost comrades.

Durant fed the boys what food he had brought from the trooper camp. While they wolfed the rations down, they explained what had become of their own food supply that Young Buzzard had been carrying on Salome.

Upon escaping Skemp's patrol, they had crept back to the wolf den and rocks in the big wash when the soldiers had left with Sunflower and Red Dust. There they had found the old dog, Lamewolf, his head all bloody, lying still in the snowbank. They had not wished such a brave fighter to have to travel the Shadow Trail without anything to eat. So they had left him their entire saddlebag full of buffalo jerky and pemmican stolen—that was to say, borrowed—from the wife of Wolfbag in the village of the Smoky Hill people.

This story of typical Indian absurdity did not amuse Durant, but it delighted Sunflower. She had worried about this—that her old pet would not have food to eat on his journey up the Dead Man's

Road of the Milky Way. Now she was happy, she said. If the pony soldier wished it, she believed she could go on and ride all night through.

Through her, Durant consulted with Blackbird and Young Buzzard, seeking to learn if they knew where to find the Fort Lyon trail. They did not, he discovered, but did know the whereabouts of a better trail.

"Where?" was the soldier's immediate plea.

Sunflower informed him that the half-blood boys said they were sitting on that trail. It ran right beside their fire, down the little dry wash. Blackbird, whose mother had been a servant at the place of the great white trader, William Bent, remembered this trail because his mother had traveled it with him many times in going to visit Cheyenne relatives at Sand Creek.

"Bent's Ranch!" exclaimed Durant. "Blackbird, maybe you've struck it bigger than you know."

Of a sudden, whether by desperation's grasp or genuine chance, the weary soldier saw hope for all of them. Colonel William Bent was the lifetime friend of the Cheyennes. He had married their women and fathered several half-blood sons by these daughters of the wolf and the wind. He was more Cheyenne than white in his heart, yet at the same time he had the trust and respect of the frontier community, and even of the military. Bent's Ranch, could they reach it, might be sanctuary even for Private Durant. The Bent influence spread south among the Comanches and the Kiowa-Apaches and even the true Apaches of New Mexico. If the old man wished, he could send Durant through that Indian country and into old Mexico and to safety from Colonel Chivington and Skemp's charges of desertion and worse. It was a chance. All of the chance, likely, that was ever coming to Private Durant.

"Honey," he said to Sunflower, "ask those boys if they are sure they can follow this trail to Bent's place. Ask them if we can go tonight and not lose the way. Ask them if we can get across the Arkansas and into the ranch before daylight." He paused, his arm tenderly about the injured child's shoulders. "I think we all better go down there if we can. You're going to get better, tended there, and likewise all three of these boys. See what they say."

Sunflower asked the questions, returned the answers to Durant.

Blackbird said they could easily be at the ranch before the sun came up. He and Young Buzzard had been planning to go on anyway as soon as the mares finished their hay. Going to Bent's Ranch was like going home for Blackbird. He could do it with his eyes shut tight. *Nitaashema*, what were they waiting for?

Durant got hopefully to his feet. "All right," he said. "I surely do hope Preacher Bleek taught you kids to tell the truth up there at that school on

Horse Creek. Yes, and to pray straight, too. I've a notion we'll need a little of both before we make it to Bent's Ranch."

Sunflower smiled and reached her hands to him to be picked up.

"Preacher always told the truth," she said. "That way he didn't need to pray so much."

XXI

It was a fine morning along the Arkansas. The passengers in the westbound stage chatted with the mindless fraternity of the wheeled traveler. Behind lay Fort Lyon, ahead Pueblo and Denver. The talk was mainly of the Indians and mainly confident. The Army, it seemed, had at last put the red rascals in their place.

One passenger, the bulky man in the redolent bear-skin coat, appeared not quite so convinced.

"I would say, miss," answered Nehemiah Bleek, in reply to the possibility put by a handsome young lady passenger of seeing any "real," meaning hostile, Cheyennes along the way, "that it isn't likely. These here Indians are fairly gun-shy. They don't admire being shot at by the soldiers and settlers."

"No," said one of the soldiers escorting Bleek. "What they admire is shooting at the soldiers and settlers."

"Yeah," said his companion. "From the back."

"Oh, dear," said the young lady from Leavenworth. "How terrible."

"We won't see any Cheyennes, miss," said Bleek. "They've been promised a treaty now after all the trouble of the summer and they don't hardly mean to see its chances ruined by any brushes with the troops. That's gospel."

"Gospel according to Saint Bleek," said the acidulous trooper. Then, brightening: "Yonder's Bent's place. I hope they got a good noon dinner for a change."

"How wonderful!" cried the young lady, craning to see the storied hostelry. "Bent's Fort, think of that! Why, it's like the history books come to life!"

"No, lady," corrected the other soldier. "Not the fort, the ranch. Fort's long gone. Old man Bent blew it up in 'Fifty-Two when the Army wouldn't buy it off of him. He's only freighting now. Trades with his relatives, the bloody Cheyennes, with his left hand, serves the white traffic along this here road with his right."

"How very interesting. You said Cheyenne relatives? I didn't know Mister Bent was part Cheyenne."

"No, ma'am, not him . . . his wife, I mean his wives, uh . . ."

"The trooper means, miss, that Colonel Bent's taken more'n one Cheyenne wife in his long years on the Arkansas," suggested Bleek. "It isn't like it is back East."

"Not hardly," said the soldier.

"My, my," murmured the young lady, and subsided until the coach lurched and turned for the river crossing to the ranch. "Oh, dear!" she squealed, as the iron rims bit into the river gravel of the sharp grade at the ford. "Will we get wet?"

Her plaint reached the hairy ears of Dirty-Face Watson, the driver. Dirty-Face hooked a bowed leg about the handle of the brake, leaned far out and down.

"Not," he bellowed profanely into the window, "if you keep the blasted door shet, lady, and your mouth along with it!"

"Oh, dear." The young woman blushed, and was not heard from again until noon dinner was on the table at Bent's.

The stop went quickly and pleasantly, however. The food was passable, the young lady fair of skin and limb. There was no hint, anywhere around Bent's Ranch, that history was about to ride into the lives of the ticket holders. Indeed, quite the opposite.

As the food was cleared away, the Cheyenne woman who had been serving the table whispered something to Bleek, who rose and followed her into the kitchen.

The reunion there was startling. In a far corner, and dark, a soldier and two small Indian children had just finished their meal. Bleek peered, not daring to believe what was hammering in his heart. But it was true. Trooper Durant and Red Dust and little Sunflower were there before him, safe in the house of William Bent. And more! From the darkest shadows of the alcove, white teeth flashed and two hitherto unseen "hostiles" stepped out into the lamplight, Blackbird and Young Buzzard.

Tears, laughs, giggles, and bear hugs were passed around briefly. Then Preacher called them all to attention. Showing them the paper from Major Wynkoop, he told them it was a "pony soldier order" permitting him to take them on the stage with him to Pueblo for a visit with Agent Colley, who would then get them all quickly away from Mashanē's country.

"Durant," he said, "you, too. Colley will stand behind you even if Wynkoop das'n't. You got to come along."

The trooper, refreshed now and realizing that Mexico was long and risky miles away, decided to put it all on the big man's word, and trust in the paper from Wynkoop to protect him from Chivington.

"It's done, Preacher," he said. "Here's my hand on it."

They shook hands, then herded the children out into the main *sala*, or big room, where the passengers were gathering their belongings to reboard the coach. Hurried introductions were made and there was some hesitation on the part of Bleek's regular Army escorts as to taking on a 3rd Colorado man who looked to them to be a deserter. Bleek did not labor the point, saying only that Durant had become separated from his patrol in a snow squall and had found the children holed up in a dry wash and had brought them down to Bent's as the best place he could think of.

There might have been more objection but for the fact that the handsome young Leavenworth lady was going out the door. Both troopers gaped after her. The young lady's profile was easily the most compelling seen along the Arkansas Road that autumn. The soldiers gave Bleek's odd new passenger list a hurried wave of acceptance and sprinted across the yard. The important thing was to be first to hand the lovely one up the treacherous step into the old Concord. Bleek and Durant exchanged a pair of relieved looks.

In the general movement to get the stage on its way, they were able to get the children marshaled and calmed into the idea of mounting the white man's "inside wagon." None of the Indian youngsters had been in a stagecoach, or dreamed to be in one. They were frightened, but greatly excited, too. In their high feelings, Bleek was able to see the hand of that God he did not overly preach about or pray to. When he thought no one was watching, he bowed his head and muttered something that ended with "Amen."

But it was too late for prayers. The fresh teams were just being fastened into the tugs, the hangers-on at Bent's gathering around to wave the usual farewells, when the ranch dogs commenced to bark and run out toward the river.

All eyes shifted to the three horsemen splashing over the shallows of the Arkansas. An old Cheyenne helper who aided Dirty-Face Watson in hooking on the teams shaded his failing eyesight. His peering squint centered upon the middle rider.

"Mashanē . . . !" he cried, and turned and ran whimperingly for the rear of the ranch house.

Chivington rode up to the group by the stage. His cold face scanned the waiting passengers. If he took especial note of Nehemiah Bleek, Durant, and the Indian orphans, the fact did not reveal itself. "All of you people," he said, "will please go back into the ranch house and stay there. This place is under military quarantine. No one leaves."

Bleek marveled at the man's control, his utter lack of surface emotion. But he was frightened by it, too. He held Sunflower, who he had carried from the house, still closer to his broad chest.

Chivington swung down from his horse. He towered half a head over the brawny missionary. "Well, Preacher"—he nodded—"we meet again." As there was nothing to say to that, Bleek said nothing. In the silence the children crowded in under the tail of his bear-skin coat, like cubs to the mother.

"You and Durant are under arrest," continued Chivington. "You will accompany me on my march. Is that little girl sick? No matter. She will stay here at Bent's place with the others. That's the little Arapaho girl who speaks English, is it not?" Without waiting for Bleek's reply, he looked at Sunflower. "Child," he said, "you talk for these other children. They must understand that my soldiers are all around this ranch and will shoot anyone, man, woman, or child, who tries to get away. If you keep them quiet, none of you will be harmed."

Sunflower said nothing. She bobbed her head and blinked her brown eyes, however, to show that she had heard Mashanē.

Bleek was breathing a silent thanks to the Lord at this point. If it were only Durant and himself who must be hostage to Chivington, this was a blessing. But again his prayers were countermanded by the unpredictable Chivington.

"Beckwourth!" he called to one of his companions.

The man rode forward, halted his horse. He slouched in the saddle after the manner of the old mountain man that he was, and Bleek knew him instantly. This was the famed mulatto scout, Jim Beckwourth, now along in years and no longer the legend he had once been. But the old Negro still knew more about Indians than any man alive, saving only Bridger and perhaps Carson, and he rode with the 3rd Colorado for that reason.

"You recognize any of these children?" Chivington now asked him. "Stand away from them, Bleek."

Preacher told the children in Cheyenne not to be afraid. Old Jim Beckwourth was a kindly man, and a friend to the Indian.

"Why, sure," drawled the old scout, grinning and nodding at Red Dust. "*Hau, nis'en.*" He chuckled. "Now you ain't fixing to say you don't rekollect old Uncle Jim Beckwourth, be you, Mahesie?"

The mixture of pure Cheyenne and mountain man argot was troublesome to Chivington. "You know the boy, Beckwourth? Or are you just mumbling something to earn your supper?" he demanded.

"Oh, I reckon I know him, all right, Colonel. This here is a hostile child, sure enough. Name's Mahesie, Red Dust. He's the primest apple of his uncle's eye, and I allow his uncle is somewhat of a big warrior."

"What the devil are you saying, you old fool? Get it out, man."

"Why, yes, sir, Colonel. This here skinny kid is the nephew of Roman Nose."

At the name of the great Cheyenne, Chivington's eyes leaped to Bleek. His voice remained low, but the set of his heavy features did not match the levelness of the words. "You should have told me that, Preacher," was all that he said.

Bleek did not answer him. He put his arm about the slender shoulders of Red Dust and said quietly to him in Cheyenne: "Do not be afraid of Mashanē, boy. Your uncle gave you into my care and I shall not let any harm come to you. Remember that, Mahesie. I give you the word of our Lord God Jehovah for it."

The boy was watching Chivington. It was doubtful he even heard Bleek.

"What are you saying, there?" asked the officer sharply. "Beckwourth, what did he say to the boy?"

Before the mulatto scout could answer, Bleek stepped forward and brought out the Wynkoop order.

"What I said, Colonel, was that I have here a signed paper for the safe conduct of these here little ones of mine. It's from Major Wynkoop and it says I can take my children on up to Agent Colley at Pueblo, and neither you nor Major Anthony or anybody else is going to harm them or to halt me on my way with them."

Chivington stared at him a moment. He did not look at the paper. "May I see the order, please?" he asked, eyes never leaving Bleek's face.

Bleek passed it over.

The giant officer took it in both hands, still not

181

looking down at it. Slowly he tore it into shreds and threw it away.

"Was there anything else you had to say, Preacher?" he asked quietly.

XXII

Chivington rested his command at Bent's Ranch all that afternoon. His pickets were ringed completely about the station with orders to shoot anything that moved outside the stockade yard. As darkness came on, he lit fires between each picket station and doubled the soldiers on guard.

It had been announced that the troops would move out under cover of night and march on down to Fort Lyon. Durant and Bleek would be taken along as military prisoners. So would the nephew of Roman Nose, to be held for his value in prisoner exchange with the Cheyennes or, as Bleek was convinced, some other more sinister use. Wynkoop's two soldiers would also be returned to Fort Lyon and would serve as armed guards for the prisoners *en route*. To expedite the prisoner transportation problem, the Pueblo stage would be commandeered and turned about for Fort Lyon again. The remainder of the passengers, the young Eastern woman and the others of Bleek's children—Sunflower, Blackbird, Young Buzzard—would remain at the ranch with

Bent's several Indian and mixed-blood employees and patrons in a house arrest situation policed by a strong guard of troops to be left behind. No further information as to Chivington's plans was released. Pressed on this matter by the Leavenworth lady, whose loveliness had not gone unnoted by the commander of the 3rd Colorado, the huge officer would only bow and smile graciously.

"Routine patrol operations, ma'am . . . nothing else, I assure you. No need for concern. Won't you join me for supper? My staff and I would be most flattered by your company."

Bleek, of course, accepted not a word of this. For one thing, Chivington had far too many troops with him—nearly 600—for any routine patrol of the Arkansas stage road. For another thing, Colonel J.M. Chivington was not given to routine patrols. He was given to nothing routine. And so Nehemiah Bleek was not fooled and, in the end, his fears forced him to a desperate decision. Suddenly, sitting there on the long bench by the kitchen doorway watching Mashane and his officers over their after-supper cigars and their small talk sparring for the flutter of the Leavenworth lady's thick lashes, Bleek knew that he must not let Red Dust be taken to Fort Lyon. The boy must escape Bent's Ranch.

What foulness awaited him in Chivington's custody no man could say. But Nehemiah Bleek had given his word to this boy's uncle to shelter and cherish him as a son—and Nehemiah Bleek would never permit a son of his to go with Mashanē to Fort Lyon.

There were but minutes left before departure. How might it work? Who might he trust? On the wooden loafer's bench with Bleek were Beckwourth, Durant, Red Dust, the two Wynkoop troopers, and Dirty-Face Watson, the stage driver. All had been fed in the kitchen, ordered subsequently to wait where Chivington could see them.

Fate, or Preacher's canny foresight, had brought him to seat the boy between himself and Dirty-Face, on the end of the bench nearest the kitchen exit. Catching the driver's eye now, Bleek nodded his head the least fraction. Dirty-Face scowled, looked across the room at Chivington, then returned the nod as carefully.

"Soldier," said Bleek to the Wynkoop trooper beside him, "the boy wants to relieve himself. Is it all right if I take him outside?"

"Sure, I reckon." The trooper started to rise, but the stage driver beat him to it.

"Hell, stay put, soldier. I'll go with them. Got to check the teams, anyhow."

The trooper hesitated, but it was warm in the room and that girl was pretty as sin and Dirty-Face Watson had been on the Pueblo run for years and, besides, the stockade yard was crawling with 3rd Colorado cavalrymen. The kid couldn't possibly get away.

"Yeah, well, thanks," he said, easing back down on the bench. "Make it quick, eh?"

The driver grinned, and old Jim Beckwourth drowsing at the far end of the bench opened one rheumy eye and closed it just as quickly. If he saw the Cheyenne boy get up and go out through the kitchen with Bleek and the stage driver, he reacted only with a movement to seek a position of greater comfort on the hard bench.

It was perhaps five minutes later that Dirty-Face Watson rushed back into the room to interrupt Chivington in a toast to Leavenworth's most lovely daughter with the fearful admission: "Me and Preacher, sir, we just let that Injun kid give us the slip out in the yard!"

On the heels of the confession, Bleek entered from the kitchen to confirm the escape.

Chivington, never the same man twice, seemed almost pleased with the news. Calling in the commander of the guard detail to be left at the ranch, he informed him of Red Dust's flight, assured the nervous officer that the boy could not possibly get far but that no risk of his escape to carry word of the Bent's Ranch quarantine was to be assumed or tolerated. "Take care of him where you find him, Captain," he said. And, calling his officers after him, he strode out into the ranch yard and ordered the waiting troops to mount up. Within minutes the long column of dusty cavalry-men fell into formation, forded the Arkansas, and were gone from the sight of the watchers at Bent's Ranch. With them went the captured Pueblo stage and its silently fearful passengers.

Midway of the night march to Fort Lyon, driver Watson halted the Pueblo stage. The right brake shoe was dragging, he said. The coach's 3rd Colorado escort, a boy lieutenant and eight volunteer troopers, had orders not to stop, not even to smoke in ranks, not even to talk more than necessary. But the lieutenant could recall no order about smoking out of ranks, or halting for stagecoach repairs. "Go ahead," he told Watson. "Pry it loose. Take your time. We ain't going no place that won't wait."

Dirty-Face climbed down, began fussing and cussing at the rear wheel.

"Preacher!" he called. "Can you lift up this here wheel whiles I knock the shoe out? I reckon them soldier boys can spare you. Less'n they wants to hoist it."

The guards in the coach decided they would not labor after hours. Bleek got out complainingly, but quickly.

Off to the right, perhaps only ten yards on the river side of the road, the 3rd Colorado escorts smoked and talked unhurriedly. They did not seem concerned. It was going to be a long night any way they marched it.

It was also a notably dark night. And, the guard

troopers inside the coach later swore, it was full of reassuring and familiar voices. Like that of driver Dirty-Face Watson inviting Preacher Bleek to ride the rest of the way with him up on the box of the coach. And like that of the Horse Creek missionary assuring driver Watson that he would be "mightily pleasured" to accept the invitation, "as the air in the coach was a little close for a man in a bear-skin coat." Or at least so he was quoted by the two Wynkoop troopers in their subsequent courts-martial for dereliction of duty.

Had the guilty guards given thought to the matter at the time, they would have realized that it was a frost-cold midnight for even a man in a bearskin coat to desert the passenger compartment of a Concord coach for the wind-whipped exposure of its driver's seat. But the men did not give thought to it, and, if their other prisoner, Private Durant, did so, they did not recall Durant's warning them. The loss was not discovered until, in the blackness of next dawn, the pickets that Chivington had set out around Major Anthony's post at Fort Lyon checked the coach through their lines and found the Reverend Nehemiah Bleek to be among the missing.

For his part, Chivington took the news reasonably enough.

"Very well," he told his reporting aide. "The crazy devil won't bother anything. He has lived with the Indians so long he thinks like one of them. He simply got scared and ran off. We'll find him sooner or later." He paused, still seemingly calm. "Put the driver, Watson, and those two guards of Wynkoop's under arrest with Durant," he said. "If I can, I mean to hang the four of them when I get back."

XXIII

In the rocks and grasses of the brushy point where the stage had halted for brake shoe adjustment, and where Preacher Bleek had freed Red Dust from the luggage-boot of the Concord coach— in which Preacher and Dirty-Face Watson had hidden the boy back at Bent's Ranch—the two fugitives hugged the earth like the parts of the night they prayed they would be taken for.

Past their hiding place, when the stage had gone on out of sight, clanked and crowded the seemingly endless ranks of 1st and 3rd Cavalry troops following Chivington toward Fort Lyon. The dust, the horse sweat, the laughter, curses, complaints, and crudities of the white riders struck at the noses and ears of Preacher and the Cheyenne boy, and clutched, too, at their hearts. But at last the rear guard of the column had passed along the road and all was quiet at Brush Point of the Arkansas.

Bleek stood up sighingly.

"All right, praise the Lord," he said. "We're saved." He grinned his rare grin and added: "Now all we got to do is figure out what that means."

But he knew what it meant, and he had planned in the beginning what he and the boy must do. From Wynkoop he had learned that a very large camp of southern Cheyennes under Black Kettle and White Antelope, with some few lodges of Arapahoes under Left Hand, was at the main forks of Little Dried River, variously called by the whites the Big Sandy or simply Sand Creek. Knowing of this camp, and of no other in the immediate vicinity that might be reached by reasonable swiftness on foot, he and the boy must cut across country and find these friendly people. They were at peace with the Army and had camped on Sand Creek at the express direction of Major Anthony with whom their chiefs had talked only that past week. Here Bleek could leave Red Dust secure in the belief the boy would be returned to his uncle, Roman Nose.

What happened to him did not matter. Bleek believed he could care for himself, but it was clear that he could no longer shelter the Cheyenne boy with any certain safety. He told Red Dust of this decision and the boy accepted it with the quiet fatality of his dark race.

"I heard my uncle tell you that you must bring me to the people of Black Kettle and White

Antelope, if there was any trouble over me or over my care. Now I know there is great danger. Soldiers have tried to kill me. Mashanē has made me a prisoner, and would take me to Fort Lyon. Whatever you say, Preacher, I will do. You are my father."

Bleek nodded, humbled. "Sometimes, boy," he said, "I wish I was an Indian."

"Many times lately, Preacher," answered Red Dust, "I have wished that I was a white boy."

They set off northeasterly away from the river. The pace Preacher set was severe. They had far to travel and could move only during the dark hours for fear of being seen by a prowling cavalry patrol. They could not be sure, either, what Chivington was about. Would he rest his troops again at Fort Lyon? Or would he keep them marching, and, if so, in what direction, toward what purpose, and how rapidly? They were certain of but one thing: with Mashanē on the hunt, all things evil were possible—and the movement by forced march and in secret of the entire 3rd Colorado Cavalry regiment must be an evil thing.

They walked until dawn, then lay up in some rocks and slept like prairie wolves. It seemed to Red Dust but an hour before Preacher was touching his shoulder.

"Come on, wake up, boy. Dusk is gathering again."

"*Ai-eee!*" shivered the youth. "It will be cold this

night, Preacher. Where did the day go so fast? I only closed my eyes."

"It's a gift of the young," said Preacher. "Come on."

They went forward through the twilight, guided by stars that only Preacher knew and by landmarks in the prairie with which no other of its shy denizens save the coyote and the kit fox were familiar. With midnight they struck the lower, or south fork, of Sand Creek.

"Getting there," murmured Preacher, and turned downstream.

It was now necessary to find the Indian Road crossing of this stream, so that they could pick up the Cheyenne trail to the Sand Creek camp and not blunder wide of the village in the darkness. But the way was not familiar now, and the pace slowed. Dawn was not far away when, on a rise just before the descent to the crossing, Bleek touched Red Dust's arm and said: "Look down there toward the stream."

The boy squinted downward, drew in his breath.

"Many ponies," he whispered. "Many riders."

"That's Mashanē," said Bleek flatly. "I know it, but we can't be certain without scouting in close. There is just time to beat them to the fording place, I think."

Red Dust went forward with the big missionary, not arguing, not complaining. If Preacher said there was just time to scout the crossing, and they must do it, then it would be done. What else might Red Dust do? He was a lost boy in a strange and alien land. Very small boy. Very far from home boy. Very much afraid boy. But Maheo was watching over him. Maheo would protect him. And big Preacher would look after both of them. *Ezhesso*, thus be the way of it!

They were first to the south fork crossing, as Preacher had said they would be. Examining the trail by starlight, Bleek told the boy the sign was all old, all the hoof prints unshod. "Indian horses," he said. "All from yesterday. Come on, hurry."

The missionary chose their hiding place with all the cunning of an old wolf ambushing difficult prey. He bedded them on a point that rose above the ford and was rocky, hence would not be ridden through by horsemen. The point was also heavily grassed and downwind of the trail. Their scent would not carry to the cavalry mounts.

"Breathe into your cupped hands, boy," said Preacher. "Then no cold air vapor will rise to give us away. Make yourself small in that grass. Quickly. Here they come."

Red Dust felt every pore of his skin grow small and wart-hard. The beating of his heart against the frost-rimed dirt of their cover became smothering. He could hear the horses coming now. The *thud* of their shod hoofs. The musical *tinkling* and *ringing* of the iron shoes striking here a pebble, there an exposure of bedrock. Closer they came. Now it was the *jingling* of bit chains, spur chains, sword chains. The *creak* of saddle and girth and stirrup leathers. The very breathing of the horses. There! Look there!

Four horsemen—two officers and two scouts. But it was the near horseman, the one who loomed against the widened eye of Red Dust as a giant from some other, nether earth who struck panic into the boy. It was Mashanē.

The horsemen halted at the ford. In the stillness the voices carried with the breaking cleanness of icicles.

"What do you think, Colonel?"

The questioner was the second officer, Major Scott Anthony. The man hand-picked by Chivington to replace Major Wynkoop, who sometimes treated Indians fairly. The man who but a few days gone had given tobacco and assurances of peace to Black Kettle and the other chiefs at Fort Lyon.

"I'm not sure, Major," answered Chivington. "Beckwourth, get up here. You, too, Bent."

The scouts came forward, Beckwourth leading. But Jim Beckwourth, the legend, was too old now. The comrade of the days of Bill Williams, Big Throat Bridger, Broken Hand Fitzpatrick, and Uncle Dick Wooten had ridden too many dark trails, shivered through too many cold nights. The mulatto hunched himself in the saddle. What teeth remained to him were clenched against the freezing wind that cut along the creekbank and rattled the dry brush of its winter bed.

"I cain't he'p you no more, Colonel," he said. "I'm that blue I cain't get outen the saddle. Eyes gone to watering on me something fierce. Cain't hardly make out my own tracks no more. I'm done, I'm done."

Chivington ignored him instantly; he had ceased to exist, to have ever lived.

"Well, Bent?"

Robert "Jack" Bent was one of old Bent's boys, the son of the Cheyenne squaw, Owl Woman. He raised his hand for silence now, stood in his stirrups, listening intently.

"Wolf, him howl," he said in his half-breed's English. "Injun dog, he hear wolf, him howl, too. Injun, he hear dog and listen, then him hear something and run off."

Chivington made nothing of the half-breed's broken language. He was angered at the Indian talk, which he considered spurious in style as well as content. He pulled his revolver and put it under young Bent's nose.

"Jack," he said, "I haven't had an Indian to eat for a long time. If you fool with me, and don't lead us to that Sand Creek camp, I'll have you for breakfast."

The half-breed did not look at him. He merely nodded, pointed ahead toward the ford, grunted that they should go on quickly—daylight was coming.

Chivington at once told Anthony and Beckwourth to go back and bring on the troops, which had halted down the trail. He and Bent would scout ahead and locate the camp. Anthony swung about and was gone. Chivington and the half-breed splashed over the stream, disappeared on the far side. After a moment, Preacher rose up from the grasses.

"Boy," he said, "they are going to attack Black Kettle's village up on the north fork. We will try to beat them there and warn the People. There is little time."

"*Wagh!*" said Red Dust. "I am ready."

"Let us go, then," urged Nehemiah Bleek. "Stay closely by me and run with no noise. If you fall, I shall go on without you."

Bleek had made a serious miscalculation. While he delayed at the crossing of the south fork to scout Chivington and Anthony, columns of the latter's dismounted troops were already going over the fork lower down. These troops the missionary now found were positioned between him and Red Dust and the Cheyenne camp on the north bank of Sand Creek proper. Moreover, the boy and the Horse Creek schoolmaster could actually hear the sounds of the Indian pony herd and knew that they were very near the village. Desperate now, they raced to the west, trying to get around the dismounted troops, poised and waiting for daylight to attack. Here, they encountered even more dangerous blockage—Chivington's mounted forward patrols had gone over the fork above the crossing. And while they lay panting in the prairie grass hiding from these horsemen, the main forces of 3rd Colorado and 1st Colorado Cavalry moved into place behind them. They were trapped, outside of the Indian camp.

"Boy," whispered Bleek, "uncover your ears. Listen to Preacher. I say these words with a sad heart, but hear them well."

He quickly told Red Dust that they were too late to save the village. There were only minutes left before daylight. All that might be done now was to risk everything on a rush through the foot soldiers at the lower camp. If Preacher could break past them and get into the camp, the Cheyennes would at least have warning enough to seize a rifle, perhaps even catch up a pony. But to make the best of that slim hope, Preacher must run unburdened with the problem of Red Dust—he must run alone. It was a thing to decide between the lives of all those people, or the fears of one small boy. Preacher knew that Red Dust would be brave, would hide and wait outside the village in the thick brush of the stream, would stay where Preacher put him and not move until Preacher returned for him.

"Will you do this, now?" he concluded. "Will you obey me?"

For a long moment the northern Cheyenne boy appeared to be stunned. He was not able, Bleek thought, to absorb the meaning of being deserted, or the reason. But Bleek was wrong. Red Dust understood. He simply looked one more lingering second at the big white man, then before Bleek could stop him he turned and slipped away through the tall grasses and was gone into the predawn blackness. That was the whole of his farewell. Just that one long Indian look and he was gone.

Preacher knew his mistake. It had been that word "unburdened." Red Dust was a northern. The nephew of Roman Nose. That was the proudest blood in the prairie world. The boy might live, he might die, they might never see one another again. But one thing he would not be, that boy, he would not be a burden. If he reached the village, he would bear his share of the battle. If he fell on the way, he would fall alone. It was the Cheyenne way.

"Maheo," said Bleek, peering up at the paling night sky, "I just give you back one of your children. Take care of him for me."

With that, the big man was up and running for the lower village, and the chance to save at least some of the sleeping Cheyenne people.

XXIV

But Preacher Bleek did not reach the Cheyenne camp; he was struck in the head by the ricochet of a rifle bullet. He fell unconscious and lay as dead beneath a brush clump not twenty strides from where Red Dust and he had parted. For his part, the boy did succeed in crossing the sandy channel and reaching the beleaguered camp, never realizing that Preacher had fallen. Yet the lad had time only to arouse two or three lodges and to try and alert a group of old squaws who were out with the predawn grayness gathering fire-wood for the morning cooking.

The village grannies, however, with true Indian delay, set to debating the identity of the enemy, rather than running for their lives. To the old women the mass of moving figures across the streambed appeared more like a herd of buffalo than a regiment of mounted troopers. The squaws commenced to wave their blankets and throw rocks and sticks at the advancing buffalo. They were still shouting—"Go away!"—at the supposed beasts when the firing upon the village was begun by Wilson's battalion of the 1st, which had been detailed to cut off and drive away the Indian pony herds.

The terrified Cheyenne mounts the next moment

broke and ran directly down upon Red Dust. The boy was saved from certain death by trampling when an ancient white mare, with an aversion for running over small Indian lads, slowed to avoid striking him. Instantly Red Dust seized her mane and swung himself up onto her back. As he did, the old pony wheeled and galloped instinctively away from the village, back toward the channel of Sand Creek. Red Dust lay flat upon her back, shouting her on in Cheyenne, and praying.

The Indian camp was now a scene of incredible disorder. The white troops were breaking into it from both upper and lower ends. The dust and gunsmoke billowed like a pall of hell, half hiding the naked fleeing red men from the cursing cavalry soldiers, giving the stunned Cheyennes their only brief chance for escape and life thereafter. It was into and through the very wildest of this maddened clot of humanity and exploding rifle fire that Red Dust's bony mount bore him. But the old mare ran with the cunning of a coyote. This was not the first murderous trap of pony soldier crossfire from which she had been forced to flee. And, like her human owners, the panic-stricken Cheyennes, she knew where lay the only possible exit—the streambed of Sand Creek. Unlike pitiful scores of the Indians, however, the old white mare made good her race for the river. Striking the sandy channel, she leaped over its low bank, down into its bed, raced away from the screams of the dying village.

Upstream she went, then back down, ducking and dodging and scrambling all the while into and out of cover of boulder and brush clump, now atop the bank, now below its lip, wheeling all the time with the driven keen mind of the hunt-scarred stag or crafty doe bent on eluding the seemingly solid hail of enemy rifle bullets sent to kill her and all of her people.

For his part, Red Dust displayed equal intelligence and native wile. He remained with the old horse past a score of opportunities to slide off her back into what looked like better hiding places by far, than the peril of her hunching withers. So it was that he survived with her, rather than remaining behind to be stomped out of whatever covert he chose by the vicious troopers. In surviving through rifle burst and striken Indian cries of agony and death, he witnessed some of the testament of insanity that flamed within the camp.

He saw Anthony's battalion of mounted troops come into the village from the southeast. He saw a familiar white squawman, Uncle John Smith, an interpreter for Agent Colley and the father of a half-blood Cheyenne brood of his own, run out of his lodge and toward the advancing soldiers. He heard clearly the old man pleading with the troopers to stop firing. That the Cheyennes were at peace in this village. That they did not want to fight. That the hot soldier fire was murdering women and little children and old ones without any selection of target. That all of the troops knew him, Uncle John Smith, and they should believe him and stop the terrible slaughter of innocent people at once.

So appealed to, one of the officers bellowed to his sergeant—"Shoot the old fool!"—and Uncle John ran sobbingly, stumblingly back toward the lodges, trying a last hopeless time to help the Cheyennes get away alive, and to stay alive himself in that swirling madness of soldiers who were shooting at anything that moved and looked like an Indian.

Horrified, Red Dust then saw the main force of the fleeing Cheyennes start up the dry streambed of Sand Creek, the mounted troops of Anthony driving behind them and driving them thus directly into the waiting, dismounted riflemen of Chivington who had blocked the upper streambed, bank to bank, in anticipation of precisely this dreadful moment. When the Indians drew near the waiting ranks of the 3rd Colorado, they called out plaintively that most of their number, as the soldiers could see, were women and children. To this, Chivington roared his infamous epitaph: "Kill all, kill little and big!" To which blasphemy Red Dust heard a nameless soldier laugh out loud and add a cheering shout of equal infamy: "*Yee-hahh!* You tell 'em, Colonel! That's a fact. Nits make lice!"

Red Dust witnessed, too, as the old mare carried him back and forth across the firing lines, Black Kettle standing in front of his lodge pointing to the American flag fluttering from its pole to mark the teepee of the main chief, and pleading with the soldiers to see that beneath the Stars and Stripes a white cloth had been run up to say that the camp was friendly and wanted only to surrender.

Some of the soldiers laughed at him; some of them did not. All of them kept up their heavy firing.

Red Dust saw White Antelope, seventy-five years old, the most honored of the old-time Cheyenne fighting men among the southern people. He saw White Antelope proudly refuse to run when Black Kettle came limping past with his wife and urged his old friend to come with them, to try to make the streambed and get away. He saw White Antelope fold his arms across his breast and stand before the flaps of his lodge, and he heard the croaking of his feeble voice intoning the ancient Cheyenne prayer of those about to die:

> Nothing lives long, nothing stays here,
> Except the earth and the mountains. . . .

And he saw the hail of soldier bullets that cut through the fringes of the old chief's doeskin shirt, saw the noble old man buckle downward, and slide into a sitting position, dead and staring-eyed in the doorway of his teepee.

Mercifully that was the last the boy saw to remember as a separate image of the nightmare kind. He did see one more thing in the village, a strange thing, not of the nightmare kind but which left him with a bad memory all the same. It seemed wrong to him. Something an Indian would not do. Something only a white man—even a white man with an Indian wife and red children—would do. It worried Red Dust then; it worried him still when he was an old man with children and grandchildren of his own. But he never spoke of it. It would have dishonored him, made him unworthy. And perhaps, also, it was not as it seemed.

What he saw, as the old mare bore him away, was Uncle John Smith. The old squawman was alone. He had abandoned his Indian friends. Uncle John was looking for someone else, someone of his own skin color. A command of troops was driving toward him under an officer he clearly knew—Chivington. The giant cavalryman had just left his streambed slaughter pen and come to find livelier killing in the village streets. He saw Uncle John Smith in the same moment Red Dust saw Chivington. He flung up a gauntleted fist and shouted to the old white man: "Ho, Uncle John, run here!" The squawman heard and saw him. He scuttled over to him across the dead bodies of the people among whom he had lived. He seized the huge officer's stirrup and clung to it and ran along, in that way protected by Chivington.

When the gunsmoke hid them from Red Dust's view, the old man was still clutching Chivington's boot, still running by the side of his horse to save his own life. That was the boy's last memory of the Cheyenne village at Ponoeohe, the Little Dried River. After that came the rifle pits.

The old mare angled across the open streambed toward some willow scrub choking a side branch wash. Red Dust clung to her mane, riding flat to her churning withers. Ricochets screamed in every direction. Stricken Indians screamed back. There was no time, no reason for the Cheyenne boy to look at the camp again.

The people, all of them who would ever get out of the village, were already out of it. The main body had fled into Chivington's dismounted riflemen, then split around that bloody place in the streambed. These small bands had burst like scattered quail in wild flight. They went, some of them, into the nearby sandhills. Others, most of the larger groups, still tried to get upstream beyond the 3rd Colorado's blockade. But the old mare bore Red Dust away from the streambed and after those fugitives, running like wolves and coyotes for the shelter of the sandhills. So it was with the luck of the innocent that the white mare won through the carnage at camp's edge, broke past the windrows of women and children sprawled silently before the guns of the 3rd Colorado, and brought the Cheyenne boy to the momentary sanctuary of the willow brush.

The mare, panting heavily, started up the thicketed wash. Stumbling her way through the stones and débris of the narrow course, she quickly reached its upper end. Here the brush ended abruptly; the grass began again. They were out into the open before Red Dust saw the soldiers.

There were perhaps a dozen troopers. They were of 1st Cavalry, no officer with them. They had captured some Indians, three women, two older children, three small children. The soldiers appeared to be returning their captives to the village, guarding them, even protecting them.

Then an officer came up on the gallop. His uniform was of 3rd Colorado. He was a lieutenant.

When this officer saw that the men were taking prisoners to the rear, he shouted that Colonel Chivington had ordered no prisoners. From his horse, with his pistol, he shot two of the Indian women. The third woman broke from her captors and ran. The lieutenant killed her with his carbine. He then dismounted and went among the soldiers. They shrank away from him, and from the five children huddled over the first-killed women. One by one, the officer shot the children in the head. But he had only four pistol bullets remaining. He broke the skull of the fifth child with the butt of his pistol. Red Dust was sick, but he could not move to flee.

The lieutenant stopped cursing and shouting. He took a wooden-handled butcher knife from the body of one of the squaws and cut the hair from the head of the little child he had struck with the pistol butt. He reached for the hair of the second child. Now Red Dust began to cry. It was a strangled sound, half tears, half terror. It burst from him into the silence of the scalping. The soldiers, watching the grisly thing as gray-faced as the Cheyenne boy, turned their eyes toward him. So did the officer, pausing with the butcher knife in one hand, a child's hair in the other. "Kill him," he ordered the men.

But the men did not move. Not toward the Cheyenne boy. They started walking away from the officer. They began to run, not looking back. The officer cursed them, then turned to Red Dust, levering a fresh shell into his carbine.

The boy was still frozen with terror, but the old mare was not. She had seen many Indian women and children murdered. With a snort she whirled and ran back into the brush of the wash.

A crashing of branches warned that the officer's horse was but a few jumps behind. The boy believed he would die now, that the lieutenant would shoot and scalp him. But he was wrong. In the final leap before the officer's mount came up to the old mare, dark red arms reached up from the thick growth beside the trail and swept the boy from the old horse's back. The mare ran on and the officer, not having seen the boy taken from her back, drove his horse on after her. He was raging like a madman.

In the thick growth were ten Cheyenne warriors of middle-aged years. They were hard, desperate fighters. It was their leader who had reached out and pulled Red Dust from the mare's back. He was a half-breed and the boy was quickly told who he was: George Bent, another of old William Bent's dark sons by Cheyenne mothers.

"Did you see any more soldiers up there beyond the head of the wash?" Bent asked the boy. "I mean other than the ones who ran away from the officer?"

"Yes," answered Red Dust. "Many more were on the slopes of the sandhills past where I was. I could see them, and they were half a hundred anyway."

"Too many," grunted Bent. "Come on, we will have to turn back and go up the creek after the others."

The Indians got up out of the brush and ran like red shadows down the dry wash toward Sand Creek. Red Dust did what he could to keep up with them. It was that or be left to the soldiers. The Indian men could not wait for him.

XXV

It was bad going up the creekbed. Patrols and gangs of soldiers without their officers roved the field everywhere. Commanded units also moved up and down the stream hunting Indians. Through this welter of regular and vigilante troops, Bent's ten warriors, Red Dust still panting beside them, sneaked and fought their way. As they went, the boy saw more of the nightmare things he had seen in the village.

There was a major of 3rd Colorado Cavalry pursuing a Cheyenne girl, a little girl, younger than Sunflower. The officer was mounted, the child afoot. The girl fell. The major leaned down from the saddle, shot her through the head, rode on. He did not even glance back to see that the girl staggered up again and wandered off, holding the side of her face with her two hands, so that it would not fall away from the other part of her head.

An old woman had struggled as far up the stream as her strength would take her. She had fallen to her knees, her heart failing her. Four or five soldiers came up to her. They closed about her, and, when they moved away, Red Dust saw that the old woman no longer had any hair. It was dangling in the hands of one of the soldiers. The old squaw tottered to her feet. The bald skin of her head flapped down over her eyes. She could not understand why she could not see. She walked about with hands outstretched and asking: "Where are the People, where have they all gone?" She was still walking, still asking, as long as Red Dust could see her.

An elderly chief, excitedly recognized by George Bent as Black Kettle, thought his wife was dead. They saw him bending over her body in the streambed, then he left her, going on alone. Some soldiers came and shot down into her body. George Bent counted nine shots fired at her in this way. The half-breed flinched with each shot, as though the lead were going into his own flesh.

Everywhere were prowling soldiers, scalping or mutilating or shooting into the Indian dead. And the Indian dead were everywhere. They lay in the level wide bed of the stream's dry sand. They lay drowned with their own blood in the random pools of standing water that were the creek's entire volume at the time of year. Here and there a white soldier was also seen lying still, but only a very few, less even than the fingers of two hands.

Time, in the agonizing eye of battle, suspended itself. Red Dust thought the journey up the streambed lasted the full morning. It actually required but half an hour. The only halts were to drop on panting bellies to imitate their slain fellows in the creek sand, the only cover to be taken when a soldier patrol went by. One of these times a pack of scalpers from the 3rd Colorado slid from their horses to take hair among the very fallen where Red Dust lay beside George Bent in frozen-limbed imitation of the dead.

Face down in the sand, the boy heard the actual ripping away of the scalps. He heard the talk and hard breathing of the scalpers and the sound of their feet moving toward him. In the moment of ultimate terror, a hand took hold of his own hair and raised his slight body from the sand.

But the northern boy did not twist about and begin to plead for his life. He hung dead in the soldier's hand and was saved by that and by the fact that Preacher Bleek had shorn his hair during the wagon journey to make him recognizable as a tame Indian. Another of the Colorado men laughed at the one gripping Red Dust's cropped braids.

"Hey, Bill," he said, "you down to taking them bobtail kind? Here's one a good two-foot long, with double braids and all. You can have it. I'll find me another."

The soldier dropped Red Dust back into the sand. As he did so, a very heavy rifle fire began upstream. "Listen to that!" shouted one of the men. "Colonel must have struck the main hive of them yonder past the bend. Let's get up there 'fore all the good hair's took!"

Booted feet *thudded* away. Bent raised his head. "*Nitaashema!*" he said in Cheyenne. "Let's go!"

210

Swiftly they reached the bend. Beyond it, the banks of Sand Creek narrowed and became pocked with wind- and water-gouged holes. It was this refuge that the Cheyennes called Voxse, The Place Where the Pits Are. It was here that the main flow of fugitives had fought to reach, and here that Chivington had followed them along the blood trail of their wounding by the 3rd Colorado.

"Three hundred soldiers," said George Bent to his panting warriors. "All Mashanē's men. Can we do it?"

Red Dust knew what he meant. It was to break through the soldiers surrounding the Cheyennes who had dug in at Voxse and were prepared to die there in the rifle pits. It was to reach the brave ones and to die with them.

"We must do it," answered one of Bent's band. "Those are the last of our people."

"*Nitaashema*," George Bent said again, and the men rose up and howled their war cry of the wolf and fell on the rear of Mashanē's startled troops.

By the surprise of it, the warrior band, Red Dust running with them like an orphan colt, made it into the rifle pits of their people, unharmed. But in the pits it was like a cattle-killing pen. The sand and soft stone of the bank were slippery with blood. The Indian quick lay in the same slime with the dead. After the first hour that saw Red Dust reach the Cheyenne redoubt, the stench of the dead and wounded became a separate terror in itself. The boy became ill. He retched and could not stop retching, even when nothing came from his tortured stomach save the yellow-green venom of bile. Still he would not look away from the slaughter, would not lower his head. He crouched where George Bent crouched, watching the fight, watching their people die.

It was in this time that Chivington killed the last of whatever understanding the white man may ever have made with the Cheyennes.

The soldiers would not charge the Cheyenne rifle pits to end the cruel execution. From time to time, as their officers through field glasses determined that the male fighters in a certain pit were all dead, an assault on that separate pit would be mounted. The remaining Cheyennes could not defend these separate pit takings because they had so few guns, so little ammunition. Each round must be hoarded against the last moment. They were thus forced to huddle and watch as the soldiers went into the fighterless pits and clubbed the women, children, and old persons left defenseless by the death of their men. As with the murdering of White Antelope and the scalping of the captive children, the final action at the pits was a thing that stunned the mind.

The Cheyenne women in the central pit, perhaps a score of them, despaired of life. Seeing their sisters and the children of their sisters clubbed to death robbed them of reason. They declared that the soldiers had committed these brainings because, in the excitement of rushing each pit, the troopers did not have time to distinguish among old man, woman, or little child. They cried out: "Come, now, if the soldiers are shown plainly that we are women, they will not shoot us or strike us with their rifles. Has the white man not always told us that his people do not kill or harm women and children?"

The men in the central pit were aghast at this insanity.

"Shame, shame! You know better than that. Can you not see what the soldiers have already done?"

But the women would not be held back.

"Care for the children," they begged the men, and leaped from the pits and ran toward the white riflemen of Mashanē, crying out—"Look, we are women!"—and lifting their dresses to show their forms to prove it for the soldiers as they ran.

The men of the 3rd Colorado did not recall in their memories if this were a true report, or not. But those men knew the truth of the story in one way, the way in which Red Dust and all the horrified Cheyenne people saw that high noon of the massacre at Sand Creek: the way in which the troops of Colonel John Chivington shot down on the pleading run those women made coming toward their rifle lines, and then how those troops, by clubbed rifle and close-held pistol, finished up the gruesome work even as the squaws ran into their ranks still crying: "We are women!"

After that, Red Dust's eyes were locked wide. He saw but he did not see.

When it was that the soldiers quit the fight at the rifle pits and went away downstream to loot and fight among themselves amid the spoils of the village, the northern boy could not remember. Neither would any of the Cheyennes who were there, or any of the soldiers, later agree on the hour of the retreat. Some said it was shortly after midday. Some insisted it was nearly sundown. Black Kettle himself may have been the most accurate.

"The fight lasted five hours," said the old chief. "The soldiers went away about noontime or a little later, but we stayed in the pits until the sun was low, fearing to leave because we thought the soldiers might still be waiting for us, that it was a trick. But it was not. When the dusk was not far off, we went away from there. The soldiers did not come after us. It was very cold. We all remembered that."

Red Dust stayed with George Bent. The half-breed had taken a bad hip wound. His dark eyes were glazed with pain. Each step was an individual torture. But he walked. All the wounded walked. Or crawled. Or were dragged on foot by the unwounded. There were no horses. It was only many miles and hours later in the retreat that a joyous sight was seen through the settling gloom of the winter twilight.

Men, Cheyenne young men, were coming in from the prairie to join the survivors marching up Sand Creek. The young men were the first brave ones who had run for the pony herd to secure mounts under the soldier fire from Captain Wilson's hard-fighting 1st Cavalry.

These warriors had caught up a few precious mounts, just a single horse to each man, because each man had taken but one catching rope in the suddenness of the flight from the sleeping robes in the village. But these mounts were the true gifts of Maheo, and were given over to the worst wounded and to the dying. Red Dust saw a young pure-blood cousin of George Bent's give the half-breed an old pack mare, then walk beside his half-white kinsman holding him on the horse and guiding the horse, as well, for another five miles and until the Cheyennes had made camp under full darkness ten miles up Sand Creek from the rifle pits at Voxse.

The night was freezing cold. A raw wind whipped down the channel of the stream, howled through the brushless ravine that was the only shelter for the people on that black prairie. Ice formed about the moist muzzles of the ponies. The wind kept switching farther north. By midnight the temperature had fallen deeply below freezing.

Red Dust, with the women and older children who could still walk, went out into the blackness and gathered grass to burn for fires, and to heap upon the wounded and the old and the sick, and the very young babies, to keep them from dying in the cold. None of the People had any decent or warm clothing. Most were half naked, driven from their beds that morning with no time to seize even a shawl. All had been caught in some state of undress, except the old squaws who had been out gathering wood and who had seen the "buffalo across the stream," and those old squaws were all sleeping back along the trail that night—sleeping forever.

All of the night hours the Cheyennes cried and called into the darkness so that any passing survivor might know that they were there, might come in and be with them, might not die alone on the naked prairie with no Indian hand to comfort him. But no one came in out of the darkness.

By 3:00a.m. the warriors knew that the People could not live there in that icy ravine. All were ordered up. The ponies were loaded with the sick and injured. The strongest men carried the little children. There were not many women left with the People. Of all the drifts and moundings of silent red bodies left behind in the Sand Creek bottoms at the main village, two out of three were women and children, and more women than children. In the terrible pits at Voxse alone, seventy dead were counted when the soldiers left and the survivors tottered away.

No Cheyenne knew how many other dead were left that day, how many had died in the village, how many in the fight to reach the rifle pits, how many were frozen, never to be found or counted, lost and alone on the plains and in the sandhills of Ponoeohe, the Little Dried River. The Cheyennes knew only that somewhere across that freezing blackness lay the Smoky Hill River and the camp of their relatives who had not trusted Major Anthony and gone with Black Kettle to camp in peace.

So it was that the warriors roused them out of the ravine and led them on through the blind darkness, praying to see with daylight the sight of their friends on the Smoky Hill. And this time Maheo was listening to them and leading them.

When the day broke eastward across the frost rime of the buffalo grass, they saw their friends and relatives coming through the sunrise toward them. Some young men with ponies had reached the Smoky Hill camp with news of the Sand Creek massacre. Now the friends and kinsmen were rejoined. Cooked meat and warm blankets and riding horses and medicines for the wounded were given to the refugees, and all were carried swiftly back to the camp on Smoky Hill River. There the farewell prayers and the keening of the women for their dead made a sound in the prairie morning that Red Dust would remember until Maheo gathered him to the Land of the Shadows.

217

XXVI

The Smoky Hill people made preparations to break their camp should Chivington turn his attention to them. Scouts were sent out to the south to watch for Mashanē, while other scouts rode at once for the north to carry word of the massacre to the fighting bands above the Platte, to the Sioux, Arapahoes of the north, and Cheyennes of the north. It was a tense time, and fearful.

But when the scouts returned from the south, they brought only good news. In the seven days of their traveling, no pony soldiers had been seen near Sand Creek, or Rush Creek, or any place above the Arkansas. And more. It was positively told them by some of Little Raven's Arapahoes from Camp Wynkoop below Fort Lyon, that Mashanē and all his men had marched on down the big river, down toward Major Wynkoop. He was now said to be fifty miles from Fort Lyon. He had withdrawn all of his guards about the fort and from about Bent's Ranch, and taken them with him.

The Arapahoes of Little Raven said that Mashanē was out looking for more Indians to kill, but that, when he had gotten as far as Major Wynkoop's field camp, he was not talking that way any more. His own men were camped and very quiet. The Arapahoes thought that Mashanē had been told something by Major Wynkoop that changed his mind very fast.

Robert "Jack" Bent, who was still with those soldiers of the 3rd Colorado Cavalry, had told the Arapahoes that Mashanē was going back up the Arkansas right away, but not looking for any Indians any more, but only for a place to think over what he had done. Bent had heard some of the soldiers saying that Mashanē was in very bad trouble with the big soldier chiefs of the Grandfather in Washington, D.C., about destroying Black Kettle's village. And that Major Wynkoop had told Mashanē to his face that he would never command another body of troops along the Arkansas, or any other place that the regular Army kept soldiers in all of that country. There was even talk of arresting Mashanē, but that was foolish. Who would do it? Mashanē was the commander of all of the military district of Colorado. Well, *ih hai,* good hunting, that was all of the news that the Arapahoes of Little Raven had given the Cheyenne scouts from Smoky Hill. It was better at that than any of them might have hoped.

But what of the strange-minded schoolteacher from Horse Creek? Was there any news of him down there on the Arkansas? No? Not one report? No one had seen him, or seen anyone who had seen him? Since the big fight he had disappeared, eh? And his orphans? The ones left at Bent's Ranch? Did Robert "Jack" Bent know anything of them, of the two little half-blood boys and the crippled Arapaho girl? No again. Jack Bent had not been near his father's ranch.

Well, too bad. The red-bearded schoolmaster with the grizzly-bear winter coat had been a true friend to all the Cheyennes. He had saved Red Dust, the nephew of Roman Nose. He had made a home for unwanted Indian waifs at his lonely school at The Cottonwoods. If he had been a little odd in his head, in his heart he had been truly touched by the Allfather.

As for the children, they were probably gone never to be seen again in that life. What chance was there that Mashanē's guards had withdrawn without doing something bad to them? It was too bad, all of it, but the Cheyennes could have told Preacher that his mission school at The Cottonwoods never would be there very long. What white man had ever lasted very long being kind and fair to the Indians?

On that final day when the scouts returned from the Arkansas, a council was held to decide on more messages to be sent north telling the news that the Colorado troops were going back to Denver and that Mashanē was said to be through fighting on the Arkansas, perhaps forever. In this same council Wolfbag and his wife, who was the aunt of Red Dust, asked also that the elders make a ruling on what to do with the northern boy. He seemed homesick, they said, or sick in some way that was hurting him, and they believed he should be sent home to his uncle, Roman Nose.

The boy was called in, after the Indian fairness in such matters, and asked if he wished to go home, to ride north with the new messengers even then readying their ponies for the long journey to the Powder and the Tongue Rivers in far Wyoming. Strangely Red Dust seemed to hesitate. Faced with the thing he had thought he wanted most, some inner doubt weighed upon him, nor could he say what it was. But even as he stood there, trying to answer the elders, a great shout went up outside the lodge and everyone got up and hurried out to see what was happening.

There, coming in toward the camp of the Smoky Hill people, was a horseman—and a horse that Red Dust knew in the instant of the first sighting. In his breast the heaviness was gone. The doubts and inner weighings disappeared. He laughed—the first laugh anyone in that country had heard from him—and he ran past the elders and all of the people, waving and crying out: "Preacher, Preacher, it is I, Mahesie, your son!"

But the miracle of Preacher Bleek's return on the old white mare, the same old speckled and bony white mare that had saved Red Dust at Sand Creek, was not complete. The remainder of it was now groaning and creaking into view behind the great square man in the bear-skin winter coat. It was the resurrected old prairie schooner, the Argonaut. The Argonaut with the Kiowa Ladies and Samson and Delilah whinnying and braying their welcomes to the pony herds of the Smoky Hill people. And the Argonaut with Blackbird driving the teams, proud as any pure-blood. The Argonaut with Sunflower and Young Buzzard perched on the seat beside Blackbird, waving to Red Dust and calling to him: "*Hai*! Look at us, Mahesie. We are going to Kansas and build a new schoolhouse! You can go with us, if you don't mind riding in the back with a shaggy old friend who doesn't smell too good when he gets wet!" And that was the last part of the miracle. As the children laughed, old Lamewolf poked his head out of the pucker hole of the canvas wagon cover behind the driver's seat and began to bark and growl and bare his teeth and move his tail in Indian circles to show that even he was glad to see the northern boy again.

That night, at a feast of fresh buffalo tenderloins and lump sugar from the Argonaut, Preacher held forth at much length in the big lodge of Wolfbag. The Smoky Hill people gathered inside and outside to hear the wonderful story of his escape from Sand Creek. How he had been struck in the head by the rifle bullet of a soldier and left for dead. But how he had regained consciousness to find he had only been creased by the bullet and began urgently to search for some way to escape Mashanē's prowling troops. And then how the old white Cheyenne mare had found him when all appeared hopeless, and had carried him away safely through the sandhills to freedom. Then how he had ridden the old mare down to the Arkansas across from Bent's Ranch, just in time to see the soldier guard leave the ranch and hurry away. And how he had then found his little strangers all still safely there. How they told him that the good soldier, Durant, had been helped by two of Bent's half-breed sons to get away from the troop guard of Mashanē's men one stormy night, and was now safely surrendered to Major Wynkoop's men far down the big river at Fort Larned, whence some friendly Kiowa Indians had taken him. And how the children and Preacher had then left the ranch riding the Kiowa Ladies and old black Samson and little spotted Delilah, heading for the Smoky Hill camp of their good friend Wolfbag.

But, *tòa noxa*! Wait! Now came the really remarkable part. When they left the ranch, Sunflower begged Preacher to ride by way of the wolf rocks where brave Lamewolf had died fighting the pony soldier, Sergeant Skemp. Sunflower wanted to give the old dog a decent Indian burial, with a scaffold and burning and some appropriately long prayers. But when they reached the place, there was Lamewolf, thin as a baby crane with no feathers, but alive on the offering of food left for him by Blackbird and Young Buzzard—and alive because Skemp's bullet had only made a bloody wound in his scalp, just like Preacher's wound! And he had only been unconscious in that snowbank and not dead when the soldiers took Sunflower and Red Dust away.

Now Preacher had taken out his Bible and read from it to them all, and vowed that finding the old dog alive was a sign from above. He said his Lord God Jehovah had sent that sign to give back his courage to him, Preacher, to show him that where hope does not die, nothing dies.

"*Haho*, Maheo!" Preacher had added quickly. They were all going over on Rush Creek and dig that old wagon out of the snow hole into which it had fallen. They were going to fix it up and patch the harness and put the Ladies and Samson and Delilah into the traces and start out all over again to finish their journey to Smoky Hill River. For Preacher's God had also told him that, if old Lamewolf could be alive, then the boy, Red Dust, might also have lived. And, had he done so, he would be in the village of the Smoky Hill people with the other Cheyenne survivors from the terrible fight along Little Dried River.

That was the story. Between them, the Cheyenne's Great Spirit Maheo and the white man's Lord God Jehovah had done it all. Those old gods sent powerful signs. *Nahaôn*. Amen.

● ● ●

Early next morning, the Argonaut and her orphans departed the camp of the southern Cheyenne on Smoky Hill River. It was December 8th, 1864.

A day of serene clear-skied beauty, it was as though Maheo had said to old Maxhekonene, old Strong-Faced Hard Frost Moon: "Forget your blusters and your big snows for a little while. Let these people pass."

In the wagon, yet a little weak for long walking, Lamewolf rested like a chief. On the driver's seat sat Preacher. In the rising sun his beard bristled red and golden as a chestnut burr. His bear-skin coat bulged with good treasure recovered from the Argonaut: lump sugar and rock candy for the children, dried liver bits and pemmican balls for the old dog, shag leaf Burley tobacco for Preacher—and something else for Preacher, too, corked tightly in a medicine bottle that held no medicine.

On the seat with the big white man from Horse Creek, whose inner spirit knew the meaning of Cheyenne *hotoma*, sat Blackbird and Young Buzzard. Out in front of the Kiowa Ladies and of black Samson and spotted Delilah went Sweet Medicine, the old long-maned white mare. She went as proudly as a best buffalo horse or even a first-picked war pony. And why should she not? How many aged pack ponies of the southern Cheyennes lived to carry a nephew of Roman

Nose, the greatest fighting northern Indian of them all? And more. To carry with Red Dust the Arapaho crippled girl, Sunflower, both as light and kind as a burden of gray goose down to an old mare's misused, much-curved back.

Sweet Medicine lifted up her speckled snout, blew out through her hairy nostrils, rolled a soft brown eye back at her two small riders, kicked up her ancient heels. For a little while, at least until she had led the Argonaut over the first rise and out of sight of the Cheyenne camp, she knew again the feeling to be young.

So it was that Red Dust went home, not to high Wyoming but to western Kansas. And so it was that Preacher Nehemiah Bleek, who seldom prayed and never preached, set forth once more with his little strangers, his orphans of the Argonaut. Perhaps his only epitaph was that one slowly spoken by Wolfbag, watching with his woman from the village edge until the last snow patch turned blue with distance and the gray haze of the buffalo grass blotted out the Argonaut.

"A good man," said the dark-faced brave. "I think Maheo made him with the wrong-colored skin. He should have been a Cheyenne. . . ."

FRONTIER FURY

I

At the top of the long rise the white soldier eased his raw-boned bay to a halt, sat him, hipshot, while his squinted gaze studied the fall of the wagon track toward the distant river. His silent red escorts let their slant eyes join his in frowning consideration of the flood-swollen Snake.

1st Sergeant Emmett D. Bell, H Company, 1st Dragoons, wrinkled the hawked bridge of his sun-blackened nose, spat disgustedly into the settling dust of the Colville Road. The spittle lanced into the bone-dry underfooting, its force erupting the powdered surface of the road like a miniscule artillery burst. Behind him, the foremost of the three Nez Percé scouts took note of the impact and attitude of the sergeant's expectoration.

"Twice now you have spat, Ametsun." The Nez Percé had taken what he wanted of Bell's name and made of it a good Indian word—something that sat properly in a red mouth rarely shaped to call a white man friend. "That's a bad sign. Don't you like what you see?"

"You know damn' well I don't, Timothy." Bell used the Nez Percé's Christian name. "I don't like what I see ahead, and I don't like what I see behind."

"Is it the Snake being in high water that worries you?"

"You know better than that."

"Aye." The soft bass of the Indian's mission-school English broke thoughtfully. "You are thinking of what I am, then. Of something beyond the Snake."

"That depends on what you're thinking of." The soldier's eyes narrowed, watching the Indian closely.

"Of a name," said Timothy simply.

"Palouses?"

"Aye, Palouses."

"All right, then. We're both thinking of Kamiak."

"We are both thinking of him," echoed the Nez Percé softly.

For the first time Bell straightened in his saddle, threw a quick smile at his red companion. "Well, by God, Tamason, it's a relief to know somebody else in this lousy outfit has got brains enough to be worried! Come on, let's get back to the column and give the colonel his all clear to the crossing."

"Wait." The Indian had his bronze hand on Bell's bridle. "You spoke as well of not liking what lay behind. How did you mean that, Ametsun?"

"Take a good, long look down there, Timothy, and tell me what you see."

Following the abrupt sweep of the oak-post arm with which the white man indicated the climbing swell of the prairie to their rear, the Indian shrugged deprecatingly. "I see the flag, Ametsun.

230

Then the oak leaf chief and all the pony soldiers following after it. Truly, is there more to see?"

"Nope, that's it." There was sudden bitterness in the sergeant's slow words. "The dear old Stars and Stripes up front on schedule. Backed by Brevet Lieutenant Colonel Edson Stedloe with four company officers and one hundred fifty-two enlisted men." The acid in Bell's tones etched the continuing roll call deeper still. "Five gentlemen by grace of an act of Congress, and a hundred and a half ignorant heroes by grace of not having got through grammar school, or being on the dodge from the sheriff back home. God A'mighty!"

"Amen," echoed the Nez Percé solemnly.

Bell looked at him sharply. Studying the Indian's expressionless face, he decided he hadn't meant the remark to be humorous. You take a pure savage like Timothy, one who had been ground, exceedingly fine, through old Marc Whitman's missionary mill, and you had a case about as far from funny as he could get.

"It is the soldiers behind us that you do not like?" The Nez Percé's low question broke in on Bell's side-stepping thoughts.

"That's it," grunted the white man. "With Kamiak over there in the Bitter Roots heating up the Yakimas and Spokanes with a mess of lies about Colonel Stedloe coming to Colville for war instead of peace, how else can a man feel that knows Indians?"

231

"You are sure those are lies, Ametsun?" The question was put with child-like directness.

"I don't rightly know, Tamason. But that's neither here nor there. What's here is a column of regulars supposed to be heading for Colville for a peace powwow with the red brother . . . and that column toting along two mountain howitzer companies and three of crack dragoons. And what's there is a hostile Palouse chief who's been predicting right along that we'd come just the way we're coming . . . armed to the eyeteeth and loaded for red bear." It was a long speech for the ordinarily taciturn Bell, and he concluded it abruptly. "Anyway you pull that bad-boiled dog apart, there's going to be big scrapping over the bones."

"No." Timothy's contradiction came softly, the slit eyes behind it looking far away. "If Colonel Stedloe follows his word to march only along the Colville Road, there will be no fighting. I have heard this among my people. You may believe it, Ametsun."

"Hallelujah," breathed Bell in half-mock relief, "we're saved. I read those field orders and they route us straight up the Colville Military Road. Looks like the colonel's soldier boys might get to Colville yet."

"They will get there if they stay on the road," was all Timothy said before motioning to his fellow Nez Percés, and turning his pony to follow Bell's.

The early May evening lay over the main crossing of the Snake like a blue-dark shawl. Overhead, the fat Washington stars bloomed, thick and white as Shasta daisies. Ashore, the camp's cook fires dappled the broad shift of the river with their myriad sequins. On the lamplit patch of bare ground in front of the command tent, Sergeant Bell's "five gentlemen by grace of an act of Congress" had dined at length and well, were comfortably disposed in an idle discussion of their prospects in Colville.

After a desultory half hour of small talk, Stedloe exchanged the easy patter of his normally paternal address for the brisk tones of the colonel commanding.

"Well, gentlemen, I think we'll let that do it for tonight. I've something of a surprise for you in the morning and I'd like you to have a good night's sleep ahead of it." As his youthful staff traded raised eyebrows with one another, the colonel concluded: "If there's nothing further, I bid you good evening."

Apparently there was not, and the young officers, despite their aroused curiosities, quietly arose to take their leaves. As they did so, Stedloe motioned to a particularly boyish-looking second lieutenant.

"Wilcey, send a man to find Sergeant Bell. Winston tells me the insubordinate devil sent one of his Indians on up the Colville Road this afternoon. Dammit all, I sometimes wonder who's running this command, me or Sergeant Bell."

Facing Colonel Stedloe in a sagging at ease that qualified as such only because he was, technically, still standing up, Bell covered his position with his usual bluntness.

Yes, sir, he had sent Timothy ahead. No, sir, he had not thought an authorization necessary. In view of the certain layover occasioned by the Snake's being bank full, he had thought the Nez Percé scout could better improve his shining hours by scouting the column's line of march than by building up his bottom bunions squatting around an idle camp. It was Sergeant Bell's concluding and none too respectful opinion that all was not as happy in the hunting grounds of Kamiak's Palouses as the colonel might care to imagine.

Lieutenant Colonel Edson Stedloe, whatever his limitations, was no martinet. Contrary to the grimly regulation disapproval of his staff, he himself not only tolerated but actually enjoyed Bell's unique lack of deference toward commissioned personnel. In this instance he agreed, in theory, to the sergeant's economic employment of the Indian's spare time, while in the same breath advising the dumbfounded non-com that in fact there would be no layover at the Snake. With the dropping of that little howitzer burst, he retired to his tent to get on with the really important business to hand: the laborious hand-scripting of his endless operational reports.

Long after Bell's lounging shadow had been lost to the feeble arc of the command tent lamp, the colonel's stubby quill scratched the dull litany of its squeaking progress across the yellowed sheets.

Snake River Crossing
Wash. Terr.
May 12, 1858.
Major W.W. MacKay,
Asst. Adj. General
U.S. Army,
San Francisco

Major:

On the 2nd instant I informed you of my intention to leave Fort Wallowa with about 130 dragoons and a detachment of infantry for service with the howitzers, and to move directly where it is understood the hostile party of the Palouse chief, Kamiak, is at present. Accordingly, on the 6th I left there with C, E, and H, First Dragoons, and E, Ninth Infantry; in all, four company officers and one hundred fifty-two enlisted men.

As advised to you in mine of the 2nd the announced purpose of this movement, was to seek a council with the hostile Indians at Colville, and there to mediate their differences with the whites of that settlement. However, learning that the hostile Palouses were in the vicinity of Red Wolf Crossing of the Snake River in Nez Percé lands, I have reconsidered my earlier plans and now intend to march directly for Red Wolf Crossing. I have not thought it advisable previously to acquaint my staff with this fact since the new route directly enters the hostile treaty lands and there exists among them (my officers and men) some unwarranted feeling of doubt as to the real intent of the reportedly aroused Indians.

However, my own intelligences assure me that the Spokanes and Yakimas will not unite with the Palouse chief Kamiak (who is personally wanted on several white murder charges) and that there is definitely no danger of a general uprising at this time.

I shall accordingly issue the revised order tomorrow, the 13th, and the column will move at once on Red Wolf Crossing. I am entirely satisfied the new route will heighten the originally desired effect of intimidating the various restless tribes into accepting our direction for an immediate hearing at Colville. I shall keep your office advised with regular field dispatches, but you may assure General Clarkson of an early and peaceful settlement of the complete matter.

I have the honor to be, very respectfully, your obedient servant,

E.S. Stedloe,
Bvt. Lt. Colonel
United States Army

Once well away from Stedloe's tent, Bell removed his canteen and tipped it skyward. When, five full seconds later, he brought the container away from his smacking lips, it was not the wholesome redolence of soft mountain water that assaulted the evening air.

Twenty strides later, passing Lieutenant Gaxton's tent, he was perfectly aware of the young officer's hail, chose nonetheless to ignore it.

"Sergeant Bell!"

This was an order, now, not a greeting, and Bell halted his slow, dragging steps.

"Yes, sir?" The sergeant, pausing in his loose slouch across the fire from the officer, didn't offer either to salute or sit down. Lieutenant Gaxton looked up, frowning. And with ample reason. What he saw would have stiffened the neck of the least proper of Congress's gentlemen.

First Sergeant Emmett Bell crowded six feet two without the benefit of his thick dragoon boot soles. His arms, heavy as wagon tongues and half as long, hung the best of the way to his bent knees. His complexion, rare in a sandy-haired man, was as dark and sun-lined as a prairie Sioux. The slovenliness of his dirty blues, together with the dust-red bristle of his short beard and the more than faint air of fusel oil that impregnated his entire person, completed the picture of the factual frontier cavalryman—drunk, dirty, and disrespectful.

Gaxton turned his eyes away from the waiting non-com and coughed heavily. "Sit down, Emm. There's something I've been wanting to tell you for a long time. And don't say anything about this damned cough. Randall says it's nothing to worry about."

"Well, that makes either you or Surgeon Randall a cold-deck liar," grunted Bell, sinking to his haunches and letting the charge come backed by his slatey eyes. "You've got lung fever, Wilse. I know that bark. The way you've been baying the past six weeks would make a 'coon hound hoarse."

"It's a funny thing, Emm"—the reply came only after a long look between the two—"but I never could get past you. You could always give me a headstart and be waiting to help me across the finish line. I guess the only time I ever did beat you was with Calla."

"Forget it!" Bell jumped the short words. "Let's

not go to turning over wet hay. What did Randall tell you, Wilse?"

"Six months . . ."

Bell, busy packing his pipe, was not too busy to throw a guarded, eye-tail glance across the fire. One look was enough. The skull-tight pallor, the bright flush over the cheek bones, the snake's glitter of the eyes, it was all there. Bell had seen too much of it among the Nez Percés. A man hacked away with that sick-dog bark for a few weeks and then one day the back of his hand came away from his mouth with that bright smear on it.

"Listen, Wilse, you're playing around with a rifle-squad salute and a led horse with nobody in your saddle but a black blanket."

"I know, Emm, but I've got to make it up to Colville."

"Oh, the hell with Colville!" Bell, missing the tenseness in the young officer's words, snapped back irritably. "What's so damn' important about Colville? There's nothing up there that somebody else can't take care of for you."

"That's what I wanted to talk to you about, Emm." The tension in the sick man's voice increased. "Calla's up there."

"Oh, God . . . not Calla . . ." The words came out of the big man as if they were being cut out of him with a knife.

"God forgive me, Emm. I did it for . . ."

"God may, Wilse." Bell's interruption had the flatness of dead anger in it. "I never will."

With the words the sergeant was on his feet, the scarecrow hulk of his shadow hanging over the smaller man. A pine knot, shifting in the fire, held its ruddy torch to the hovering face long enough to show the wide mouth soften, the odd, opaque gray of the eyes uncloud.

"Emm, wait! I didn't tell you why Calla came out. Emm . . ."

The lobar wrack of a coughing spell broke the young officer's plea, and, when the spasm had passed, there was no other sound in answer to it. Bell had gone.

The white-faced man by the fire slumped weakly back. Presently he coughed again, wiping his mouth with the back of his hand before moving to stir the graying ash of the flames. The fitful flare of the disturbed coals lit the back of the reaching hand, briefly limning the bright smear upon it.

In front of the tent he shared with the remaining three first sergeants, Bell found a small fire still burning. Crouching alongside its lonely glow, he sat for many minutes staring out across the black and moonless rush of the river. The shift of the firelight seemed to play deceiving tricks of softness and sentiment with the immobile lines of the set face. Yet, perhaps, the illusion was not entirely one of seeming. Or of playing. Or of deceit. For in the end no man may turn his mind at long last homeward without the weary mile posts of memory marking their paths across his features.

Bell took the oilskin packet from inside his shirt. Unfolded it slowly. Brought the dingy envelope to view. With equally distracted precision he removed the single page of the letter and spread it on the firelit sands. He read it with his lips moving, as a man not seeing it but knowing it by heart.

Refolding the letter, the sergeant returned it to the envelope. For a moment he studied the addressed side, his lips moving across the treasured legend.

Miss Calla Lee Rainsford,
c/o Gen. Henry Clay Rainsford,
The Sycamores,
Lynchburg, Va.

After another moment he turned it over to the back side, revealing the soiled embossing of the formal letter-head:

United States Military Academy West Point
The Class of 1854
Second Lieutenant Emmett Devereaux Bellew

This time Bell's lips didn't move until long after his eyes had left the envelope, and then only

241

as he spat acridly into the smoking fire bed. "To the class of 'Fifty-Four," he announced, skying the battered canteen, "and to First Sergeant Emmett D. Bell thereof . . ."

II

The morning of the 13th came on, sweat-hot and glass-clear. Accordingly the members of the advancing column got their first real bath in a week. By early forenoon every man in the command had sweat a quart and Bell, at least, had drunk one.

Despite the merciless sun, noon halt found the men in excellent spirits. Stedloe's dramatic announcement of the shifted course and real purpose of the command had filtered through his enthusiastic staff and on down to the greenest buck in the outfit.

Bell, scowling at the picnic-outing atmosphere of the whole thing, thought of Timothy's grim warning about staying on the Colville Military Road and cursed bitterly. The idiots! Bucking blithely ahead into treaty-forbidden red lands as though Kamiak and his damned angry Palouse were so many beef-fed, reservation bootlickers!

The afternoon march began as briskly as had the morning's. But late afternoon, with five miles still facing them to the Nez Percé crossing at Red

Wolf, found the column's blistered bottoms beginning to drag. Stedloe, in no great rush and exercising his good professional eye for such enlisted symptoms, called the halt at 5:00p.m., a matter of perhaps ten seconds before 1st Sergeant Bell would have felt compelled to call it for him. The remaining daylight was spent looking to the lathered horses, policing the spotless company streets, and furbishing the colonel's precious howitzers.

An hour after dusk, Bell, feeling the better for his supper of three pipes of shag-cut Burley and a half canteen of bourbon, was lying with his back to the welcome slope of the tent wall. For lack of a better recreation he was adding his usual silence to the regulation campfire talk of his fellow non-coms—that endless and oathful rehash of the glories of past campaigns (a painful few military, the hog's bulk of them amatory).

Presently the chevroned orators had run through their short supply of new lies and had, by mutual consent, turned the floor of the following silence over to the rush and stir of the passing river and to the out-of-tune sawings of a nearby cricket.

"Sarge . . . ?"

Although the least number of service stripes among them would have trebled Bell's, the others reserved this address for their red-bearded junior.

"Yeah, Mick?" Bell responded.

"Play us a tyune, bye." Keg-chested, Airedalehairy Sergeant Erin Harrigan put the request in his turfy County Donegal brogue. "I can't abide the div'lish black mutterin' of that miserable river."

"Nor me, the sawin' of thet cricket, yonduh." Bull Williams, rolling his tiny eyes, protecting the reference by forking the first two fingers of his right hand and holding them away from himself. "Back home they say a cricket singin' in the house means a death in the family. Play us a tune like Mick says, Sarge. I got the fantods."

Bell looked at the giant Kentuckian disgustedly. To Sergeant Bell's way of seeing things, the burly hillman, both in bulk and brilliance, was humanity's closest approach to a Hereford. The fact that he had chosen to attach his dumb-brute devotion to 1st Sergeant Bell did nothing to endear him to that resistive-tempered individual. But Bell assumed it was given unto each of God's likenesses to bear some hopeless burden through life and wearily accepted Bull Williams as his.

"All right, Bull. What'll it be this time? 'Old Smoky' or 'Bluetail Fly'?"

"Atop of Old Smoky!" Williams brightened like a child handed a nickel with no strings. "Play it slow, Sarge, so's I can do the words of it."

"God in heaven! Not that dirge again!" Sergeant Victor Demoix was a fiercely mustached ex-hussar of the French army with a Gallic preference for settling all arguments with the handiest piece of edged steel.

"Shut up, Frenchy." Bell knocked the pocket lint out of his harmonica, ran a wheezy scale or two, and settled down to the serious work of "Old Smoky."

On the second, dolorous chorus, Williams, eyes closed, thick body swaying, began to sing.

> On top of Old Smoky, all covered with
>   snow,
> I lost my true lover from a-courtin' too
>   slow . . .

As the oddly beautiful voice of the huge Kentuckian faded, Bell rapped the spittle-laden reed of the mouth organ against the calloused heel of his hand and shook his head wonderingly.

"If the poor dumb ox could only think like he can sing!"

"He's got yez to do his thinkin' fer him," said Mick, "and that's a good thing."

"Good for what, in God's name?" demanded Bell irritably.

"And yez have him to do yer singin' fer yez," continued the Irishman, ignoring Bell's temper, "and that's a good thing, too."

"Maybe," grunted Bell, "but all the same that voice gives me the creeps. God never meant an animal like that to have that voice."

"Aye," muttered Mick uneasily. "In the body of a murderin' bull, the blessed throat of a bird."

"*Et un ame de boue!*" added Demoix angrily.

"Tut now, little man," the squat Harrigan clucked reprovingly at Demoix. "I've warned yez about spoutin' that heathen tongue of yers. Now yez'll be forcin' me wance ag'in to be askin' the dear teacher whut yez said!"

". . . and a soul of mud," translated Bell.

Any further comment was interrupted by the hip-swinging approach of Stedloe's orderly.

An ambitiously proper soldier, needle-neat and not yet twenty, Corporal Roger Bates was listed "all business and no belly" in Bell's caustic catalogue. He ate clean, kept clean, and slept clean, and was by his own oft-stated conviction "officer material of the clearest water." He drew up at the sergeants' mess with all the dignity possible to a size 28 chest in a 42 shirt.

"Colonel Stedloe to Sergeant Bell!" he announced dramatically. "And will the sergeant please report at once!"

Bell, glancing up slowly, looked squarely at him without apparently seeing him at all. Williams and Demoix bent their attentions to a speculative regard of the river. Harrigan felt compelled to relieve the silence.

"Faith now, lad. Will yez never learn? Now yez jist watch yer Uncle Erin this wan more time. It's the last I'll be showin' yez of how to address yer superiors in this man's army."

With elaborate patience Harrigan arose and drew off from the fire, to return a moment later in a perfect, mincing mimicry of Bates's running-walk approach. Hitting a rigid brace in front of the reclining Bell, he bellowed delicately: "Git up off yer big dead end, yez drunken slob! The Old Man wants to see yez on the double!"

"Thank you, Sergeant Harrigan." Bell's sober salute was a minor miracle of dead-pan earnest. "Please accept through me the sincere gratitude of the entire service. The United States Army may well be proud of such memorable devotion to dire and dangerous duty as you have only now displayed in getting through to this command with Colonel Stedloe's message. I congratulate you, sir!"

"Oh, bless you, General, sir!" Harrigan's words broke pathetically. "Remember me when the next Commission Board is sittin', sir!"

"That I will, Sergeant, that I will . . ." Bell's reply trailed off after the departing slouch of its maker's shoulders. "You're very clearly officer material. As any fool can plainly see."

Corporal Bates stood a moment, torn between his urge to blast the remaining three rascals and his indecision as to just what Sergeant Williams meant to do with the barrel-swung butt of that issue musket. By the time it became evident that the Holstein-size non-com had it in heart and hand to try the venerable walnut against the quivering indignation of the Bates buttocks, it was already too late.

Because, during his four years on the North-west frontier, Bell had painstakingly learned the guttural intricacies of the Chinook dialect and had demonstrated a repeated ability to get along with the quirky red men, Stedloe had long since turned the post scout force over to him. These Indians, all Nez Percés, found in the gaunt sergeant's shortness of tongue and temper and tart readiness of acid humor a common bond of hard-core understanding. Bell, as lonely as most men of his patently dangerous disposition, was glad enough to accept the frank regard of his Nez Percé admirers at face value.

As the sergeant had guessed it would be, Stedloe's current call concerned the Indian hue of the campaign's present complexion. Did Sergeant Bell think that Jason and Lucas, the two remaining scouts, could successfully take the column past Red Wolf, or had they best hold up for Timothy's return? Was the sergeant aware of the current rumor that the Nez Percé tribe wanted to embroil the Army with the hostiles of Kamiak's federation, and thus come out top dog on the territory's Indian pile? Would Bell give any credence to such a ridiculous fable, and, if so, did he have complete confidence in the loyalty of their own Nez Percés? Particularly in Timothy, who was known to be a blood chief among them? Beyond that, had the sergeant heard anything from his Indians about the Army's confidential report that Brigham

Young's Mormons were arming Kamiak's group? And that the Coeur D'Alene mission priest, Father Joset, was issuing ammunition to the hostiles? Finally, did Bell have any idea how many active followers Kamiak might have at present, or any information about the Palouse chief's reported threat to start his uprising if the troops came toward Colville in major strength or, particularly, if they chose to come by any course other than the Military Road?

Bell, agreeably surprised at Stedloe's earnestness and the heartening extent of his information, replied in characteristic style. The colonel was damned well right he had heard about the Mormons and Father Joset. The former rumor was 110 percent correct, the latter unadulterated hogwash. As to the idea of the Nez Percés being eager to bring about a clash between the troops and Kamiak, take some and leave some. Timothy had as much as admitted that some such sentiment was rife among a minority of his tribesmen. Coming to his own Nez Percés, he wouldn't trust Jason and Lucas any further than he could pitch a buffalo bull by the back end. By the same token, he would put his last dime on Timothy and expect 8¢ change.

Regarding Kamiak's strength, he had only Timothy's report that Father Joset estimated the organized hostiles at somewhere near 1,000, and that there were indeed sizeable elements of

Yakimas, Spokanes, and Coeur D'Alenes in that number. Lastly, as to Kamiak's threats to open up if the troops came in force or left the Military Road, the colonel would have to bite his own chaw off of that plug. Bell's idea would be that, if Stedloe stuck his curly head across the Snake at Red Wolf Crossing, he'd pull it back with a Palouse haircut.

Stedloe thanked him, disagreed with his closing recommendation that the column should hold up on the Nez Percé side of Red Wolf until Timothy got back, advised him the command would march at 5:00a.m., and directed him to convey that intelligence to his fellow non-coms.

Bell came to what was supposed to be attention, forced one dangling hand halfway to his forehead, and awkwardly backed out through the colonel's tent flap.

The weary camp was quieting down as the big non-com bent his long strides for his own fire. Here and there a last bed of cooking coals was still flickering fitfully. On the picket lines, the artillery mules tossed at the last of the chaff in their nosebags while beyond them the scattered shadows of the dragoon horse herd grazed on the river bottom.

Drifting up behind the solitary figure at the fire outside the non-coms' tent, Bell settled alongside it. The nodding figure came awake, its red-rimmed, lake-blue eyes burning resentfully.

"Damn yer red-lovin' soul, Sarge! It's enough to give a dacint, Christian man the Nez Percé shakes, the way yez feather foot it around!"

"Never mind the Nez Percé shakes, Mick. I've brought you something stronger. Where's Bull and Demoix?"

"In the tint, poundin' their hairy ears. Whut do yez mean, somethin' stronger, bye?" The squat Irishman put the query nervously.

"Palouse palsy," said Bell shortly. "Roust the boys out. The Old Man's pulling out at daybreak. Aiming to cross over at Red Wolf without waiting for my Indian to get back from up Colville way."

With the two newly aroused sergeants nodding, owl-eyed, under his terse words, Bell spent the next few minutes conveying Stedloe's orders for the early start. With the tired aplomb of the professional regular, the three soldiers took the news back to their clammy blankets. In a matter of seconds the dissonant trio of their snores was in full nasal sway.

Bell pulled his own blankets from the tent and rolled up by the guttering smoke of the fire. Shortly the heavy tones of his own exhales were adding their rich bass to the carefree quartet of old campaigner snores.

III

Bell came hard awake, suddenly prodded by the instincts that could put a man to sleeping like a log and still shuck him out of it gingery as a scared cat. The first camp-wide sweep of his narrowed eyes recorded three things: first light of the 4:00a.m. false dawn was tipping the tent rows; a sudden rash of oil lamps was pimpling the interiors of the staff canvas; a confused ruckus of muffled talk and moving figures was clotting up down by the river. Then his long legs were under him and seconds later he was breaking through the little group of stumbling troopers who were half carrying, half dragging the body of an unconscious man.

One look at the naked slimness of the figure was enough for Bell.

"Timothy!" The shouted cry of recognition was seconded by the drumfire of the barked commands. "Give me that Indian. Where the devil did you find him? Come on, for Pete's sake, speak up!"

"Fished him outen the river, Sarge. Just now." One of the soldiers found his startled tongue. "I was down there relievin' myself when I heared him holler from the other side. I could make out he was mounted and I seen him put the horse into the river. About five minutes later I seen him flounderin' in the shallows on this side, and I jumped in and fished him out. He's plumb drownded, I reckon. Horse, too. Least, the horse didn't make it to this side. I . . ."

"You worry about the horse, soldier"—Bell put the Nez Percé's slack form over his shoulder as easily as though it were that of a child—"and get the hell out of my way. This is *my* Indian!"

At Captain Randall's quarters it developed that Timothy was suffering more from weariness than water. The surgeon brought him around quickly enough and after a long peg from Bell's canteen the Nez Percé was ready to talk. What he had to say would have lifted the short hairs off any white man's neck.

Five seconds after the first, deep-grunted phrases broke haltingly from the exhausted Indian's compressed lips, Bell was shouldering aside the flaps of Stedloe's tent to rap out the grim news.

Five minutes after that, a general command meeting was in white-faced, pin-silent session. The cleared ground in front of the colonel's quarters was glaringly lighted by the hastily fed-up flames of the banked fire. On the three open sides of this shifting illumination crouched Stedloe's four company officers, Winston, Baylor, Gaxton, and Craig, along with the supply quartermaster, 2nd Lieutenant Henry Fanning, and Surgeon

253

Randall, as well as Bell's three fellow sergeants.

The colonel sat in his camp chair just outside the tent, while on the ground in front of him, facing the breath-held ring of officers and non-coms, squatted the blanket-wrapped figure of the shivering Nez Percé. Bell, overlooked in the confusion, hung his tall shadow on the tent flap to Stedloe's left. It was 4:15a.m., Friday, May 14th.

"All right, Timothy"—Colonel Stedloe's quiet nod went to the Nez Percé chief—"go ahead."

The Indian hesitated, his quick glance running around the circle of graven-faced officers.

Bell's big hand found the thin, red shoulder. "You tell them, Tamason. Like you told me and Colonel Stedloe. *Lka'nax gita'q'atxalema,*" the white man counseled gravely in Chinook. "Remember you are a chief, these are common ones."

"*Gu'tgut,*" the Indian murmured, low-voiced. "It is just that I am so tired, Ametsun." And with that, fixing his slant gaze in the heart of the fire, Timothy told his story.

It was short. Brutal. Naked. Starting up the Military Road toward Colville late Wednesday afternoon, he had immediately run into abundant war sign. Helio mirrors and blanket-broken smoke columns were flashing and rising from almost every ridge and hilltop within forty miles. The Colville Road had seemed literally alive with these and the more tangible signs of frequent, hurrying groups of armed and painted warriors. So great had been this activity that Timothy had been forced to await darkness before traveling on. Next dawn had found him but little over halfway to Colville and still pinned down by the heavy hostile traffic. Shortly after dawn he had met a line of seven wagons bound for the Snake Crossing. These were from Fort Colville and Timothy had told them of the great numbers of hostiles on their front, and urged them to turn back. They had thanked him and gone on. About noon he had met an old friend of his, Victor, the Coeur D'Alene. Victor's young men were moving to join Kamiak, and the old chief was going along to try and persuade them not to. But it was already too late. The scouts had come from the Snake, saying that the oak leaf chief and the pony soldiers were coming in great numbers, and that they had swung suddenly south, last night, to march directly for the treaty lands of the Yakimas and Spokanes and Palouses. Kamiak's prediction had come to pass and there was no holding the young men now.

Then, even as Timothy had turned back to warn his soldiers of this big trouble, he had seen it. He had seen the black smoke to the west—behind him—where he had met those wagons. When he had come up there to that smoke, there was no noise there, and nothing moved. All seven of the white drivers lay dead among their burning wagons. But the beautiful young white woman who had been riding with them when Timothy had stopped to warn them in the morning was gone. Gone, too, was the big black servant woman who traveled with her. The men were all without their hair, and the way it had been taken from them, high up and toward the front of the skull, and cut out very precisely, told any Nez Percé what tribe had done the work. No other band took hair in just that clean, artistic way. Those were Palouse scalp cuts up there. It was Kamiak who had stolen those two women from the wagon train.

At the close of his simple accounting of the thirty-six hours that had seen him cover 145 miles, eluding constant hostile war parties both coming and going, then ride his dying horse up to the roaring bank of the main Snake and swim that father of evil waters in full flood, the Nez Percé chief looked quietly around the speechless circle of his white listeners and concluded: "I have said this now, and you can believe it. I have promised to follow the flag. The flag is my life."

Despite the chief's careful admonition, however, the immediate reaction of most of the officers was one of general incredulity and suspicion, Stedloe himself joining in these attacks on Timothy's integrity. The commanding officer wound up the rough interrogation by reminding the Nez Percé that the Army knew all about the existence of the Nez Percé plot to embroil the troops with Kamiak's federation—and that his wild story about a beautiful young white woman traveling with a Negro maid servant sounded like a very shallow and bad lie to get the pony soldiers to go chasing off into the Bitter Roots and into a bad clash with the hostile Palouses.

At this point Timothy stood up.

"I brought you this," he said slowly, "for I know your hearts are bad toward my word and the words of all my people."

Reaching a thin, red hand into the doeskin pouch of his breechcloth, the Indian removed something from it and flung it upon the ground. A dropped pin would have shattered the following stillness like the crash of an eighty-foot pine. On a village street in Virginia or a plantation porch in Georgia the object might have fallen unnoticed. But on a naked stretch of firelit frontier dirt 2,000 miles from St. Louis the mutely crumpled pertness of the tiny Eugenie hat struck with stark and glaring shock.

"Good Lord"—Captain Baylor's hushed words were the first into the stunned silence "a white woman's."

"And a lady's, too, I'd say." Captain Harry Winston spoke with his usual flat literalness. "And young."

"A Southern lady," Bell corrected softly, stepping out of the tent shadows and picking up the little hat. "Am I right, Lieutenant Gaxton?"

The question, grimly escorted by the enlisted

man's slate-gray stare, marched across the firelight to bring up in front of the fish-pale Gaxton.

Before the young officer could answer, Colonel Stedloe was on his feet. "That will do, Bell. I'm asking the questions here. Give me the hat. Lieutenant, what have . . . ?"

Bell's great paw tightened around the pathetic smallness of the hat.

"I've got the hat, Colonel. And the question that goes with it." The sergeant's pike-jaw closed on the refusal with an audible snap. "Lieutenant Gaxton, there, has got the answer, sir. And if it earns me the guardhouse for the rest of my natural life, I aim to hear him come out with it."

"Orderly! Corporal of the Guard!" Stedloe's crisp shout and Corporal Bates's eager response thereto were interrupted by the low intercession of Gaxton's shaking voice.

"Bell's right, sir. You can't blame him. Nor his Indian. What they've both had to say is true. That's Calla Lee Rainsford's hat, Colonel."

"You can't mean that, Wilcey!" Stedloe's loyal Southern mind was refusing the thought that Gaxton, himself a Southerner, could be guilty of such heinous conduct. "Bringing General Rainsford's daughter out into this country? What in God's name for, sir?"

"Begging the colonel's pardon, sir." Bell's blunt reminder put its words to the common thought of

258

the restive officers. "I would suggest that Lieutenant Gaxton's private life with this lady doesn't discount the fact she is possibly still alive and certainly in grave circumstances if she is."

"How's that, Bell?"

The even, white-toothed way in which Stedloe asked it let the sergeant know that the commanding officer had reached the furthest edge of that sharply cleared area dividing his natural liking for the rebellious non-com and his West Point heritage of commissioned untouchability. Nonetheless, when 1st Sergeant Bell set his size-eleven dragoon boots to overstep a simple line of authority, he didn't mean to put them down just halfway across the mark.

"You've got seven white men murdered up there on the Colville Road and a white girl and a Negress taken captive by Kamiak's Palouses. I'd say that little problem suggested some more academic course of military arithmetic than cross-examining Lieutenant Gaxton's well-known Mason and Dixon morals."

"Oh, you would, would you, you insubordinate devil!"

Bell sensed the keenness with which Stedloe was watching him, and for the first time in his service felt uneasy. And suddenly ashamed. Stedloe was actually one hell of a gentleman. And a damned fine officer. One of the rare ones from the Point who understood and genuinely loved his men.

"Sir"—the towering sergeant's out-size feet seemed all at once to need considerable shifting—"I apologize. And I want you to understand something, Colonel. I haven't been in the ranks all my life and my temper can't seem to remember that. When I get mad, I keep remembering where I'm from, and forgetting where I am. I don't suppose all that makes any sense to you, sir. I'm sorry," Bell finished lamely.

"On the contrary, Sergeant"—Stedloe's warm-eyed reservation brought Bell's glance sharply up from its awkward regard of his boot toes—"in light of what I know about you, it makes a great deal of sense. All the same, I'll appreciate it if you can manage to remember at least to act like a sergeant while you're in my command."

IV

Bell came away from the brief council at Stedloe's tent with his mind spinning. The colonel's implied hint that he knew about Bell's commissioned background would have been enough in itself. But on top of that Stedloe had hammered the rest of it to him and the other open-mouthed members of the grim meeting. Briefly an emergency patrol was to be readied to take the field at once in an effort to find and contact Kamiak and whatever of his forces had Calla Lee captive. That was the

260

main of it and Bell took it that far in good stride. But the details relating to that patrol, its composition and proposed course, were enough to lift the fur off any first sergeant's well-haired belly.

Bell mulled them over now as he bent his long strides for the assembly ground. Even in the short space of the journey through the company street, the sergeant saw and heard enough to let him know that big trouble was overdue to bust its cinch in the Colville column. Company officers and non-coms were already barking and bellowing orders across the growing grayness, and all four companies were beginning to fall into ragged parade dress on the cleared ground between the camp and the river. Without being able to catch a glimpse of their owners, Bell had recognized the vocal trademarks of his three companions: the poodle-sharp accents of Demoix's Bordeaux baritone, the whiskey-burred terrier tones of Harrigan's Donegal tenor, and the swamp-hound bass of Bull Williams's he-cow roar.

Cataloguing the familiar details of the hurried assembly as he went along, Bell put his mind back to the nature and content of Stedloe's forward patrol. The group was to be what the C.O. designated as a "flying column." This force was to consist of ten picked men and mounts from each of the four companies, all four company officers and 1st sergeants figured in addition. The balance of the column would cross over the Snake and follow this forward element as rapidly as possible, 2nd Lieutenant Henry Fanning commanding this reserve. Failing an earlier contact of Kamiak, the forward group would hold up at the Palouse River and wait for the following reserves. Rejoined, the entire force would then press forward with all speed toward the Ingosommen— the treaty line of Kamiak's Palouse domain.

The troopers from Company E, the mounted infantry outfit in charge of the two mountain howitzers, would use double hitches of mules so the artillery would not retard the speed of the reconnaissance patrol, which (of course!) they would accompany. Expressing amazement that the cannon would even be considered for such an action, young Craig, by Bell's hard-bitten estimation one of the two cool heads in Stedloe's command, had been sharply informed that where Lieutenant Colonel Edson Stedloe went, there went his two high-wheeled howitzers. Those two guns were worth a regiment of rifles in any man's Indian campaign—by the Lord, sir!

So the advance patrol was to be a lean, mobile, essentially swift scout force, seeking far out ahead of the main force to find and engage Kamiak in amicable council relevant to returning the captive girl—without unnecessary hostilities! It was that last that put the bitter rime frost of Bell's flash grin to work. Appalled by the entire conception, the gaunt sergeant had restrained himself only with the knowledge that any further outburst on his part might result in his being left with Fanning's group of main reserves.

The one glaring flaw in Stedloe's resolve was the sudden reliance of the whole command upon the recently suspect Timothy. Upon apparently eager information supplied by the Nez Percé, that his people were encamped near Red Wolf Crossing and could supply canoes enough to get such a small force across the Snake immediately, it had been decided to start the patrol at once for Red Wolf, cross over, and strike without delay toward the Palouse—a matter of ninety long miles across entirely hostile, badly gully-cut, brush-choked country. It didn't take too much of a stretch of the sergeant's opinion of Stedloe's staff to cover their being taken with the dash and heroics of such a galloping assignment, complete with captive white princess and faithful Nubian slave women! But that his trusted Timothy had concurred in the insanity, let alone largely promoted it, hit Bell with a swift-rising chill of premonition.

The aroused camp teemed like fire-alarmed ant heap. Troopers, non-coms, officers, horses, mules, baggage and ammunition animals shouted, scurried, bawled, whinnied, and brayed as though the encampment had been lit into by 5,000 unannounced Comanches. Bell, his H Company dragoons picked and mounted in the first twenty minutes, sat his bony bay and waited for the uproar to resolve itself into a lined-out column, his tired mind trying to marshal some order out of the storybook shenanigans of the past hour.

No matter how a man turned and balanced the figures, the answers always came out in dark, red numbers. Out there beyond the Snake—or the Palouse—or the Ingosommen—were Kamiak and the combined forces of the Spokane, Yakima, and Palouse hostiles, a force that Timothy's information had numbered at better than 1,000 seasoned braves. And when the Nez Percé chief said seasoned braves, he wasn't talking about teepee Indians or mission mascots. He was talking about man-grown, hot-tail bucks with not a reservation-bred, tamed-and-saved son in a copper-colored gross of them! And right here, right here under Bell's high-bridged nose, right down there on that river bottom flat, what in God's name was there?

The big sergeant's Indian-wide mouth lifted just the least bit at the left corner. Bell could tell them what there was down there! Forty men, already tired from a week's hard ride. Four company officers, two of them so far separated from twenty-five years of age they couldn't see to that birthday standing on a three-year stepladder. And all four of them, between them, totaling three years less than ten on the frontier! Then a command head who had spent better than half his scant four

264

seasons in the Department of the Pacific riding M.P. detail on old Brigham Young and his half-hearted Saint rebellion down in the Salt Lake Valley. And if that weren't enough to pucker your bladder, you could take a look at what this rescue squad was toting along in the way of self-defense.

In that regard you'd better take the colonel's devastating howitzers, first off. And the best place you could take those beauties, as for any effect they might have on the hostiles, mental or physical, was to the nearest river bluff. With the artillery out of the way, you could reassure yourself with the knowledge that those short pattern muskets with which Fanning's following reserves would be armed could, on a clear day with good light and no wind, speed a ball nearly as far, if not as accurately, as a sick squaw could swing an egg-size rock.

Naturally, you had to be fair and admit that the new Sharps carbines that Bell's H Company had in their saddle boots were nice, long-shooting guns, and dead-accurate as a regular sergeant with a four-ounce quid of longleaf Burley. But when you got through leaving half the ammunition ration at Red Wolf Crossing with Fanning's reserves, you would have along a fine, fat issue of twenty rounds to a trooper. Bell shook his head angrily, the long slant of his jaw descending with disgust.

Looking at the now-completed form of the patrol column below him, his shadowy gray eyes scanned the rank of the waiting soldiers. The cursory examination done, he waved his gloved hand to the silent troopers behind him, started his bay moving toward H Company's position at the head of the column. As he went, the mirthless, flitting grin went with him.

There was your final laugh, by God. In a full field command of 152 enlisted regulars you couldn't pick out forty of them who had done a full hitch. Eighteen of the top-separated cream in Stedloe's dashing emergency force were bare-belly, no-beard boys; first-hitch bottle babies who had never fired a shot in anger in their stable-sweeping lives. A non-com of Bell's hock-leather cut could handily restrain his eagerness to see how they would react to a gut-bucketing charge of rawhide hostiles, firing five shots a minute from under the grass-cutting bellies of their flattened-out paint ponies.

In the leprous gray of the fog-patched morning, Red Wolf Crossing loomed, drear and desolate as the devil's dooryard. The bleakly carved banks of the booming Snake cut like a ragged war-axe slash through the low hills. The rain, a misty drizzle all night, thinned out and stopped, leaving the bare earth and sodden scrub drifting with a ground smoke of humid steam.

On Stedloe's orders, Bell accompanied Jason and Lucas to the Nez Percé camp to make arrangements for the canoes. The word in the Indian camp was uplifting only to the small hairs at the nape of the neck. Until early evening of the previous day a village of 500 of Kamiak's Palouse had been squatting across the river from the Nez Percés. Shortly before dusk three scouts had ridden in from the direction of the main crossing, forded the Snake, and disappeared into the Palouse camp. Minutes later, the hostile teepees had begun to come down and by real darkness there wasn't a Palouse within long coyote call of the Red Wolf Crossing.

Bell bore this disquieting report back to Stedloc along with fifty of Timothy's braves and two dozen of the big Nez Percé cargo canoes. Apparently both delighted with the transport vessels and undismayed by Bell's intelligence, the colonel roused up his resting troopers and with the wordless and watchful-eyed aid of Timothy's canoe men got his patrol across the twisting Snake in a really creditable two hours.

It was now 11:00a.m., Friday, May 14th. An hour was taken at this time to prepare a hot ration for the already fagged troopers. They wolfed it down, remounted, fell into column, and were moving toward the Palouse a handful of minutes past high noon. The belated sun was boring a sweltering hole through the heavy ground mists and eastward toward the land of the Palouse a fair blue sky was beckoning.

Yet, even as the blazing midday dropped behind and the long miles rolled beneath the *clip-clopping* gait of the shod horses, the temper of the sun-sodden patrol rose rather than fell. No matter what else a man of Bell's mind might think about Stedloe's gallant lads, their morale was higher than the price of ice in hell.

Outriding the jogging trot of the column's head, together with Jason and Lucas, Bell took time from wiping the cascading sweat out of his smarting eyes and shifting his aching buttocks in the iron-hard issue saddle, to wonder why. Every sign Timothy had taught him to translate had been reading wrong since leaving the oppressive fogs at Red Wolf Crossing.

For one thing, the tracks of the moving Palouse village, clear and broad at the outset, had shortly split into a dozen different trails, fanning out past the forefront of the advancing patrol like so many crazy coveys of flushed quail. And despite the fact that the big Indian camp could not have had more than a twelve-hour start, there wasn't a living sign that any Palouse was presently within sixty miles of the Snake.

Secondly, although the country toward the Palouse River was as open and easy to read as a hard-shell Baptist prayer book, letting Stedloe's uniformed troops stand out like a colony of blue herons stiffly strutting a bare sandbar, not a local Indian had appeared to ride with the column.

Lastly, Timothy, who had departed alone from the Snake to scout the country ahead of the patrol's advance, had failed to report back, and Jason and Lucas, riding with Bell, had been grunting uneasily in Nez Percé for the past hour. Sum text of their translated gutturals was to the effect that their chief's long black braids were no doubt already drying over the smoke hole of Kamiak's lodge. His lean jaw set, Bell cursed inwardly and at bitter length.

Thus, sawing raggedly between the sergeant's contained profanity and his Nez Percé companions' uncontained dark prophecies, the afternoon wore into early evening, and the early evening in its turn into a picketless and open camp on the banks of Smokle Creek midway between the Snake and the Palouse.

The morning of the 15th brought a gray, cloud-driving dawn and an early, high-spirited start. The flying column was making remarkable time, its excellent progress auguring well for the success of the projected contact with Kamiak.

Noon brought the usual short halt, along with clearing skies and a warmly brilliant sun.

But 2:00p.m. and another ten miles of roughening trail produced a sudden and chilling change in weather. It occurred without the least dimming of the bright May sun or the faintest suspicion of a cotton cloud puff in the bell clearness of the Washington afternoon.

Jason caught the first sign of the weather shift when his roving glance picked up a sun flash from the steepening hills to the column's left. Seconds later Lucas reported a similar phenomenon about two miles beyond the column's head and off to its right.

Nodding abruptly to his Nez Percé companions, the sergeant wheeled his bay and galloped him back to the head of the column. Here he pulled the animal up, saluted Stedloe and Captain Baylor, and delivered his bad news, point-blank.

There were plenty Indians, looking to be Palouse and Spokane, riding abreast of the troop movement and about two miles to its right and left. So far Bell and his Nez Percés had counted twelve small bands, a total of perhaps 100 braves.

Stedloe dutifully called a halt and gathered his youthful command about him. Bell repeated his intelligence and an admirably speedy command decision was forthwith reached to ignore it and march on. One hundred or so curious local Indians riding their flanks and points were nothing to deter forty picked dragoons and two mountain howitzers from continuing their avowed mission of inter-cepting and counseling with Kamiak and his errant Palouses.

Accordingly the patrol resumed its advance, halting only when nightfall and the Palouse River conspired to get in its way. It was into this euphemistic and brightly firelit camp that a slim, mahogany-dark bearer of grim tidings, shadowed by a squat, ugly Coeur D'Alene chief, rode shortly after 9:00p.m.

Timothy went straight to Bell, riding within twenty feet of Colonel Stedloe and his cheroot-puffing, post-supper assembly of command to do so. The properly incensed C.O. sent Corporal Bates galloping after the Nez Percé, but by the time the eager orderly had reached Bell's fire, the sergeant, tagged by the two Indians, was on his bent-kneed way to the command tent.

Bell had heard all he needed in the first string of grunts from his Nez Percé chief of scouts, together with the latter's blunt announcement of his Coeur D'Alene guest's identity, to let him know that Colonel Edson Stedloe's advance patrol was standing ear-deep in redskin-fashioned peril. And in a fair way to strangle for keeps if it made so much as one false move in the face of the deadly situation surrounding it.

V

The scene following Bell's conduction of the two Indians into the midst of Stedloe's officers, and the stark revelations there made by the red men, burned itself as indelibly into the sergeant's memory as had its predecessor subsequent to Timothy's return from the Colville Road massacre. The Nez Percé chief led off by saying he had scouted clear to the Ingosommen in the preceding day and night. There he had noted the gathering of a considerable number of Indians, but due to the presence of constantly arriving war parties had been unable to get in close enough to ascertain whether or not Kamiak had arrived with the captive white woman.

In this tight time and place he had had the great fortune to cross trails again with his old friend, Victor. He had inveigled the Coeur D'Alene into accompanying him back to the soldier camp, while the old man's fellow Coeur D'Alene elder chiefs had gone on into the war camp to spread the word that their chief had accompanied Timothy to the camp of the pony soldiers to arrange peace talks.

With this low-spoken introduction, the Nez Percé stood back for Victor. Studying the Coeur D'Alene chief from his vantage point in the darkness beyond the command tent, Bell nodded gravely. Victor was a short, powerful Indian who, despite his white hair and stooped posture, possessed a vigorous and intense dignity. He was a Christian Indian, Bell knew, one highly trusted and spoken for by Father Joset. Satisfied that Victor would indeed talk without a split in his tongue, Bell waited tensely for him to speak.

"*A'x'otck.*" The Coeur D'Alene addressed the Chinook starting word to the tent shadows that hid Bell before turning his slant eyes on the little circle of white officers and continuing in English: "To begin with, it was Kamiak who burned those wagons and who took that white woman. When you came as he had predicted, with many pony soldiers and dragging the big guns which shoot twice, you made liars of us old men who had told our young braves Kamiak would be wrong and that you would come with good hearts and without many guns."

At this point Bell caught Timothy's quick glance, returned the Nez Percé's silent nod.

"But even so," Victor was continuing, "the young men would not have made war had you stayed on the Colville Road. They wanted to talk peace with you still."

"Oh, hell!" Captain Baylor's hot-eyed interjection burst loudly. "The low-down dirty murderers kill seven innocent white men because they're dying to talk peace! Good God, Colonel, how long are we going to sit here and listen to this lying red heathen?"

"Captain Baylor!" Stedloe's command echoed the captain's angry demand. "I want to hear this Indian out. When he's done, you can exercise your profanity to your heart's desire. Meanwhile, I'll thank you to keep completely quiet. That goes for all of you!" The C.O.'s mild brown eyes were snapping. "Go on, Victor. Captain Baylor apologizes for his lack of courtesy."

Bell looked at Colonel Stedloe, making a mental

reservation to let out the belt of his respect for him one more big notch. For all his sad hound's eyes and drooping mustaches, the Old Man was all man when he needed to be.

"As I was saying," the Coeur D'Alene resumed after touching his left hand to his brow toward the commanding officer in the sign-language gesture of respect, "the young men would have brought the woman to Colville. But then you took these soldiers and these two big guns and you left the Colville Road. So the warriors have been gathering around Kamiak for three suns. They are over there on the Ingosommen right now. In the number of many over a thousand. All armed. All big for war. And so, *x'ol*! To finish the story. Kamiak will keep the white woman now, and tomorrow he will kill the oak leaf chief and all the pony soldiers with him. *LqLa oL'q*! The Palouses will strike and they will win."

When the Coeur D'Alene stepped back, passing his right hand in front of his mouth and downward to signify that he was cutting off his words and had finished, Colonel Stedloe thanked him and turned, solemn-eyed, to his officers. Wasting no word or gesture, he put the Indians' report up for discussion. His staff fell at once to a heated arguing of the patrol's situation, Timothy's and Victor's questionable reliability, the true whereabouts and probable fate of Calla Lee Rainsford, the real intent of Kamiak's hostiles, their actual location, strength. The net result of this one- and two-bar bickering was a split vote.

Captain Oliver Baylor and Lieutenant Wilcey Gaxton held for a continued bold advance toward the Ingosommen with daylight. Captain Harry Winston and Lieutenant Davis Craig voted as firmly for a pat stand on the Palouse until Fanning came up with the main body of troops—a conjunction that should be effected late the next afternoon.

Following this deadlock, Stedloe, speaking in chips-down earnest, revealed for the first time the full headquarters background for his expedition. In brief, he was to make a reconnaissance in force of all the hostile tribes, warning them to come into Colville and peacefully surrender their wanted members, or face the alternative of a full-scale military campaign to force them to do so. Further, that Colonel C.G. Wrightson was even now assembling this punitive force in San Francisco and would follow Stedloe into the field at once, should his power peace threats break down.

By this time, used as he was to the whirlpool confusion of the Army's Indian policy, Bell felt himself beginning to lose contact with the whole drift of the situation. Holy Murphy! It was no wonder the poor red devils couldn't make heads or tails of how they stood with the white brother. Every time some well-meaning missionary or Indian agent would give him a piece of issue beef, the Army would slap it out of his mouth, and then step on his fingers when he reached a hand to pick it up.

Further ruminations along this angry line were interrupted by Craig's aroused rejoinder to his C.O.'s remarkable statement.

"Well, good God, Colonel!"—the young lieutenant was hotter than a baker's apron—"that offer would include Kamiak himself! He has a dozen murder charges standing against him from Indian Agent Boland's on down. Surely you wouldn't expect him to bring his hostiles into Colville for any such idiotic bait as a peace talk based on him and his best friends getting strung up on the nearest cedar!"

"That'll do, Craig. Hysteria isn't going to help us now." Colonel Stedloe, his paternal manner of patience back in firm grip, spoke calmly and reassuringly. "What we're after here is a reasonable decision as to our present danger, if any, and to the situation of Miss Rainsford among the hostile Palouses."

"Well, Colonel," Baylor brought the point of the meeting to hard bearing, "that leaves it right on your oak leaves. Two for. Two against. What do you say?"

"I've got to think, Baylor . . ." Stedloe's voice trailed off in the direction of the wandering indecision in his worried glance. "If only we could know that these Indians are reporting the truth as to the hostile strength. If we could know just that. If there were some sure way of ascertaining . . ."

At this point the colonel's fretful eye fell on the lounging figure of 1st Sergeant Bell. The tall non-com's slate-gray glance pounced on the commander's warm brown one like a duck hawk on a wounded drake. The big hand shifted to the sunburned forehead in the least of flicking salutes. None of the officers caught the gesture save Stedloe, but the relief in his cornered grimace was patent and instant.

"Gentlemen"—the good, crisp authority of the senior officer in command took over—"I'll ask you to give me a few minutes alone. Meantime, get double pickets out at fifty and one hundred yards. Picket all the stock and put every man to sleeping on his carbine. Corporal Bates will have coffee ready in twenty minutes."

The officers departed to leave Stedloe alone with Sergeant Bell and the Indians.

"Begging the colonel's pardon, sir." Bell's deep voice dropped in on the muffled tread of the last of the retreating officers. "I'd like the colonel's permission to make a suggestion."

"Eh, what? Oh, you still there, Bell? Well, well, out with it, man. What's on your mind?"

Stedloe's studied surprise put the big sergeant's flick grin to snaking its caustic way across the wide lips. The old boy would sure never ask an enlisted man for his opinion on a tactical decision, but if there were a spare non-com left over after the junior officers had had their say and fallen flat on their collective cans, that non-com could rightly expect to get himself heard. At any rate he could if he shaded six two with his dirty socks on, had a red-bristle beard and murky gray eyes, and called himself 1st Sergeant Emmett D. Bell.

The sergeant seldom wasted words. He squandered no syllables now with Stedloe. The Palouse war camp was reported to be a bare fifteen miles northeast. Why not send a reliable white observer up there to check the Indians' information? Naturally this was no job for an amateur. The colonel had better send his best man. Sergeant Bell took leave to suggest that his best man was Sergeant Bell.

Since the suggestion, as clearly the big non-com had meant it to, coincided with the column commander's own major worry, Colonel Stedloe agreed at once.

Minutes later, with his staff hastily reassembled, he announced that he was dispatching 1st Sergeant Bell and the Nez Percé, Timothy, on a scout to determine the true strength and location of the hostile forces and, if possible, the whereabouts and welfare of Miss Rainsford. As a concession to Lieutenant Craig's quick suggestion, he also agreed to send Victor back to Kamiak with Stedloe's request for a council next day, terms of such talk to be the immediate release of Miss Rainsford against the column commander's word to retire at once to the Snake.

It was now 10:00p.m. Sergeant Bell had estimated his return at about 2:00a.m. Pending the information brought by this return, the final decision would be taken.

Leaving the stubborn staff still arguing the makeshift arrangement, Bell withdrew. Padding silently behind him, half trotting to match his reaching strides, went his gargoyle-faced followers, Timothy and Jason and Lucas.

With the shadows of their departures scarcely passed, the powdery *ca-lump, ca-lump* of Victor's unshod pony echoed briefly over the premonitory hum of the aroused camp. The Coeur D'Alene chief's bulk hung suspended for a moment between the bat-cave black of the crouching hills and the pale, anxious wink of the camp's watch fires. Then it was gone, swallowed up by the formless felt of the early moon dark.

At his fire, Bell spent a frowning five minutes. Then, having reached his hard-eyed conclusion, he glanced up to where Timothy and his two Nez Percés waited beyond the jumping light of the flames. In response to his gesture, the Nez Percé chief came forward, obediently dogged by the frozen-faced Jason and the grinning Lucas.

Seeing the two following him, Timothy chopped his right hand back and down. "*Me'tx'uit!*" he barked in Chinook. "Stay where you are! Ametsun wants to talk to me."

"Let them come," said Bell quickly. "We're all in this together."

"Just so, Ametsun," acknowledged the Nez Percé. "I only thought you didn't trust my brothers."

"You trust them, don't you?" Bell's sharp question was seconded by his narrowed gaze.

"I trust them," responded the Nez Percé simply.

"*Lka'nax*," growled the white man. "They are chiefs, then."

Saying it, he watched the Indians, seeing from their immediate little nods that he had made the right point. Jason and Lucas came forward to squat beside their chief, the left hands of both going silently from their foreheads toward the white soldier. Bell returned the gesture, fell at once to talking with Timothy.

"All right now, Tamason. You heard the colonel and the officers talking. What do you think about this mess? First off, about our scouting the Palouse camp?"

"There will be no trouble in that. We have scouted together before, you and I. Your skin is white, Ametsun, but your feet are red. We will make no noise."

"Good," grunted the sergeant. "Now then, what about our chances of seeing anything once we are there? Can we get an accurate idea of their strength?"

"Yes. There will be a big council when Victor returns. All will be at the fires, eager to hear what is said."

"How about the girl? Any chance of locating her?"

"Very little."

"All right." The white man's lips flattened. "Tamason, you know I trust you?"

"Yes, Ametsun."

"And that when you said there were a thousand braves in that camp, that I believed you?"

"Yes."

"Well, then, why do you suppose I worked on Colonel Stedloe to let me go up there?"

"I don't suppose, Ametsun. I know."

"Well, am I right, or not?"

"I think you are, my brother."

"That white girl won't have much of a chance if those bucks decide to jump us tomorrow?"

"I believe that."

"And they are going to jump us?"

"Victor says so."

"How about you?"

"I, too."

"All right, then. Do you think we can do it?"

"No."

"Good. I don't like to see a man overconfident." Bell's scum-ice grin touched his mouth corners. "We'd best go right now, then, eh? Before friend Victor gets too far ahead?"

"Yes."

"Good." Bell turned to Timothy's two frowning comrades. "Jason. Lucas. Listen to me. Do you want to do something tonight that your people will be telling your great-grandchildren about, ten times removed?"

The two shrugged, palming their hands, Jason frowning, Lucas grinning wolfishly.

"If we do it, there will be extra pay? Perhaps some old blankets or a team of crippled mules? Many big smiles from the oak leaf chief?" Jason, the elder and more sober of the two scouts, put the queries.

"If we do it, my friend," Bell corrected, "Colonel Stedloe will hang the lot of us from the front gate at Fort Wallowa."

"Oh, well"—Jason palmed his hands again—"in that case, let us be going. You said I was a chief. Would a chief be concerned with a small thing like the displeasure of one pony soldier chief? Or a thousand Palouses?"

"Lucas?" Bell turned quickly to the other brave.

Jason's squat companion spread his loose-lipped grin another six teeth. "This thing you intend to do? It will make Kamiak very happy?"

"Very," Bell assured him. "If we are able to do it, his spirit will be spitting on us from the Land of the Shadows for the next ten thousand moons."

"I'll go." The Nez Percé shrugged. "A little matter of three spotted mares and a prime young Yakima squaw he outdid me on last spring."

Bell was on his feet. "All right, then. Let's get out of here."

"*He'nau'i*," agreed Jason.

The three red men followed Bell to their picketed mounts, the half dozen wire-thin cayuse scrubs that made up the Nez Percés' little string of picked scout ponies. Each was unshod, bare-backed, haltered only by a feather-light horsehair hackamore. The white sergeant looked them over, quickly nodded his satisfaction.

Where these potbellied little brutes were apt to be treading before the night was many hours older would be the last place in Washington Territory for the merry *clink* of a stirrup buckle or the queasing *squeak* of saddle leather.

Swinging up on a steel-blue roan, Bell took the lead ropes of the two spare ponies and guided his little group quickly out and away from the camp, keeping his clouded gray eyes sharply out for Stedloe or any of the junior officers. No time, this, to be answering academic questions about the extra mounts or the unauthorized use of Jason and Lucas.

Well out of the short, stabbing range of the fires, he halted his mount to let the others come abreast of him in the pocky gloom.

"Well, here we go," he muttered tersely. "From

here on, Timothy leads and nobody asks any questions. Is that clear?"

"It's clear, Ametsun." Timothy made the answer for his fellows. "There will be no questions."

In the moment of silence pressing in on the soft heels of the chief's statement, Lucas, the incorrigible, provided the demurrer. "Well, just one small question, cousin," he vouchsafed pleasantly. "Not much of a question, really."

"Well, brother?" The Nez Percé chief didn't keep him waiting. "If you had a mind, what would be in it?"

"Nothing," declared Lucas earnestly. "Really nothing. Just that I don't remember anyone saying what it is we are going to do."

Bell opened his mouth to set the limp-witted member of the expedition straight—found his words blocked by the velvet hand of Timothy's deep bass.

"Oh, nothing, cousin." The Nez Percé chief's tones were in masterly mimicry of his vapid companion's. "Really nothing. Just that Ametsun has it in mind to lift that white girl out of Kamiak's lodge while Victor is making his big peace oration at the council fires."

VI

For the first hour Timothy held the ponies on the rhythmic, mile-rolling lope that is the Northwest cayuse's natural way of going when let out to move as he will. It eats trail dirt at a pace that would choke a thoroughbred in the first forty furlongs.

Fortune and the Nez Percé chief's shrewd boldness also favored their progress. Stedloe's column had been advancing in its northeasterly course along the well-traveled track of the old Lapwai Trail. This broad, relatively level path led on from the Palouse River toward the Ingosommen and the reported hostile camp. Timothy had chosen to guess that the Palouse would have no scouts along the Lapwai at such an hour and date.

Fortunately for the long braids of his two cohorts and for Bell's short stand of auburn scalp stubble, he chose to guess right. The uneasy sergeant had started to ask him if he meant to gallop them right on through Kamiak's teepee flap, when the Nez Percé slid his gelding to a stop. Wasting no least Chinook guttural, the chief laid it out for them, tether-short and tack-sharp.

They were now on the south bank of Otayouse Creek. It was unsafe to follow the main trail any farther, either afoot or ponyback, and unwise to follow any trail farther by the latter means. From here they would make it via soft moccasin and big medicine. Or not at all.

Jason would stay here in the creek clearing, holding the ponies in readiness. Lucas would accompany him and Bell. No, there was no need for concern over the former's addle-pate. The squat one might talk like a fool but he fought like an idiot, and that was what was most apt to count before this night's shade was rolled up by the coming sun. So from where they now stood it was a scant mile and a half up the Otayouse to where it mouthed into the Ingosommen. And from where it mouthed into the Ingosommen a 1st sergeant could conveniently spit into the middle of Kamiak's main council fire.

"*A'kxamit,*" concluded the Nez Percé abruptly. "Do I have your attention, Ametsun? You understand?"

"We sneak this creek a mile and a half, hitting Kamiak's camp where she joins the Ingosommen." Bell kept his recitation grunt-short. "After that we pull up our crotch cloths and turn it over to Choosuklee."

"Amen," echoed the reverent Nez Percé, thus agreeing to the white soldier's use of the Chinook name for his Christian-taught Jesus Christ. "After that it is in His pale hands."

"How about our guns?" asked Bell. "You reckon we ought to leave them here?"

"Aye, leave the guns. The knife has the best tongue for talking in the dark. Just bring the knives."

"*K'a'ya*"—Lucas grinned—"not me. I'll take the stone axe, cousin."

"You'll take what Timothy tells you." Bell broke the order sharply.

"He can take the axe," said Timothy. "Every artist to his own brush. There's no sound to a good stone in a soft skull."

With the words, the Nez Percé chief was turning away through the darkness, heading swiftly up the starlit track of the creekbank sand. Bell fell in behind him, tailed by the bowlegged, gross lump of Lucas's shadow. Indian-file, the three trotted forward through the tunnel-like gloom of the creek timber. There was no more talking now. No questions. No answers. No loose grins. The time for empty smiles and slack tongues was long gone.

Belly down, Bell lay in the beetling brow of scrub pine cresting the river bluff, overlooking Kamiak's war camp on the Ingosommen. The scene below was one of pagan wildness, holding even the irrepressible Lucas in unnatural silence.

The confluence of the Otayouse and the Ingosommen formed an amphitheater of mountain meadow a mile long by half as wide. Shouldering down to the edges of this grassland and probing its ragged fingers out into it, ran the black cloak of jack pine and spruce that formed the continuation of the cover in which Bell and the Nez Percés were presently hidden.

Close below the bluff upon which they lay, the Ingosommen cut the scythe-sharp swath of its course, while directly beneath their hiding place the precipitous gorge of the Otayouse knifed the rearing bluffs. Just beyond the noisy rush of the confluence, not 200 yards from the bluff's base, sprawled the pole-peaked mushrooms of the war camp.

Rough-counting the smoke-dirty apexes of the cowskin cones, Bell caught his breath in mid-intake. Putting the frontier slide rule of red calculus to the number of lodges in that meadow—two adult braves per smoke hole—a man came up with the nape-bristling figure of 1,200 trail-age bucks! The sergeant let his held breath go softly free.

Emmett Bell was a man who liked his odds long and his whiskey strong. In a tight scrape, be it settlement saloon brawl or outpost Indian scout, the sergeant was rarely the one to run a close tally on the opposition before winding up and wading in. Nor did he mind, if that were the way the luck of the evening went, being knocked on his sinewy backside. But holy cripes, 400 to one wasn't precisely his idea of picking a daisy patch to park his butt in!

Pressing his chest deeper still into the pine

needles to blot up the sudden trickle of sweat coursing his breast muscles, he bent his nervous gaze on the milling scene about the spark-ballooning council fire. In a crouching circle, their corded bellies gleaming copper-dull in the bouncing light of the flames, squatted Kamiak's first-line faithful, the 600-odd cobalt- and vermilion-smeared flower of the Palouse tribe. Ranging behind these, stood the remaining 500 to 600 warriors of the Yakima Federation, principally Spokanes and Yakimas with a sprinkling of reservation-jumping Coeur D'Alenes, Klikatats, Pisquose, and Ochechotes. Back of the outermost fringes of this crowding ring, the chosen few squaws selected to accompany and service this restless group waited and watched their war-painted menfolk. There were no oldsters, no children, no papooses. In the center of the flamelit circle, a single Indian faced the sullen ranks of his fellows, gesturing and speaking dramatically.

Watching now, Bell was struck with the preternatural stillness of the listening braves. He had seen just enough treaty talks to know that an Indian crowd had one, constant peculiarity: given words they did not care to hear, they made no vocal sign whatever, squatting like so many dumb lumps of inhuman red clay, not even the dust shuffle of a moving moccasin arising to break the spell of their slant-eyed resentment.

The white man flicked his eyes away from the

scene below, caught Timothy's answering glance as he looked around. Both men nodded, needing no words to convey the common thought—that was Victor speaking down there. And he was speaking to a silence as glass-brittle as wind-carved lake ice.

"Good Lord, Tamason," Bell's hoarse whisper broke excitedly, "how in God's name are we going to get Miss Rainsford and her nigger out of that swarm? There's six hundred lodges down there if there's three, and we don't even know for sure which one they might be in."

"I know which one," said Timothy unexpectedly. "Victor told me. Kamiak is a great one for new squaws. It seems he took a fancy to the black woman. He keeps her constantly in his lodge. And he keeps the white woman there to wait on her." Bell's ferrous laugh interrupted the Indian, making his conclusion come with inquiring dignity: "What is it, Ametsun? Have I said something funny?"

"Only to a damyankee who's lived half his life in the South," muttered the white soldier grimly. "Go on, Timothy. Now all we have to do is guess which one is Kamiak's lodge, and of course"—again the acid laugh—"that's a hair cinch. With only six hundred to choose from, any fool could do it."

"Aye," Lucas broke in, "it's a good thing you have one with you."

"One what?" growled Bell unthinkingly.

"One fool," said the whimsical Nez Percé. "I know which is Kamiak's lodge."

"Which one, cousin?" Timothy's arrow-fast query shot in ahead of Bell's.

"Well, you see he stole this Yakima squaw from me. The one I was telling you about. The young one with the eyes like black stars and the breasts like sun-big melons. *Aii-eee*, those plump . . ."

"*Ho'ntcin*," snapped Timothy, "be quiet, you fool. We want only to know what the lodge looks like, not your Yakima sow's bulging paps."

"I was just telling you," defended the injured Lucas. "I trailed Kamiak down to the Bitter Roots when he took Tsikin. It was there I saw the lodge. It's that big red one down there to the left. Off by itself there, almost in the trees. You see it?"

"I see it," breathed Bell. "And by God, there's our first break. Close to the river. On our side of the camp. And on this side of their damned horse herd. With good pine cover right up to its cussed back poles."

"It's a miracle," announced Timothy soberly. "We might almost do it. Choosuklee has his gentle hands over you, Ametsun."

"Let's hope he keeps them folded," grunted Bell unfeelingly. "Come on, let's get down there."

"One minute," advised the Nez Percé chief. "I want to hear the last of Victor's talk. He is finishing now."

"Hell, don't tell me you're a mind-reader."

Bell's jab was caustic. "We can't hear him from here."

"A hand-reader," replied the chief, straight-faced. "An Indian talks with his hands, always. Even while he's talking with his mouth, too. There, now"—the Nez Percé pointed toward the distant figure—"he's finished. And I can tell you he has spoken the true word as he promised the oak leaf chief."

"And you don't have to tell me what they think of it, either." Bell's rejoinder was burred with disgust. "Even a white man can read *that* silence, brother."

"You're right, Ametsun. Kamiak will talk now and there will be plenty of noise. All for fighting. All for killing the pony soldiers. You'll hear it now, and it will be the big noise. By it we shall know the Palouses mean war."

"Yeah, and by it," said Bell dryly, "you and Lucas and I are going down there and crack that lodge."

"Aye," agreed the Nez Percé, "the noise will cover us like a blanket over signal smoke. There, now. You hear it? That is Kamiak coming forward down there. In the bright red three-point blanket. You see him? You hear that noise, brother?"

Bell's eyes followed the Indian's gesture to focus intently on the tall, strikingly garbed figure of the Palouse leader. And no more had they done so than his ears were bringing him the deep

292

swell of the rolling, angry roar that greeted the hostile chief's appearance.

"*Staq! Staq! Staq! Staq!*" The belly-rumbled cadence of the frenzied chant cannonaded up against the bluff top, unnerving Bell with its thousand-throated savagery, jumping his question at Timothy.

"*Staq?* That's the attack word, isn't it, Tamason?"

"It's the war word," corrected the Nez Percé. "Not just any attack. The *real* word, Ametsun. Let's go now, and may Choosuklee go with us."

"Amen," seconded Bell, fervently borrowing the Christian Nez Percé's trademark rejoinder as he slipped over the bluff top to follow its red originator down the nearly vertical belly of the granite incline.

By the time the sergeant and his slant-eyed companions had dropped down the bluff side, waded the shallow Ingosommen, and wormed their ways through the pine timber to within fifty feet of the rear skins of Kamiak's big lodge, the commotion at the council fire was in full cry. Evidently the hostile leader had made his pitch short and to the lance point, for his followers were already circling to the first drum throbs and throat barks of the *staq* dance.

With the aid of the pine-filtered starlight, Bell could make out the contours of the lodge with little difficulty—at least, with little enough to see they had run into their first rut. In front of the entrance flap, her shadow squatting against the blurred ground line, a lone Indian woman sat guard over Kamiak's new black squaw and her high-born white servant. The sergeant's warning went guardedly to Timothy.

"Damn it to hell, there's a squaw sitting out front there."

"It is nothing," breathed the Nez Percé. "But we must work fast. Others of the squaws may be leaving the dance soon. Lucas and I will take care of that one out there. We will go in now. You count twenty breaths and follow. Go in under the rear skins. Don't look for us. We'll be on watch in front. Get your woman and go out fast."

Bell started his whispered reply, found himself talking to the pine trees. Timothy and Lucas were gone.

Feeling his belly pinch in small and hard as a green persimmon, the white soldier counted his twenty tightly drawn breaths, then went forward, navel flat, through the meadow grass. At the rear of the lodge he paused, listening for any least sound out front.

There was only the night rustle of the river breeze nodding the meadow hay. Slashing downward with the knife, he slit the taut lodge skins and snaked his head and right shoulder inside.

"Who's there? Answer or I'll cry out."

The husky throatiness of the voice drove into the pit of Bell's stomach like an eight-pound war axe, reeling his memory backward across the years, freezing his tongue. Before he could free it a new, harsh voice joined its mistress's.

"Lawd, Lawd, we's done foh now! Oh, missy, Ah jes' cain't stand no moh. Ah's gwine ter yell, missy . . ."

Bell writhed on through the slit skins, his whisper hissing ahead of him: "Shut that old fool up, Miss Rainsford." The fierce command, knifing the teepee gloom, brought a gasp of relieved astonishment from the captive girl.

"Glory be, a white man." The low cry, for all its surprise, was held carefully down, letting Bell know Calla was in good control of herself.

"Sergeant Bell, ma'am. First Dragoons, with Colonel Stedloe. That's Lieutenant Gaxton's outfit, ma'am."

"Lawd Gawd, missy, dem Injuns'll kill us sho now."

"Be quiet, Maybelle. The soldiers have come to take us away."

"Ah ain't gwine ter go. Iffen dem Injuns ketches us sneakin' away, dey gwine ter scalp us sho, jes' like dey warn us. Ah gwine ter start yellin' foh dat ol' Marse Kamiak right now."

"Miss, either you keep that nigger quiet or I'll kill her." Bell's voice fell harshly, the flat anger of fear in it.

"Maybelle."

The white girl's warning was blotted out by a squat shadow looming in the starlight of the teepee opening.

"Tamason says too much noise in here," grunted Lucas, stepping toward the moaning Negress. "He says the black one better rest, now." Bell winced at the sodden *thump* of the war axe. "So now she rests. Let's go, Ametsun."

"Damn you, Lucas. Now we've got to carry that black cow."

"No." The quiet denial came from Timothy, joining Lucas in the flap opening. "The black woman stays here. I can tell by the change in the drums up there that the dance is nearly done. We have only minutes now, Ametsun."

"Damn it, Tamason, we can't just leave her here. She's human, black or white."

"She is safe here," said the Indian, finality in his tones. "Kamiak has taken her to squaw and he will treat her well."

"Sergeant." The white girl's suppressed cry leaped with indignation. "I won't leave Maybelle here. She's going if I do."

Bell's tired mind caught desperately at the sudden shift of the situation. Damn! A man could squat there in that fish-stinking teepee of Kamiak's all night, and, when first light hit those river bluffs over there, he'd still know Timothy was right. That darkie had to stay where she was.

And then, when he'd gotten that far, a man could peer through the lodge dark at the faint bloom of that lovely white face yonder, and know that he couldn't leave the Negress no matter what.

"All right, ma'am." The soft agreement went to the white girl. "Give me your hand, here. Lucas will take your woman." Turning to the silent Timothy, his deep voice dropped lower still. "*Ntaika*, Tamason," he used the formality of the Chinook phrase, "we two are brothers, you and I. That's the way I ask it of you."

"*Iu*," responded the Nez Percé, "I reproach you for your foolishness."

"*Tsk'es*," murmured Bell, "I stoop before you."

Ignoring the white soldier's gratitude, the Nez Percé called softly to his fellow tribesman. "*A'lta*, Lucas. Come, take the black woman and carry her. Go ahead of us, now. By the way of the Otayouse. We'll follow."

With his usual grunted grin, the powerful brave shouldered the unconscious Negress and disappeared back out through the entrance flap.

"Come on." Timothy nodded to Bell. "Bring your woman and let's go. Out the back slit. After me."

With the Nez Percé chief's command, Bell felt the reaching hand of the white girl brush his arm, slide in turn down its sinewed length to fall, cool as a snowflake, into the callused bed of his palm. "Let's go, Sergeant." The murmured laugh was as cool as the touch of the tiny hand. "I haven't a decent thing to wear but I don't suppose we'll be meeting anyone really important."

Timothy led the way across the Ingosommen and into the yawning mouth of the Otayouse's gorge. Here he paused a moment to study the Indian village. The *staq* dance was still in progress, but from its whirling tempo even Bell could guess its end was not long distant now. They had maybe five minutes, no more.

"Choosuklee still has his hands above you," muttered Timothy, putting his words to the thought in Bell's mind. "They haven't missed the woman yet. Let's go while our Lord still shields us."

Bell started to answer in agreement but his words were forestalled by a sudden commotion among the cross-stream dancers. Even at the distance the white soldier could translate all he needed of the screaming squaw's outflung gestures.

"*Yukpa't*," advised Timothy. "Let's depart from this place. That squaw comes from Kamiak's lodge."

"*Yukpa't*, and then some," said Bell grimly. "They'll be running our tracks harder than a hot-nose hound on a grounded 'possum."

"Aye, but it's a good dark night. They'll have to follow our feet with their fingers."

"You reckon we've got a fair chance to make the horses, then?"

"Aye. Unless we stand here talking all night."

"I'm talked out," said Bell. "Let's drift." To the waiting girl he added: "Come on, ma'am. We're going to trot a spell. Do you still want my hand, or can you see the way now?"

"I can see, thank you. The sand seems very white."

Bell liked the way she said it, keeping her voice down and not blubbering like so many women would have. Well, he'd known Calla was tough. And ten parts tomboy. That'd been the reason he'd thought he could get away with the daft idea of snaking her out of Kamiak's camp in the first place. Now, by damn, she'd made good her part of his half-crazy hunch. From here on, it was up to him to do as much for his part of it.

For the next half hour there was no more talk, Timothy forcing the pace along the narrow ribbon of the Otayouse's bank sands.

Behind the trail-watching eyes of the Nez Percé chief, the thoughts of the time and place were galloping at war-pony speed. *Tea! Well enough!* All had gone too easily thus far. Ahead now, just a little way, the horses waited. And beyond them the huddled camp of the pony soldiers. But then what? What would the first sick light of the Ingosommen sun bring to the oak leaf chief and his little band? To the good, brave Ametsun and his quiet young woman? To Jason and to Lucas, and to Timothy, their chief?

The knife-slash of the Nez Percé's mouth twisted grimly with the answer. He had a word for it. A hard, dark, Chinook word. *O'megt.* To be killed. To die. Death.

Behind the silent red man the mind of Calla Lee Rainsford, too, was running desperately. Who was this invisible, deep-voiced Army sergeant? What was he doing up in this god-forsaken country with these two throat-grunting savages? Where were they actually taking her? Toward whom? Or what? Safety? Recapture? Endless, blind flight? Breath sobbing, the white girl fought back the tears of breaking nerve. The even, white teeth ground into the ripe lower lip, the chiseled loveliness of the slender jaw quivering with the effort. Daughter of a regular Army general and service-bred by family clear back to the First Continental Army, Calla Lee Rainsford was damned if she was going to bawl or break down in front of a clay-common, enlisted man and a naked, heathen Indian!

And back of the girl, 1st Sergeant Bell beat back the weariness of five days of forced marching. Choked down the whole, hopeless nightmare of the reëntrance of Calla Lee Rainsford into his life. Forced his mind away from the girl and himself. Drove it back and repeatedly back onto the only thing that could count now—the somehow survival of forty-six white men and one lone, Southern gentlewoman against the renegade Kamiak and his 1,200 war-trailing hostiles.

Any way a man wanted to cut up that little carcass, the butchering was certain to give him plenty to do beyond worrying about what a high-flying Southern belle was going to think when daylight and Stedloe's Palouse River camp let her find out what had really become of her precious 2nd Lieutenant Emmett Devereaux Bellew.

The temporary relief of arriving at the horses to find Jason with all six mounts ready for the trail was abruptly dispelled by the Nez Percé's disclosure that Lucas had not yet come in. Timothy took Bell aside and expressed his fear that the squat buck had deserted, asking nonetheless that Lucas be given a few minutes of grace. Bell had no more than grudged the request than the broad-shouldered brave came shadowing into the creek clearing, explaining that he had heard them on the trail behind him and had thought they might be the Palouses, had accordingly waited for them to go on past before following them in.

Bell turned at once to helping Calla up on the pony that was to follow Timothy's in the traveling order. With the girl safely aboard and moving off after the Nez Percé chief, he stepped back to permit Jason and the others to pass him and fall in behind Calla. Waiting nervously for the Indians and the Negress, he called out to the invisible Jason: "*Ka'ok'o*, Jason! Didn't I tell you to mount that woman up and send her next?"

"Softly, Ametsun," came from Lucas. "She doesn't want to come. She says she is afraid of you."

"I'll make her afraid, damn her charcoal-colored soul!" The sergeant moved back through the gloom until he could make out the figures of the two mounted Nez Percés, and that of Calla's servant, standing motionlessly by her pony.

"Here, you!" The command curled out like a bullwhip. "Get your stubborn black bottom up on that pony. What the hell's the matter with you, Jason?" The angry charge crowded atop the order to the waiting Negress. "You're not getting simple-minded, too, are you? Help that girl onto that pony!"

"No!" The refusal was edged with anger. "That girl doesn't need any help onto any pony!"

Before Bell could make anything of this rebellion, the woman bounded up onto the skittering cayuse in a leg-throwing, graceful way that not even the creek gloom could hide from the startled white man.

"*O'tx'uit*, stay where you are!" snarled Bell. "Who is that woman?"

"Tsikin," answered Lucas with ready pride, "Little Chipmunk, my woman that Kamiak stole from me."

"Where in God's name did you get her?" demanded the amazed Bell. "And where the hell is Miss Rainsford's black girl?"

"Oh, the black one is back there in front of Kamiak's lodge where I left her. I thought as long as I had to carry one of them, I might as well take the one that belonged to me."

"Lucas thought that taking Tsikin would fool Kamiak more than taking the black woman," defended Jason loyally.

"In a pig's eye!" snapped Bell. "He meant to bring this squaw the whole damn' time!"

"Can you blame him so much, Ametsun?" The elder Nez Percé's question dropped softly. "He went with you, unafraid. He loaned you his life when he didn't have to."

Cursing the luck that had put the Nez Percé idiot's heavy-fronted cow on guard this particular night, the white soldier was duly shamed by Jason's velvety reminder.

"I wouldn't have known her in that dark," put in Lucas helpfully, "save for those breasts. *Aii-eee!*"

Ignoring Lucas, Bell addressed his apology to Jason. "It's true what you say, brother. The fool's heart is good. Let's say no more about it. I'll figure out what to do with Little Chipmunk when we get back to camp."

"You won't have to, Ametsun." It was Jason who dropped the little shock into the stillness. "We're not going back to camp. Lucas and I think we'll do you a favor for calling us chiefs. We're going to stay out here in the hills and scout for you. Good bye, Ametsun. Look for us tomorrow."

"Damn your treacherous red souls!"

Bell's choking growl was answered only by the fading hoof clumps of the ponies and by the sodden spatter of the thick Washington dew disturbed by their ghostly passage.

Wheeling his roan, the white sergeant kicked the little beast viciously, sent him scrambling up the main trail after Calla and Timothy. Three minutes later, he pulled in behind the white girl's loping mount.

"Where are the others?" Timothy's call back came at once, his keen red ear counting out the hoof sounds and coming up three ponies short.

"Oh, I sent them around by the other trail to split our track in case Kamiak got to pushing us." The white soldier's too-loud rejoinder came in deliberately light English, and was followed just as deliberately by an angry string of Chinook: "The bastard curs have deserted us. That was Lucas's squaw who was guarding the lodge. He brought her along instead of the black woman. They wouldn't come with me. Said they wanted to stay back and scout for me."

The silence rode in heavily ahead of Timothy's answer. "Perhaps they will at that, Ametsun," he said at last. "They are strange ones, you know. And it is a good idea for somebody to stay back."

"Kick up your pony," grunted the white man. "We've seen the last of those two, or a dead dog doesn't stink."

VII

Bell had told Stedloe they would be back by two. It was more nearly three when they rode down on the smoking fires of the patrol's camp. There would be another hour and a half of murky semidarkness, but the first pallid fingers of the coming light were already feeling their uncertain ways along the eastern crests of the Bitter Roots.

Looking toward the Army encampment, there was little to see save the tendrils of wood smoke from the banked fires. The rest—men, animals, and equipment—lay shrouded in the creeping sop of the river mists. But peering intently through the lessening dark, the fatigued eyes of the sergeant saw something else.

It was one of those tricks of the tired mind wherein the inner thought is mirrored briefly over the outlines of fact. Bell's mind now projected above the eddying Palouse fog a red granite block, slab-like, dull, darkly polished. In the brief moment it stood there, wet and cold in the drizzle of the Washington false dawn, Bell noted the stone-cut symbol of the crossed cavalry sabers above the Gothic lettering of its terse legend.

On this spot, Sunday, the 16th of May, 1858, Lt. Col. Edson Stedloe and his entire command of four company officers and 152 enlisted men of the 1st Dragoons and 9th Infantry were massacred by an overwhelming force of Palouse, Yakima, Spokane, and Coeur D'Alene Indians under the Palouse chief, Kamiak. There were no white survivors.

Bell shook his head, cursing softly. When he looked again, the mists were once more solidly over the river's bend, and Timothy was at his elbow.

"You spoke, Ametsun? You saw something down there? What is it, brother?"

"Nothing . . . I hope," said the white man heavily. "We'd better sing out now. I've no mind to let one of the Old Man's Palouse-happy outposts do Kamiak out of the privilege of drilling me."

"I was just going to suggest it," said the Nez Percé. "We're getting in too close already."

The sergeant reined in his roan, sent his hoarse challenge into the clotted fog: "Hello, the guard! Sergeant Bell here. We're coming in."

"Halt where yez are!"

The muffled counter-charge came with heartening promptness, being followed by Harrigan's familiar thick form together with some further cogent advice: "All right, laddy buck. Let's have that word ag'in!"

"It's me, Bell! You god-damn' flannel-mouth baboon! Get your finger out of that trigger guard and call us on into camp."

"Sarge! Ah, Sarge, bye, it is yez! God bless yez, lad, we thought . . ."

"Quit thinking and take us on in, Mick. My time's shorter than a grizzly's temper."

"Right yez are, Sargint!" His natural relief showed joyously in Harrigan's bellow to the invisible Williams: "Hi, yez there, Bull! Yez broad-beam buffalo! Sarge is back. Pass the word and come up on the double."

Bell could hear the deadened passing of the alert, then the gigantic form of Bull Williams was hulking before them. The brutish non-com groped eagerly to the side of Bell's mount, his great arms reaching up to encircle its rider's waist, the clumsy hands moving up to pat and stroke the sodden chevrons.

"Gosh A'mighty, Sarge! Don't yuh run off on me ag'in. When I heahed yuh had gone up theah among them cussed heathen, I neah had me the . . ."

Bell disengaged himself from the bear crush, reached out to pat the thick shoulder. "Save the fantods, Bull," he said gently. "I'll see you and the boys as soon as I've talked to Stedloe. You look sharp now, boy, and hold this post. Mick's going to take us in." Without waiting for the giant hillman's answer, he called to the Irishman: "All right, Mick! And watch your language this time. We've got a lady with us."

For the first time the two sergeants swung their eyes away from Bell.

"Hail Mary, full of grace," breathed Harrigan, "it *is* a woman. Yez'll forgive me, ma'am. I . . ."

"A lady," Bull's awed stammer unmeaningly corrected his companion. "A honest-to-Gawd white lady."

"It's Calla Lee Rainsford, boys." Bell's dry reply braced the backs of both staring soldiers. "I reckon the Old Man wouldn't want you to keep her waiting."

Following Harrigan through the graying dark, Bell was aware of the passing blobs of huddled soldiers, and of their suppressed, fog-thick comments.

"Jeez, it's Sergeant Bell! He's got back!"

"Yeah, the Injun's with him, too."

"And a woman, too, by God."

"A woman, fer hell's sake?"

"Sure, a woman, dogface. Must be that girl we're after."

"Yuh mean thet Rainsford gal the Palouse grabbed? Naw!"

"Naw, hell. You know any other white females runnin' around loose up here, you cussed bird brain?"

"Jeez!"

"Damn it, Slim, maybe now he's got the girl, we

won't have to fight them lousy hostiles. How the hell you reckon he done it, anyhow?"

"Who the hell cares? He done it, didn't he?"

"*Aw,* sure, he knows all about them stinkin' Injuns. I reckoned he'd bring her back right along."

"You reckoned no such thing, you lyin' jackass."

The voices faded with the anxious shadows of their makers, as the lamplit cone of Stedloe's tent bulked ahead of Bell. Touching Harrigan's shoulder, he murmured quickly: "You take the girl on in, Mick. The Old Man'll want to see her for a minute. I'll hang back till they're done. Understand?"

As Harrigan nodded, Bell turned to Calla, raising his voice.

"You go along with the sergeant now, ma'am. That's Colonel Stedloe's tent yonder."

Before the gruff direction was well out of his mouth, the girl was at his side. Her slim hand found his once more, the warm pressure of its grasp seeming to wrap itself more around his heart than his answering hand.

"Aren't you coming, Sergeant? I'd like to thank you, you know, and I haven't even seen you yet."

Bell pulled back roughly, turning away from his questioner and from the pale light of the lamp now being turned up to new life before Stedloe's tent.

"Go along, ma'am. Have your say with the

colonel and let me have mine. You're wasting time that can mean men's lives." He hadn't meant to put it so hard, wanting only to avoid being with her in the lamplight ahead, and to have her out of the way when he faced Stedloe. "You understand, I guess, ma'am," he finished lamely.

"No, I don't!" she flashed back at him. "There's no point to his fooling around with me when you've got your report to make. Come along, Sergeant"—the pressing hand slid up to his corded bicep—"I want to make my own report to Colonel Stedloe when you've finished yours. And mine'll be about you, soldier."

Bell broke away from her angrily, but Stedloe's face, rumple-haired and sad-eyed, was already swimming through the lamplight.

"What the devil? Is that you, Bell? Get in here, man. Where in God's name have you been?"

Bell's chronically short supply of patience was run out by the C.O.'s irate greeting, and by the realization the growing lamplight had him trapped beyond retreat. His answer came snapping with sarcasm.

"Escorting a guest of Lieutenant Gaxton's down from Colville, sir!" Jaw set, he took the girl's arm and stepped forward into the full light. Hitting one of the dodo-rare, proper braces of his enlisted career, he announced belligerently: "First Sergeant Bell reporting. Miss Calla Lee Rainsford, The Sycamores, Lynchburg."

"Miss Rainsford . . . !" Stedloe's astonished recognition, fast as it started, ran a shaded second to the girl's.

"Emm! Oh, Emm, it's you!"

With the cry Calla's wide eyes ignored the colonel, riveted their unbelieving stare on the yellow-limned swartness of Bell's craggy face, her lithe figure hanging, shock-bound, in its first quick turn of discovery.

Looking for the first time in five years on the charcoal-eyed beauty of the Southern girl, Bell felt the rush of the blood to his temples, the wringing grip of the nerve fist around the core of his belly. His stumbling words came behind the awkward drop of the clouded gray eyes. "Yeah, Cal, I guess it is."

When he had said it, he looked up at her like some gaunt hound who had come home, bottom land muddy, to be caught sneaking past the sacred boundaries of the sitting room rug.

Then she was against him, her hands clutching the rough lapels of his open shirt, her dark head pressing against the bareness of his dirt-streaked chest, the hot tears coursing their channels through the caked trail grime. He stood an instant, confused and vacant-eyed, then his long arms were around her as the short red beard buried itself fiercely in the high pile of her tumbling curls.

"Cal! Cal! Oh, Cal, girl . . ."

Colonel Stedloe, having coughed three times,

turned the momentary twinkle in his brown eyes to sterner measures, and to one of his infrequent, stiff-backed little flights of humor. "Colonel Stedloe to Sergeant Bell. Begging the sergeant's pardon, sir. Did you have a report for me?"

"Yes, sir. Excuse me, Colonel." Bell released he girl and stepped back. "As soon as you say, sir."

Calla moved away from him to meet Stedloe and by the time the latter had delivered his paternal, clumsy hug and formal, forehead kiss, his junior officers were beginning to appear out of the fog and crowd around the embarrassed girl.

What Kamiak's sullen savages had left on Calla of her original gentle womanly attire was something less than white law allowed. Now belatedly aware of this devastating state of undress, the girl pressed her crossed hands to the tattered remnant of the clinging camisole, seeking in small-handed vain to cover the full, half-naked breasts.

Stedloe, throwing his campaign coat hastily over the gleaming, bare shoulders, gave his ogling staffers a few seconds to get rid of their first bursts of curiosity and compliment, then quietly asked the girl to retire to his tent and rest while his officers and he heard Sergeant Bell's urgent report.

With a dazzling smile thrown to the tall non-com over the hungry eyes of the C.O.'s staff, Calla disappeared in obedience to the request, leaving the officers to fall on Bell with their questions.

In the fifteen minutes of hushed discussion following Bell's report, the staff voted the only move it now had—to hold fast to the Palouse River campsite, waiting for Fanning to come up with the main column and gambling, meanwhile, to keep Kamiak off with peace parleys. Timothy was dispatched with an express to Fanning.

Bell came away from the meeting with one satisfaction. Stedloe and his dashing command were at last very aware of their true situation, and of Timothy's real character. But they had learned, too late, that the Nez Percé was one Indian who talked with a tongue as short and straight as a Sharps' shot.

To the east now, as far as fifteen miles or as near as 500 yards, an overwhelming force of aroused hostiles crouched behind the thinning river fog and waited. Crouched and waited for a pitiful few pony soldiers to ride forward. Or backward. Or any way. Or maybe no way at all. Perhaps waiting only for daylight and the lifting of the mist. But waiting. And crouched. And ready to jump.

VIII

With but a lone hour of half darkness remaining between the patrol camp and broad daylight, Bell dismissed any thought of sleep. The sergeant felt his first duty to such an historic occasion was to wash his hair. After all, it wouldn't do for even an improper soldier to allow a lousy Palouse to catch him scaly-headed. If 1st Sergeant Bell's auburn topknot were scheduled to be dangling from Kamiak's scalp belt ere sundown, he'd be damned if it dangled there dirty! And, anyway, it was Sunday and there was a lady in camp.

At the stream he shucked out of his filthy shirt and leggings, soaped himself, lay gratefully back in the gently rinsing backwater of a pine-sheltered sandbar. Ten minutes later, full-stretched in the silence of his tent, the leaden flood of fatigue released by the cool wash of the river waters rose swiftly up and bore him under. When he awoke, it was to the muted ringing of the instinctive alarm system frozen into him by his four winters in the Indian Northwest. From the deeps of exhausted slumber to full consciousness was only the matter of an eye wink to a man who'd been taught to sleep by Nez Percé experts.

"Who's that? Frenchy? Bull? What in tunket time is it?"

314

Even as the questions rolled, Bell's nostrils were expanding to a scent never in the world born of saddle-sweated 1st sergeant. And seconds later his vision, adjusting to the tent gloom, was confirming the hasty diagnosis of his nose.

"Calla! What the devil!"

"Shhh." The warning slid tensely in ahead of the throaty laugh. "Remember your regulations, Sergeant. A general's daughter in enlisted quarters."

He looked at her a long moment, his eyes continuing to push back the semidarkness. "I can remember a lot more than that, Cal." His answer, when it came, matched the low-voiced tension of hers.

"Like when you weren't a sergeant?" she asked quickly. "And wore one bar instead of three stripes?"

"Like when you were seventeen," he answered slowly, "and engaged to Emmett Bellew's best friend."

"Is that all you remember, Emm?"

"I remember when I was a lieutenant," he grunted.

"And I remember," she murmured huskily, "when I was in love with that lieutenant."

"We were kids then, Cal. And crazy, that's all." He said it with the monotone finality of something long gone and best forgotten.

"Are you sure that's all, Emm?"

"That's all," he echoed, the dull tread of

remembered heartache in his tones. "You were engaged to cousin Wilse, remember? And I was the damyankee ingrate making sneak love to his Sunday girl." His anger was out in the open now, hammering at him to hurt this girl who had come so unwanted out of his past, to taunt him with its compounded failures. "So I was in love with you that night," he snarled suddenly. "I did what I could about it. I got out. What more do you want of a man, Calla? To go crawling back to Army tradition eyewash? I made my jump, and, so help me Hanna, I aim to land where it takes me. And on my own two feet."

"I want you to come home with me, Emm." The simple words fell gently, the girl's quiet face backing their appeal.

"Home." The gaunt sergeant's bitterness flared anew. "What home is left for me back there? What can I expect from my kin after what I've done to them?" Softening, the hoarse voice slowed. "When I first met you that night after graduation at the Point, you were engaged to the boy whose father picked me out of a Saint Louie gutter. Who took me into his own house and home like I was a blood son, and broke his heart trying to make a gentleman of me. It wasn't anybody's fault that my mother was the old colonel's only sister, and the low-flying family hussy she apparently was. Nor that all anyone ever knew about my father was that he was a Northern rake hell who left my

316

mother with nothing but me and his name and no marriage license. But it's nobody's fault but my very damn' own that I've become the disreputable, dirty drunk I have. I'm a bastard, Cal, and I've spent the worst part of five years and fifty drums of rotgut whiskey proving it. I think I've done a ringtail job of it, and I don't aim to see you nor anybody else stand in the way of my finishing it. Now, if you still want to play me that dear old 'Home Sweet Home', go ahead and strike up your tune."

"I don't think you heard me, Emm." The girl's clear eyes held his wild ones steadily. "I said I wanted you to come home . . . with me."

"With you?" The words labored through the compressed trap of the wide lips. "Cal, you . . ."

"I don't mean anything else, Emm Bellew." The interruption came, chin-high and half-defiant. "I wish to glory you had half the sense about women your cousin Wilse has! He and I broke our engagement right after you disappeared. I told him about you, right off. He took it without a peep, being a real Gaxton. When he was assigned out here, he kept mum about you a long time. Finally, last month, he wrote me you were here. Said he'd been trying to straighten you out. Had been waiting for you to . . . to . . ."

"To sober up and turn myself in as a deserter," Bell broke in bluntly. "Is that it, Cal?"

"Yes . . . oh, Emm!"

"Save it, Cal. He'd have had a longer wait than Lot looking back at his wife."

"I got Dad and Colonel Gaxton to pull their rank," the girl was continuing, ignoring his acid retort, "and get me Army transportation past Salt Lake. When I knew you were here, I had to come. The others all want you back, Emm. But I just want you. They've had you before. I never have. And I do . . . now."

With the dropping murmur of the last word, Calla moved a step away from the tent entrance, partly raising her arms toward the soldier, pausing in mid-stride, her lips parted in that Mona Lisa smile that has invited men to madness since the year one.

Bell, letting his head settle forward, put his eyes to drinking of the waiting girl like a tall horse that had been long without water. Calla Lee Rainsford was twenty-two, tall, full-figured, graceful as a willow wand in moving water. Her hair, tumbling in deep waves past her shoulders, was night-black, soft and summery as an August wind. An ivory-skinned woman, her face had about it the oddly pagan look of an Inca altar carving. Under the low forehead heavy lashes swept the long slant of the brilliant eyes. The nose was short and fine, the mouth full and wide, the chin firm. It was a face to hit a man's heart with a jolt that would carry clear past his bent knees.

"Come away from that flap, Cal. Let it drop."

Bell didn't hear his own voice, the order falling harshly as his eyes kept drinking.

Her body, erect as a drummer boy's, seemed yet to consist of nothing but crouching lines. Like a startled cat's. The coarse Army coat, draping from the rounded shoulders, was fastened high at the throat, seeming to hide all, yet hiding nothing, every sensuous line of the moving body beneath it being seized and sculptured by the rough cloth.

"Come on, Cal. Move in here. To me."

"Emm, oh, Emm." Deep, that voice, and wild. As mountain water around satiny rocks. Putting a man's blood to pounding like Cheyenne drums.

He stepped back as she swept toward him, still not directing his actions, his clouded eyes following the sway of her body. At the contact, the warmth of her came to him through his clothes.

Moving to meet her, arms spread, his nostrils were all at once full of the heated, fresh smell of her. And then he had hold of her. Their locked bodies surged back, the force of him throwing her against the giving slope of the tent wall, backward and down.

With a muffled cry she fought him furiously, twisting one arm across his straining face to hold him from her, the fierce motion breaking the blanket pin at the throat of the Army coat, flaring the crude garment, bursting one of the full breasts into curving half view.

Bell, his slitted eyes widening, dropped his

hands slowly from behind the girl's back. In the tiny second of freedom this allowed, Calla writhed back and away, the snake-swift blow of her flattened hand smashing across Bell's flushed cheek as she did so.

He stood a moment, swaying and growling like an angry bear, one hand moving in awkward, abstract motions across his distorted jaw. Then the livid white of the anger gave way to the dark rush of the shame, and the moving hand dropped away from his face to hang motionlessly.

"I'm sorry, Cal girl." The voice was thick with control. "I'm not your boy any more. I'm crazy like this now. No good to you, nor anybody. Get out of here and don't come back . . . ever. You hear, girl?"

She was turning now, clutching the torn coat savagely, reaching for the opening, her acknowledgment coming wrapped in an angrily deep husk of bitter humility. "Never, Emm! Not ever as long as I live!"

Pulling back the flap, she stood framed for a moment in the growing grayness of the dawn, her black eyes once more sweeping across the tent. Only for an instant she let them linger on the fist-clenched, head-hung figure, her glance dropping hopelessly, nonetheless, even in the brief moment of its stricken accusation.

She was gone, then, for all his belated, stumbling rush to the tent entrance and the intense, tongue-tied humbleness of his tardy urge to cry out after her. She was gone, and in her place was only the grim light of the growing day. The grim light and the swift-mounting stir of the awakening camp. The stir and the jarring return to hard reality it brought to the harassed Bell. The reality of the day and of its somber date.

Sunday, May 16th, 1858. End of the Indian Trail for Lieutenant Colonel E.S. Stedloe and his rash-dashing, forty-man command.

IX

Moving like blue-gray ghosts, Bell and Lieutenant Craig shadowed forward under the patchy cover of the lifting river mists. At the outer picket post 200 yards across the Palouse they found Harrigan and Williams in good spirits. The two sergeants had shared the watch since 2:00a.m., hadn't heard so much as a pony whicker or a bird whistle to indicate there was an unfriendly Indian within owlhoot distance of Stedloe's stalled patrol. The bland assurance was no sooner uttered than the raucous, barking cry of a startled magpie shattered the morning stillness.

"So help me, Sarge"—Harrigan's grin went to Bell—"that's the first bloomin' thrush we've heard the whole of the bloody night."

"Shut up," grunted Bell. "That's a human thrush."

"What is it, Emmett?" Craig's low query came as his eyes trailed Bell's to a quarter mile distant thicket of lodgepole pine. "Palouse?"

"Nez Percé," said the sergeant, following his short growl with a staccato echo of the alarmed bird cry that had his companions looking at him in head-shaking wonderment. Was there no end to this bad-tempered non-com's talents?

Before any of them could put words to their admiration, however, Bell's chattered answer was being picked up by the hidden songster up the trail. After another short-bursting magpie reply from the sergeant's side of the harsh exchange, the big man turned abruptly to Craig.

"I don't know who it is over there, Lieutenant, but I've given him the all clear to ride out. We'll see in a minute. It'll be a Nez Percé, one way or another."

The fulfillment of Bell's prophecy brought a grunt of surprise even from him. "I'll be damned to hell, Lieutenant. It's Jason."

"Our Nez Percé?" asked Craig, quietly eying the Indian horseman's galloping approach.

"Our Nez Percé." Bell nodded. "Chalk me with a clean miss. I thought the red son was long gone."

Jason's iron-faced report removed whatever trace of starch might have been left among the members of the forward post. Kamiak and his hostiles were slowly riding the Lapwai not half an hour behind the Nez Percé. They would be up to the river in a matter of minutes.

How was that? Were they painted? Oh, yes, they were painted, all right. What colors? Charcoal and ochre, of course. What had Ametsun expected? Clean colors?

"Black and yellow," Bell asided grimly to Craig. "That's their war colors, Lieutenant. We'd best pull back across, *pronto*."

The brassy thin echoes of "First Call" were still bouncing back from the cross-river hills when Bell and his company commander hurried up to Stedloe with their relay of Jason's information. The command was already assembled at the colonel's tent and began at once to interrogate the returned Nez Percé. Their queries added nothing to what the Indian had told Bell and Craig until the former tacked a brusque demand onto the staff's questions.

What, the lean sergeant growled, the hell had become of Lucas?

Jason's reply, although failing to entertain the anxious staff, put Bell's grin to smearing his wide mouth. The feather-headed one, Jason vouchsafed, had made a gall-bitter discovery shortly after they had parted company with Ametsun. Little Chipmunk had not been wasting her talents in Kamiak's teepee. Already she was seven moons gone to the Palouse chief's noble cover. Pro-foundly moved, Lucas had knocked the Yakima squaw off her pony with the haft of his axe, commended her to hell and the back trail to Kamiak's camp, and taken off with the spare mount in the general direction of the Snake, suddenly overwhelmed with the idea of riding back to the main column of pony soldiers to acquaint them with the fact 1,000 or so of his red-skinned relatives had his friend and fellow chief, Ametsun Bell, pretty well snowed under at the main crossing of the Palouse.

For the benefit of the nerve-tight staff, Bell put face value to this unexpected show of loyalty, estimating it might easily mean an unhoped-for early arrival of Fanning and the reserves—perhaps (stretching the perhaps mightily) as early as late forenoon. In any event the command could use it as a bargaining point when Kamiak showed up across the river. Providing no more time was squandered deploying the forty Sharps carbines along the near side of that sluggish watercourse.

Openly and unabashedly consulted by Stedloe, backed by the agreeing head nods of Craig and Winston and the annoyed grimaces of Baylor and Gaxton, as to the best disposition for the troops, Bell had some short suggestions, all of which were at once put into effect.

This was a question of Indian play, now. Of white man's bluff. And red man's bet. Of Palouse poker, with Kamiak showing four cards to a flush on the board and Bell playing a lone ace in the hole named Fanning. "According to Academy" and "West Point Hoyle" were deep in the discard. If a long 1,000 hard-gambling hostiles were to be backed down, even for a few hours, it would be by the quirky rules of a shuffle they understood and could answer to. And that shuffle wasn't in Army American. Nor King's English. It was in Five Tribes, bastard Chinook. And Bell alone could deal in that language.

Accordingly, the scowls of Gaxton and Baylor to the contrary, the white table was set to the sergeant's bob-tailed orders. On either side of Stedloe's tent, which was pitched in the center of the tiny, half-moon meadow fronting the crossing, the mounted troopers were stationed at regular ten-foot intervals, the short, dull-gleaming barrels of their carbines unbooted and lain athwart their horses' withers. The four company officers and their sergeants, also mounted, were stationed slightly in advance of their respective commands. In the center of this thin, resolute circle, ten feet in front of the dropped flaps of his tent, Stedloe took his nervous ease in the lonely isolation of his omnipresent camp chair. Flanking him, right and left, stood Bell and Jason, their hackamored Nez Percé ponies drooping listlessly behind them.

Glancing quickly over the tight-jawed array, Bell knew he had done what little he could to copper his lone ace. The idea, always with Indians, was the big face. Bold. Quiet. Ready.

Beyond that, a man could know that having Calla out of sight in the tent might help somewhat, and even a bad lot like Kamiak would think three times before front-charging forty picked white rifles in broad daylight.

After bolstering his belly with those three little bites, a man could only pull up his belt and hope Kamiak wouldn't be late for breakfast. He wasn't.

The white sergeant could sense the hypnotic effect his bald effrontery was having upon the watching troops. Not a man or a mount moved in the frozen line, all eyes, human and animal, being bent unblinkingly on the striking figure of the infamous Palouse.

Bell's wolf-wide mouth pulled down at the corners in a passing grimace of understanding. Striking was scarcely the word for that Indian. Six three if he were an inch, the hostile messiah towered over the short statures of his retainers. His shoulders were as wide as Bell's, his belly as flat and muscle ridgey. His head, high-held and hawk-lean as a Hunkpapa Sioux's, featured a mouth that appeared to hinge somewhere behind the small, flat ears, a tremendous, arching nose made unlovely by God to begin with and subsequently laid half over toward his left cheek by a deep lance slash, and an undershot jaw as long and sharp-hooked as a steelhead salmon's. As for costume, save for a cartwheel war bonnet, elk-skin breechclout and moccasins, and the blood-red three-point blanket carelessly draping his Appaloosa stud's withers, he was as naked as the day that witnessed the grim accident of his birth.

His two companions were lesser men by far, and at the distance offered nothing of note in appearance.

"Kenoukin. Kenoukin." Jason's excited whisper at his elbow turned Bell's eyes from the advancing hostiles. "That's Kenoukin, Ametsun."

"I saw him last night, brother," Bell acknowledged. "Thanks just the same."

Then the sergeant stepped forward, his voice booming ahead of his upflung arm. "*O'txuit!* Stand where you are! How do you come now? And don't lie. I can read the color of your paint."

"*Palau!*" responded Kamiak, checking his gaudy stallion, his voice heavy as summer thunder. "We come to talk!"

"Talk English, then," advised Bell, straight-faced. "My chief doesn't hear Chinook."

"All right," Kamiak complied with the requested tongue, "we're coming, now."

"*L'taqt,*" remonstrated Bell, cutting his hand sharply downward. "We'll meet you over there. And look well, meantime, on these guns we have." Bell referred to the carbines, Stedloe's beloved howitzers having been put carefully out of sight on his express insistence. "They're the new ones that look short and shoot long."

"I see them," answered the Palouse. "They look like fine guns."

Ignoring the hostile leader, Bell's short words went to the colonel. "Come on, sir. Here's where we face the red scut down."

"I hope you know what you're doing, man." The C.O. was taking his horse from Jason with the statement. "I don't like to put the river between us and our rifle line."

"The hell with what I'm doing," grunted Bell, gesturing toward Kamiak. "It's what he's doing that'll cut the beef for this barbecue."

But when Kamiak had said he'd come to talk, he'd been stating the literal fact. After half an hour of politely cautious pointing and counter-pointing with the Palouse chief, Bell had heard nothing but a wordy, boastful jumble of the latter's prowess in war, and a routine rehash of all the wrongs any white man had ever done any Indian. At last, the sergeant turned to the chief's gargoyle-silent henchmen in a last effort to learn something.

The first of these was an elderly, quiet-faced Spokane, accoutered with the occupational foofaraw of a tribal medicine man. He was a pleasant-looking, sane-eyed sort of a fellow and, to Bell's slight relief, wearing the cobalt and chalk-white paint of a man of peace. He replied to the sergeant's question as to what he was doing on this ground by addressing himself, quite properly, to Stedloe. His people, he said, had been informed that the soldiers had come into their lands to make war upon them. And if this, indeed, were their purpose, the Spokanes were prepared to fight.

Stedloe answered carefully that he had come into their country for the purpose of passing through it on his way to Colville, where he had hoped to meet them all and to have talks that would terminate in a firmer rule of friendship for all—white and red.

The medicine man smiled and nodded, raising his left hand toward the colonel. This was good talk and he heard it. He would tell his people.

Encouraged, Bell turned to the third Indian. As he did, Jason touched his arm.

"That's a real bad Indian, Ametsun. Watch that one. His name is Malkapsi. Under that shirt his heart is black as a dead bear's liver."

Bell took a second, long look at his man. Malkapsi was a Coeur D'Alene, a young, bone-thin warrior and, by his trappings, a chicf of standing. With a face narrow enough to pass for an axe blade on a cloudy night, eyes as puffy and oblique as an Eskimo's, lips as thin and bloodless as a day-old knife cut, and a receding chin that exposed a set of yellow, hand-filed upper teeth, the Coeur D'Alene chief was patently no less than Jason had named him—a real bad Indian.

Bad Indian or no, he was a good talker. The words flowed out of him, thick and bitter as gall

329

bile. What had the Indians done to the soldiers that the soldiers should come now to seek them? If the soldiers were going to Colville, why did they not take the main road? If they had done so, not one of the Indians would then think of molesting them. Why did they go to cross the Snake so high up? Why direct themselves, then, upon the remote places where the Indians were only peaceably occupied in digging their winter roots? Was it the Indians who had been to seek the soldiers or the soldiers who had come to fall upon the Indians with their two big cannon? Let your chief answer those questions, tall man with the red hair!

Bell didn't play to the rising passion in the Coeur D'Alene's charges. Wheeling his horse, he saluted Stedloe.

"I'm afraid that's it, Colonel. You can see what they've got in mind. I think we may as well go back."

"I agree, Bell. Tell them we shall talk again when the priest, there, has kept his promise to take my word to his people."

Turning to the Indians, the sergeant gave them Stedloe's directions. The Spokane medicine man nodded soberly. Kamiak said nothing, only continuing to look over the heads of Bell and his fellows toward the cross-river line of rifles. Malkapsi at once began to curse and threaten.

Bell put his horse's shoulder into that of the

Indian's cayuse, leaned in his saddle until his square jaw was a scant foot from the Coeur D'Alene's snaggled teeth.

"Do you know me, Malkapsi? Ever hear talk of me from the Nez Percés? Ametsun Bell?"

The Indian shifted his glance, hawking after a sullen moment to spit disdainfully into the ground in front of Bell's mount. "I've heard you don't talk much. That's a bad joke. You wander on like a homesick squaw."

"Did you ever hear I don't lie?"

"Perhaps."

"Well, hear this then," the white soldier said. "I've heard you're a real bad Indian. That you carry lies to Kenuokin and the Palouses about the white soldiers. I've heard this, and see that you remember it when the medicine man is speaking Colonel Stedloe's true words to the Spokanes."

"I hear you, Redbeard," sneered the Coeur D'Alene, "but what are you saying?"

Bell looked at him steadily, the opaque dullness of his eyes holding the nervous brightness of the Indian's. "I am saying that, if fighting comes of our talk here, I myself will kill you for it."

With the warning, Bell gave Kamiak and Malkapsi his broad back to look at, while touching his forehead to the Spokane medicine man. "Good bye, father. May your tongue be strong. There's no winner in a bad war."

The three Indians were still sitting their ponies, slant gazes tracking the white men and the Nez Percé in motionless quiet as Stedloe, Bell, and Jason put their mounts splashing back across the murky Palouse.

X

On their return to camp, Stedloe at once ordered the troops to dig in and prepare to stand where they were. With the men at work on a line of shallow rifle pits facing the river, Bell asked permission to take Jason and scout back along the line of approach Fanning must take, hoping thus to determine the proximity of the relief column and to ascertain whether any considerable hostile bands had gotten between that force and the forward patrol.

Permission granted, the big sergeant and the owl-sober Nez Percé swung up on their raunchy cayuses and departed. Half an hour later they were sitting their lathered mounts atop a three-mile rise and gazing southwest at as fine a sight as ever regular sergeant and native scout laid longing eyes to.

A mile beyond their ridge, moving at a brisk canter, the climbing sun flashing off musket barrel and harness metal, the maroon and white guidon of the 1st Dragoons snapping, color to color, with the Stars and Stripes, came 2nd Lieutenant Henry B. Fanning and the tight-ranked balance of Stedloe's Colville column.

Dispatching Jason to bear the news to the river camp, Bell rode down and joined the column. After giving the brief details of Stedloe's position to Fanning, he asked about the lieutenant's trip up from the Snake. The young officer, a quartermaster of supply by experience and hence no very able informant, reported no signs of Indians on his advance along the patrol's track. His advanced position was due to a warning a band of Nez Percés from Red Wolf Crossing had brought into his first night's camp out of the Snake, a warning that the whole country beyond the Palouse was aswarm with Kamiak's hostiles.

The night just previous, about 4:00a.m., the Nez Percé, Lucas, had found their camp with the news of the patrol's grave situation. Camp had been broken at once and the march resumed through the morning darkness. An hour later the other Indian, Timothy, had found them.

At this point the Nez Percé chief had taken over the guiding of the column and the other Indian had dashed off down the back trail toward the Snake. Timothy had disappeared ahead of them with daylight, had been seen no more since.

This conversation was no more than concluded when the missing chief rode into sight. Bell at once rode to meet him, the two of them swinging back, north, to outride the relief column's head. From the Nez Percé, Bell learned that Lucas had been dispatched to gather a force of Timothy's Red Wolf Nez Percés, and to guide them forward with all speed "to aid the pony soldiers and make liars of those who whispered the Nez Percés sought to destroy their white friends." He had also instructed Lucas to send three Nez Percé riders to Fort Wallowa with the news of Stedloe's peril.

Bell grunted softly when the chief finished. "*Lax-o'ita,* my brother. We shall do to ride together, you and I. You have done well."

The Nez Percé looked at him quickly, his slitted eyes flicking from Bell back to the column head with the slight gesture of his shoulder rearward. "I follow that flag, Ametsun. That's all. Now it's in a very bad place but I am still with it."

Riding a little way in silence, Bell turned to the Nez Percé chief. "I've never asked you, Tamason, but maybe I won't get another chance. What do you see in that flag? You've spoken of it enough for me to know that, when you look at it, you see more there than your brothers."

The chief didn't answer immediately, letting his little pony pick its own way up the dusty track while his slant eyes moved ahead, up and away and far beyond the long-rolling ridges.

"Well, Ametsun, you can't blame my brothers. When they look on that gay banner of the pony soldiers, they don't see what I do. They have no eyes for that bright cloth on its round-topped lance haft. They can't feel the blood and the snow of its stripes. They can't touch the deep blue of its sky or reach the bright glitter of its stars. Well, *wuska*, let that be the end of it. If they can't see the flag, how can they follow it? But I can see it. I have always seen it. From the day the old chief, Menitoose, my father who walked with Lewis and Clark, drew its design and color upon my first boyhood shield, I have seen it. The old man bade me take the emblem and walk behind it with its image in my eyes for all the days of my life. I have done that bidding. Where that flag goes, Tamason will follow it."

The white man, embarrassed by the Indian's simple faith and by the childish statement of its context, tried to make his hard grin lighten the sudden, strange sense of inferiority he felt to this half-naked savage. "You're a good Christian, Timothy. . . ."

"Aye, Choosuklee is my Lord."

"Well"—Bell's grin widened—"you're going to have to follow that blessed bunting of yours farther than your Lord might like."

"And where is that, Ametsun?"

"To hell, brother," answered the tall sergeant softly. "Because that's where it's going to lead you. And before ever another sun sets on it, too."

"Amen." The Nez Percé nodded, kicking up his pony. "Choosuklee will show me the way."

• • •

An hour later, with the command rejoined at Palouse Crossing, a decision was hastily reached to attempt to push on to a more defensible position before Kamiak could argue his way past the peace efforts of the old Spokane medicine man. In this regard the objective was a small lake described by Timothy as being five miles up the main road of the Lapwai and a mile west of that broad trail. Beyond that point the Lapwai entered a rocky defile of some length, offering a perfect trap for a hostile ambush.

The column march was hence resumed, the first slow hour bringing the nervous troops to within sight of the defile named by Timothy as the point of turning toward the lake. And bringing them within sight of something else, too. Something that put the saddle sweat to streaming down every horse-clamping leg in the command. Bell, leading the column with Timothy and Jason, caught the warning metal flashings and feather sproutings only a breath behind his two red companions. His abrupt back wave was picked up by Stedloe and relayed to the close-following column. With the troops halted, the colonel and his staff rode forward to Bell's position.

"What is it, Sergeant?" The C.O.'s edgy question followed his peering eyes. "I do wish the red devils would show themselves soon. This waiting is intolerable."

"Keep your eyes peeled, Colonel," the sergeant admonished, nodding toward the shouldering walls of the defile. "You'll get your wish quick enough. They're clotted up in those rocks thicker'n tick birds on a bull's bottom."

"Damn it, Bell, I can't see a blessed thing!"

"You will." The lanky non-com shrugged. "Timothy had them pegged. If we'd gone into that slot yonder, they'd have been as all over us as squaws on an issue beef. They'll pour out of there in a minute heavier'n a winter rain in Portland."

The sergeant had no more than predicted the red storm than it broke under a thunder of war screams and startled pony neighs that had the dirtiest face in the command looking whiter than a newly washed baby's backside.

"Tell the troops to hold their fire, Colonel," Bell's low call went to Stedloe. "This is a bluff charge. Nerve stuff. They always pull at least one. Tell the men to hold off till they're under a hundred yards. If they pass that, give them everything at once."

"Relay that order, Baylor!" The C.O.'s command jumped instantly. "You go with him, Wilcey. Craig and Winston stay with us."

By the time the two officers had reached the troops with the bellowed warning, the rocks around the defile's mouth had spewed forth no less than 500 howling warriors, the van of which was now not over 200 yards from Bell and his advance group. It looked for the moment as though Stedloe and his 150 adventurers would be swallowed up in one vast, gulping bite. But Bell had gauged the Indian appetite for soldier meat almost to the foot. One hundred and twenty-five yards from the waiting white troops, fifty from the advanced Stedloe, the front line of charging hostiles pulled their galloping cayuses to a rock-showering halt, the following hundreds piling up behind them like an angry red wave dashing headlong against the thin dike of feathered rocks in front of them. Behind these, moving their ponies out from the screen of the hillside rocks, sitting them in full and silent view, another 700 or 800 savages were now visible.

"Let them stew a minute," advised Bell tersely. "They're not set to fight just yet or the others wouldn't have hung back there on the hill. They still want to palaver."

Implementing the sergeant's claim, a dozen gorgeously painted chiefs rode forward to within thirty yards of Stedloe and his group. "Spokanes," asided Bell. "Now we'll hear how loud that old medicine man talked."

The ensuing parley followed the precise pattern of the earlier meeting with Kamiak, Stedloe replying to the same questions as to his presence with the exact straightforward answers he had given before. The Spokanes, either satisfied or feigning satisfaction, advised the commander that while his words were reassuring they could not at the same time allow his soldiers to proceed to the Spokane River, the boundary of their tribal lands. Stedloe replied he had no such intention, was only moving to better water for his many pack animals, and would turn back the next morning.

The Indians again seemed content and began waving back the results of their parley to the waiting hundreds on the hillside. The pony soldiers were turning back. They sought only friendship and a council, not a fight. They had come into this land only because they had lost their true way to Colville. It was even as the medicine man had said. The white chief's words had a good sound. What had Kamiak to say?

Apparently Kamiak had more than a little. No sooner had the hopeful trend of the talk been hand-signed to them, than the Palouse chief and his Coeur D'Alene lieutenant, Malkapsi, began to gallop the front of the restless warrior line, haranguing the painted braves to cover their ears and not to listen. In response to their barking exhortations the packed ranks of their followers began the chant that had blossomed Bell's spine with perspiration the night before.

"*Staq! Staq! Staq! Staq!*"

"Good Lord! What a beastly sound! What is it they're yelling about now, Bell?"

"War, Colonel. They're going to fight, sir. *Staq* is the last word on the subject, Timothy tells me.

We're wasting our time and risking our precious necks up here as from right now."

Stedloe nodded, turning to the Spokane chiefs. "You talk of peace while your brothers shout for war. Go back and tell them we'll fight. But tell them we still want peace. Tell them they'll fire the first shot."

The white truce party returned at once to the waiting troops, and Stedloe solemnly instructed his command that they would have to fight. Since the ground they were on was badly suited for a stand, every effort would now be made to reach and take a strong position on Timothy's lake. Not a man was to return the hostile fire until given orders to do so.

The troops turned at once to the left and west, pushing up the rising, broken ground between them and the water. During this tedious and exposed advance, the whole, boiling mass of the hostiles foamed along the right flank a scant 100 yards out, taking the opportunity to dazzle the white soldiers with their superb horsemanship and to acquaint them with the fact they had ammunition to burn and first-class rifles to burn it through.

No fire was directed into the troops during this time, all of the considerable volume of the hostile fusillade being thrown over the command's line of march, along with the bitter torrent of Indian invective and insult that Bell knew to be such a part of the red man's mental buildup to the climactic charge. And sneer as he might personally at such heathen yelling and screaming, the sergeant had only to look about him to see the effect it was having on Stedloe's column. Having done most of his life's reading from the open books of men's faces, Bell didn't need glasses to translate chapter and verse from the chalk-white pages hurrying past him as he outrode the flank of the retreating force. General Panic wasn't in command here, yet, but he was taking a man a minute away from Lieutenant Colonel E.S. Stedloe—even before Surgeon Randall had swabbed his fuming nitric acid into the first bullet furrow.

Notwithstanding the gross and growing fear of the men, the lake was reached without further incident. Stedloe at once arranged his companies in defensive order with their backs to the water, the entire command remaining mounted and arms at the ready. The two howitzers were wheeled into position and stripped, the pack and ammunition mules, now crazed with the Indian pony smell, being herded close and hard-picketed behind the outer line of nostril-flaring dragoon horses.

At this point, the crowding, solid ring of the Indian lines parted to let the familiar, hatchet-headed form of Malkapsi through. The renegade Coeur D'Alene wanted to inform the white chief that his lies had failed. The Spokanes had lost their case. None of the others believed that the soldiers came in peace with two big guns and this far off the Colville Road. Furthermore, far from being satisfied with the column's turning back short of the Spokane River, large hostile forces were even now racing to cut it off from the Snake River. The white soldiers were penned up like pigs, and they were going to die that way. Slashed through their pale, hairy throats with clean Indian steel!

As the Coeur D'Alene's flamboyant diatribe rose to its full pitch and flower of phrase, another figure rode up to join it from the hostile ranks.

Bell, sitting his mount alongside Timothy, muttered to the Nez Percé: "That's the medicine man who talked peace with us earlier. I thought he talked straight then."

"He probably did," said Timothy. "That's Qoe'lgoel, The Owl. A good Indian, Ametsun. But what's one owl among a thousand fish hawks?"

"Damn it to hell, Tamason, what do you suppose is keeping them off of us? They could have cut us to pieces two hours ago!"

"Who can say? Perhaps it's the day."

"Where the hell's the day figure into it?"

"You've forgotten, Ametsun."

"The hell! It's the Sixteenth. What's that got to do with the price of pony soldier scalps?"

"Sunday." The Nez Percé nodded soberly. "The Lord's Day, Ametsun."

"Thank God," murmured the sergeant with fervent irony. "I'd plumb forgotten. So help me, Timothy, I think you're getting limp-witted in your old age!"

"Don't thank our Lord like that, Ametsun. He's still riding with us. You'll see."

Bell, readying another impious blast at his red comrade's literal concept of Marcus Whitman's prayer book hogwash, had the agnostic earth cut out from under his heathen feet before he could open his profane mouth. The cutting was being done in the voice of Malkapsi's newly arrived fellow, the Spokane medicine man.

"Hear me, my brothers!" The old man's words carried clearly in the sudden hush. "A few among us have done what we can. I name Victor and Vincent of the Coeur D'Alenes among these. And Jacques and Zachary. We have failed, but this one thing we have done . . . just today there will be no fighting. Tomorrow they will give you battle. But they have promised not to defile this day by fighting. We could do no more. But today, this is Sunday."

For the remaining five hours of afternoon daylight the command sat their saddles, muskets and carbines loaded and unbooted, expecting each minute of the entire time to produce the continuously threatened Indian charge. The dragoon horses, pushed unmercifully for five days and without a decent feed or water in three, were rapidly becoming unmanageable under the ceaseless screaming and firing of the galloping hostile horsemen. The pack mules, always more susceptible to the alien odor of both Indians and cayuses, were requiring the attention of the complete 9th Infantry company to keep them on picket and under their various loads.

With the whole column—mule, horse, and man—at the exact outside of the breaking point of ordered array, sunset brought an unexpected delay of execution. With the first shade of evening, the hostiles began pulling back into the hills and within ten minutes there was neither sight nor sound of an enemy horseman within five miles of the tiny lake.

After waiting another half hour in saddle, Stedloe ordered camp made and disposed his command for the night. Every mount—pack and cavalry—was picketed under load and saddle, and each trooper billeted with his charged carbine or musket for a blanket. Double sentry lines were run around the entire perimeter of the huddled camp, the men not on guard duty sleeping in company groups within hand's reach of their ready horses.

Back of this thin bulwark, Colonel Stedloe and his staff sat the night away planning the retreat to the Snake. In this course there were now no demurrers. The low supply of ammunition, the overwhelming forces opposed to them, the absolute proof of their own eyes that the Spokanes and Coeur D'Alenes, tribes hitherto without a spot of white blood on their hands, had joined Kamiak's rebellion held the discussion strictly to ways and means of extricating the command from its present trap.

In this regard it was proposed to send another express to Wallowa via Jason and Timothy asking for reinforcements. The Nez Percé chief bluntly refused the mission, stating he had already sent a good man in the same direction and that, furthermore, that man had a twelve-hour start. The country behind them would be swarming with hostiles by this time and there was no sense of either him or Jason getting killed to prove it. If Lucas could not get through, Jason or Timothy would never do so.

This rebellion brought a momentary reflaring of the command's original suspicion of the Nez Percés' loyalty, Captain Baylor heatedly pointing out they had no assurance beyond Timothy's own that Lucas had been instructed to carry such a message and, even granted he had, no real hope at all that the already discredited Lucas would fulfill his mission.

Stedloe, after a brief discussion with Bell, announced his readiness to stand behind Timothy and his statements, adding that the sergeant and the two Nez Percés constituted the column's sole remaining scout and Indian-contact force and hence could not at the moment be spared. Under this agreement, the final marching orders were arranged with the departure hour scheduled for early, pre-dawn darkness of the following morning. The troops were to be in saddle and moving at four, the remaining short hours to be employed in rehearsing every man with his and his animal's position in the line of the retreat.

Bell, long-legging his weary way among the ground-sleeping troopers, headed for H Company's section and his own picketed bay. At the bony mount's side, he felt along the stirrup leathers for the treasured rawhide thong. Seconds later the familiar silhouette of the battered canteen was topping the horse's hipshot rump, and the first of the corn of Old Kentucky in forty-eight hours was running the corroded gamut of Bell's gullet. Following the long sigh and grateful smack saluting the canteen's return to the saddle horn, the sergeant cocked a professional eye eastward to the low set of the stars over the ragged spine of the Bitter Roots.

It was hard onto 2:00a.m., Monday, May 17th.

"Damn the whole, lousy mess to hell," grunted 1st Sergeant Emmett D. Bell, reposing his gaunt length in dust. "We're all dead and we might as well lie down and admit it."

XI

The column was formed and moving toward the Palouse by 4:10a.m. On Timothy's advice a route was taken diagonally through the hills and bearing directly for the crossing, this to avoid the obvious possibility of Kamiak's having ambushed their previous day's line of march up the main trail of the Lapwai. Due to the lack of any roadway through the cut-up brush and timber of the new route, progress was necessarily difficult and dangerously slow.

Since the issue was now apparently resolved, there could be little use for scouting, and Bell was reassigned to his regular place with H Company, his two Nez Percé scouts riding with him. The marching order was straight out of the regular field-command handbook, having been determined by Stedloe and his staff in final disregard of the pleadings of Bell and his Nez Percés for a closer grouping.

Looking back along its tenuous, broken length, the sergeant groaned audibly. Timothy, his quick glance tracing Bell's, spoke softly.

"It's about time for you to spit again, Ametsun. That's a bad way to march back there."

Bell grinned, shifted his cud of long leaf. As long as he'd known this red rascal, he hadn't been able to figure him for certain sure. Either he was what he appeared to be, stick-straight and dull-serious, or the deadestpan Indian cynic in the business. In either event he seldom missed his point, and he didn't miss it now. Bell spat, and spat hard.

"Plumb bad, Tamason. Look it over and get a prayer book express off to old Choosuklee."

The Indian nodded, saying nothing, both men twisting anew in their saddles to regard the object of their disaffections.

Their own Company H Dragoons, under Lieutenant Craig, held the advance, as usual. Then Captain Baylor and his Company C Dragoons. Following these came the twenty-five men of Captain Winston's Company E, 9th Infantry, with the two howitzers, next the pack and ammunition train, and finally Lieutenant Wilcey Gaxton's Company E Dragoons. And then came the part to shift your cud and spit about: the dragoon companies were carefully holding an ordered separation of over a thousand yards! Blessing Stedloe's faultless West Point form with another acid benediction of burley, Bell swung back around in his saddle, his humorless grin going to Timothy. "You in touch with your Lord yet, brother?"

"My hand is always in His," responded the Nez Percé soberly.

"Well, squeeze it, then," counseled the sergeant.

"There's room enough between those companies to hold a county fair with a half mile horse race on the side."

As soon as daylight allowed (about half an hour from Timothy's lake) the harassed column was aware its sneak departure had been a little too noisy. The distant hills lining both sides of the march were covered with thin stringers of moving Indian horsemen and, shortly after these were sighted, Sergeant Williams rode up from Gaxton's rear guard company to report a very heavy hostile concentration off both flanks of the column's rear.

Stedloe, taking Bell and the Nez Percés, at once rode back to check the giant Kentuckian's report. Arrived at the rear, neither Bell nor Timothy could make sense of what they saw. Bull Williams's hostile concentration was heavy enough, all right, but it was acting as queerly as a Tolouse goose, not a rifle shot or a war cry disturbing its rapidly growing ranks.

The excitement among the hostiles was evident but it was almost certainly not of the grade of full *staq*. It was more as though Kamiak had gathered his brightly clad hundreds to wave and bid the pony soldiers an extravagant, demonstrative farewell.

"I give up, Colonel. I've never seen the likes of it. Maybe Timothy can make something of it."

The column commander's questioning gaze joined Bell's with the latter's statement, both men waiting for Timothy to speak. The Nez Percé shrugged.

"I can only say this . . . something has happened. Something they didn't plan on. The Indian is not like you. He makes a plan, and then if something unthought of occurs, he is defeated. He has to stop and make a new plan. They're defeated over there right now. They'll have to get a new plan. Choosuklee has given us a little more time."

"We can use it," said Stedloe, breaking out one of his rare, stiff little smiles.

"Heads up," grunted Bell suddenly. "Here comes your something, Tamason. And by the flap of that crêpe hassock it looks like Sergeant Bell owes your Lord another apology."

"Good heavens," exclaimed Stedloe excitedly, "it's Father Joset!"

"Choosuklee's right-hand man," said Bell acidly. "That is, if Timothy will settle for Marc Whitman being his left-hand one."

"Amen," echoed the Nez Percé, "the Black Robe is on the right today."

The Coeur D'Alene mission priest slid his slobbered pony into the rear of Gaxton's company, coming down off the wind-broken little beast in a leg-over step-down that would have done credit to the slickest Indian rider in the Northwest federation.

He delivered his information with a brevity and modesty that added up to everything of solid honor and Indian sense Bell had heard of the man. He had come in all haste from the mission, ninety miles to the north, in response to Chief Vincent's dramatic appearance there following a twelve-hour night ride from Kamiak's camp on the Ingosommen. The Coeur D'Alenes had felt the famous Jesuit's presence in the war camp might stave off the upcoming slaughter of the trapped white troops.

Père Joset took respectful leave to hope the same, in the identical breath reminding Stedloe of his months' earlier warning to him that the dispatching of any considerable military force to the north of the Nez Percé River would bring an Indian uprising, and further adding that despite his night-long efforts among Kamiak's aroused hostiles an attack upon the white force was imminently certain.

He inquired further if Stedloe had had the report that he, Joset, was arming the hostiles and, upon Stedloe's admission of the fact he had, denied the allegation bluntly, adding that from his own information he was certain the rumor of a Nez Percé plot to involve the white troops with the tribes of Kamiak's Yakima federation was true. In this regard he had started early last month to ride to Wallowa and personally warn the colonel. At the last minute, Vincent had reported a Nez Percé plot to ambush the priest's party and incite an inter-tribal war.

Colonel Stedloe expressed his gratitude for the priest's amazing ride and, further, his astonishment at the hostile attitude of the Indians. After a few moments of continuing earnest discussion, Father Joset asked the officer if he would not consider one more parley with the hostile chiefs, informing him there was yet an outside possibility of a peaceful retreat, since some of the less inflamed chiefs felt Stedloe had broken off the preceding day's talks with undue abruptness.

Glancing along the waiting line of the halted column, Bell grimaced bitterly. There wasn't a snowball's chance in hell's back furnace of holding the command up. Stopped not over five minutes, the crazed pack mules were already beginning to break line, the excited, nerve-shot dragoon horses being of little or no use in curbing them. The sergeant's thoughts were quickly repeated in Stedloe's unhappy refusal.

The colonel was sorry, but the priest could see for himself it would be impossible to hold his frightened pack animals. The column had got to move, and move at once. Father Joset, the steadiest man Bell had ever watched, now suggested the talks could be held in motion, without halting the column, and to this Stedloe gladly agreed. The priest rode back at once, promising to return with as many of the hostile leaders as would follow him.

He returned in half an hour, highly disturbed.

He had been able to find only Vincent and Victor, the Coeur D'Alenes. Their hopes would now have to be pinned on these two elder chiefs.

Colonel Stedloe repeated his promises of the previous talks to the Coeur D'Alenes, adding the further guarantee that the whole idea of the Colville council would be dropped until such a time as the Indians were convinced of its benefits. At this moment and for the first time in the entire series of cloudy parleys, Bell felt a last, half chance truce hanging in the delicate balance of the Coeur D'Alenes' agreeing nods.

He had no sooner responded to this fleeting hope when even its slight string was brutally snapped. It was one of those weird, unreasonable by-plays that no one not deeply familiar with the real thinness of the mission veneer smeared over the basic uncertainty of the Indian character by the various Christian proselyters on the Washington frontier could understand. And even Bell, an Indian veneer peeler of five years' good standing, got hit by the flying chips of frontier varnish now exploding off the unpredictable Jason.

The Nez Percé subchief shoved his pony forward the moment Vincent's handsome face broke in a smile of understanding toward Stedloe. The next instant, before the dumbfounded whites could intervene, the Army scout had laid his heavy, four-foot quirt squarely across the Coeur D'Alene's mouth. The force of the unwarned blow nearly unhorsed the visiting chief, but Bell, spurring forward, caught him and held him on his sidling pony. As he did, Jason's angry accusation was snarling its way into the stricken Indian's bleeding face.

"You talk with a forked tongue! I've struck you now, proud man! Why don't you fire?"

Victor, moving his pony forward to come between the enraged Nez Percé and his fellow Coeur D'Alene, found himself included in the shouted charges.

"And you, too, you dog! I saw you lift your rifle just now to fire on the oak leaf chief!"

By this time, Bell and Timothy had the raging Jason's pony pinned between their shouldering mounts and Stedloe was addressing his white-faced apologies to the visitors. The Coeur D'Alenes, under Father Joset's rapid Chinook address to them, agreed to overlook the incident and to return to the hostile lines with their final peace effort.

But where the hearts of the two old Coeur D'Alenes were good, they were no better than the eyes of the watching hostile hundreds. The Palouse warriors had seen the Nez Percé scout attack their emissary, and translated the action literally. Even as Vincent and Victor were touching their foreheads to Stedloe, a young Coeur D'Alene warrior broke from the waiting hostile ranks and whipped his pony forward. His black eyes snapping, the youth hauled his mount to a leg-stiff halt, shouting his warning to Vincent.

"Depart, uncle! Come away now! The Palouses are all through waiting! Kamiak has said for them to fire!"

With the two chiefs turning to follow the excited boy, Victor sent a last hand wave to Colonel Stedloe. "We are sorry, my brother. But we don't want to die here in the middle, and it is too late now."

"It's never too late to die, brother." Bell held his soft curse under breath, his smoky-gray eyes following the dust of the departing ponies. "And right here is where me and a hundred and fifty other enlisted heroes drop dead to prove it."

XII

The first, long-range shots from Kamiak's hostiles were splattering the rocks around Gaxton's rear company before the dust of Vincent's and Victor's ponies was halfway back to the Indian lines. With typical and even (Sergeant Bell grudging the fact) admirable methodicalness, Colonel Stedloe ignored the opening fire to pull his fat, brass stemwinder from inside his campaign jacket. Twelve hundred hostiles or no, it was of primary importance that the hour of the onset of the Battle of the Tohotonimme be duly noted for future and precise inclusion in his field report to Headquarters Operations.

"Eight three, Sergeant"—the watch was being carefully restored to its particular pocket—"please ride up the column to your company and tell Craig to resume march and hold all fire. Pass that word to Baylor and Winston on your way up. I'll see Gaxton. Remember, Bell . . . not a shot in return until the order is changed."

"Yes, sir"—Bell was wheeling his bay—"anything else, sir?"

"No, I'll be up directly. I want to watch this back here a bit."

Saluting, Bell sent his mount galloping up the left flank of the slow-moving column, shouting Stedloe's orders to Baylor and Winston.

"Colonel Stedloe's orders, sir! Resume regular march . . . hold all fire!"

The two captains flicked their yellow gauntlets in understanding, relaying the shouted command in quick turn to Sergeants Demoix and Harrigan. Looking back, Bell could see the non-coms wheeling down the flanks of their companies, could hear their hoarse yells bouncing back and forth across the narrow gully in which the column presently found itself.

"Close up! Closed company! Column speed. Hold your horses down. No fire! Repeat. Hold your fire!"

By 8:30 the hostile fire had built up to a

continuous roll, the entire weight of it directed at Gaxton's rear company. Glancing back from the occasional slight rises in the gully's floor, Bell could see the Indian riders galloping back and forth from hillside to hillside across the lieutenant's rear, their range still too long to result in anything save accidental casualties. The ugly grimace this maneuver brought to the sergeant's bearded face was turned with his hard words to Lieutenant Craig at his side.

"The colonel's making a hell of a mistake holding his fire, Lieutenant. Those red buzzards'll think we're bluffed clean down to our boot socks. In five minutes they'll be seeping up our flanks and in ten they'll have us headed."

"I'm right with you, Sergeant," the youthful officer receipted the grimace along with the sentiment. "And I don't like the looks of that big hill ahead. If they pass up and get on that, we're trapped. We can't go any place but right under it."

"Yeah"—Bell's grim retort dropped all thought of rank—"and, if they try it, guess who'll get the fun of running them for it!"

"Company H, for sure."

"Company H for hell." The big sergeant grinned. "Take a look back there, Lieutenant. Here they come!"

As Bell spoke, the main force of Indians to the column's rear closed up and launched a full-scale charge into Gaxton's company. At the same time, two lesser forces split off and came bombarding up the flanks of the column. The distinctive hollow booming of the issue muskets began immediately, letting the forward column know that Stedloe had released Gaxton's company to fire. Seconds later, Bell could make out the colonel's slight figure galloping up from the rear.

Stedloe brought the news that Gaxton had had his horse shot from under him and taken a rifle ball through the arm. He was now remounted and his company in good order but suffering casualties by the minute. Baylor and Winston had as yet taken no casualties but the Indians were massing on their companies and they'd been given orders to make short counter-charges out of column line to keep the foe off balance and to attempt to prevent them from gaining any elevation along the route—their now obvious intent and purpose.

Further orders had been given to close up the company gaps, there still remaining several hundred yards between companies. It was to be hoped that Baylor's and Winston's side charges would keep the hostiles from heading the column in any force. The no-fire order had been changed to fire permitted only on the counter-charging necessary to clear the Indians from the line of march. Even as the order and the hope were released from the colonel's compressed lips, Bell knew both were futile, and for the next two brutal miles through the trackless brush his knowledge was bloodily born out. Encouraged by the light fire from the troops, the hostiles were constantly charging, using their favorite prairie-wolf tactic —whirling in to point-blank range to draw a counter-charge, fleeing before the charge until they had it pulled way out of line, then turning on it with savage fury to drive it back in.

The engagement was now entirely general along the line, with Baylor's and Gaxton's companies having sustained five murderous charges and with Winston's group of mounted infantry, howitzer, and pack string rapidly beginning to lose all semblance of an ordered command.

During all this wild time, Bell had had occasional glimpses of Calla in her borrowed corporal's uniform—hastily donned that morning at Timothy's suggestion that it would serve to give her anonymity among the crowding troops—being moved up as the battle progressed, from Gaxton's company to Baylor's to Winston's, in rapid succession. Now, in a brief lull as Stedloe and Craig studied a large force gathering off their left flank, he looked anxiously around for the Southern girl.

Sharp as his hurried glance was, it swept over the girl twice before flicking back to spot her on the third pass. Well, by God, that was good, anyway. Bouncing along back there as the ninth man in H Company's third squad, she was about as safe as she could get in this crazy hour and place. If he could miss her at fifty yards, it was a good bet the hostiles could do likewise at 200.

At that moment, she caught his eye upon her and waved, following the wave with a mock salute and a summer-lightning flash of a smile that would have lifted the powder smoke of any man's Indian battle. Before Bell could wave back, her horse was rearing in terror at the sudden lash of Indian lead that announced the attack from the new force on H Company's left, and in the hot work of repulsing the hostile slash he lost sight of her.

That he ever saw her again was more a tribute to the guts and gallantry of Lieutenant Davis Craig than to any military right Company H had to survive the following Palouse maneuver, a maneuver that, ironically, the young lieutenant had himself predicted an hour and a half before. In seconds, now, it became apparent that the charge of the left-flank group had been a feint, for no sooner had it broken than a much larger group of hostiles bucketed out of the hills to the right, wheeled sharply south, and raced for the high hill at the column's head that Craig had marked for Bell in the beginning.

Stedloe, measuring up fully to the sergeant's unaltered estimation of his basic coolness, at once ordered Company H forward: ". . . to beat the Indians to that hill and, failing that, to beat them off of it!"

Bell, picking the order up from Craig, threw it down the ranks as he slammed his spurs into the bay and drove him after the jumping flag of the lieutenant's horse, his eyes sweeping the right-hand hills as he went—and opening wide with the tail end of the sweep! *Aii-eee*, brother! Trust Kamiak not to send a boy on a man's errand.

That six-foot buck in the lead of the racing hostile warriors—cartwheel war bonnet, three-point blanket and all—was nobody but Kenuokin himself! The headlong dash for the hill, although closer than a straight-razor shave, was won by the dragoons, a victory that proved as short-lived as Guxton's first horse. Kamiak, abandoning the race the moment it was apparent he had lost it, swept on around the base of the hill and disappeared beyond its far side. Topping the elevation a few moments later, Bell cursed at length and wickedly.

No wonder the red son hadn't held up to bicker about the hill they were on! Facing them now, for the first time revealed by their new elevation, stood a second and higher hill, its brushy crest not over 150 yards from their uncovered position! And the van of Kamiak's whooping henchmen were already piling off their scrambling ponies to dive into the rocks and scrub of its commanding top.

Craig, realizing he must take this new position, left Bell and one squad to hold the present ridge and, with the remaining three squads deployed in open skirmish line, at once went after Kamiak. The assault, probably due to its quickness, was successful. With lethal reservations. The hostiles, no longer fearful of the dragoon charges, fell back only from the hill's apex, setting up their new lines just below and completely ringing Craig's troops. The lieutenant and his men were as flat-pinned as so many blue and gold butterflies on the exposed roundness of their granite and scrub-brush exhibition case.

With H Company split and isolated, the savages turned the full fury of their attentions on the remainder of the column. Winston, to whose company Stedloe had escorted Calla when Craig went forward, was the nearest to the lieutenant's beleaguered troops—about 800 yards north and still trapped on the gully's floor. Baylor and Gaxton, both of whom had succeeded in closing some ground, were still cut off from each other and from Winston's group.

The chain of command being thus shattered, the fighting now became completely broken and independent, the inevitable, deadly result entirely clear to all concerned—if the several sections of the command could not be speedily reunited the Battle of the Tohotonimme would go into the history books as of 10:15a.m., Monday, May 17th, 1858.

Into this next-to-last *extremis* of the Colville column, as indeed it had since the first, fateful camp at the main Snake Crossing, now stepped the reed-slender, mahogany-dark figure of the Red Wolf Nez Percé, Tamason.

Shortly after 11:00a.m. the first slight break in the deadly situation occurred, setting the stage for Timothy's remarkable ride: Captain Winston and Colonel Stedloe succeeded at that time in fighting their way with the howitzers and packs to Craig's hilltop position. The howitzers were at once stripped and brought into action. Their effect, contrary to Bell's earlier hard-bitten cynicism, and supporting the colonel's laughed-at pride in them, was little short of electric. While even Stedloe would have admitted that perhaps not a solitary Indian was injured by the noisy bursts, the fear and confusion temporarily occasioned by them among the crowded ranks of Kamiak's hostiles were obvious and instant.

It remained for the slow-drawling Winston to see the true and momentary nature of the diversion. "Colonel, those devils breaking and running like that mustn't fool us. Both Kamiak and Malkapsi were present at Wallowa last summer when you held that demonstration." At the mention of the demonstration—due to the fort gunners' faulty marksmanship, a well-touted exhibition of the howitzers' deadliness had fallen flat—the colonel's face reddened, but Winston continued: "They'll rally their people quick enough, I'm afraid."

"Yes, sir"—Craig's earnest voice joined the discussion—"Harry's right, Colonel. The reservation bucks in that bunch will have them back on us in ten minutes. It's the wild Indians that have broken. I don't mean to sell your cannon short, sir."

While this conversation was going forward among the officers atop Craig's hill, Bell, who had brought his squad over from the other hill when the howitzers first opened the way for the maneuver, was lying off to one side of the anxious group, belly-flopped amidst a jumble of granite boulders. By his side the ever-present Timothy was letting his slant gaze join the sergeant's in scanning the still broken ranks of the hostiles below.

Suddenly Bell's gray eyes narrowed. Another moment of careful searching and his words were snapping at the Nez Percé chief. "Tamason! Do you see what I see down there?"

"Aye, the field is almost clear between us and Captain Baylor. And Lieutenant Gaxton has fought nearly up to the captain. It's too bad they cannot see it from down there where they are. Is that what you mean, Ametsun?"

"You're damn' right that's what I mean! Go get Stedloe, brother. And jump it!"

Seconds later, the colonel, along with Winston and Craig, had joined Bell in his rocky look-out, the big sergeant's rapped-out greeting at once widening the eyes of all three.

"Look down there, sir! Your damn' howitzers have opened them up clean down to Baylor's boys. And Wilse is damn' near up to the captain!"

"We were just discussing it, Bell." Stedloe's voice was held down with its customary calm. "But Captain Winston and Lieutenant Craig feel they'll close up again in a few minutes. I'm afraid we haven't any reason for a celebration yet, Sergeant. Perhaps if Baylor could see the opening . . ."

"That's the hell of it," interrupted Craig bitterly. "They can't see a thing for the base of this damn hill we're on!"

"That's just what I mean, Lieutenant!" Bell broke in excitedly. "If they can't see, neither can the Indians that're pinning them down. We've got a thousand-yard slot right up this hill as open as the devil's front door. If the colonel can keep his howitzers blasting for another ten minutes, we can get a rider through to Baylor!"

"By God, Colonel, Bell's right!" Craig was on his feet. "They've got a chance to get up here if we can get word to them."

"I'm sorry, gentlemen." The C.O.'s refusal fell softly. "There isn't a man in the command who'd have a chance in a thousand of getting down this hill alive."

"Not a white man, maybe . . ." Bell dropped the statement slowly, his eyes holding Stedloe's.

"What the devil do you mean, Bell?"

"He means me, Colonel Stedloe." The deep bass of the Nez Percé's voice came from behind them, pivoting their combined glances in time to see the scout swinging up on his roan gelding. "I see the flag down there and I'm going to it."

"Get off that horse, you fool Indian!" Stedloe's angry command trailed the wheeling pony. "That's an order, Timothy! Bell! Stop the idiot . . . !"

The colonel's order and entreaty were lost alike in the shower of rotten granite chips churned up by the plunging descent of the Nez Percé's scrambling pony, and in Sergeant Bell's soft-muttered benediction.

"There's nothing in all hell will stop that Indian, Colonel. Nothing short of half a pound of Palouse lead, anyway. God help him, I wish I had his guts."

Stedloe broke his eyes from the lunging slide of Timothy's gelding, turned their earnest brown-ness with sudden warmth on Bell, his thin hand finding the big sergeant's shoulder with the look.

"Yours will do until they issue a better set of intestines," he said softly.

While the anxious eyes of Craig's and Winston's hilltop commands watched helplessly, Timothy completed his suicidal dash to Baylor's company, apparently without a scratch. An instant later the watchers on the hill saw another tiny figure dart across the 400 yards that still separated Baylor's and Gaxton's companies. Even at the distance Bell could make out the rider wasn't Timothy, but knew from his side-swinging, crazy way of hanging to a horse that it was an Indian, and concluded with a wry grin that Timothy had dispatched Jason to do his bit for the Nez Percé chief's precious flag.

Following the contacts of the Nez Percé riders with the separated companies, Baylor and Gaxton began to drive at once for the base of Craig's hill, their lines of attack approaching one another diagonally. The Indian pressure on their flanks was unrelenting but Kamiak saw too late the purpose of the pincers. He was able to rally about 200 braves and throw them onto the base of the hill just as the two companies, in full dragoon charge, arrived at the same point.

Caught between the desperate tongs, the hostiles took their first considerable casualties of the day. A round dozen were killed and two score wounded—among the former, disastrously, Jacques, Zachary, and old Victor, three of the five friendlies among the chiefs of the hostile command.

Baylor and Gaxton, scarcely breaking the momentum of their conjunction, turned their troops up the hill and, assisted by a counter-charge down the slope by Craig and H Company, succeeded in reaching the top. With this achievement, the several sections of the command were unified for the first time since leaving the lakeside camp seven and a half hours earlier. For the first time, also, a pause was gained to look to medical attention and to check battle casualties and issue rations. The time was 11:25a.m.

The medical inspection and casualty survey revealed unexpected good news: thirteen troopers slightly wounded, four moderately, none seriously, one missing and presumed killed. This slight lift was immediately let down by Lieutenant Fanning's report that the last of the water had just been issued to the wounded. On top of this Captain Winston turned in his figures on the pack string —twenty-four animals and their packs lost, half of the remaining forty head suffering bullet wounds and well near out of service.

All these facts waited silently before Fanning's fateful revelation. Without water the command was as dead as though its scalps were already cut and dried. It was quickly brought out that the only hope in this direction must be placed upon Timothy's information that the main Ingosommen lay only three miles to the south and west in its looping course from Kamiak's war camp to the north. With utterly no alternative, Stedloe ordered his command regrouped and the advance toward the Ingosommen begun.

The start down the far flank of the hill was made at 11:55, Baylor and Gaxton holding the flanks as before, Stedloe leading with Craig's H Company, Winston, with the precious packs and howitzers, in between. Included among the "preciousnesses" was the almost forgotten, white-faced figure of "Corporal" Calla Lee Rainsford.

Immediately the course of the past morning's

struggle assumed the innocent-fun aspect of a Sunday school picnic. Where Bell thought he and his comrades had been bucking the heat of hell's front yard in the earlier advance, he was now made to realize they'd hardly been up to the devil's mailbox. With Kamiak and Malkapsi screaming them on and with the holding counsel of the Coeur D'Alene chiefs dead and gone, the hostiles swarmed in on the white soldiers like bottle flies at a bull gutting.

At five minutes of twelve, E Company was sliced clean away from the rear of the column and minutes later Lieutenant Wilcey Gaxton was vomiting his life out, with three Palouse slug holes gaping where his belt buckle should have been. Inflamed by the death of a "soldier chief," the hostiles tore into the leaderless company. After eight hours of absorbing the main enemy pressure, Company E broke as wide open as a rotten melon. The bulk of its men succeeded in reaching Winston's section but as an organized command E Company was off the books. And in meeting the wild charge that had driven its survivors into his rear, Winston lost twenty-five of his remaining pack animals.

Baylor's troop, which had been sheared off by the same onslaught that broke E Company, was now in equally desperate straits in trying to regain the main column as a unit. Captain Oliver Baylor, for all his rash temper and dramatic flare, was a fighting officer of the first bloody water. He proved it now by taking his company straight through 500 enraged hostiles to make contact once again with Winston's forces. And he proved it, too, by taking a .50-caliber, smooth-bore ball through the base of his throat sixty seconds before his inspired riding had brought his men through.

The column was now dead-halted in open, undefendable terrain, still two and a half miles from water. One company was broken, and two leaderless, Lieutenant Gaxton was dead, Captain Baylor dying. At least thirty-five troops were heavily wounded, several of these beyond any doubt mortally. The packs and ninety percent of the rations were strewn over the crimsoned granite talus of Craig's abandoned hillside and the ammunition count was down to six rounds a man. It was time for Sergeant Bell to spit again.

XIII

With the perverse red military logic that had saved many a white command before them, the hostiles, their disorganized foe surrounded, waterless, nearly out of ammunition, and literally shot to pieces, now broke off the engagement and pulled away from Stedloe's bleeding column.

Watching them go, Bell was as nonplussed as the greenest dogface in the company, but Timothy, his lean form as usual shadowing that of the big sergeant, had his customary grasp of the glass-simple Indian psychology wrapped firmly around the peculiar antics of his fellow redmen.

"It's the packs, Ametsun." He shrugged. "Pretty soon you'll see them now. Fighting among themselves back there on that hillside."

Even as the Nez Percé spoke, Bell could see the first of the racing red warriors putting their lathered mounts up the broad incline down which the white column had just fought its bloody way, and along the grassy slopes of which were scattered the bulk of Captain Winston's cut-off pack animals and their precious loads of equipment and supplies. And in his mind the thought was forming just as Timothy was putting his soft words to it.

"If the colonel will move quickly now, we may be able to reach that last big hill, there"—here a slight shoulder hunch ahead of the low-voiced conclusion—"and up there we can at least die like men."

Almost before the echo of the Nez Percé's final phrase was lost among the groans of the wounded and the ceaseless neighings of the terrified cavalry mounts, Bell was saluting Stedloe with the terse hope of the Indian scout's discovery.

"Begging your pardon, Colonel, but Timothy says, if we hump our backsides, we might just make it up that butte yonder, while the Palouses are

371

scrapping over our packs. You see them clotting up on that hill we just left? That's why they pulled off of us. To divvy up Captain Winston's supplies. We've got maybe twenty minutes, sir."

Stedloe, who with his remaining officers had just reached a decision to abandon the drive for water and move the command to an adjacent small hill for its final stand, at once grasped at Timothy's straw.

"Craig, you were with Mullins and his map survey in here last fall. Do you recall that butte? It's big enough to be on the charts."

"I believe that's Pyramid Peak, Colonel. I can't be sure, but if it is, there's half an acre of level ground on top with a fifteen-foot vertical drop-off of basalt and granite around the north and east perimeters. The south slope is fairly steep as you can see from here, but you could drive a wagon up that long west ridge. I really can't say it's Pyramid, though. All these damn' buttes look alike to me now."

"Beg Colonel's pardon," Bell broke in abruptly, "but Timothy'll know all that and he's already said we might make it if we jump fast and long."

"Bell's right!" Winston's ordinarily quiet voice barked harshly. "We've no time to review Mullins's survey. And we'd best stick with this damn' Indian. He's led us straight so far."

"Agreed, Craig?" Stedloe turned the low question to H Company's commander.

"Agreed."

"Fanning?" Even a lowly supply officer rated his equal vote under the colonel's calm thoroughness.

"Yes, sir, as fast as I can, sir!" The white-lipped youngster managed a pale grin.

"That's it, then," said Stedloe. "Let's go, gentlemen. H Company first. Fanning and Baylor's C Company next. I'll go third with what's left of Wilcey's troop, and Winston and the Ninth last. All clear?"

The "all clears" moved hurriedly with their respective givers to their waiting horses, and within five minutes of Bell's first advising of the god-given respite, the ragged column was galloping for the base of the long western approach of Pyramid Peak. And within another, lung-bursting fifteen was pushing the last of the panting horses onto the desolate, billiard-smooth top of the lonely butte. Taken off their greedy guard by the surprise dash, Kamiak's war-whooping Palouses went streaming after it minutes too late, the command reaching their barren objective without further casualties.

But to Kamiak, Malkapsi, and company, collectors of Army materiel and pony soldier scalps, the temporary loss of revenue was scarcely serious. There were still very much in business and proceeded now to prove it by the enthusiastic recklessness with which they invested their considerable resources completely around all four approaches to Stedloe's waterless tableland.

Kamiak had lead money to burn. He was out to paint the newly established little Army town of Pyramid Peak a bright, Indian red. With fresh, white blood, of course.

The 3,600-foot cone of Stedloe's butte lay, hot and naked, athwart the slanting rays of the five-o'clock sun, its treeless, deep-grassed shoulders thrusting 1,200 feet above the crowding neighborhood of lesser hills that hemmed it on every side. On its hard-won summit the surviving troops of the Colville column lay on their gnawing bellies among the rank grass ringing the perimeter of the tiny mesa, their red and fearful eyes straining to catch the first signs of Kamiak's third assault against their granite bastion.

Twice now, once at 2:00p.m. and once at 4:00, the hostiles had come swarming up at them on foot, being each time driven back with heavy losses, but each time throwing the flood tide of their attacking wave higher up the basalt walls of the command's barren prison. The third attempt, now clearly readying below, might mark the last white shots.

The ammunition ration, by Fanning's last careful count at 4:30, stood at four rounds per man, and Bell, peering through his weedy cover at the red force massing the south slope, grimly concluded the young supply officer had made his last inventory—for that or any other day. Nor was the tall sergeant's optimism fattened any by the fact that he and fifteen H Company troopers were stationed along the exact quadrant of the mesa that must bear the brunt of any hostile assault mounted up the south slope. Not only must bear it, but were not over thirty seconds from so doing. Kamiak was ready and he was coming.

The red lines seemed to grow out of the slope rocks by a literal magic that had even Timothy blinking his slant eyes. Where dozens had been visible seconds before, hundreds now sprang war whooping up the sunbathed incline. And this time Kamiak was putting his bottom dollar on the red line, he and Malkapsi leading it with a picked group of 100 mounted warriors, the first employment of horsemen in the past several hours.

"There's their first little mistake," Bell grunted to Timothy, indicating the advanced group of galloping ponies. "If we can down a dozen of those cayuses right at the top of that rock slide . . ." He pointed out the steep pitch of the spot, fifty yards below them, and the Nez Percé nodded.

"Aye, Ametsun, that's the place. Tell the men."

"Hold your fire, boys!" The sergeant's shout caught the nervous troopers shouldering their carbines. "Wait'll those lead bucks hit the top of that slide right below us, then give it to them in the horses' guts. Don't sight on a man. Hold low and let drive square into the ponies. And let drive when I holler. All of you."

The other sections of the white line were already lobbing long musket fire down into the mass of the charging Indians, wasting powder and lead as though they had a fort full of both to burn, completely ignoring the pleading curses of their officers and non-coms to hold down and pick their shots. But Bell's men, steadied with the picture of the burly sergeant and his slim Nez Percé companion kneeling, fully exposed now, on the mesa's rim and cradling their carbines as casually as though they were waiting for the trap master to throw up the tame pigeons, clamped their gritting teeth and waited.

"You take Kamiak," said Bell to the slit-eyed Timothy. "I'm shooting Coeur D'Alenes this afternoon."

"Malkapsi?" asked the Nez Percé, raising his gun.

"With a capital M," grunted Bell, his gaunt cheek sliding into the stock. "I made him a little promise back at the Palouse."

"May your word be as good as usual," murmured the Indian. "Now, Ametsun?"

"Now," snapped Bell. "Let them have it, boys! Low down and reload lively!"

Kamiak and Malkapsi, with perhaps thirty of their wildest riders, were just heel-hammering their foam-flecked ponies across the top of the rock slide when H Company's long delayed volley cut into them. The effects were as gratifying as

Timothy might have arranged through an entire month's negotiations with Choosuklee and the powers of faith other than that associated with the short barrel of a Sharps carbine.

At least fourteen horses dropped in the first murderous blast, those of both Kamiak and Malkapsi among the number. But the dropping was the least of it. As they went down, kicking and screaming, the loose surface of the incline beneath them sent them bounding and hoof-thrashingly down among the crowded ranks of the following horsemen, knocking down fifteen or twenty more unwounded mounts and adding the falling, bouncing figures of their own and their riders' bodies to the cascading, bloody mêlée.

The spectacular breaking up of their spearhead of ponies slowed the following dismounted braves enough to allow the timed-fire shots of H Company's reloaded carbines to begin to arrive among them—and aimed fire with a Sharps at sixty yards, nervous troopers or no, is convincing. Additionally some of the backing musket fire from the other companies was getting home at the pistol-blank range. Shortly—about eight or nine belly-drilled braves later, to be exact—Kamiak's faithful decided (with notable lack of formal conference) to call it an afternoon.

Twenty minutes later there wasn't a painted face within Sharps shot of Colonel Stedloe's arid retreat, and the only Indians to be seen were those whose bones would bleach the bare cone of Pyramid Peak till hell cooled down and died out. Among these, unfortunately, was neither Kamiak nor Malkapsi.

The main body of the Indians was shortly afterward noted to be reassembling along the banks of the main river south and west of the butte, where it was soon evident a major council was in progress. A considerable number of the hostiles, however, remained stationed among the scrub of the lower slopes and continued to lob a long and steady fire onto the mesa top.

With dusk, a number of mounted riders were seen to leave the creek camp and go among the braves still on the firing line. The loud calls and barking signal cries of these presently informed the anxious white command, via the running translations of Timothy, that the fighting was to cease for the night and be saved for a better day. No man among the watching whites had the least doubt as to the identity of that better day. It would be tomorrow.

On Stedloe's butte, the unnatural hush of the early darkness was broken only by the groans of the severely wounded and the low-pitched commands of the officers and non-coms. Here and there little clots of frightened, huddled troopers squatted together and whispered in the fireless dark.

Sergeant Bell, his own wounded accounted and

cared for, found himself with his first spare time since snaking Calla out of Kamiak's gaudy red lodge. His thoughts, naturally, turned to the Southern girl and to the weird warp of circumstances that had brought her to this Washington mountain top 3,000 miles from her genteel Virginia home. She was presently assisting Surgeon Randall with the wounded, he knew. As indeed she had been the whole of the long march from Timothy's lake. Knowing too well what the sight and sound and touch of a beautiful woman meant to these lonely men, even in the bloom of health, Bell knew that Calla Lee Rainsford had repaid her debt to the officers and men of the Colville column many times over in these past bloody hours.

Hers had been the soft lap and gentle hand that had cradled the mortally wounded Baylor's head as sunset had brought the last, ugly rattle into his torn throat. Hers the slow touch and lingering smile to ease the wrenching pain of Demoix's lung-shot strangle. And of Bull Williams's gaping belly wound. And the picture of her lovely face, clear and high-colored in the afternoon sun, or white and faint in the gathering night gloom, had been the last vision to close the tortured eyes of more than one agonized enlisted man on that bare and stony butte.

"Timothy."

"Aye, Ametsun," came the Nez Percé's answer out of the darkness at Bell's side.

"Go tell the girl I want to see her when she's done. I'll be here."

"Aye, Ametsun, I'll bring her back."

"Just tell her where I am. She'll find me. I want to see her alone."

"I knew that, brother." The soft reproach of the Indian's answer faded with his departing shadow, leaving Bell to face the further loneliness of his darkening thoughts.

Five troopers were dead. Two more, dying. Bull Williams and Frenchy Demoix, hopelessly wounded. Thirteen other troopers clean down with bad bullet holes. Another two dozen cut up with flesh wounds and out of effective action. Gaxton and Baylor, whose rash courage had held the column together all morning, gone. The men had been without food for sixteen hours, without water for eight. Company E Dragoons without a leader, C, little better off under the beardless, battle-shy Fanning.

Two first sergeants, a brave but green dragoon lieutenant, a slow-thinking infantry captain, and a barracks-bred, over-cautious artillery colonel were all that remained of leadership to the nerve-broken men huddled in the crawling dark of Stedloe's butte.

Bell hunched his shoulders, the shiver of raw fatigue shaking him with its sudden chill. Damn. It was a hot night, but a man's fingers and feet felt like they'd been half frozen. Funny about that cold. Damned funny. He'd seen his share of men shake to it before now. Plenty of them. But damned if he'd ever expected to live to see Emmett Bell frostbitten by it.

That was fear cold, mister. And it would freeze a man to death quicker than a snowdrift.

Bell came up off his haunches, his eyes swinging through the gloom to the half sound that had startled him. "Who's there? That you, Cal? Answer fast, girl!"

"It's me, Emm. Oh, Emm! Emm!" She was up to him then, her tears coming with her breaking voice, hard against his sweated shirt.

"All right, Cal baby. It's all right. Don't cry, honey. Don't let down now, baby girl." His voice, thick and deep with the huskiness of his own emotions, stroked the sobbing girl like a great, awkward hand. "It's over for tonight, honey. All over now. You're going to stay right here with me. . . ."

"Emm, just hold onto me. Hard. I can't stay with it, Emm. I just can't."

He took her in his arms, gingerly and overly careful, as he might with a month-old child, carrying her as easily as a feather pillow.

"Here's my pack, Cal. And blankets." With the words he placed her gently down, his old grin coming through the darkness. "Not much of a boudoir for the prettiest girl in Lynchburg, but there's plenty of fresh air and it's awful quiet."

She didn't answer and he sank down beside her, easing his aching neck against the support of the pack, letting his long body go limp with the first relaxation in forty-eight hours. As he did, he felt the slim nakedness of the reaching arm slide over him, the soft, sighing nestle of the dark head as it sought and found the hollow of his shoulder.

"Let's don't talk, Emm"—the whisper came to his ear just ahead of the searching lips—"we've said it all before. That very first night on the plain, at the Point. A million years ago . . ."

"We've said it, Cal"—his face was turning with the promise—"all of it. Let's both remember it now, from here out."

"From here out, Emm boy. From here . . ."

The soft, full lips came into the wide, hard ones, shutting off the sigh and its vow. His heavy arms tightened slowly and relentlessly across the yielding curve of her back. Not eagerly and passionately like a man who has seized tonight and means to have it now, but reverently and protectively and finally. Like a man who has grasped tomorrow, and means never to let it go.

XIV

Bell had not meant to sleep but his next memory was of Harrigan's broad paw on his arm.

"*Psst,* Sarge." The Irishman's whisper was held down so as not to awaken the sleeping girl. "Where the hell have yez bin? I've crawled twicet around this blasted mountain feelin' for yez."

"What's up, Mick?" Bell demanded. "I must've dozed. What the hell time is it?"

"Eight o'clock," came the grim reply, "but all ain't well, Emmett bye."

"How's that?"

"Hell to pay, lad. And the divil holdin' all the due bills." By this time Bell was moving away with his fellow non-com. "First off, right after yer Injun come to git the gal for yez, we caught the other red scut hollerin' down to them slimy Palouses."

"You mean Jason? What the hell was he hollering about?"

"I don't mean Kimiak, bye. We didn't think nothin' ot this red bird's yellin' until yer Injun comes up and hears him. He was jabberin' in that heathin Chinook and we wasn't payin' him no mind."

"For God's sake, Mick, get on with it."

"Take it easy, Sarge." Harrigan was pushing Bell's fierce grip from his arm. "Ye're gettin'

383

jumpier'n a pet 'coon. I'm tellin' yez, jest listen. Yer Injun grabs this Jason the minute he hears him, hands him a cut acrost the kisser with his backhand, and tells us the buzzard has been eggin' the enemy on. Hollerin' . . . 'Courage, brothers! Ye've already killed two chiefs and seven pony soldiers!' . . . and stuff like that."

"The hell!"

"Percisely." Harrigan's thick voice rose in pitch. "And when yer Injun braced him, he jest shrugs and says what the hell? The white men up here are all dead come tomorrow, anyway, and he's jest tryin' to build up a little social good will with Kimiak's lads so's maybe they'll remember he's a fellow countryman come tommyhawk time tomorrow."

Bell shrugged. "Oh, hell, that doesn't mean anything. Sounds pure Indian to me. Typical of them, Mick. What'd you do? Tie him up?"

"Yeah, and stuffed his yap. Timothy's idee."

"Well, then, that's that. What the hell did you come to roust me out for?"

"Well, no, that ain't quite it, Sarge. Just half of it. When we git this bird trussed up and stuffed, lo and behold, the other one's clean flown."

"Good Lord! Not Timothy!"

"Gone as a goslin' down a fox's gullet."

"By God, I don't believe it!"

"Believe it or else, lad. It's why Lootenant Craig sent me to locate yez. He's up to Surgeon

Randall's spot, with Capt'n Winston. Wants yez over there right away. They were powwowin' about some bug the lootenant's got up his bottom about gettin' offen this bloody mountain, when this Injun trouble broke."

"Well, c'mon, Mick. Lead the way. How's Bull and Frenchy?"

"Both spittin' blood. Frenchy kin still move but Bull's sittin' ag'in' a rock grabbin' his belly and holdin' his breath. Surgeon says if he lets go to scratch his head, he's dead."

"You talked to him?"

"Yeah. You'd best see him. He's got some crazy notion yez were killed. It'd break an Orangeman's heart to see the big ox sittin' there grievin' about it. Not a sound, mind yez, jest sittin' there mutterin' . . . 'Old Sarge, old Sarge' . . . and the tears runnin' off his jaw like water."

"All right, Mick"—Bell's voice tightened— "let's get done with Craig, first. Bull'll wait, I reckon."

"He will for yez," agreed Harrigan. "There's Randall and them, jest ahead. I'll be tellin' Bull yez'll be along."

Craig wasted no time in bringing Bell up to date. He and Winston and Randall had been to see Stedloe earlier on Craig's idea of leaving the butte. The colonel had refused, outright. As he saw it, any descent, even though initially successful, would bring an immediately following pursuit and running fight with the hostiles and in this resolution their ammunition supply—now just over two rounds per man—would be utterly squandered. To further argument he had proved adamant, insisting the command would stand on the butte where at least it could make its last shots effective, and even might, possibly, arrange some sort of surrender truce with Kamiak's besiegers.

Returning from this refusal, the three officers had run headlong into Jason's treachery and Timothy's apparent disaffection. They now wanted Sergeant Bell to evaluate Timothy's disappearance and to furnish his opinion, based on his knowledge of the red men, as to the possibility of getting off the butte and out through the Indian lines. And they intended returning to Stedloe with that evaluation and opinion for a final try at convincing the commanding officer of the soundness of Craig's projected retreat. It was acknowledged, naturally although a bit wry-facedly, that 1st Sergeant Bell had more influence with Colonel Stedloe than any commissioned man on his staff.

Abruptly returning Craig's frankness and confidence, the big sergeant stated that he still had faith in Timothy and believed he must have dropped down to scout the enemy lines, that the column could expect no quarter from the hostiles, and that Stedloe's implied hope for a survival truce was impossible of fulfillment, and that Craig's insistence on a forced night flight was the command's final 500 to one chance.

Three minutes later he was expounding the same views to Stedloe while Craig and the other officers waited in hard-faced silence. Unexpectedly the C.O. broke down.

Fanning had just come in to report that the men had broken into the liquor commissary, had been drinking for the past hour, and were getting out of hand. In view of this, some activity seemed imperative. If Sergeant Bell would now go out with Lieutenant Fanning to commandeer the liquor supply and destroy it, Stedloe and the remaining officers would begin at once to map plans for the descent. Bell was to come back immediately to lend his scouting experience to the mapping.

With the liquor gathered up and cached, the men temporarily buoyed up with the orders to ready for departure, and a hasty visit to the dying Sergeant Williams under his drawn-up belt, Bell returned to the command council.

Under his belt, also, was something else. Something that at once attracted the refined nostrils of the teetotaling Stedloe.

"Sergeant Bell!"

"Yes, sir. Mission accomplished, sir."

"Bell, I told you to destroy that whiskey, not surround it!"

"It's destroyed, Colonel. Leastways hidden, sir . . . uh, what's left of it."

"Bell, you're not drunk?" The colonel's soft question speared the sergeant's grin in mid-spread. "I want your word on it. I'm depending on you in this. We all are. You'll not fail me now, man?"

"No, Colonel . . . both times," said Bell, setting his long jaw on the denial before letting a shade of the grin return. "I must've spilled some of the nasty stuff on me, pouring it out. I'm as ready as a ripe banana, sir. What're the orders?"

Stedloe shook his good, grave head hopelessly. This boy was one for the books—but not the Academy books. Half inebriated all the time, all inebriated half the time, and rebelliously insubordinate, drunk or sober, he was a shame and a disgrace to his uniform. And if he only had a hundred like him right now, a column commander could walk down and spit in Kamiak's Palouse face!

"Craig will give you the details, Sergeant. You can go along with him now. But before you leave, there's a little something I want you to hear. And you other gentlemen, as well."

With the words, Stedloe was turning to his staff, the three officers watching him closely as he concluded: "This is the order of the retreat. Remember it. C Company to take the advance, with Lieutenant Fanning. Ninth Infantry next, with Captain Winston. Then H Company, with Lieutenant Craig." Stedloe broke his orders to swing his quiet brown eyes on Bell, his three staffers following the look and the suspended statement with puzzlement. Catching Bell's frowning glance, the colonel held it for a long three seconds. "Then E Company," he said at last. "With Lieutenant Bellew!"

With Bell's tall shadow dogging his hurried movements, Lieutenant Craig made his way from one company to the next, calling each outfit together and repeating the general orders. The column was moving out. No equipment was to be taken save musket or carbine, and ammunition. All metal harness was to be wrapped with torn cloth and all loose, metal-buckled tack—canteens, scabbards, trenching shovels, axes, anything that might possibly make a noise in traveling—was to be left behind, right down to spurs and spur chains. Every trooper was to ride with his right hand on his mount's nose. The horses bearing the wounded were to be muzzle-wrapped.

Thus briefed, the squad corporals began at once to check their men and mounts and to fall them into rough company order. Craig and Bell, with a picked squad of regulars chosen by the latter, went on about the grim business of the main issue—faking the camp to look normal after their departure. This project was one upon which the dour sergeant had insisted as the minimum guarantee of a successful getaway, and Craig gave him no question on it. As a matter of fact, neither the young officer nor any of the rest of the staff had called the obvious question on Stedloe's peculiar reference to Bell as Lieutenant Bellew, all accepting the sergeant's new rank along with his running fire of suggested orders without a murmur.

Thirty-three of the command's horses had been killed and it was now necessary to Bell's strategy to eliminate another dozen. These were all the gray and other light-colored animals that were quickly cut out and picketed around the perimeter of the mesa—where prying Palouse eyes might note them even in the present darkness.

While Craig and the sergeant went about their labors, other work squads were busy with equally grim chores: the knocking down and caching of the howitzers, the collecting and burying, in a shallow common trench, of the trooper dead, the tight lashing of the severely wounded on the few remaining pack mules, and the hurried movement of strings of led horses over the burial sites of the colonel's beloved artillery and of his honored dead.

When a similar treatment was proposed for the considerable pile of packs and supplies being abandoned, Bell objected at once. The idea was to stack these as neatly and obviously as possible to charm the well-known red cupidity. The Indians' fighting over the division of these spoils might easily mean an hour of vital pursuit delay.

Shortly before 9:00, Craig and Bell returned to

Stedloe to report the column in readiness. Winston and Fanning, already there, nodded their silent agreement. Surgeon Randall announced the wounded ready to move, with the exception of 1st Sergeant Williams.

Questioned at once on this exception—Stedloe's orders had been explicit: no wounded left behind—the surgeon explained the non-com was all but cut in two with four hopeless abdominal wounds and that to move him a foot would be to kill him.

"I can't bring myself to give that order, Edson. You'll have to do it, if it's done. The man can't possibly live an hour, and he wants to stay. I'm sorry."

"Gentlemen?" The C.O. turned the soft question on the others.

"Let the poor devil alone," said Craig slowly. "Randall knows best. A dead man can't help us down that mountain."

"I talked to him just now," Bell's deep voice added. "He wants to help by staying here. I'd let him, Colonel. He's cold clear up to his kidneys."

"How about Demoix?" Stedloe turned again to the surgeon.

"Demoix might make it. I've got him ready, in any event."

"All right." There was no hesitation now in the commander's agreement. "Let's get on with it. So you still want to scout that western slope before we start, Bell?"

"We've got to. That west slope looks too good to me. The easiest way down and the only damn' one they haven't got watch fires burning behind. I think it's a trap. Kamiak was born a lot of yesterdays ago, Colonel."

"All right, Bell, get to it. The rest of you look to your men and ease the wounded as well as you can."

Bell left at once, declining any company. He was gone ten minutes. Then fifteen. And finally, twenty.

The only sounds from below were those of the night winds in the serviceberry bushes, the occasional sleepy twitter of a bullbat, and the distant mutter of the drums from the river camp of the Palouses, pitched along the Tohotonimme at the south base of the butte.

On the mesa top 140-odd hopeless whites cocked their straining ears and waited. Waited for the first triumphant war whoop that would announce their scout had found his trap. Found it, and stepped squarely on its trigger-light, Indian-set bait pan. Stepped on it and snapped its ringing jaws hard shut on their last, thin chance of escape. Twenty minutes stretched endlessly to thirty. And then to forty-five.

To the nerve-torn watchers on the hill, Bell's soundless reappearance, minutes before 10:00, came as a distinct jolt. A jolt occasioned by a most unnatural phenomenon. Tall white men very

392

seldom throw thin red shadows on moon-dark nights. But Bell was throwing one now. A reed-slender, wordless shadow that stepped quickly past him to touch its sober forehead toward the dumbfounded Stedloe and his staff.

"Timothy! God bless my soul!" gasped the colonel, his simple candor riding ahead of the dark suspicion due to follow the first surprise.

"Never mind your soul, Colonel." Bell's cynical reminder spiked the little pause. "You'd better bless this Indian's!"

"And you never mind your insubordinate tongue!" snapped Lieutenant Craig, his temper breaking under the sergeant's acid coolness. "Where the hell did you get this Indian, and why in God's name did you let him follow you back here?"

"And *you,* Lieutenant Craig"—Bell's hard advice broke in a perfect imitation of the young officer's outburst—"never mind your little silver bar. I'm talking to Colonel Stedloe."

"Go ahead, Bell. Answer Craig's question." The C.O.'s voice showed a touch of West Point spine. "After all, Timothy's been gone for two hours and the Lord alone knows what doing."

"*Me,* and the Lord," amended the big sergeant softly. "As for Craig's questions, Tamason speaks better English than I do, Colonel. I'll let him talk."

And the Nez Percé chief talked. Low. Deep. Simply. The throaty gutturals of his mission-school English falling, swift and short, their soft delivery slowly lifting the nape-hairs of Stedloe's dry-mouthed staff.

At the bottom of that long west slope down which the colonel intended taking his troops, Timothy had encountered Sergeant Bell, advising him to go no farther providing he still held his short red scalp in some esteem. Beyond the base of that slope the Palouses had driven their horse herd, hiding at least 800 of the nervous, uncertain little mounts among the scrub pine bordering the Tohotonimme at that point. And beyond the horse herd, waiting to respond to its first alarm of inquiring neighs, Kamiak and Malkapsi lay with a big force of picked warriors. *Any* of the white officers, the Nez Percé stressed quietly, could thus see what their advance down that slope would have brought them into.

Now. Beyond that. Would the officers look carefully at the way in which the enemy had his signal fires burning. To the north, just a few. To the east, just a few. Look out for those places. They looked thin, and were swarming with warriors. Then see that darkness to the west. No fires there, at all. And as Ametsun Bell had warned—Timothy himself had trained him, had he not?—that was the worst spot of all.

So. Where were the fires brightest? Where were the drums beating? Where was the last place the pony soldiers would think of going down? To

394

the south naturally. Down there where the lodges lay. Down there where even Sergeant Bell would never have looked. And what was down there? Nothing. Nothing save a dozen squaws feeding the big fires and a few old chiefs pounding the buffalo hides. . . .

At the end of the Nez Percé's tooth-setting disclosures Stedloe and his staff occupied themselves with the most pressing necessity of the moment—letting their held breaths go in sibilant unison.

Before they could gulp a fresh lungful, Sergeant Bell was putting his brief valedictory to the suspected scout's address. "I'll save you all the time of hashing over Tamason's chewed-up loyalty. This Indian's been wading in ambushed hostiles up to his crotch cloth for two hours. Nobody asked him to and he knew full well nobody'd believe he'd done it. Not even me." Bell paused, letting the silence grow a little before concluding. "So he took me on two little trips . . . one, just across the creek, due west . . . one, a half mile down it, straight south. Gentlemen, I can smell horse sweat and road apples when they're blown at me eight hundred deep. And I can see an empty village when I'm looking at one in bright firelight. Any questions?"

XV

At 10:00p.m., Colonel Stedloe with Fanning's company of dragoons and Winston's 9th Infantry moved in orderly silence over the rim of the mesa. There was a muffled shifting of loose rock as their mounts struck the steep slide where Bell's carbines had broken the back of Kamiak's last charge, and then pin-drop stillness. The first companies were successfully away.

Lieutenant Craig, collecting the last of his outposts and enjoining Bell to follow him in unbroken order, went next. When the settling of the rock trickle below told the sergeant H Company was safely past the slide, he turned abruptly to the lean trooper at his side.

"Get going, Clay. Take the lead and hang your horse's nose onto H Company's cruppers. Jump it, now."

"Hold on, Sarge"—the bearded soldier pulled his mount back—"I thought you was supposed to lead this here quadrille."

"I said get going, Corporal." Bell's command leaped through the gloom with ugly shortness. "I'm aiming to be the last man off this hill. Now, move."

Corporal Sam Clay was a Carolina man and a six-year regular. And four of those six years had been spent as a buck private under the untender tuition of 1st Sergeant Emmett D. Bell. He went. And after him went the sixteen survivors of Gaxton's company, E Dragoons, Bell counting them carefully over the rim and giving each mount a slap on the haunch and each anxious rider a soft reminder: "Watch the man in front of you, soldier. Don't let your horse hang back, and keep your hand on his nose when you go by that village down there."

With the last man and mount over the edge, Bell waited a tense two minutes until the final, faint movement of the granite below told him Corporal Clay had gotten E Company past the slide. Then he turned noiselessly away from the rim. As he went, a less moon-dark night would have limned the slight, frosty grin that turned with him.

Below the slide, Corporal Clay picked up the gait of his troop, soon overhauling the ghostly rumps of Craig's H Company. Another five minutes of slow-walking progress along the sharp-falling face of the south slope and the column was unaccountably halted, word at once relaying back from the head of the line that Colonel Stedloe wanted Sergeant Bell up front. The hostile village lay just ahead and the C.O. wanted the sergeant alongside the guiding Timothy when the passage was made.

The message, passed back along the muffled line of E Company, was shortly returned with an ugly postscript. Sergeant Bell was not among those present and accounted for.

This intelligence had no more than been passed back up to Stedloe than a shifting night breeze brought the answer to the question already framing the column commander's grim lips. From the north, that breeze came. From the north and across the abandoned mesa top. Dropping softly down the darkened south slope. And bearing on its mountain-scented breath a sound known to every last member of the Colville column, and to not a few of the reservation hangers-on among Kamiak's swart-skinned followers: the soulful and ardent, if not artistic, harmonica playing of 1st Sergeant Bell.

"Faith and be Jazus!" The muttered expletive broke from Sergeant Harrigan, who had ridden forward with Captain Winston to check the reason for the delay. "The crazy, blessed idjut has stayed up there with old Bull. And listen to thet bloody tyune he's playin', will yez, Colonel? Thet'll be Sarge's idea of somethin' funny."

" 'Rock of Ages.' " Stedloe murmured the words like a man talking in his sleep and not hearing his own voice.

"The drunken devil." The clipped phrase fell in Captain Winston's flat monotone and was followed with the softly qualifying afterthought: "But God, what a bellyful of guts."

"Not drunk, Harry. Not this time." The thought

came, surprisingly enough, in Stedloe's patient voice. "I know the man. He's playing to cover our withdrawal. And to make up for his own memories. There's a story, there. I'll tell it to you if we get out of this."

"Emm, oh, my God, it's Emm."

The muffled delay of the cry burst from the stunned Calla. Riding with Fanning and Stedloe, she had been the first to leave the butte, had not seen Bell since he left her sleeping at eight o'clock, had only now realized the tense discussion concerned him.

"Don't worry, Miss Rainsford"—the gallant lie came from young Fanning—"he'll make out. He's got more lives than a three-toed cat."

"He'll need them," grunted the unimaginative Winston. "We can't wait for him."

"I'm going back." The suppressed cry sprang from Calla. "It's just a little way. Colonel, I'm going . . ."

"No, miss." It was Timothy's iron hand that found the distraught girl's bridle with the low-voiced denial. "Ametsun Bell planned it this way. I was to tell you when we were past the village. He knew we had no chance unless the Palouses were made to think all was well on the hilltop. Many of those Indians waiting back there know Ametsun Bell. They know his music on that mouth reed. They will hear it and nod. And go on waiting."

"Oh, Emm . . ."

"Timothy's right, ma'am." Stedloe's hand found her arm with the gentle insistence. "We'll go along now."

"And quickly," added the Nez Percé, before the girl could answer. "While Kamiak and Malkapsi are still grinning about that music up there."

"Column resume," said Stedloe to the waiting officers. "On the double once we're past the village. Single file and slow walk until we are. Right, Timothy?"

"Aye," said the Nez Percé, turning his roan pony. "*Kela'i*, Ametsun." The low farewell, with the quick touch of the red hand to the forehead, went to the now brooding silence of Stedloe's butte. "We shall meet again along that other trail."

Bell laid aside the mouth harp, reached in the dark for the hallowed canteen. "How do you feel, Bull? Easier, now?"

"I couldn't pin a grizzly, Sarge"—the huge man's words brought a groan of pain, deep and soft, like a wounded animal's—"but I allow that theah last drink helped summat."

"Want another?"

"Yeah, maybe. Hold mah cussed head for me. I cain't seem to get it offen this rock no more."

Bell passed his thick arm behind the massive head, held the canteen steadily.

"That's enough, you dumb ox! You'll have it

pouring out that hole in your belly. This isn't issue rotgut, you know."

"Mah Gawd, I know that. That's sourmash whiskey, Sarge." The brutish non-com's voice seemed to gain from the fiery draft. "Wheah'd we get it?"

"Surgeon Randall's best. That's officer whiskey, boy. Can't you feel it in your dumb belly?"

"Sarge . . ." There was fear in the heavy voice now. The unreasoning, nameless fear of a four-year-old, alone and lost in the dark. Childish. Pathetic. Turning Bell's stomach with its perfect faith. "I cain't feel nothin' in mah belly. I'm cold up to mah elbows. Lemme feel your hand again, Sarge. Jest this oncet more. . . ."

Silently Bell felt forward, bringing his hand to rest in the huge sergeant's. Feeling the clammy weakness of the great, groping fingers, he shuddered.

"You cold, too, Sarge?"

"Naw, just nerves, Bull."

"Not you, Sarge. You jest ain't had yer quart today."

"Nor yesterday," said Bell aimlessly. "I'm about caught up, though, I reckon."

"How many left, Sarge?"

"A couple."

"I'll split you."

"You're split, Bull . . ."

Bell held his head again, tipping the canteen.

Feeling the liquor splash his steadying hand, he pulled the container away from the slack mouth, eased the burly head back on the boulder.

"You never could hold your whiskey, you big dummy. That's all for you."

Draining the canteen with steady gulps, he shied the empty container toward the nearest of the picketed horses. At its muffled bounce, the animals headed up and nickered.

"And that's for Kenuokin," he grunted. "Just to remind the red buzzard he's got a bunch of ragged-bottom dragoons cornered up here."

"Sarge . . . ?"

"Yeah, Bull?"

"How long the boys bin gone?"

"Couple hours. You been dozing off and on."

"Yeah."

"Aren't you sleepy again?"

"Naw, jest cold . . ."

Bell slid his hand out of the Kentuckian's rigid fingers, moved it up to the huge shoulder, recoiled quickly at the marble coldness. "I'll get you another blanket, boy."

"Naw, listen, Sarge. You got to go. You was only goin' to stay a few minutes."

Bell nodded, without replying. He'd said that, all right. Hours ago. When he'd thought the big ox couldn't last ten minutes. Now it was crowding midnight, the column clean away and long gone. And still the tremendous brute hung on.

"Yeah, Bull. I'll be going pretty sudden . . ."

Bull was dead. Maybe another five minutes. Maybe another five hours. But dead, anyway. Just as dead as though God had already reached down and gathered him up. Time was wasting for both Bell and Bull Williams.

"Sarge . . . ?"

"Yeah."

"What you doin'? Thet's yer Remin'ton, ain't it? Why you wrappin' it?"

Bell looked down at the heavy, rolling-block Dragoon pistol. Folded the torn blanketing over it again.

"It's my Remington, Bull. I'm fixing you a gun to leave with you, boy."

"The old last shot, huh, Sarge?"

"The old last shot, Bull."

"I ain't goin' to need it."

"I reckon not."

"Sarge, play us a tune 'fore you go."

"Sure, Bull, what'll it be?" The left hand was feeling in the linted jacket pocket. The right, easing the wrapped pistol into the cross-legged lap.

"You know . . ."

"Yeah, boy. I know."

"And slow, Sarge"—there was that old touch of child-bright eagerness in the sudden plea, wrenching Bell's chest, hardening his wide mouth—"so's I can do the words."

"Sure, Bull." The left hand was placing the harmonica to the dry lips, the right, dropping to the motionless lap. "Second chorus, boy."

"Yeah, second chorus."

The reedy thinness of the opening bars echoed with eerie lonesomeness across the deserted dust of the mesa top, startling the drooping horses. On the second, mournful chorus the big Kentuckian began to sing.

> On top of Old Smoky, all covered with snow
> I lost my true lover from a-courtin' too slow
> Now come all young ladies and listen to me
> Don't hang your affections on a green willow tree
> For the leaves they will wither
> And the roots they will die
> And leave you . . .

The blanket-muffled shot reverberated dully, its flat tones not even disturbing the horses. Pulling the smoking weapon from its folded cover, Bell placed it gently near the slack hand alongside the granite boulder.

Like you said, Bull—he nodded silently—*you won't be needing it.*

With the raw powder burns of the shrouded

shot still blistering his pistol hand, Bell set himself one last duty before leaving the mesa.

In this direction he was guided by his knowledge of Indian psychology and not, as some later detractors were to claim, by his sardonic sense of humor, or by his well-known agnosticism. His self-imposed labor cost him twenty priceless minutes, and Sergeant Bell wasn't the one to squander time like that for a laugh, or to prove his doubts of a living deity.

With an abandoned shovel, two canteen straps, and an unearthed pair of the oaken howitzer shafts, he worked in driving silence, pausing frequently to cock a straining ear to the stillness of the slopes below. There was a limit to the illusion a dozen cast-off dragoon horses and a harmonica-playing first sergeant could create. Sooner or later Kamiak and company were going to start wondering about the astonishingly good behavior of 140 frightened men and a like number of nervous horses on that mesa top!

When he had done, stepping back to drop the shovel and survey his handiwork, he had a reasonable facsimile of what he wanted—a crude mission cross planted squarely in the middle of Stedloe's deserted butte.

Grunting his satisfaction, Bell turned away. If he knew the child-simple Indian mind, that cross would do its work. The fear reserved for the symbol of the crucifixion by the Northwestern savages was complete. There would be no scalping among the stark bodies of the colonel's abandoned dead.

At the western mesa rim, the sergeant pulled up his gelding, stood forward in the stirrups, ears tuned to the night sounds along the slope. A moment later he was sliding off the bay and flopping, belly down, in the welcome cover of the rank rim grasses.

There were no night sounds coming from that slope. At any rate, not the right ones. His stomach drawing in like drying rawhide, Bell peered through the parted grasses, gray eyes scanning the unnatural quiet of the western decline.

Then of a sudden, pupils expanding under the severity of the lower darknesses, he was seeing it. Seeing it and understanding the stillness of the night hawks and of the serviceberry birds. Seeing it lapping slowly up the west slope and, as he turned quickly, along the south as well. There was no mistaking the ragged, extended lines of that creeping shadow. The red night crawlers were out and moving. Kamiak was coming up!

Rolling back from the rim, Bell bent double and raced for his pack. There it was but the work of a moment to shuck out of his heavy dragoon boots and bulky service shirt. Another moment and his fingers were easing the trim tightness of the Nez Percé moccasins around the outsize bareness of his feet. After that it took only seconds to belt on the skinning knife, sling the short Sharps carbine over his shoulder, slip across the mesa top, and over the precipitous drop of the north wall. Ten minutes of leaping, brush-torn descent and he was standing 800 feet below the mesa rim on the deserted north side of the butte. And seconds after that he was hearing the war whoops and belly screams that announced the Palouse assault over the west and south rims.

With the disappointed howls and barking signal cries from above telling him Kamiak's faithful had discovered their empty trap, he reslung his carbine and set off around the north slope—heading west. He traveled now at a long-swinging dog-trot, finding the open grasslands of the lower inclines fairly level and free of gully washes.

Shortly he sighted the dark line of scrub pine marking the course of the Tohotonimme ahead. Slowing his pace, he speeded up his mind, the wild gamble forming in it beginning to fall into hurried place as his figure entered the screening gloom of the trees.

Just ahead, its position marked by the drowsy *tinkling* of the bell mare's musical neck piece, lay the main hostile horse herd. Eight hundred or 900 half-wild, white-hating Indian cayuses. There were your odds, brother, and they were long enough to satisfy even 1st Sergeant Bell. Still, maybe not too long. If a man could get to that bell mare—

but, cripes, that was a little daisy that would take some careful picking! And a big piece of luck.

He ran into his needed chunk of fortune almost as its necessity was forming in his mind. And it was a bigger chunk than he could have asked for. As he melted into the fringe of the pines, a low voice hailed him in Chinook. Turning, he was in time to see the silhouetted cartwheel of a Coeur D'Alene war bonnet following him.

"Hold up, brother!" the guttural order foreran the chief's gliding approach. "Name your name and follow along with me. The white dogs have gotten away and Kamiak has sent me to gather up those down here!"

"Omatchen!" hissed Bell, picking a known Coeur D'Alene's name out of the thin night air. "Who calls me?"

"Malkapsi, you fool. Didn't I just leave you up on top there? Why have you come down?" With the questions the Coeur D'Alene was up to Bell, his ugly, axe-blade jaw poking forward through the dark.

"To run the horse herd off, naturally, you fool!"

Bell threw the growling retort into the renegade's hand-filed teeth a shaving of a second ahead of the clubbed, steel butt of the carbine. Malkapsi's tiny eyes had time to jump wide open, and that was all. The next instant the gunstock was splintering his gaping jaw and the spreading eyes were glazing closed.

Bell caught the swaying figure, easing it to the ground. A hasty ear pressed to the hostile's deerskin shirt picked up no discernible heartbeat. Ametsun Bell figured he had kept his promise to Malkapsi.

The sergeant now had what he needed to approach the Indian horse herd safely—deerskin and eagle feathers reeking of the familiar and friendly Coeur D'Alene body odor. Seconds after downing Malkapsi he had donned the chief's shirt and bonnet, was rapidly circling the close-packed herd, south toward the *tinkling* of the bell mare's luring ornament.

The shirt and bonnet were a plenty tight squeeze for the towering Bell but with them and Kamiak's bell mare that horse herd could be scattered till hell wouldn't have it. Not hell, or the pursuing Palouses, either. Those bell-broke hostile ponies would follow that lead mare wherever Bell might boot her. And where Bell was going to boot her was far away and long departed from Kamiak's Tohotonimme war camp!

XVI

With the fog-sopping dawn of the 18th, Stedloe halted his fleeing column safely across its fateful, former fording of the Palouse. There had been no sign of pursuit to that gray hour. However, there was as yet only a scant handful of miles between the fatigue-drunk troopers and their heaving, hollow-flanked horses, and the wind-swept emptiness of Stedloe's deserted butte. No time could be taken to graze the wind-broken mounts, and very little to water thcm. Nonetheless, their first drink in twenty-four hours had a heartening effect on both man and mount.

While the last of the lathered horses were still standing hock deep in the shallows of the stream, Timothy rode in to report a high dust cloud rolling down the Lapwai Trail from the Ingosommen. He didn't like to arouse false hopes in his fellow soldiers, said the Nez Percé, but he would think from the size of that cloud that no more than 200 or 300 could be riding under it! At the same time he could not be sure. It was a damp morning and many ponies might make only the dust of a few. It was no time to be squatting on the exposed banks of the Palouse, waiting to find out.

As if to put the lie to the Nez Percé's cautiously hopeful report, and the truth to his stern warning to move on, a veritable rash of smoke signals began to top the bare hills to the north and east. This hostile hint was more than enough for the haggard survivors of the Colville column. It was still sixty-eight miles to the Snake.

To the hoarse calls of the officers and the dispirited echoes of their non-coms, the straggling column was reformed, and for the next four hours the failing mounts were forced to a laboring gallop straightaway down the brush-girt track of the Lapwai Trail. With the advance of midday, the climbing sun drove into the backs of the fleeing men with the deadening power of a giant sledge, sapping their little remaining strength and pulling the Palouse water out of the dehydrating troopers as from so many saddle-jolted sponges.

By 1:00p.m. and the branching of the Lapwai toward the distant Snake, men and horses had reached their limit. In the spotty shelter of a jack-pine-fringed creek, crossing in from the east, Stedloe called the halt.

And it was in this haven of sweltering shade and brackish branch water that the disorganized column got its first uplift in forty-eight hours of hell. Shortly after the halt Timothy spurred his pony down from a neighboring ridge to announce a lone Coeur D'Alene chief galloping the Lapwai a mile to the north. The distance was too long for positive identification but the solitary rider was astride a white pony and there was something familiar to the Nez Percé in his swinging, upright seat. Timothy couldn't say who the hard-riding stranger was, but he could say he had seen him before.

Lieutenant Craig at once took a squad of skirmishers out to cut off the newcomer's approach. This party was scarcely gone from sight over the first ridge than it reappeared, the tall

Coeur D'Alene riding in its jubilant midst. As the returning riders broke into view, the watching Timothy's stolid face split wide in an expression never before noted thereon by any of Stedloe's command—a flashing, lightning-brief, purely dazzling smile!

"Ametsun! *Ho-hoho!* It's Ametsun Bell!"

And Bell indeed it was. Cartwheel war bonnet, Coeur D'Alene deerskins, Palouse bell mare, and all!

No Cæsar returned triumphantly from Gaul ever received a comparable salute. Private, squad corporal, company officer, and column commander, all joined in the rousing cheer that greeted the dour non-com's return from the dead. Alone among the company failing to aid the vocal reception, Calla sat her artillery mule in silence, letting the tears cascading her dirty cheeks splash their own grateful word of welcome. Looking over the heads of Harrigan and the rest of the intervening backslappers, Bell waved his understanding to the girl, sending the bright rareness of his quick smile to receipt the unspoken message in her tear-stained grimace. A man could understand, at a moment like this, that it's pretty hard to talk through a soft mouth full of salt water!

But Bell had brought other news than good. And longing as his arms might to be around that slim waist, they'd have to ache a spell yet. Keeping to the ravines paralleling the main trail, he had been able to avoid the hostiles while at the same time scouting their pursuit. About an hour ago the Indian force had swung west to angle toward the Snake. Their present course would bring them back into the Lapwai eight miles short of Red Wolf Crossing. And right into the rocks of the Smokle Creek headlands. As pretty a spot for an ambush as any tired scout would care to think about.

There were some 350 warriors in the pursuit party, all Palouses and personally led by Kamiak. It was Bell's guess the chief's Spokane, Coeur D'Alene, Yakima, and other allies had suffered a temporary loss of their appetite for white meat following Stedloe's astonishing escape from the mesa trap, and the division of the spoils abandoned in that escape. Also contributing, no doubt, was the thoughtful delay occasioned by Bell's running off of their horse herd.

Under the terms of the sergeant's blunt report no option remained save to race the hostiles for the Smokle Creek headlands. If the troops could beat the Palouses to that dangerous point, the day would be long spent and the precious safety of the Snake River but an hour's short ride away. It was a long, long chance, and the battered column took it at a floundering gallop.

With four o'clock and the hulking landmarks of the Tah-To-Uah Hills behind them, the troops were slowed to a stumbling, rank-breaking trot. But the headlands of the Smokle were in sight. Another eight miles and they would know. Hope, that cat-lived spur that was as much a part of the dragoon's equipment as his clumsy boots, began once more to straighten the seats of the sagging soldiers.

And then, rolling ominously up from the unexpected direction of the low hills to the south, came a moving dust cloud that could denote no less than 100 fast-traveling riders.

Timothy and Bell, pushing their mounts to the nearest hilltop, were back in ten minutes with the stark news.

Whoever those riders were, they were Indians. And their line of gallop was going to cut them into the Lapwai a good way short of the Smokle headlands.

Again there was no course but to push on. To retreat was unthinkable. To leave the marked trail, northward or southward, was out of the question. It was now quite clear the wily Kamiak had split his forces, sending half of them to the south, holding half of them to the north, aiming, obviously, to bring the two jaws of his running trap hard together somewhere short of the Smokle rocks. And aiming to have the last of the desperate pony soldiers between those jaws when they closed.

White-faced and raw-shot with fatigue, Colonel

Stedloe put his hoarse orders to his hollow-eyed officers. The column fell raggedly in and stumbled forward.

Ten minutes and two miles later they pulled their foam-caked mounts to a halt and prepared to deploy for the firing of their remaining two rounds per man. The upcoming Indian attackers had shifted their course to bear straight for the stalled column. The Colville force had come a long way from Stedloe's dreary butte, and had almost come all the way. But this would be as far as they were going. This would be the end of it.

The next instant, with the flat-galloping Indian ponies nearing 400 yards and extreme range, Timothy gave a great shout and dashed his rat-tailed roan straight for the onrushing horde of painted braves. And the next second Bell was standing in his stirrups and yelling like a schoolboy at his first stake race. The swinging gestures of his wildly pointing arm, along with the bass bellowing of his cracked voice, were aimed at a memorably squat and ugly figure quirting a lunging Nez Percé cayuse out of the foremost line of warriors and down upon Timothy.

"Lord A'mighty, Colonel, that's Lucas!" Bell's triumphant shout went to Stedloe. "God bless the ugly idiot, he's done it! Those are our Nez Percés!"

"Good Lord, there must be two hundred of

them!" Craig's boyishly exultant voice joined Bell's. "Would you look at them, sir? I never thought I'd be so god-damn' glad to see Indians again in my life!"

"Thank God," muttered the colonel, his voice dead flat, the reins falling loosely from his slack hands with the words. "Thank God . . . and our Nez Percés."

With the appearance of Timothy's tribesmen the issue of the passage of the Smokle headlands was as dead as last year's dog salmon. Kamiak, no more than any other Indian Napoléon, before or since, would ever risk openly engaging a fore-warned enemy of nearly equal numbers. What matter, now, that he had won the race for the Smokle rocks? What matter that his followers had spent the past hour arguing the manner in which the wonderful Sharps carbines of the pony soldiers were to be divided? In truth, no matter now.

Sitting his Appaloosa stallion among the granite boulders from which he had expected to lead his warriors down upon the last of the white troopers, the big hostile shrugged, hunching his scarlet blanket higher against the chill of the rising wind, the resilient shift of his thoughts demonstrating that Indian elasticity of adjustment that Bell had so often marked and admired among them.

Yonder came his long-chased prey, to be sure. Worn down. Beaten. Ready for the kill. But, alas. With them also came the cursed Nez Percés. Those fools. Those damned fools. Riding up like heroes at the last minute. Robbing the Palouses of their victory. Spoiling the carefully spread hostile tales of a planned Nez Percé treachery to the soldiers. And the real pity, the real Big Pity, was that he, Kamiak, war chief of the Yakima Federation, had been within minutes of achieving the greatest Indian victory of them all over white soldiers! But now? *Iki! E'sa?* Was it bitter as gall? Should a chief feel that way now?

No. There was more to it than that. He had inflicted on the soldiers their most humiliating defeat. The name Kamiak would put the cold sweat down their pale backs for a long time to come. *Kape't.* It was enough. *Wuska.* Let that be the end of it. It was time to go home.

Turning to his waiting subchiefs, Kamiak gave the word and the sign. There were no dissents, the subchiefs in turn grunting the low order back into the packed ranks of charcoal and ochre-blazoned faces. *Kape't. Wuska.* It was time to go home. Kamiak had said it.

When, with the lowering gray of the eight-o'clock northern dusk, the tattered Colville survivors filed past the Smokle rocks to enter the broad, granite track that marked the final fall of the Lapwai Trail toward the Snake, the Palouses were gone.

The Palouses were gone and in their place three solitary Nez Percé warriors sat their hunching cayuses on the skyline of the Smokle ridge, their slant eyes studying the march of the blue-and-gray-clad troops below. Timothy, and Jason, and Lucas. Hesitating now that their work was done. Wondering which way to point their ponies. Watching in stony-faced silence the fading of the flag toward the west and Red Wolf Crossing.

In the minds of two of the watchers there was nothing but what their cherty eyes were seeing: the rag-tag, broken passage of the ill-fated Colville column. But in the mind of the third were many things not seen with the eye alone. Timothy was seeing the empty places in that column. Captain Baylor dying with the dusk on Stedloe's butte. Lieutenant Gaxton dead in the hot sun of the Tohotonimme gorge. Sergeant Williams holding his belly and bleeding to death while Ametsun Bell played his reed pipe in the lonely blackness. And Sergeant Demoix left with his mortal wounds and a loaded pistol somewhere along the morning darkness of the Lapwai Trail.

He was seeing, and hearing again, the brave but empty words of Colonel Stedloe in congratulating his troops on their survival, and in predicting (only Timothy knew how foolishly!) that their stand against Kamiak's rebellion would pave the way for the warless dissolution of the hostiles' Yakima federation. He was hearing, too, those final words of the good, quiet Ametsun Bell. Telling him, Timothy, that his alone was the honor and reward for the saving of Stedloe's men. But telling him, too, that he must not expect this honor ever to come to him. It was not in the ways of the white soldiers to say that an Indian had led them out of the Palouse wilderness!

Timothy had nodded, then, knowing the gray-eyed chevron soldier spoke the truth. And he had nodded again when Ametsun had told him he was going to his home to the East, beyond the Shining Mountains. Going there with the girl, to make his peace with the Army that he had served so well. And going with Colonel Stedloe's promise of complete official backing, and the patient-eyed commander's hopeful prediction of full military pardon in the end.

But rehearing and seeing all these fleeting things, the Nez Percé was seeing something else above them all. Something whose image had never left his narrow eyes. Something whose identity was even now being put to him in the guttural acrimony of Jason's dry words.

"Well, Tamason, there goes your pretty flag. Do we sit here all night chilling our buttocks with this Bitter Root breeze, or do we go after it?" The sun-blackened leather of the chief's face held its chronic mask of blankness a long three breaths. Then its wind-carved wrinkles were breaking to the deliberate fall of his words. There was nothing of bitterness or of contempt in his quiet speech, but only the bare honesty of reality.

"It's a fools' flag, my brothers. And those who follow it with them are fools. The red you see upon it is Indian blood. The blue is the empty sky they trade us for our lands. Those white stars are their promises, high as the heavens, bright as moonlight, cold and empty as the belly of a dead fish."

"Aye, maybe so, cousin." Jason's lead-faced seriousness acknowledged the accuracy of his chief's analysis, while at the same time challenging it. "But my belly, too, is cold and empty as a dead fish's. And the food is there. Where that flag is."

"Aye! That's a true thing!" Lucas, the irrepressible, was adding his bright penny's worth. "Let us go after that food. Let us follow that flag."

Timothy was quiet then, his gaze looking not at his waiting companions, but out across the desolate thickening gloom of the Snake River highlands. After a moment he waved his slender hand turning his slat-ribbed roan with the gesture.

"All right, my brothers," was all he said, the deep bass of the agreement as soft as the night wind stirring the young May grass. "Let us follow the flag."

About the Author

Henry Wilson Allen wrote under both the Clay Fisher and Will Henry bylines and was a five-time winner of the Spur Award from the Western Writers of America. He was born in Kansas City, Missouri. His early work was in short subject departments with various Hollywood studios, and he was working at M-G-M when his first Western novel, *No Survivors* (1950), was published. While numerous Western authors before Allen provided sympathetic and intelligent portraits of Indian characters, Allen from the start set out to characterize Indians in such a way as to make their viewpoints an integral part of his stories. Some of Allen's images of Indians are of the romantic variety, to be sure, but his theme often is the failure of the American frontier experience and the romance is used to treat his tragic themes with sympathy and humanity. On the whole, the Will Henry novels tend to be based more deeply in actual historical events, whereas in those titles he wrote as Clay Fisher he was more intent on a story filled with action that moves rapidly. However, this dichotomy can be misleading, since *MacKenna's Gold* (1963), a Will Henry Western about gold-seekers, reads much like one of the finest Clay Fisher titles,

The Tall Men (1954). His novels, *Journey to Shiloh* (1960), *From Where the Sun Now Stands* (1960), *One More River To Cross* (1967), *Chiricahua* (1972), and *I, Tom Horn* (1975) in particular, remain imperishable classics of Western historical fiction. Over a dozen films have been made based on his work.

"I am but a solitary horseman of the plains, born a century too late and far away," Allen once wrote about himself. He felt out of joint with his time, and what alone may ultimately unify his work is the vividness of his imagination, the tremendous emotion with which he invested his characters and fashioned his Western stories. At his best, he wove an almost incomparable spell that involves a reader deeply in his narratives, informed always by his profound empathy for so many of the casualties of the historical process.

Center Point Large Print
600 Brooks Road / PO Box 1
Thorndike, ME 04986-0001 USA

(207) 568-3717

US & Canada:
1 800 929-9108
www.centerpointlargeprint.com